BIG GIRLS DON'T CRY

BIG GIRLS DON'T CRY

FRANCESCA CLEMENTIS

PIATKUS

For more information on other books
published by Piatkus, visit our website
at www.piatkus.co.uk

Copyright © 1999 by Francesca Clementis

First published in Great Britain in 1999 by
Judy Piatkus (Publishers) Ltd of
5 Windmill Street, London W1P 1HF
email: info@piatkus.co.uk

This edition published 1999
Reprinted 1999

The moral right of the author has been asserted

*A catalogue record for this book
is available from the British Library*

ISBN 0 7499 3143 4

Set in Bembo by
Phoenix Photosetting, Chatham, Kent

Printed and bound in Great Britain by
Mackays of Chatham PLC, Chatham, Kent

For Freya Collis and Tasha Clementis.
May they grow up always feeling beautiful, special and loved.
And for Neal Clementis, because he's great too!
And for Steve, just because …

Prologue

David Sandhurst watched his mice with a paternal fondness. Huffy and Puffy returned his gaze without judgement. It amused him to come up with names for the animals appropriate to the drugs being tested on them. Of course, Oxymetabulin's original purpose to prevent the escalation of asthma attacks had long since been discarded. As with many medical discoveries, it was an unexpected side-effect of the experiment that was proving to be the breakthrough that Perrico Pharmaceuticals' investors had long been awaiting.

David opened the cage and carried the mice over to the scales. They knew the drill and stood still while David took the measurements. He smiled as he checked back on previous recordings. Perfect. Exactly as he had predicted.

A casual observer would have seen a thirty-four-year-old scientist too absorbed in his work to care about his appearance: the stained white laboratory coat and faded jeans, the dark hair that flopped randomly over his forehead, drooping on to severe metal-rimmed glasses, the fingernails that seemed to carry three weeks of indefinable grime.

The casual observer would have been mistaken. The white coat protected a Versace shirt and the jeans were by Armani. It had taken twenty minutes and several applications of mousse and spray to achieve that carefully tousled hair structure. On closer inspection, his glasses bore a tiny, discreet YSL logo. The frames were minimal to prevent anyone being distracted from his dark blue eyes. He had even learned to resist his instinctive fastidiousness and cease to manicure his nails after being accused of foppishness by the one rare woman who had resisted his approaches.

Not that such vanity detracted from his serious approach to his work. David Sandhurst was as ambitious as a man needs to be with £100,000 a year tastes and a £25,000 a year salary. Until now, he had only managed to finance his expensive lifestyle with the co-operation of a female bank manager who willingly extended his overdraft on a regularly upward spiral in exchange for David's fingers-crossed promise of dinner ('one day *very* soon').

But his fortune was finally in sight. His work on Oxymetabulin had coincided with the exciting discovery in the USA of the 'fat' gene in a mouse. This gene appeared to control the hormone responsible for increasing and reducing the body's energy consumption in the same way that a thermostat regulates temperature. If it wasn't working efficiently, the mouse would either be too fat or too thin. Within a short time, an American team had succeeded in producing a protein that actually worked directly on this gene, 'turning up' the mouse's fat burner and leading to rapid weight loss.

If your one overriding problem happened to be obese mice, your prayers were about to be answered.

Unfortunately, it is a well-known fact that mice do not make a significant contribution to the multi-billion pound diet industry. They do not buy slimming foods, magazines, books or videos. If they are fat, they do not spend thousands of pounds having the fat sucked out of them nor do they join gyms or have their jaws wired by private surgeons. They do not swallow pills by the bucket load nor do they fly to a spa in Arizona for a fortnight every six months or so. They do not need two completely separate wardrobes of clothes for their fat days and thin days. They do not pay for injections of liquidised lambs' foetuses and they seldom send away £29.95 to a mail-order company for plastic knickers that claim to dissolve the fat on their backsides. All in all, they are a pretty poor target market for such a revolutionary discovery.

But what about people and, in particular, women? To be able to offer a pill that would allow them to eat what they wanted, exercise as little as they liked and still enable them to lose weight with no effort whatsoever? In surveys carried out by some of the major women's magazines, over ninety per cent of women said that the one thing most likely to make them happy would be to lose a stone. They rated weight loss higher than being given £5000. More desirable than a glittering career. More comforting than a lovely secure home. More important than love. Overweight or not, almost all Western women believe that their lives would be improved by losing weight and they would do or pay anything to achieve this goal.

Small wonder that the mouse drug had inspired such a frantic race for a safe and effective human version.

Ironically, Perrico had not even considered entering the race. They were small players in the pharmaceuticals market and could not afford the millions of pounds of necessary investment. They continued with the lower-profile work on asthma treatments that David had been recruited to develop straight after university. Oxymetabulin was the result.

Oxymetabulin had turned out to have a few minor but significant positive effects on asthma but all the mice injected with the drug had lost weight. At first this was considered a potential problem. Unexplained weight loss can often be a indicator of serious illness. Then David discovered why the drug was having this effect. Quite by accident, David had stumbled on a compound that cranked up the mouse's metabolic rate.

There was absolutely no reason to believe that such a compound would work on humans. After all, the American protein was apparently no closer to demonstrating an impact on human subjects. It was unlikely that David's modest discovery would be any more effective. And working in a small laboratory in London with limited resources, he was never going to be able to develop the project sufficiently to reach the human testing stage.

His desperate need for glory and the dwindling co-operation of his bank manager drove him to take a huge risk. Against all ethical rules and guidelines, he administered a controlled dose of Oxymetabulin to himself. He felt he had nothing to lose and everything to gain.

A month later, he had lost twelve pounds and become destined to gain the attention of the whole world.

Chapter One

The need had been growing since lunchtime. Marina Riesenthal had played the Fat Woman's game of not overeating in front of others, toying with grilled fish and a salad in the hope that her new client, Paul Jerome, would interpret her fifteen-stone bulk as the result of a rare glandular condition.

'Fancy a liqueur, Marina?' Paul had asked. 'I will if you will.'

Marina succumbed and the conversation got vaguely dirty over the third Cointreau as Paul talked to her about the women in his life as if she were another man instead of just the sexless companion that she usually represented.

Marina recognised that this was a man only worthy of a thin woman's fantasy. She had learned as a fat teenager that all men who were neither social outcasts, congenitally ugly nor of psychopathic tendencies were permanently out of her league. She lived with it. As the waiter took their glasses away, Marina looked at Paul appraisingly. Everything in the right place. Dark brown eyes that matched his hair and not an ounce of fat on him. Clearly very fit. Christ, what must he think of her great wobbling mass? She hid her genuine attraction towards him by rearranging her piggy features into a grotesque parody of sexuality that made Paul laugh out loud.

'Fancy a cigar, Paul?' she asked. 'I will if you will.'

And they did.

Paul exhaled his cigar smoke in perfect rings. 'That was a great lunch, Marina. The first of many, I hope.'

Marina widened her eyes in mock-coyness. 'You're the client,

1

Mr Jerome. If you absolutely insist I accompany you to fabulously expensive restaurants then I must comply. After all, there are plenty of other account directors at TNSW willing to suffer like this if I'm not.'

Paul laughed. 'Yes, but they're all *boys*, aren't they? I've always preferred female company myself.'

Marina thrilled at being acknowledged as a woman. She drew deeply on her cigar, a recent habit that she'd acquired in an attempt to bring her perceived personality into line with her actual physical size. A few moments of companionable silence passed. The intimacy almost made her weep.

A while later, Paul caught her in a daydream. 'Are you thinking what I'm thinking?'

Marina delivered her best conspiratorial smile. 'What are you thinking?' (I doubt very much that you even noticed those two portions of Death by Chocolate that the waiter has just carried to the next table. And it's unlikely that you were wondering if you could smuggle a portion into the ladies' room and flush the toilet constantly so that nobody will hear you eating. That's what I was thinking.)

Paul looked around him. 'I was thinking about how lucky we are to be able to make a living like this.' He looked at Marina curiously. 'Do you know what I like about you?'

Marina cringed inwardly. She knew that it wasn't going to be her beautiful eyes despite the ten minutes she'd spent applying kohl pencil around the lids to make them look bigger. She knew that it wasn't going to be her dress sense despite having spent over £100 on an expanse of glorious silk fashioned into an allegedly 'hip skimming, figure-flattering, bosom-camouflaging' tent. She knew that it wasn't going to be her five feet ten inch height that, on a less bovine woman, would have been the perfect complement to Paul's own six feet two inch elevation. 'Surprise me,' she said dryly.

'I can really talk to you. Not just about business although you certainly know as much about Sparkleeze and the kitchen cleaning liquid market as I do. No, I can talk about anything. Like with a friend. Or a sister.'

It wasn't his fault. He didn't realise how hurtful the friend/

sister comparison can be to a woman who longs to be regarded as a sultry siren, a brainless bimbo, a sex object, anything but a friend or a sister.

Still, Marina was satisfied that lunch had been a success from a business point of view. And you could never have too many friends. And Paul hadn't looked at her enormous stomach once. Perhaps he hadn't noticed? Ha ha.

Of course he had noticed. He'd noticed everything about her. He liked her. She made him laugh, made him feel warm. She sparked off in him the sort of feeling that preceded or implied physical attraction. And yet ... Surely not ... No, this woman was very, very much not his type. What he meant by this was that she wasn't *anyone's* type, so she couldn't possibly be his. Now that he had that definition clear in his mind, he could restore Marina to the correct place in his mental classifications as 'chum'.

Except she refused to stay in her place.

She resisted the lure of sweet shops on the way home that night. She was still buzzing from her achievement at bringing in a £3 million account and establishing a good personal relationship with the client.

The Friday night torment began the moment she placed her low-calorie cardboard food substitute in the microwave. She heard the voice whispering above the annoying hum of the oven as it irradiated her dinner to a deserved death. 'Why are you eating that? You don't want it, it won't taste good and you'll still feel hungry afterwards. What's the point?'

Marina tried to ignore the words nagging her from within. She put into practice all the tricks she'd been taught at Slim-4-Good years earlier: she ate a carrot, she ate another pound of carrots; she drank a pint of water; she stared at a photograph of an anorexic lingerie model in a magazine; she visualised herself in a bikini that didn't require industrial joists to support her mammoth chest; she chewed every mouthful of her Lite Veggie Risotto twenty-five times; she manicured her nails; she took a bubble shower (terrified of getting stuck in the bath, she only ever took showers now); she conditioned her magnificent corkscrewed hennaed hair and gave herself a face pack; she stood in front of the mirror and announced to her reflection as seriously as she could: 'I am a beautiful woman.'

It wasn't working. The need was escalating into a desperate craving. She found herself rummaging through the kitchen cupboards wondering what she could make with a box of Bran Flakes, a sachet of slimming hot chocolate flavour drink and a tin of powdered low-fat milk. She gathered them all up in her arms, grabbed a jug of water and the washing-up bowl and carried them through to the living room.

Marina tipped the cereal into the bowl, emptied the powdered milk and fake chocolate powder on top of it and splashed over the water. She plunged her hand in and squished the mixture into a crunchy mud. It felt like dead leaves crackling between her fingers as the dark slime oozed into speckled clots that stuck to her nails.

She snatched up a handful and crammed it into her mouth. Her eyes closed in a fake-chocolate ecstasy. Handful followed handful until Marina's face was streaked with greasy stripes. She didn't care. She knew what she looked like, with or without dirty marks. Her face was an anonymous round thing with too many chins, too much fat cheek, too heavy eyelids. All the pre-Raphaelite hair in the world could not make her look anything other than middle-aged.

She was thirty-one.

By 8.30, the bowl was empty, licked clean, the last mouthfuls leaving behind a soapy aftertaste of washing-up liquid. Marina didn't notice. She was already beginning to panic. No more food in the house. No more food in the house. She was breathing more heavily now and pacing the floor trying to talk herself out of the next inevitable step.

The inevitable won. Marina snatched a coat and ran out. The icy December snap made no impression on her well-insulated frame. She half-ran along the street, carefully avoiding her reflection in the dark shop windows. Focused on the distant beacon of the twenty-four-hour supermarket, she mentally planned her itinerary around the aisles.

She breathed in as the automatic double doors opened and admitted her to paradise. She enjoyed a moment of relief that she

4

didn't get stuck in the superfluous turnstile that the shop had recently installed, no doubt just to humiliate her.

It would have contravened her own bizarre but consistent standards to fill a trolley with indulgences so she took a basket instead. She headed straight for the ice cream so that it could begin its sensuous melting process as soon as possible. She glanced over the cabinets sampling every flavour with damp eyes before her shaking hand settled on Double Chocolate Cream Caramel Crunch. And Toffee Cookie Fudge. And Belgian Choc Chip Cappuccino.

On to snacks and biscuits where Marina meticulously chose family-sized bags of salt and vinegar crisps, tortilla chips and cheese puffs. She was gaining momentum as she hit her favourite section. Cakes. She whispered a silent prayer (or was it a curse?) to God for sending the world Mr Kipling. One by one, she selected a coffee gateau, a chocolate fudge brownie dessert, a treacle tart, a box of fondant fancies, another box of fondant fancies, a cherry cake, a walnut cake . . .

'Moo Cow?'

Marina dropped the walnut cake into her basket and tried to remember whether she'd washed the chocolate stains from her face before coming out. She found a smile somewhere deep in her memory and presented it to her friend.

'Susie! What are you doing in this neck of the woods?' She quickly took in Susie's fitted red suit, her twenty-five-inch waist, her perfect blonde bob. She looked like the PR executive that she claimed to be despite actually being a secretary. Gorgeous. If she hadn't been her oldest friend, Marina would have hated her.

The smooth image was tweaked only by the heap of carrier bags crawling up Susie's arms. Susie never went out without a list of requirements for her family who seemed to have insatiable material needs. Whether these needs were determined by the family or by Susie herself, Marina had never managed to educe. Susie never went anywhere with just one purpose, one destination. Unless at least four tasks were achieved, then an outing was deemed a waste of time. When working, the lunch hour was earmarked for strategic shopping. Merely spending the hour eating lunch would be an unforgivable indulgence.

'I was on my way home and realised I was out of bread so I

stopped off here.' She looked into Marina's basket curiously. 'Where's the party, Moo Cow?'

Marina heard herself laugh too loudly, too animatedly. 'It's not a party exactly. No, what it is, funnily enough, is that, well you know I mentioned I had those friends with all the children . . . no? Well it must have been someone else I was telling, well anyway, they're popping round tomorrow afternoon to pick up some Christmas presents and you know what kids are like, so fussy, but you can't go wrong with cakes and crisps and the like, but then I didn't know what sorts they would all prefer, kids being kids, so I thought the best thing would be to get lots of different things, just to be on the safe side.' She came up for air.

Susie raised her eyebrows. 'I hope they're hungry. My God, you must be expecting the entire von Trapp family. Their parents must be more tolerant than I am. I won't let Alice and Frederick near all that junk food. God, Moo, I remember how miserable you were as a fat child, I couldn't see my kids go through that.'

Marina knew that it wouldn't be long before the precocious twins rebelled against Quorn burgers and 'fun' packs of raisins to become accomplished secret bingers just as she had done at their age. She didn't voice this certainty. 'So, everything all right, Susie?'

'Well, had a flare up of the old IBS yesterday. Had to go to the doctor. Got a prescription though God knows what good it'll do. And did I tell you that I've been getting these pains in my head? That's how brain tumours start, you know. And haemorrhages. The doctor said they were probably migraines. Told me to take paracetamol. I think he's just too mean to send me for a brain scan now that he's gone fundholding.'

Marina tried to regard Susie's hypochondria for what it clearly was – the cry for attention of a woman who didn't get enough attention elsewhere. The sobbing of a mother who devoted twenty-five hours a day to pleasing everyone else and wouldn't pause for reflection unless a genuine pain (of imaginary source) brought her up short. Unfortunately, Marina just felt irritated. Hypochondria was yet another door closed to her.

She wished that she had the confidence to have irritable bowel syndrome and brain tumours instead of tummy aches and headaches. There was no point in a fat person going to the doctor. Whatever the symptoms, her weight would be blamed. 'Sprained ankle? Must be all that extra weight putting you off balance. Chest infection? What do you expect when you put all that strain on your lungs? Nasty rash? Must be your body reacting to all the greasy food you eat. Broken arm? Shouldn't try to load so much lard on to your fork, Fatty.'

Susie looked at her watch that didn't have any numbers on the face and consequently made telling the time difficult. 'Is that the time? Must dash. I've got to sew labels on the twin's games kit. Oh and they're supposed to take something in for "Show And Tell". They'll expect me to think of something different for each of them. They'll ask Ken but he'll get it wrong. It's always up to me. And Ken'll be pacing the floor. You know Ken. He's like a hunter-gatherer, waiting to be fed the minute he gets through the door. If his food isn't on the table when he gets in, he becomes positively Neanderthal.'

Marina couldn't imagine Ken grunting or beating his chest. She thought he was more the muted sighing and silent suffering type, weary after a hard day's statistical research. Nevertheless she allowed Susie to continue in her fantasy that she was married to Conan the Barbarian.

Susie was prattling on, oblivious to Marina's distraction. ' So, you're still OK for tomorrow night, then?'

Saturday night. What about Saturday night? Marina quickly remembered an invitation to dinner that she'd accepted in a moment of weakness. She assumed her enthusiastic voice. 'Oh, dinner. Yes absolutely. Can't wait.'

'That's good. And you're not on any of your silly diets at the moment, are you? Because I've got this fabulous recipe I want to try for lemon sorbet. A zillion calories, of course. I'll have to diet myself after a slice of that.' She patted her non-existent stomach in mock shame. 'That'll be all right, won't it?'

Marina smiled painfully. 'Sounds great.'

Susie looked at Marina properly for the first time. 'What's wrong?'

Marina tried to pull her gurgling terrors into a coherent line of thought. Just as she was about to speak, she noticed Susie glance at her watch. It was a discreet glance, not meant to offend but the effect was the same. It reminded Marina brutally that Susie had commitments, had other people who needed her, had purpose. It hurt.

She smiled tightly. 'Nothing's wrong. Just a bit tired. I mustn't keep you.'

Susie looked guilty. She *looked* guilty but she *felt* envious. She envied Marina her freedom; no commitments, no needy others making demands on her precious time. Her only worry was what cakes to buy for some visiting kids – kids that she could send home as soon as they became difficult.

She smiled equally tightly. 'We'll talk on Saturday. Sorry if I upset you by mentioning diets. I know you don't like talking about . . . things like that. Anyway, I thought you were happy the way you are. You are, aren't you?'

Ecstatic, Marina thought. 'I'm fine Susie, honestly.'

'Great! Well I'll leave you to your shopping then. You take care. See you Saturday, Moo.'

Susie leaned across to kiss Marina, her thin lips drowning in a rice pudding cheek. As she walked away, Marina silently answered all the questions that her friend hadn't thought to ask. Yes, business is going great. Yes I did win that new client I told you about last week. No of course I'm not seeing anyone at the moment. Yes I am earning more than you and Ken put together now. Yes I do look rather like Demis Roussos in this designer tablecloth I'm wearing. Yes, I do still stay at home and read third-rate romances most Saturday nights. Yes I do sometimes feel that my life is an utter failure. And yes, I do mind being called Moo Cow. It hurt when we were eleven and it hurts even more twenty years on.

She knew she was being unfair. Susie didn't mean to appear selfish. She was just saturated with other things. When they met up for their nights out, Susie was the most attentive listener and the most sensitive of advisers. She just couldn't function outside of her rigid compartments. Right now, she was in family providing/mother/housekeeper function. She couldn't offer supportive friendship in this mode. It required a leap of concentration for which Susie did not have the energy.

Marina watched Susie picking up bread, eggs and cornflakes on her way to the checkout. She marvelled at Susie's total indifference to the chocolate display in front of the till. In fact, she envied anyone who could shop without fear, who could look at a food counter without being consumed with sweaty desire. Finally, Susie left and Marina could return to her shopping.

She'd finished with the cakes section and was now moving up and down the other aisles, scanning labels with an expert eye, looking for new delights and old favourites to tempt her. She found her arm reaching out, of its own accord, towards tins of syrup sponge, baked beans with pork sausages, ravioli, fruit cocktail in heavy syrup, packets of trifle mix, savoury rice and pasta, a large frozen lasagne, a box of muesli. When she could get nothing more in her basket she struggled towards the till, where she added six or seven bars of chocolate. She felt obliged to explain to the uninterested check-out girl about the non-existent party she was planning. 'I mean, personally, I don't like all this sweet stuff, but if that's what the kids want, what can you do?'

The girl looked bored. 'That'll be forty-two pounds seventeen.'

Marina handed over the cash and picked up her shopping bags with an anticipatory smile. She walked home quickly, resisting the temptation to take a chunk out of the walnut cake right there in the street. It was only the possibility of being caught in yet another illicit situation by Susie that stopped her.

She rushed through her front door and emptied the bags on to the living room floor. Her breathing was fast now and she was having difficulty tearing her way into the packets. She ripped open a bag of crisps with her teeth and pressed a fistful into her mouth. Her bulky body folded awkwardly on to the floor and she finished the rest of the crisps in a more relaxed state, licking off the salt and vinegar powder before letting the soggy potato residue dissolve on her tongue.

In an attempt to add a semblance of civilised order to her feeding frenzy, she liked to alternate sweet and savoury 'courses'. She decided on the fondant fancies next.

When she was sixteen her mother, always effortlessly thin, had caught her eating a whole box of fondant fancies in her bedroom. The look of disgust on her mother's face had stayed with her. She had vowed then that, when she left home, she would eat whatever she wanted, whenever she wanted. Ever since, the fondant fancies always entered the stage early during a typical binge for Marina.

Delicately nibbling away at the soft pink icing, her little finger probed for the small knob of white cream. She mashed it against the roof of her mouth, luxuriating in its evocative synthetic tang. She dropped the small square of sponge back in the box and moved on to a yellow fancy. Then the chocolate. Ending up with eight pieces of naked cake, she quickly sprayed oven cleaner over them and threw them into the bin so that she wouldn't return to them in the middle of the night. It almost made her feel in control. In her opinion, plain cake was a sheer waste of calories.

She went into the kitchen where she placed the frozen lasagne in the microwave and put on two saucepans of water, one for the steamed sponge pudding, one for the savoury rice. No longer caring about her sweet/savoury intentions, Marina started on the chocolate fudge dessert. Using her finger, she spooned the rich sugary topping into her mouth, barely tasting one scoop before shovelling in the next. The microwave pinged, signalling that the lasagne was cooked. She decided to pretend that she was a normal person so she served it out on to a plate and ate it with a fork and spoon.

She scraped the melted cheese and bland white sauce on to the spoon and slurped it noisily while oily puddles gathered at the corners of her lips. Rolling up the top layer of lasagne into a thick white sausage, she abandoned the cutlery and forced the whole doughy clump into her mouth. She mixed the next two layers of meat sauce and white sauce into a mottled gravy and dredged it in. She repeated the ritual until the plate was licked clean.

Next the muesli, one of her favourite eating moments. She poured a small quantity into a dish and delicately picked out all the nuts and pieces of coconut, the apricots and other fruits and seeds. Piece by piece she chewed the healthy morsels. She then discarded the oats and grains into the rubbish before pouring out a second helping. It killed almost ten minutes before she reached the bottom of the box. And it was fun.

Now she was ready to attack one of the tubs of ice cream which was melting satisfactorily. She dunked chunks of walnut cake into the creamy liquid, savouring the clash of sensations as the ice cream curdled with the cake's buttercream filling. Her flat was now a tip of discarded wrappings and contaminated sponge remnants. Marina was eating more and more quickly, anxious to cram as much in as possible before nausea and stomach cramps prevented her from finishing the feast.

The savoury rice had boiled into into a clump of goo, studded with pieces of indeterminate vegetable in primary colours. Its blend of E numbers and dubious-sounding additives gave it a unique school dinner flavour that helped to eradicate all memory of her £50 lunchtime fish salad. She ate the beans and fruit cocktail straight from the tins.

Time was running out. The steamed syrup sponge was ready and the thought of it was making Marina feel queasy. Gamely she opened the tin and heaped a few dense spoonfuls into her crisp-and buttercream-ringed mouth. She couldn't finish the pudding. She looked frantically at the untouched chocolate bars. It was against her rules to leave any comfort food unopened in her flat overnight so she simply had to get through it all.

She tried to concentrate on her breathing to stop herself from being sick. Filled with self-loathing, she ripped the paper from the chocolate and forced the brown opiate towards her bloated face. After the third bar, she began to gag. She lay flat out on the floor, her stomach stretched with pain. She pulled herself up with some final deepset vestige of motivation and reached for the magazine she had been reading the previous day. The pages opened at the article on dieting and Marina skipped to the relevant section.

Underneath a photograph of some smiling big women was the text that had attracted her attention: '5F – Fat Feminists Fighting the Flab Fascists. The new anti-dieting group are currently challenging media stereotypes of female beauty. 5F have already scored some notable successes with women who could barely remember a life not dominated by food and weight issues. With 5F's counselling and group sessions they were transformed into confident people, who could eat without feeling guilty and who were happy, yes *happy*, with their size twenty lives ...'

Marina didn't believe that this was possible but she dialled the helpline number anyway. As she waited for her call to go through, she surveyed the fallout of her binge. Crisp and cake crumbs formed psychedelic patterns in the ice cream splodges on the carpet. Flecks of rice and meat competed with the loud floral print of her dress. She tentatively moved her hand to her face where she recoiled from the dried icing that had settled into the chasms between her chins.

Suddenly sensing something wet trickling over her lips, she had a horrifying suspicion that she was dribbling. Tracing the moisture back to her eyes, she was surprised to recognise her own unfamiliar tears.

Just as she was about to give up holding on, her call was connected. A strong, reassuring female voice answered.

'This is the 5F helpline. My name is Gail. How can I help you?'

Marina heard a strange voice that she eventually identified as her own shouting down the phone in despair.

'Just help me! Please, somebody help me!'

Chapter Two

Marina fondled her glass of champagne and tried to ignore the fact that she looked remarkably like an expensively upholstered armchair in her £190 drop-waist Paisley-print dress. In an attempt to prevent anyone trying to sit on her accidentally, she waved her arms around a lot, giving the impression that she was drunk or suffering from one of those fashionable nervous diseases known by their initials.

She laboured to keep up a superficial conversation with the other two people in the room. One was a big Sindy doll. She was a PR executive working for the same company as Susie (another glorified secretary, thought Marina) and her husband was in construction marketing (a brick salesman, she decided bitchily). Sindy Doll could have been Susie. Same blonde bob, same smudge-free make-up accentuating the utterly regular features on the same bony face, same eyes unencumbered with telling laughter lines, same body constructed entirely of angles without a single curve. Brick Salesman could have been Ken. Same weak features, same mouth dragged down by apathy, same rounded shoulders, same flat hair with incipient bald patch. They were all thin, the lot of them.

Susie flitted into the room in a tiny black sheath with cap sleeves that made her look like a bat. Marina scrutinised the line of the dress looking for evidence that two hideous children had once sought sanctuary behind that narrow, taut abdomen. Not a bulge could be seen. If anything, Susie's stomach bordered on the concave. And whatever structure held up that perfect bust at the perfect angle, it certainly wasn't cantilevered the way Marina's bras had to be just to stop her bust from sweeping the floor. Susie smelt of perfume, hairspray and new clothes. She smelt of physical confidence and sexual self-awareness. She smelt like the prettiest girl in the class.

'Moo Cow, come and meet someone.' Susie dragged Marina from the depths of the sofa until they were both standing, both a little puffed from the exertion. Marina followed her friend into the kitchen where Susie's hunter-gatherer Ken and another man were locked in work-talk.

Marina wanted to faint or die or disappear. She was about to be partnered for the evening with someone who looked like a film star. She could hardly bear to wait for that moment when the stranger acknowledged her, that unpreventable look of horror and embarrassment on his face when he realised that he was being paired with the fat lady. Why did Susie keep doing this to her?

'David, this is my friend that I was telling you about. Moo Cow, this is David Sandhurst. He's a research scientist at Perrico where Ken works. You won't believe this but you two have a lot in common.'

I believe it, thought Marina wryly. We probably both go to the same gym and share a fondness for morning jogs and All-Bran for breakfast. I can tell these things.

She smiled bravely, in the sure knowledge that God was not going to be kind to her and send her a stroke or heart attack to save her from total mortification. She adopted her professional persona and held out her hand to the poor man as he turned round to greet her properly. 'Marina Riesenthal . . .'

'But everyone calls her Moo Cow!' Susie interrupted cheerfully. David ignored the interruption. 'Pleased to meet you Marina. Ken and Susie have told me a lot about you.' He took her hand and not for a second did his eyes wander below her face. Marina felt reassured while remaining fully aware that her bulk was so great that even the most inefficient peripheral vision could scarcely avoid the rest of her mass.

Susie hovered excitedly as the two shook hands. 'Wait till David tells you what he's working on, Moo. You'll die.'

Wishing a similar fate on Susie, Marina turned away until she and David were physically excluding all outsiders from their conversation. Susie left them to it. Her job was complete and she had another hundred jobs to do. She never stood still. Too much to do. Lives to organise. Order to restore. Impossible standards to maintain.

'She can be a bit over the top, I'm afraid,' Marina apologised. David smiled and Marina immediately lost her appetite in a flurry of collywobbles. He whispered conspiratorially. 'That's all right. I've known Susie for a while now. You get used to her. You've known her for years, haven't you?'

'Over twenty, actually. Hard to believe, sometimes.'

David looked at her quizzically. 'I hope you won't think I'm being rude ...'

Marina took a sharp breath, having a wider experience than most of just how rude 'rude' could be. '... but you and Susie don't seem to have a lot in common.'

Marina breathed out quickly. 'You mean because we look so different?'

'Not at all. I just mean as people. From what I hear, you have a fantastic career, you travel all over the world with your job, you have a lovely flat, you're not tied down with family in any way. You've achieved so much. Whereas Susie ...'

Susie had a job rather than a career. She had a husband and children instead of an eating disorder. She had a big sprawling house instead of a tasteful, compact shoebox. She had a life instead of an actuality.

David continued, 'I know I shouldn't be saying this to her best friend, but she is a bit, well, shallow.'

Marina felt indignant on her friend's behalf. 'Then you don't know her as well as you think. She's not shallow so much as ... preoccupied. She simply doesn't have the time to spare for philosophical discussions. She's a working mother, you know. And she doesn't just work full-time – she's on committees for voluntary work, and she's involved with the twins' school associations. And she gives dinner parties at least twice a week. And have you seen the garden? That's all her work.'

David looked taken aback by this catalogue of frenetic activity. So did Marina. It was only when she itemised Susie's life like this that she spotted the thread of desperation weaving chaotically through it. She didn't have time to analyse this fresh insight because David seemed anxious to appease her with a sincere apology.

'I didn't mean to offend you by criticising your friend. I was just making a casual observation. I'm sorry.'

'No, *I'm* sorry. You're right, in a way, that we don't appear to have much in common. I went on the defensive because I thought ... well, that you were talking about something else. Of course we're different people to the teenagers who swapped bubble gum stickers and swooned over David Cassidy. We've grown in separate directions. But the one thing Susie and I will always have in common is our past. If that makes sense to you.'

David considered this. 'I have to say that I've never understood women's friendships. They always seem to be based on something tenuous – a coincidence of working environment, a shared love of Mexican food, a hatred of men. I suppose I'm really a bit jealous. Men never seem to form those bonds that last years and transcend all changes in status or circumstances. I don't seem to have friends as such. What I have is the odd drinking companion who likes watching old Spurs matches on video or work colleague who has as little to go home to as I do.'

Marina was no longer holding in her stomach or clenching her buttocks. She was even drinking her champagne without a trace of self-consciousness. She was relaxed and enjoying herself in this man's company.

Marina recalled articles she had read in magazines as a teenager which dictated that men love to talk about themselves and are flattered by a woman's attention. She decided to follow this advice and hoped that she didn't appear coy. 'So what exactly are you working on that's going to make me die?'

David looked excited. 'Well, it's still at a very early stage, but I seem to have stumbled on a drug that causes fast weight loss.' He waited eagerly for Marina's reaction.

Bang, the balloon popped. Marina was the fat woman again. She saw immediately that she was merely a useful experimental subject, someone who would obviously have an overwhelming interest in any issue related to weight control. The only reason that he hadn't paid any attention to her body was because he didn't need to. He knew that she was enormous. He had already learned from Susie and Ken that she weighed a sufficiently massive number of kilograms to fall into his sphere of research.

She cleared her throat before answering. 'That's fascinating. I would imagine that such a drug could make its inventor very rich considering that over fifty per cent of women in the UK alone are overweight.'

'And the other fifty per cent *think* that they are overweight,' David joked.

Marina laughed politely without pleasure. She was aware that this handsome stranger was looking at her with a thoughtful expression she had never encountered before. She knew about freak show curiosity and judgemental disdain, but this scientist was appraising her like … like an exhibit. She didn't understand what was going on and she didn't like the uncertainty.

Several seconds of heavy silence followed during which they both fiddled with their clothes and pretended to listen to the Phil Collins CD that Ken thought appropriate, taking into account the mean age of the gathering.

They both jumped when Susie's bright voice summoned them into the dining room where the next course of the nightmare was about to be served up. Marina found herself placed in between David and Ken. Relieved at least to be spared a continuation of Brick Salesman's diatribe on the government's lack of support for cement manufacturers which he had started earlier, she gave her full attention to Ken.

'So how's work, Ken?'

Ken looked startled and Marina thought she must be shouting, a tendency of hers after a drink or two. 'Er … good actually. I expect David has told you about the exciting development. It'll really put Perrico on the map if it works. '

'He mentioned something about a new drug, yes.'

'The fat pill. Oh, I mean, sorry Moo, that's just what we call it. I'm not saying, you know …'

She knew.

Susie floated in bearing a platter of raw vegetables and two tiny dishes of dips. 'Now tuck in, but don't go too mad – there's a huge main course and a positively sinful pudding to come! Make sure you leave room.' Marina was starving. She had got through the day on only an apple, two Ryvitas and a Valium that she had taken to help her sleep through the worst of the hunger pains in the afternoon. She felt that she could have eaten all the crudités as well as the ceramic dish in the shape of a Savoy cabbage and still had room for a side of beef. Still, she comforted herself that at least fat people were allowed to eat raw vegetables without attracting accusing looks from fellow diners.

They all oohed and aahed obediently and pretended to be spoilt for choice between a cauliflower floret and a mange tout. Marina watched Susie and Sindy Doll pick at their starters and copied them, floret for floret. She noticed that all the men were helping themselves to warm bread rolls and buttering them liberally. Five hundred calories before they've even picked up a fork and they don't care, she thought resentfully.

She observed David shovelling bread into his mouth as if he hadn't eaten for ages. The truth was that he *hadn't* eaten for ages. But no one could have guessed why.

Marina was forced to concede that the dip was delicious. You could say what you liked about Susie's anorexic attitude towards portion control but she had a way with sauces and dips. They were always sinfully creamy and tangy. Susie recognised her talent and consequently refused to divulge any of her recipes.

It was her culinary mantra: 'I have a secret ingredient – you wouldn't believe me if I told you!'

Marina was almost relieved that she didn't have the recipe – it was one less delicacy to add to her bingeing routine.

The trouble with raw vegetables (apart from the subsequent flatulence) is the impossibility of chewing them quietly. Marina found herself sucking the broccoli until it was mushy enough to bite through without drawing attention to herself. The whole exercise made conversation difficult and only Phil Collins punctuated the hum of pulsing jaws.

Susie, who declared herself 'stuffed' after the second stick of celery, decided that enough eating had been done and that it was time for proper dinner party chat. Please God, don't let her start on about slimming pills, Marina prayed silently. 'Has David told all of you about his amazing discovery?' Susie asked her guests. Nobody replied, everyone too busy attempting to remove bits of baby corn from between their teeth with their tongues.

Susie carried on, oblivious to Marina's grim expression. 'Oh David, you're too modest! I would have thought you'd have announced it to the whole world by now. David's invented a pill that makes you lose weight and it doesn't matter what you eat or how much exercise you do. Isn't that fantastic? I'm trying to persuade him to give me some to try so that I can get rid of my *enormous* thighs but he won't be swayed.'

There was an awkward pause while Susie stared at Ken expectantly. Ken stopped picking his teeth and delivered the required lines. 'You haven't got enormous thighs, Susie. You haven't got enormous anything. You're as slim as a model.'

Susie laughed in surprise as if she hadn't trained her husband to produce this response on cue many times over the years. 'Oh, you're just saying that. I'm as fat as a horse! Anyway, David's going to be terribly famous and he's going to make Perrico a stack of money. Don't be shy, David. We're all agog with excitement.' David sighed. Much as he loved attention, he preferred to show off on a full stomach and he had already guessed that it was going to take a lot of bread rolls to compensate for the meagre meal ahead.

But he knew his duties as a guest. 'There's really not much to say at this stage.It definitely works on mice and it appears to work on people although testing is still at a very early stage.' Ken choked on a piece of carrot, aware that David had already tried the drug on himself, breaking every rule and ethical guideline in the book. Sindy Doll became animated as she considered all the possibilities. 'So would it work on anyone, no matter what they weighed, or only on the absolutely gross?'

Marina drank a full glass of wine down in one miserable gulp. She was not having a good time. This conversation was probably going to embrace every synonym for 'fat' through the alphabet from 'adipose' to 'Zeppelin-like'.

David was considering Sindy's question. 'In principle, it should work on anyone. Everyone burns off fat at a certain rate. If you are underweight, your fat burner is a little over-efficient. If you are of the correct weight, then your thermostat is correctly tuned. If you are overweight . . .'

Then you're a greedy pig who deserves to be the size of a missile silo. Marina switched off from the lecture. She'd read all the books, all the articles. She knew all about fat burners and faulty thermostats. And dodgy thyroids. And genetic predispositions. And hormonal problems. She also knew that, in common with many other obese women, she was big because she compulsively ate thousands of calories up to the point when she became too weak physically to continue eating. They could switch her thermostat up to a level capable of causing nuclear fission but she would still eat until she was sick.

'Moo Cow?' Susie's voice roused her from her thoughts. Everyone was staring. A question had been levelled at her and she hadn't been listening. Great. This would confirm their suspicions that fat people are all stupid. She shook her head with a big smile as if she were a scatterbrained girlie caught enjoying a suitably inappropriate daydream. 'Sorry, I was miles away! What did you say?'

Susie repeated the question patiently. 'We were all wondering what you thought of David's miracle pill. I mean, of course, you'd want to take it, everyone will want to take it, but what sort of effect would it have on your life?'

Marina considered this carefully. She sensed five pairs of eyes scrutinising the monster before them and trying unsuccessfully to picture her without a hundred or so surplus pounds. She surprised herself with her answer. 'I'm not so sure that everyone would want to take the pill. I'm not even sure that I would want to try it myself.' They all laughed riotously at the absurdity of her disclaimer: the fat woman saying that she wouldn't take a magic weight-loss pill! Hilarious! Ridiculous! Marina read their thin-person's minds: for God's sake, if they had the sort of weight problem that she had, they'd inject themselves with toxic waste if there was a billionth of a chance that it might slim them down without actually killing them. And if it did kill them, well, better dead than fat.

David stopped laughing first. 'No, seriously, Marina, I'm

interested in your opinions. What do you think people's attitude will be?'

Marina snorted. 'You know damn well what their attitude will be. You are playing to the very depths of women's insecurity. Most women will pay anything for it, they won't even consider the implications of what they're doing.'

'What are the implications apart from the prospect of a good figure without having to struggle for it?' David asked.

'That's exactly it!' Marina pointed out excitedly. 'If you don't have to struggle for it, then ...' she tapered off, not having the slightest idea where her argument was going.

Susie knew precisely where the argument was going. 'Oh Moo Cow, that's just so bloody typical of you. Everything has to be difficult. You won't ever make things easy on yourself. I remember when we were doing O-level Maths and Julia Drummond got hold of the exam paper in advance. You were the only one in the class who didn't buy a copy and you were the only one who didn't get an A.'

Marina remembered the humiliation of that C grade well. 'What is so wrong with not wanting to cheat?'

Susie looked at her in disbelief. 'What is so wrong is that everybody cheats when they get the chance. By *not* cheating when you have an easy opportunity, you are choosing to make life harder than it has to be. God, there are plenty of occasions where you just have to deal with what's being dealt to you. When there's a simple way out, what is so wrong with taking it?'

Marina never cheated. Except on diets where she was capable of lying to herself about that teensy chocolate gateau she ate in four mouthfuls when she was standing by the kitchen door. She could also 'forget' the odd 500 calories of dry roasted peanuts eaten in the car. She even half-believed the fib that calories didn't count if you ate them standing up or if no one saw you eat them.

But her biggest cheat of all was the lie that she was now telling. A pill to make her thin? Who was she kidding? Of course she would take it. She wouldn't tell anyone though. She'd claim that she was losing weight on a super-strict diet and that she had finally discovered willpower. But the lie had been spoken and she had to keep it going. 'I just think that it's tampering with nature. It could

21

have all sorts of dangers to our bodies or to future generations that simply wouldn't show up immediately. Like Thalidomide.'

The Sindy doll's voice was brittle as she laid into Marina. 'Are you saying that it's natural to be hideously overweight? Or that it's healthy? Surely it's better to take something to get down to a normal weight, even if there are risks, than to have strokes and heart attacks because all your arteries are clogged with grease and your organs can't bear the strain of so much extra weight?'

Marina could feel herself redden with this transparent attack on her own body. Susie leaped to her defence. 'I think that's being a bit mean to Moo Cow. Some people can't help being on the large side. Take Moo. She hardly eats enough to keep a sparrow alive and look at her. It's probably glandular or something like that. And anyway, what you're forgetting is that some fat women are happy the way they are. You can't force someone to get thin if they don't want to.' She tossed a supportive, conspiratorial smile towards Marina who cringed at this naive judgement.

Susie continued. 'But I have to say, Moo, that you're being very blinkered in your refusal to even consider this pill. It's like I've always said to you. I know how well you've done in your career but you've had to work like a maniac to get there. You've said it yourself – thin, pretty women always have an easier ride to the top. I'm not saying that it's your fault that you're overweight, but you've never really tried to sort yourself out. Just think how much easier your life would have been if you'd just addressed the problem with real commitment.'

She softened, aware that Marina might be feeling self-conscious at this public undressing. 'Sorry. I just get carried away because I hate watching you have to fight for everything. You deserve an easier life. And I'd love to see you settle down. I hate thinking of you all alone.'

Every muscle in Marina's body was tense. She was developing a headache and a backache and she desperately wanted to go to the bathroom but was terrified that she'd be talked about if she left the room. She practised some controlled breathing that she'd learned from a pregnant secretary and waited for the tension to leave her.

Ken intervened at this point. 'Perhaps Marina doesn't need a man as much as you do, Susie.' A glance was exchanged between the two which seemed weighed down with meaning. Marina made a mental note to probe Susie on this when they next went out. Susie's lips thinned to a needle-thin red line. She recovered well and began collecting the plates that had hardly been used. 'I'll just go and get the main course. Perhaps you could help me, Ken?' Ken rightly interpreted this request as a direct order and obeyed without hesitation. He followed his wife into the kitchen where angry mutterings could be heard above the soporific lull of Chris De Burgh who had taken over the cabaret from Phil Collins.

David started to speak, much to the annoyance of Sindy (and Marina if she was being honest) who was trying to hear what Susie and Ken were rowing about. 'I hope I haven't embarrassed you, Marina. It must seem as if we're all getting at you but I didn't mean it to have that effect. The thing is, no matter how much we all pussyfoot around it, you *are* larger than average and my pill could transform your life, I think for the better. I'm genuinely interested in what you think about it.'

Marina sighed. 'David, have you ever heard of a group called 5F?'

David looked puzzled. 'Are they in the charts?'

Marina laughed despite her misery. 'They're not a pop group. They are an organisation of like-minded women all opposing social pressures to conform to slim stereotypes. 5F stands for 'Fat Feminists Fighting the Flab Fascists'. They ... we ... are all over-weight by contemporary standards but are all happy to be that way. They ... we ... eat what we like, never weigh ourselves and refuse to be browbeaten by the fashion industry and the tyrannical rules laid down by the glossy women's magazine dictatorships.' She was impressed by her own eloquence even though she was merely reciting, parrot-fashion, the text of the article she had read a few days earlier. Her first 5F meeting was not for another week and she hadn't decided definitely to attend until this evening's debacle.

David seemed thoughtful. 'So this group of women all eat what they like? They're not following diets? They don't have strange binge/starvation habits? That must mean that their weight doesn't fluctuate like that of the average dieter. ' That thoughtful expression entered his cold blue eyes again. Marina was temporarily distracted as she tried to interpret the strange look.

She cleared her throat and answered the question. 'That's right,' she said confidently, unsure of the facts but longing for this to become the reality for her.

David sank even more deeply into his thoughts. 'Interesting,' he murmured.

Just then, Susie re-entered the room triumphantly bearing a small serving dish topped with a single roast chicken. 'I hope you're all hungry!' she cried merrily.

Marina exhaled in despair as her suspicion was confirmed that this chicken was to serve all six of them. Only the thought of a detour via McDonald's on the way home gave her the strength to appear and sound grateful for the chicken wing that sat, lonely and undernourished, in the centre of a plate surrounded by three new potatoes and thirty-seven peas. She knew that there were thirty-seven peas because she counted them.

David let himself into his small flat and tentatively switched the lights on. He sighed in gratitude that the electricity had not yet been cut off. He sat down and emptied his pockets of the leftover rolls that he'd rescued from the bin during a secret visit to the kitchen. There were five. With a lot of self-control, he could make them last through Sunday all the way to Monday breakfast.

David Sandhurst had no money. Absolutely, literally no money. This did not mean 'no money' in the sense used by people who can only afford two weeks instead of three in St Lucia. It meant 'no money', no access to money, nothing to sell, a complete shutdown of all credit sources. On Monday, David's salary would be paid into his bank account and he would begin again the futile battle of living within his means until the next payday. He would juggle his creditors, alternating the lies and excuses for non-payment that would defer final demands for a little longer.

He wasn't overly worried. Things always worked out for him. Eventually.

David was born with exceptional gifts. He had an exceptional intellect. He was exceptionally attractive and exceptionally charming. He had always been destined to change the world. He should have been – *would* have been – a prodigy. But from birth, he had been blessed, or cursed, with the two blissfully destructive 'Ls' that would prove the defining elements of his life: luck and laziness.

Perhaps the two were not bestowed simultaneously. Perhaps the former was simply the inevitable precursor of the latter. It was the continual manifestation of good fortune, always at the most apposite moments in David's frenetic life, that allowed him to indulge and yield to the siren call of laziness that curbed him from truly realising his potential.

From school days when academic work came easily to him and the minimal amount of homework produced consistently high results, he decided that any further application of his energy would be wasteful. If he could hit seventy per cent to produce an 'A' grade without working up a sweat, what was the point in going the extra distance for another twenty per cent? There was no A-plus grade, no further reward, no point.

And in time, he made an even more astonishing discovery. Even when he did *less* than the minimal amount of work required, he still over-achieved. Because he was lucky. If he only revised three out of five topics, then those three would be the topics covered in the exam. If, distracted by a new book/TV programme/girlfriend, he didn't revise at all, he would always go down with an utterly genuine illness that would excuse him from school without suspicion.

Jobs came along just when he needed money. Friends came along when his own company (rarely) bored him. His parents died and left him a small inheritance just when he was about to have his flat repossessed.

Lucky.

But this reliance on luck and his inability to explore personal resources in the face of adversity occasionally left him in dire states of limbo. Like now. Since making the Oxymetabulin discovery, he had already written the next ten years of his future history. He was going to make a fortune, an absolute fortune, once the drug hit the market. OK, it would take a while, there were procedures, protocols and the rest, but the drug worked and the whole world would want it.

So he started spending his fortune. Before he made it.

He had twelve credit cards all up to their credit limits, three bank loans (for non-existent car, non-existent fitted kitchen and non-existent holiday to the Caribbean) and four personal loans from companies who didn't ask as many questions as banks (and charged extortionate interest rates accordingly). For all this debt, he had little to show apart from a bulging wardrobe of designer clothes. This sad, unknowing man spent nearly all his (borrowed) money on carefully-planned, spontaneous, expensive, expensive gestures to impress women. He flew them to New York for long weekends ignorant that, with his looks and charm alone, the women concerned would have been just as happy with a night in, a pizza takeaway and a slushy video.

One could be generous and interpret this unnecessary extravagance as proof of an appealing lack of confidence that belied the original impression of utter arrogance and self-absorption. Or one could be realistic and acknowledge the man's stupidity when it came to human relationships.

Anyway none of this mattered. Soon he would have enough money to be as stupid as he wanted. Because Perrico had promised him a £250,000 bonus once the Oxymetabulin trial had been successfully completed.

In the meantime, his months followed an uncomfortable routine: once his salary cleared into his bank account, he paid the minimum amounts demanded on half of his credit accounts. Once *that* money was cleared, he would draw the money *out* of them and fuse that to pay off the other cards. Once *that* money was cleared, etc. Throughout this cycle, he allowed himself only the odd ten pounds here and there to buy the absolute essentials.

It was only his undisputed success with women that actually kept him alive. He encouraged them to cook (very big meals) for him and buy him little gifts (with good resale value).

His greatest humiliation was the Friday night trip to Sainsbury's when all the perishable produce was reduced for quick clearance. He pushed his elbows in front of frazzled, hard-up housewives in the battle for cheap chicken pieces and half-price stewing steak. He filled his basket with bent tins and jars of obscure foreign concoctions that could only be sold to the conservative Finchley shoppers at a third of the original price. While he never spent less than ninety pounds on a shirt, he refused to buy a tin of peas unless it was reduced to under fifteen pence.

But the struggle was getting wearisome. He needed to speed up the Oxymetabulin trial if he was going to persuade Perrico to advance him a little of his bonus. Unforeseen problems were holding him up but tonight had proved a vital step in his acceleration programme.

It was as he had thought. Marina held the key. She had to. She *had* to.

Chapter Three

The Christmas decorations in TNSW's reception were tastefully monochrome and expensive. Red baubles subtly embossed with clients' logos dangled from the massive spruce that shed needles every time a Louis Vuitton briefcase flounced past.

Andy Cline winked at the beautiful, well-spoken and utterly stupid receptionist who would only hold on to the job until the Chairman of Sparkleeze tired of sleeping with her. Like many advertising agencies, TNSW regarded itself as 'full-service' and if that service occasionally extended to offering jobs to clients' mistresses, then so be it. Andy was tempted in the girl's direction himself but valued his career prospects over a transient lust that could easily find satisfaction elsewhere among the crammed pages of his GQ address book.

He made his way through the building without disturbing the Christmas tree. Today was going to be a good day, largely due to the fact that Marina was away from the office (cue jokes in the Gents about the building's foundations having a day off). That expensive lunch with Marina's secretary a few weeks earlier had paid off and she had happily kept Andy informed of her boss's itinerary.

Apparently Marina was away on unspecified personal business. The secretary hinted, *sotto voce*, that gynaecological matters must be involved, that being the only possible reason for all the secrecy. The very mention of 'gynaecological' put Andy right off his soup.

Andy took the opportunity to call a Sparkleeze group meeting in the boardroom, inviting Rick Gifford, the MD, along as acknowledgement of the new account's importance to the agency's economic future.

The meeting was scheduled for ten thirty, leaving him a couple of hours to plan his agenda. It was all very tricky. Marina had won the account almost single-handed. She had met Paul Jerome at an awards dinner and, sensing his dissatisfaction with his present agency, invited him into TNSW for a pitch. Although she and Andy had given the presentation together as New Business Managers, it was plain that this was Marina's show.

Andy didn't understand it. He knew women but he knew men too. Paul Jerome was a man's man like himself, he was sure. Surely he was as repulsed by Marina's appearance as any normal man. Yet he seemed to listen to her, respect her, even (gulp!) like her.

The account was won and Rick gave it to Marina to head up. Andy was to work under her on Sparkleeze while attempting to bring in a similar chunk of new business to match his rival's achievement. The inducement was unspoken. A place on the board was soon to be available following the retirement of an old codger of thirty years' service who had only come into the office for the last five years to pick up his top-shelf magazines.

One place. For one board director. Andy or Marina. It wasn't supposed to be a contest based on value of business brought in but, clearly, the unexpected gain of Sparkleeze had done Marina a lot of good. For God's sake, Rick had even taken Marina out to lunch last week. Alone.

Yes, action was necessary. There was no way that Andy could find and win a sizable new account in the immediate future. He was going to have to do something more subtle. He picked up the phone, dialled Sparkleeze and, efficiently masking any malevolent intentions from his voice, asked to speak to Paul Jerome.

Five minutes later, Andy walked into Rick's office without knocking, the one member of staff who ignored the MD's preference for formal office behaviour. It was an unconscious acknowledgement of a shared past that included adjacent (and occasionally shared) beds at public school. Rick looked up and spoke with a blend of mild annoyance and comfortable familiarity. 'Come in,' he said pointlessly.

Andy sat himself on the hard, backless chair designed to keep meetings brief. He put his feet on the inflatable coffee table that was so unpleasant, you just knew it was fashionable. His pitch was casual. Professionally, deliberately casual. 'I've just asked Paul Jerome to pop in this morning for a bit of a team bash, thought you might like to sit in.'

Rick's face didn't betray his recognition of this underhand tactic. They'd played this game since the age of six. Andy would act as if they were intellectual equals and Rick would perpetuate the charade. His question was reasonable but loaded.

'Without Marina? I thought she and Paul Jerome were surgically joined by the personal organiser.'

Andy shrugged. 'She's not in today, women's things or some such nonsense, and this can't wait.'

'What can't wait?'

Andy smiled. 'Just a brilliant idea I've had for the Sparkleeze launch. We'll need to move fast if we're going to bring it off.'

Rick looked at him appraisingly. 'I thought Marina was going to be back this afternoon. Surely it could wait until then?'

'Paul Jerome can only make it this morning.' The lie was smooth, implausible and went unchallenged. 'I'll fill Marina in later on.' He interpreted Rick's lack of response as a tacit approval of the new agenda and left the office quickly before the impression could be corrected.

At ten forty, Andy walked into the boardroom with cream cakes for everyone. A cheap trick but it never failed. The atmosphere lightened immediately. The team bonded, Rick included, through the communal indignity of trying to eat eclairs without squidging cream out both ends. Without understanding why, they all found meetings with Marina tense occasions. No one liked to look at her body or talk about anything remotely related to food. Kit-Kats weren't snapped and passed around. Secretaries didn't leave out plates of the Danish butter cookies so loved by all the staff. Last night's dinner was never discussed. No matter what Marina achieved in her professional capacity and no matter how much she contributed to the personal wealth of her colleagues in profit-related bonuses, she continued to be defined only by her weight.

As any good advertising person will tell you, a point of difference is not always a positive attribute. Anything that sets a product apart from its competitors must be able to stand up to the most rigorous scrutiny. If it is a new enzyme in a detergent that gets clothes cleaner than the other powders, you can spend three million pounds showing blackcurrant juice being zapped under a microscope, you can find a word that rhymes with your enzyme and pay Elton John to sing a jingle glorifying the discovery and you can invite consumer journalists on an all-expenses paid junket to the Caribbean just to watch you doing some laundry. It is the marketing dream.

On the other hand, if your point of difference is that you are the only unattractive person in an industry where looks are all, if you are the beast in a world of babes, if you are the only woman addressed as 'love' instead of 'darling' by overpaid cockney photographers and faux-Northern art directors, well, you bluster on with your campaign and hope that nobody has noticed that your packaging is fatally flawed. Such was Marina's epic voyage towards sure rejection.

Andy, on the other hand, gloried in his not-too-handsome-to-alienate-his-male-peers looks. His skin bore the barely-perceptible traces of a ferocious adolescent skin complaint. His dark hair was shiny and one might have suspected that some oily veneer had been added. His features hinted at a Mediterranean heritage that he played down. All in all he should have been ugly. But he wasn't. He was pleasantly noticeable, even attractive to those women with no self-esteem who saw the glorious possibility of abuse behind his cruel jokes.

And he wasn't fat.

His breathtaking self-confidence made him shine and today he was radiating. Today he was fun guy, good bloke, bringer of cakes, dispensing his Old Etonian *noblesse oblige* to the working class high-achieving graduates who flocked to TNSW, hoping that their council estate names like Wayne and Kevin would be considered ironic in a post-modern way.

He shone among this gathering because he had orchestrated it so. Even Rick looked to him to take control of this meeting. And as if by magic, at the very moment that Rick glanced impatiently at his watch, the boardroom door opened and an anonymously attractive flunky showed Paul Jerome in.

Andy sauntered over to Mr Sparkleeze and shook his hand. 'Paul! Glad you could make it at such short notice. Come and meet the team.' With a proprietary hand on Paul's shoulder, Andy made all the introductions. At the end, Paul seemed puzzled. 'Where's Marina?'

Andy laughed, trying not to notice a dark glare from Rick. 'Off having some women's problems, so I've heard. Don't worry, I'm just as good and twice as pretty!' Everyone laughed. Except Paul. And Rick. Andy continued. 'We're a close-knit team here and, anyway, she'll be happy as long as every word is minuted in triplicate. You know Marina, a stickler for her paperwork. I'm more of a proactive man myself. So let's get down to it.'

They all sat down around the asymmetric table which had enough legs and joints to threaten the manhood or tights of every person who desperately sought legroom below the matt lime green surface.

Andy turned the lights out and switched on the slide projector. 'As I was saying to the bridesmaid just as I caught her coming out of the Ladies with the groom ...' he began to weak laughter. 'Whoops, wrong occasion!' He cleared his throat and readjusted his features into a serious expression. 'The purpose of this meeting is to review the current proposals for Sparkleeze and explore new possibilities in both the above- and below-the-line schedules.'

Everyone shifted uncomfortably in their seats. The schedules had been approved weeks ago. Marina hadn't mentioned anything about any changes. Above- and below-the-line? What was he talking about? It had been decided from the start that only straight advertising would be used in the first instance. Below-the-line activity, covering the range of marketing tricks from free samples to gimmicky PR ploys, was to be looked at after the first wave of the launch.

Rick's expression gave nothing away. Andy continued.

'As you all know, research showed that the time was right for a range of cleaning products aimed at both male and female usage – the modern couple: Mr *Loaded* and Ms *Cosmopolitan*. Two campaigns were developed aimed at the two target markets and we all have high hopes for the campaign's success in the coming months.'

There was a 'but' coming, everyone sensed.

'But, it occurred to me last night that we have never truly explored the possibilities of a unified approach, aimed at the commonalities shared by the modern couple. If men and women are finally pooling resources and sharing household chores on an equal basis, then why not assume that both sexes share the same attitudes towards cleaning, the same antipathies, the same dread of domestic slavery.

'Let's not patronise women by suggesting that they need less persuasion since they are genetically predisposed to drudgery. And let's not insult men, many of whom have looked after themselves and their flats since leaving home, by enticing them with *Men Behaving Badly* endorsements and carefully worded household hints.

'Let's face it – we're, all of us here, young, free and single, male and female, in or out of relationships, but we all have something in common. And what is that?'

'We're all wondering where the hell you're going with this idea?' offered a junior executive who had, with his first and last informal offering, sealed his permanent move to recruitment advertising.

Andy laughed emptily at the junior who was crushed by the death sentence that the mirthless noise was clearly delivering. 'Very funny. Before anyone else chooses to bless us with a sorely under-rehearsed stand-up routine, let me answer the question. Sex. That's what we have in common. Thinking about it, looking for it, getting it if we're lucky.' (He paused for laughter; some of the men obliged, none of the women did.) 'It's a common denominator and one that countless other consumer categories have been exploiting for a long time.

'So why doesn't the surface cleaning market take that great leap into the new millennium? Why don't we make housework sexy?'

Nobody dared answer. Nobody dared second-guess where Andy was going with this. They were all aware of the power struggle going on between Marina and Andy and everyone was careful to keep their cards unmarked until the outcome was more certain. Only two people could safely contribute to this discussion: Paul Jerome because it was his product and Rick Gifford because it was his agency.

Rick went first. 'We've had man and woman exchanging seductive looks and suggestive comments in front of the sink. What's new?'

Andy smiled. 'That's not real sex. That's safe sex. I'm talking about the raw stuff of male and female fantasy. Lust. Illicit wantings ...'

Rick interrupted. 'There's a limit to just how much you can show going on over a worktop.'

Andy shook his head. 'I'm not talking about the kitchen. Now I've got another question for you all. What is the next best thing to sex?'

'Cars.' The answer slipped out the mouth of a junior before he could stop himself. Fortunately for him, this was the correct answer. Andy pointed at the hapless body in triumph. 'Exactly! Cars. And it's not just men either. In the latest issue of *Advertising Today*, they're publishing the latest research that proves that modern women are becoming as interested in cars as men have traditionally been. Cars. Don't you see? Cars – the commonality.'

Nobody saw. What was the connection between sex, cars and window cleaner?

Andy clicked on to a sequence of slides. They showed a montage of scenes taken around London at some of the capital's busiest road junctions. The audience was more baffled than ever. They were looking at the least sexy, most unsavoury aspect of urban motoring – the squeegee merchants. Andy sensed a bristling of resentment on behalf of the filmed motorists being intimidated into an unwanted and inferior windscreen wipe from a series of dysfunctional adolescents. 'Very sexy', someone muttered.

Andy stopped the film. 'Sorry, did someone say something?' There was no answer, the thought of mortgage payments overwhelming any desire to participate in a no-win debate.

Andy smiled. 'Well, whoever it was, he was right. There is nothing sexy about some yobbo hurling a filthy sodden sponge across your windscreen and redistributing the grime in streaks right across the driver's sightline. But I'll tell you what *is* sexy ... rather, I'll show you.'

He restarted the film and, immediately, the room heated up. A scant step short of pornography, skilfully-lit images assaulted the eyes. Page-three girls pressed their treasure chests across soapy windscreens, wiping the foam away to reveal cosmically happy drivers. As they opened their side windows, the model reached into a logo-covered backpack and presented the lucky motorist with a free sample of Sparkleeze. The small, perfectly-formed bottle was handed over like a sexual favour and received with a smile seldom seen on a man who's just been given some window cleaner.

The women in the audience fidgeted. As if on cue, the screen images changed. This time the motorists were female. And the page-three girls morphed into Chippendale castoffs with chiselled faces and abdominal muscles that rippled like sand dunes. The men in the boardroom smiled indulgently at this sop to women's sexuality. They glanced at their female colleagues with the barely-concealed sniggers of schoolboy voyeurs.

The women's response was not as Andy had anticipated. Their expressions were of strained tolerance as if they'd been confronted with a toddler's tantrum. Irritated. Bored. Trying to appear amused.

Like many men, Andy had watched the burgeoning numbers of girly parties enjoying male strippers and totally misunderstood what was going on. He naively assumed that they were screaming with uncontrolled lust at the (horribly unsupported) thrustings of strange naked men's bodies. He didn't realise that they were screaming with hysterical laughter. He'd been fooled by the ads that employed pumped-up, unsmiling boy-men to seduce office workers and housewives alike into purchasing things they already purchased. He completely overlooked the fact that the ads were themselves made by men and therefore totally fallacious in premise.

Poor ignorant Andy, you might think. Although pity would not have been appropriate for he was cocooned by a comforting swathe of male empathy. The lads in the boardroom silently congratulated Andy for this brilliant egalitarian gesture. They didn't notice the women's reactions because they were too busy concentrating on holding in their stomachs in the face of the perfect male images assaulting them. And since, in the absence of Marina, all the decision-makers in this room were male, nobody really cared what the women thought.

The film ended and everyone faced inward around the table again, all looking at the client for a response.

'What do you think, Paul?' Andy asked.

Paul Jerome looked thoughtful. His male appreciation of the Sparkleeze starlets had been observed but he was not forthcoming in praise for the idea. He flicked through a folder in front of him, stopping at a page full of figures. 'Well, of course, it's a great concept. I like it, I like it a lot. I just don't see where the money's going to come from. I mean, I'm looking at the budget here and I can't see any contingency cash available. I suppose it could be considered in the next wave of promotional activity but I think Marina had ideas for that ...'

Andy interrupted firmly. 'Look, Paul, I know Marina sold the campaign well to you, but I'm offering you a media opportunity, an event, an impact that a thousand pages in *Housewife's Gazette* or whatever will simply never deliver. You need to be doing this on the day the product comes out, not in a year's time when the launch is yesterday's news.'

Paul sighed. 'I take your point, Andy, but I repeat my first question. Where's the money going to come from?'

In response, Andy passed round some impressively-produced colour charts. The figures were complicated but the strategy was simple. Andy explained. 'My "Junction Jostle" could be hitting road junctions in all the major cities within a month and paid for simply by cancelling eighteen per cent of the advertising campaign.' There were some mutters which Andy had expected. 'Yes, I know, I know, it seems a lot. But think about it – a few ads shaved from each paper, each magazine. Who'll really notice?'

Rick could no longer sit and watch silently. He didn't like to argue with a colleague in front of a client but clearly no one else was going to challenge this sweeping condemnation of the months of planning gone into producing this campaign recommendation.

'Who'll really notice? Andy, you of all people know that

EVERY ad increases the potential of reaching our target audience. You can't just butcher the campaign without affecting the outcome.'

Andy's irritation at being challenged by his pal was evident. 'I was about to say, Rick, that I realise you can't just slash budgets haphazardly. So I made friends with the latest media analysis software and came up with this.'

A chart flashed up on the screen on the boardroom wall. Everyone looked at the numbers blankly. Rick spoke on everyone's behalf. 'Would you care to interpret this for us?'

Andy smiled his most charming smile. 'I won't bore you with the maths but I will leave you computer printouts offering all the data you need. In a nutshell, if we carefully and selectively shave a few corners from the schedule and replace them with a forty-eight-town blitz of "Junction Jostle", we will be INCREASING our reach overall.'

There were no whoops and cheers.

A bespectacled minion with no confidence but a solid grounding in media planning cleared his throat, took his career into his hands and spoke up, making the point that was clear to all. 'The thing is, Andy, that Marina negotiated the prices for the whole campaign on the understanding that there would be no cancellations. What you're suggesting is that Marina goes back to every publication, every TV, radio and poster company, and renegotiates.'

Andy shrugged. 'And your point is ... ?'

Rick intervened before he lost yet another member of staff to Andy's killer stare. 'The point is that the media would be within their rights to make things very difficult with us for making any cancellations at this late stage.'

Andy looked boyishly surprised. 'I thought Marina had the media wrapped around her little, or should I say, big finger. Once she realises that this plan is an improvement on the original, I'm sure she'll do whatever is necessary.'

Paul Jerome considered the figures before him. 'It's difficult, I realise. I mean, it's a great idea but we do have promotional plans for later on and I don't like to be responsible for souring relationships with the media ...'

Andy raised his hand to stop the client from finishing what was sounding ominously like a once-and-for-all veto. 'Like I said, I have complete confidence in Marina's ability to pull this off with no adverse consequences.'

Rick felt driven to ask an obvious question. 'Why don't we just wait till Marina gets in and ask her?'

Andy looked pained by the suggestion. 'I wish we could but I need to have a decision on this by lunchtime. The organisation I've got lined up have had another company approach them with a proposal which would commit their entire roster of young men and women through August when the launch is scheduled. They need a definite "yes" this morning. That's why I had to call Paul in at short notice. I really hate doing this without Marina but I had no choice.' He paused and looked down at his hands as if struggling with his conscience before continuing. 'I couldn't believe it when I came in this morning and found she was off on some secret jaunt and was completely unobtainable. Obviously it must be something very important for her to absent herself at such a critical time for Sparkleeze, but I don't see why she had to switch her mobile phone off.'

Sharp intakes of breath greeted this concrete proof of Marina's gross dereliction of duty. I mean, being fat was bad enough but switching off her mobile phone during working hours? Only a man or a really, really pretty woman is allowed to treat the unwritten rules of executive life with such cavalier disregard.

Paul Jerome rubbed his eyes wearily. 'I suppose the decision is mine to make. I'm unhappy about doing this without Marina's input but, if you are completely happy that this can all be achieved without too much upheaval, then... I think we should do it.'

Andy smiled his first sincere smile of the day. Happy? he thought, I'm ecstatic. 'Good. That's settled then. And don't worry about Marina. I know she'll be as excited about this change of direction as we are when I brief her.'

And if his fingers were crossed as he spoke, no one noticed. Except Rick.

Rick and Andy were both born on the same day thirty-nine years earlier. It was this realisation that drew the unlikely pair together at Eton. It was a fairly trivial bond on which to base a lifetime of friendship but, for two men painfully incapable of self-expression, the mutual understanding of each other's emotional inadequacies offered a quiet and continuous comfort.

Andy suffered from severe eczema which left him open to the potent cruelty of children who teased him without mercy. Rick was the only boy who accepted his overtures of friendship and, for this favour, Andy forgave Rick for being cleverer than himself. It was the only time in his life that Andy allowed himself the mistake of allying himself with someone whose measurable superiority would always reflect badly on the underling.

What did Rick get from pairing himself off with this socially inferior creature? Well, in childhood, he got a worshipper, someone who would constantly reassure him that he was a person with perceptible qualities. And, as Andy's skin cleared up and he gained confidence, Rick gained a buddy of polished social skills who uncovered an innate talent for attracting girls.

And Andy repaid his debts. There was always a 'friend-for-my-friend', a double date for the shyer Rick. He shared his better clothes and better chat-up lines. (Funnily, when it counted, Rick found his own girl. And married her. And had children. All by himself.)

So Andy and Rick grew up together, occasionally deviating from each other's meandering paths through privileged maturity but always finding themselves touching souls at critical life junctures.

As it had to be, one of them did better than the other. In this coupling, it was Rick. Not because he was a massive amount cleverer or more ambitious or even luckier. It's just the way it went. Andy's choices led him on a more winding itinerary to career success and, by the time he got there, Rick was a permanent step ahead.

Rick gave Andy the job at TNSW because he was the best man for the post, first, and his friend, second. The potential of joining Rick on the board and, once and for all, ironing out the professional inequalities between them, was a massive motivation for Andy to take up the position.

And now he was thirty-nine. And that meant only one thing.

He would soon be forty. That awesome age where milestones are assessed and checklists compared. By the time I'm forty, I'll have written my first novel, made my first million, that sort of thing. Andy's ambitions were previously undefined but his lack of achievement in *any* field hit him like a sucker punch.

He had no wife, no kids, no big house, no big car, no job title that would raise eyebrows of admiration, no reputation beyond the narrow field of London advertising agencies. Unlike Rick. Rick had all of those things.

Andy wasn't happy. He had eleven months to go before he hit forty. By then, things were going to be different. *Had* to be different if his life was to have made any sense.

He wasn't asking much. He didn't expect to be Prime Minister or married to an It-girl. He wanted a seat on the board and someone to share it with. Like Rick. He didn't begrudge Rick his successes, well, not much. He just wanted the same. It was only fair. They were the same, after all.

And so it would be. He had a dream and a plan. And Marina was not going to spoil it.

Chapter Four

It was hard to go unnoticed when you occupied the same amount of space as two average people. It was easier when everyone else in the room was as big if not bigger than you. Marina relaxed immediately on realising that she was by no means the largest one here. She stood by the door for a few moments until she was greeted by an imposing woman who flew towards her like a Wagnerian diva.

'You must be Marina. I'm Gail Bathurst. We spoke on the phone.' She grabbed Marina's hand and clasped it warmly between both her own moist hands. It was all a little too touchy-feely for Marina, who had to make an effort not to recoil.

Gail didn't wait for her to answer. 'Welcome to 5F. First time is always the hardest. We've all been there. All you have to remember is that there is nothing that you have experienced that someone else hasn't gone through as badly as you. There's nothing that you have done in the name of weight loss, however appalling, that someone else can't top. But it all changes from this moment! We're going to show you how to be free to eat what you like without hating yourself afterwards.' She paused for dramatic effect before making her wildest promise yet. 'We will teach you how to eat cake without guilt.'

Now *that* I don't believe possible, thought Marina. She hated herself for the twang of pleasure she felt in noticing that Gail weighed a lot more than she did. Or perhaps she just looked bigger because of her astonishing presence. Her hair alone must have added a couple of pounds in weight as well as a few inches in height. There were at least four shades of red exploding among the unruly spikes that stuck out like a peacock's tail. Her face was stunningly made up although the dark matte foundation had settled into the bottomless creases of her face like slashes of war paint on an angry Apache.

Before Marina could say anything, she was being pulled into the centre of the room like a prize-winning heifer at a cattle auction. Gail clapped her hands and the room fell into a respectful silence.

'Women! We have a new member with us tonight. Someone who has taken that momentous step towards liberation from the shackles of weight oppression.' Everyone clapped and whooped except Marina who had retained an aversion to audience participation since being dragged on to the stage during a pantomime when she was eleven and already weighed ten stone.

Gail continued, 'Let's all welcome Marina to our group in customary fashion.' Before Marina could bolt out of the door, she found herself being hugged and kissed by a crowd of complete strangers with whom she had nothing in common but a self-loathing and an unhealthy attitude to food. The crowd finally broke away and separated into small groups. Marina eyed the exit longingly. Gail noticed her discomfort and grabbed her hand again. 'You can't run away from us, not now that you've found the courage to join us.' She looked around then yelled in the direction of a less threatening woman chatting comfortably in the heart of the gathering.

'Teresa, come and talk to Marina before she loses heart and abandons our cause!' Marina was reassured when the woman approaching them threw a sideways glance of criticism towards Gail which suggested a similar antipathy to the leader's expansive routine.

'My name's Teresa,' she said, offering her hand for Marina to shake, 'Teresa Stoddard.'

Marina took the hand and shook it warmly, enormously grateful that she wasn't about to be hugged again. 'Marina Riesenthal,' she replied.

Gail flitted away, pleased with her apparently successful conversion of a new fanatic to the cause.

Teresa noticed that Marina was trying not to stare at the women around her. 'I bet you've never seen so many fat women in one room before. Not even at Weight Watchers!'

Marina looked embarrassed. 'I wasn't thinking that.' (Of course she was.) 'I was actually wondering what they all do that allows them to spend a Thursday morning here. Don't they have jobs?'

Teresa smiled. 'Let me turn that thought around. Don't *you* have a job?'

Marina bristled with indignation. 'Of course I do. I'm an account director in an advertising agency.' She cursed herself silently for needing to boast. She found it difficult to remember that there was nothing for a fat woman to prove in this environment.

Teresa continued. 'So what are you doing here on a Thursday morning? Nothing to do at work?'

Marina closed her eyes for a second, not daring to think of what machinations were going on at TNSW in her absence. 'A lot to do, actually.'

Teresa repeated Marina's initial question back to her. 'So what are you doing here?'

The response came quickly and easily. 'This was more important than anything else I had to do.'

Marina was surprised by the strength of her own assertion. Teresa wasn't. She took up the theme and continued it. 'That's exactly why Gail holds occasional meetings during office hours, to test our commitment, to force us to establish priorities in our life and make sure that our own well-being and happiness come first.'

Marina was impressed by the logic although still nagged by a realisation that her own happiness was wrapped up in a career which she was putting in severe jeopardy by coming here today. Still, she liked Teresa. She always judged people quickly and was seldom wrong in her first assessments. She appraised her companion's appearance unobtrusively, using the skills common in anyone who is accustomed to being stared at.

The woman was about her own age but she wasn't flaunting a particular style that could set her in a particular era. She was of average height but her bulky figure made her appear taller. Actually, Marina wouldn't have described her as fat. She was a big woman, certainly, maybe around twelve or thirteen stone, but well-proportioned and dressed flatteringly in a classic, classy out-fit. The immaculate cut of her blonde hair and the subtle golden highlights that betrayed no hint of darker roots spoke of a dedica-tion to weekly salon visits. She even wore proper grown-up make-up that gave her the illusion of cheekbones. Marina was almost breathless with admiration.

'So what are *you* doing here, Teresa? You seem so ... unneu-rotic, happy with yourself, happy *in* yourself. You just don't seem the type to be needing all this self-help, new age stuff.'

Teresa laughed deeply. 'Think about it Marina, the whole point of 5F is to make us happy in ourselves. I've been coming here for a year now. When I joined, I was a mess. You think I'm unneu-rotic? Let me tell you what I did that finally pushed me to join.

'My husband was away on business for a couple of weeks so I went on one of the usual starvation diets to try and lose a stone before he came back. I stuck to the diet meticulously for ten days then I went out to lunch one Friday with a client and blew it. I ate three days' calorie allowance in two hours. So what did I do?'

Marina trawled through her memory bank for a purgative inci-dent that she could possibly recount to a stranger. 'Made yourself sick?' she suggested.

Teresa snorted. 'I wish! If I stuck an umbrella down my throat, I wouldn't throw up. My body has an in-built mechanism that prevents any food from being expelled until the last iota of fat has been extracted and applied with cement to a thigh or hip. No such luck. I got home and decided that, since I'd ingested three days' worth of calories, I'd make them last three days.'

Marina shrugged. 'So you starved yourself for three days? I've done that before.'

Teresa shook her head. 'God, no! I haven't got the willpower to fast. No, I took a sleeping pill the minute I got in that after-noon and went to bed. Then, as soon as I woke up, I took another one. And so on all through the weekend, until Monday morning when I got up and went to work, my dieting con-science appeased.'

Marina was horrified. Although she considered that the greater part of her life had been spoiled by her weight problems, she had at least remained conscious and carried on experiencing life throughout (give or take the odd few hours of Valium-induced oblivion that she preferred to call afternoon naps).

'You're shocked, aren't you?' Teresa asked.

Marina reassembled her face. 'No, not at all. Well, yes, I suppose I am. It just sounds like a temporary death, opting out of life for a period of time.' She shuddered.

Teresa nodded, although she was no longer looking at Marina. Her eyes were locked on to another scene, a place she didn't like to see. 'I was quite pleased with myself at first. Then it hit me. That Monday morning, everyone was asking each other what they did over the weekend. The weekend hadn't existed for me. It was neither good nor bad. It was nothingness. The panic gripped me and wouldn't let go. There was only one thing I could do, one thing that always made things better. I rushed out and bought a bag full of chocolate and sat in the toilets cramming it into my mouth. Suddenly I couldn't breathe. I started to cry and I didn't stop for twenty minutes.'

For a few moments, her face was ugly with suffering but relaxed from dropping an act which involved every physical and emotional muscle. Then like a before-and-after daytime television makeover, she was transformed back into the lady of groomed poise. 'Anyway, I was at rock bottom and I remembered an article I'd read about 5F. It didn't sound my sort of thing at all, but I had to do something. So here I am a year later. Still fat but certainly happy ... happier at least.'

Marina didn't feel happy. She felt unaccountably depressed by all these flailing emotions. She had enough trouble keeping her own under control. Scrambling for a safe conversational subject, she recalled Teresa mentioning a husband. She asked what he thought of all this. Teresa raised her eyebrows to assume a studied ironic demeanour. 'Typical man, you know the sort! Says he loves me whatever I weigh but actually prefers me on the large side. Of course I don't believe him but it's decent of him to maintain the facade. Fortunately I don't have to worry too much about him chasing slim, pretty young things because I can keep an eye on him. We work together, you see.'

'What do you do?' Marina asked, relieved that this was turning into a straightforward chat.

'We've got our own company. It's a direct marketing consultancy. We're a perfect team – I do all the work, he makes all the contacts! It suits me because I don't like golf.'

Marina was about to dispute this division of labour as surely being just a little too deconstructed for a feminist palate when Gail's voice called them all to order. She clapped like a bossy headmistress until they were all paying attention.

'Ladies, ladies. Brunch is about to be served. Please could you all make your way into the orangery.'

The buzz of excitement that greeted this announcement of food made Marina feel nervous. She hated eating in public at the best of times but eating in this worthy company was looking to be an ordeal.

Gail was blessed with a sixth sense that enabled her to spot a potential escape route for a new captive. She loped purposefully forward, forming an impenetrable moving wall between Marina and the door. 'Marina, darling, walk through with me, why don't you! I always like to accompany our new girls into the feast. You don't mind, do you Teresa?'

With a swooping arm, she swept Marina away from Teresa's protective shield of normality. Marina's eyes took one last desperate look at her guardian, who was receding from view like the last lifeboat from the *Titanic*. As she was in the presence of the group's leader, she was first through the door of the orangery. The sight that greeted her was straight out of a 1920s Russian propaganda film exposing Western decadence.

Trestle tables were pressed up against every available patch of wall, every square inch of the surfaces crammed with food. The catering manager had clearly gone to Europe, located the Fattening Food Mountain, scooped it up into a refrigerated container truck and hauled it back to High Holborn. Cakes were piled up like Ferrero Rocher pyramids; thick hunks of meat glistened like a caveman's fantasy; cauldrons of curry steamed ominously, reflecting the splendours of the hotel ceiling in the mirrored pool of ghee globules pulsating on the surface; mounds of cheese and butter competed for places on the dairy platter that represented an entire herd of cows' lifetime creative output (with the notable exception of yogurt); Belgian chocolates filled offensively empty spaces like fat punctuation marks; jugs of hot chocolate fought to be noticed from under the camouflage of whipped double cream.

But this was not the complete story. There was also fruit of every variety: mangoes, grapes and pineapples heaped in gravity-defying towers; hotplates overflowed with perfectly-cooked vegetables and fragrant steamed rice; boiled potatoes filled the air with their earthy scent of comfort; poached salmon and grilled chicken dazzled with their clean lines.

It was the choice that was so scary. Everything was here. Fat food and thin food. It all looked fantastic because, to Marina, *all* food was fantastic. Marina felt quite, quite sick. She didn't want to have to choose what to eat like this. She couldn't make up her mind if this was a fat day or a thin day. She craved solitude and starvation. She didn't want to be here. She wasn't one of them. Eating like this was to be done in private where no one could hear you cry afterwards.

She felt something being pushed into her hand. It was a beautiful plate. Gail smiled at her reassuringly and pushed her towards the first table. 'Marina. All you have to do is take whatever you want. *Whatever* you want. Eat what you want and *leave* what you want. Go on. You can do it.'

Under the spotlight of fifty pairs of encouraging eyes, Marina took a deep breath and picked up a serving fork. Her hand was sweating as it hesitated over each plate, shaking, indecisive as she veered maniacally from healthy to unhealthy choices. Finally she dared to spear a portion of Chinese duck. She hadn't had duck for ages and she really fancied it. She lifted it aloft like a hunting trophy and manoeuvred it gingerly towards her plate. As it thudded on to the reinforced porcelain platter, a sigh of approval pulsed along the crowd like a Mexican wave.

She added steamed rice and some vegetables on to which she defiantly placed a knob of butter. It was what she wanted. What she wanted, not what she needed. When she ate, she enjoyed the taste as she had never enjoyed food before.

Rick contemplated his fortieth birthday with indifference. The age milestones meant nothing to him. His life had other touch-stones. Or maybe he was kidding himself. Maybe it was precisely his fortieth birthday that was concentrating his mind on his failings.

No, not failings, that was the wrong word. His envy.

Because he envied Andy with a savagery that he could hardly stand. And an intensity that Andy would never believe. Or understand.

Chapter Five

It was Christmas Eve at Marina's parents' house.

The television was on but the volume was too low to be able to hear exactly which festive song Cliff was singing. Marina sat in the armchair that had been hers throughout her adolescence. Her hips fitted the permanently-rounded canyon in the seat cushion perfectly. She sat and stared at the bowl of Quality Street that her mother had probably counted.

'Have one if you like.'

Marina jumped at her mother's voice. As on many occasions in this house, she felt that her thoughts had been invaded and she resented the knowledge that somebody knew her that well.

To look at Nancy and Donald Riesenthal and then to look at their daughter, Marina, was to ask oneself some serious questions about evolutionary theory.

They were both under five feet two and their combined weights totalled less than Marina's fifteen stone. They both suffered from what seemed to be the only example of cosmic justice dealt out to older thin people – wrinkles that a bloodhound would be proud to be seen wearing. Like siblings, their hair was uniformly grey and unruly.

What distinguished each from the other was the light that shone from their eyes. Donald's eyes radiated with a gardener's love and wonder at the constant surprises and warm reassurances of Nature's cycles. Nancy's eyes were dull from an inability to widen her field of vision beyond the nearest ring road.

She was a feminist tragedy. At fourteen, she had run away to

Spain to participate in the Civil War, mainly because she couldn't stand her parents. It had sparked off a long flirtation with communism which ended when her lover got some local rebel pregnant.

She had returned home and became a history teacher, vowing never to entrust her soul to a man again. And she kept her promise, even when she surprised herself by marrying at the age of forty-one. She met Donald Riesenthal when they were both canvassing for the Labour Party. They never said 'I love you' to each other. But each was grateful for the companionship and neither wanted to face the prospect of living alone again.

When Nancy became pregnant at the age of forty-four, her transformation became complete. She felt that she had compromised her principles all those years earlier when her infatuation for a man in uniform had quashed her desire to change the world. She had sacrificed a lonely third of her life to bitterness. She felt that, if she could have found a soul mate earlier on, they might have changed the world together. As it was, Donald and Nancy shared a life of cream teas, church fetes and the occasional documentary on BBC2.

So when Marina was born, Nancy redefined her principles. Her daughter was going to have an easy life. She would have a husband and children. She would have material security and get all the women's bits out of the way as early as possible in her adult life. Only then could she have the freedom to explore herself.

It made sense to Nancy in a way that it never did to anyone else. Marina put the whole insanity down to a particularly harrowing menopause that had left her mother somewhat dotty.

And so it was that the woman who had once planted explosives on a rail track near Barcelona now spent her Saturdays looking into Kwiksave's windows in the hope that she might see a wedding in the church opposite reflected in the sparkling glass. Dreaming.

Donald was not in the house to rescue Marina from her mother. For as long as Marina could remember, her father had spent most of his waking days in his greenhouse or on his allotment. Nancy always said that the constant supply of organic fruit, vegetables and flowers in the house was a tribute to his skills and dedication. When Marina was still a child, she began to sense that perhaps it was more a tribute to Nancy's own innate skill at driving people to seek refuge out of hearing distance from her quiet, judging voice.

'Did you hear what I said?'

Marina reluctantly abandoned her thoughts and concentrated on the inescapable reality that was her mother. 'Sorry, Mum. What were you saying?'

Nancy produced one of her trademark sigh-tuts that generally preceded a comment on her daughter's weight, her husband's absence or the sad decline of TV comedy since the death of Sid James. 'I could see you were looking at the Quality Street and I assumed you were too embarrassed to ask for one so I just wanted to save you the trouble. God knows, a chocolate is the last thing you need but, after all, it is Christmas. So go on, have one, if you want.'

Marina reacted as she always did to one of her mother's frequent jibes at her weight. She was struck by a dual impulse: the urge to stuff handfuls of the forbidden fruit into her mouth in full view of her tormentor and a sudden firm resolve to starve, develop anorexia nervosa, die and really make Nancy sorry. Of course, she just took a chocolate apologetically and ate it as quickly and quietly as she could.

To assuage her guilt at feeling she hated her mother so much, she tried to make the sort of conversation she knew Nancy liked. 'So, Mum, have you seen anyone lately?' In daughter-mother shorthand, 'anyone' meant any of Marina's old grammar school friends, all of whom had pleased their mothers by sublimating any urges to have a life of their own. They married young (but not too young) to someone suitable, had children quickly (but not too quickly) and had already had their hair cut and permed into a bouffant crown that would see them without controversy into middle age and beyond.

Nancy sighed (this time without the tut) and began the soliloquy that she rehearsed incessantly between Marina's visits.

'Well, let me see. Did I tell you that Janet Griffin had a girl, eight pounds four ounces, called Kylie-Jade?' She paused but not long enough for Marina to reply. They both knew that replies weren't expected anyway. Or needed. She continued wistfully. 'It

51

was only two weeks ago but she's already got her figure back. Of course, she has to with that handsome husband of hers. If a woman wants to keep a husband, she has to work at it. The same goes for a woman who wants to *get* a husband. You may think you're a feminist but in truth you're just lazy. You can't be bothered to put in the work necessary to find a good man.'

Marina waited for the sigh-tut. It came.

'Then there's Alison Danson. She's got a little job now that the twins are in school. She helps out Mr Patel in the newsagent a few hours a day. Doing well, too. If she keeps up the hard work, apparently, Mr Patel said he'd think about letting her do the cash and carry run for him by the summer.'

Wow, thought Marina. I may be responsible for millions of pounds of multinational business but I doubt very much if I'll be doing cash and carry runs for anyone this summer or any summer. What a crashing disappointment I must be to my mother.

'And Linda Alderton. She helps her husband out with the family business. He's letting her do a bookkeeping course in the evenings but, do you know what, she still has a meal on the table for him every evening before she goes out ...'

Marina glanced at the door, silently praying for her father to make an appearance to save her from the inevitable wedding story.

'Oh, I haven't told you about Gaby Rushforth's wedding ...'

Marina managed to get through it by remembering the box of shortbread that she had smuggled into her bedroom. Stuff 5F. She was going to binge and she didn't care how much she would hate herself later.

It was Christmas morning at Susie and Ken's home.

Susie was just finishing talking to Marina. 'Thanks for the present! As always, it was my best! You're the only person who can buy me earrings. Ken always compensates for his lack of inspiration by buying me a hunk of gold that would get me mugged if I ever wore it.'

Marina laughed, enjoying her first rush of non-alcohol-induced warmth that Christmas. 'Thanks for the books, Suse. No one buys me books any more.' She didn't mention the low-calorie cookbook that her mother had given her that morning.

'That's OK. I just bought you all the books I wanted to read myself, so you can pass them on to me when you've finished them!'

'When will you ever get the chance to read with everything on your plate, Susie?'

There was a brief silence and Marina wondered if she'd said the wrong thing. Susie sounded different when she started talking again.

'You're right, now you come to mention it. Well, maybe I'll make a New Year's Resolution to spend some more time on myself. And I know *exactly* what I'll spend that time doing.' She chuckled. 'Anyway, must dash. Merry Christmas Moo! Don't eat too much! Love to your mum and dad. 'Bye!'

Marina was aghast at having the snippet of potential gossip dangled before her and then snatched away before she could chew it. She wished she had secrets of her own to withhold. Apart from food-related ones, that is. Christmas Day seemed longer than ever.

Susie put down the receiver and looked around her normally impeccable home. It was a seasonal Armageddon: wrapping paper lay across the polished wood floor like dead bodies; games opened and unplayed littered the marble coffee tables; hyperactive children fought over the TV remote control; a husband listened to *Tristan und Isolde* in blissful oblivion through headphones; walls screamed at her, covered in oversized gilded Christmas cards of classical reproductions and all unsigned but embossed with the senders' names and addresses; a closed kitchen door called her like a siren to a day of slavery; bloody Noel Edmonds smiled demonically at her from an hospital where, sadly, he was not a patient.

'WILL YOU SHUT UP!' she screamed at Alice and Frederick. The room became silent. 'Thank you.' She smiled gratefully but the smile didn't quite make it to her eyes. The twins stormed off upstairs to sulk and to open the selection boxes that Susie had expressly forbidden her mother to buy them.

Ken blinked and smiled weakly to acknowledge the outburst without having to take off his headphones. Before Susie could yell at him for being so selfish and finding pleasure in this domestic war zone, the phone rang. She picked it up and assumed a voice of unassailable good cheer.

'Hello! Merry Christmas!' On hearing the voice at the other end, she spun around so that Ken would not be able to see her face as she spoke. 'What are you doing, calling me today of all days?' she hissed.

'I just wanted to tell you that I love you and that I'm wearing your present.' He fingered the watch with real affection. He would sell it as soon as the shops opened again. It would buy him breathing room and, for that, he was *truly* grateful.

His soft, cultured tones melted Susie's anger. She lowered her voice and spoke in her best mistress-voice.

'David, sweetheart, I love you too, but we have to be careful. Ken will start to suspect.'

David stopped himself from laughing. He worked with Ken every day. The man would never suspect anything. He had neither the imagination nor the depth of feeling needed either to suspect or care very much that his wife was having an affair with his colleague and friend. He spoke in the tones that one of his lovers had compared to Richard Burton. 'Darling, have you opened my present?'

Susie thought of the rather cheap bracelet that she had opened in the bathroom that morning. She tried to mask the disappointment. 'Oh, it was lovely, David, lovely. I loved it.' As a master of deceit, David sensed immediately that her enthusiasm was audibly muted, but he wasn't bothered. 'I thought of you as soon as I saw it,' he said, wickedly, thinking of the man in Oxford Street brandishing a dirty suitcase full of suspiciously low-priced 'quality' gold jewellery.

'Who is it, Suse?' Susie jumped in terror as she felt Ken's hand on her back. She whipped around to face him, her hand clenched over the receiver. She quickly collected herself, the result of experience gained over the six months of her affair. 'It's David, darling. Calling to wish us a happy Christmas. Do you want a word?'

'No, that's all right. Wish him all the best from me.' He disappeared into the kitchen where she could hear him opening a can. She was torn between continuing the sweet illicit talk with David and yelling at Ken to stop enjoying himself.

'Are you there, Susie?' David was whispering through the earpiece. Ken won a reprieve and was allowed to relax for a little while longer.

'Sorry, sweetheart, Ken was hovering. What were you saying?'

'I was telling you about the research. About how we are ready to start human trials ...'

'Oh, right.' Susie felt let down by this unromantic turn to the conversation.

'... and I was thinking about your friend Marina.'

'Moo Cow? What has she got to do with it? You heard what she said, she wouldn't take a fat pill, she doesn't believe in an easy life.' Susie heard a hard, unpleasant edge to her voice that she hadn't noticed before. She just knew that she didn't want Marina to have anything to do with her lover. There was a balance at stake here, something complex and fragile that might not survive the entry of another participant, whatever her role, however close the friendship.

David heard the unspoken warning and backed off. It could wait. 'It was just a thought, that's all. Anyway, we can talk about it when we meet next.' He knew that would do it. It worked. Susie leaped at the proposal. 'When? Where? How about the day after tomorrow? I can tell Ken that I'm going to the gym.'

David tortured her by considering it for what seemed like ages. In fact he was checking to see that the woman in his bed had still not stirred. Finally he gave her the answer that would sustain her through the nightmare of Christmas. 'That will be wonderful. I'll count the hours,' he purred.

They prolonged their goodbye as lovers do with a reluctance that is nauseating or endearing, depending on your own particular situation in the love stakes.

Susie put the phone down, wiped away a tear and focused her distracted mind on how she was today going to adapt her famous recipe for white sauce that formed the base of every dish she produced.

She smiled to herself and enjoyed the thrill she always got from imagining everyone's faces if they discovered her secret ingredient.

It was Christmas afternoon in Teresa Stoddard's house.

Teresa and her husband, Rod, sat alone opposite each other across a table that was straight out of a *Vogue* Guide To Stylish

Christmas Entertaining. The glamour of the surroundings was wonderfully out of keeping with the music accompanying the meal. 'Sounds Of The Seventies' took Teresa and Rod back to the days when they met in college. As they dined on a spectacular crown of turkey, they waved their forks in time to Sweet and T Rex. They la-la'd along with the Bay City Rollers and played air guitar with their Christmas crackers.

Rod broke off his tuneless, but enthusiastic, version of *Crazy Horses*. 'Do you remember what we were doing the first time we heard this, Terry?'

Teresa let out a filthy laugh that made a lie of her carefully presented elegant appearance. She picked up her glass of champagne and pointed it towards Rod challengingly.

'How am I supposed to remember when you got me drunk on cheap cider first!'

Rod threw a stuffing ball at her in mock indignation. 'Excuse me! That cider may have been cheap but it left me with no grant money for the rest of the month.'

'Huh!' Teresa retaliated with an accurate lob of carrot into Rod's glass. 'You didn't need any money. You moved into my room and lived off my chocolate biscuits!'

Rod rose from his chair like a volcano. Even after twenty years, Teresa still loved to see her husband stretch to his full height. He was a six-feet five-inch bear: big, broad and utterly decent. There was nothing mediocre about this man. All was pronounced and special. His tobacco hair stopped suddenly at his face to form a full ginger beard that looked preposterously false. His eyes were so green, he was frequently accused of wearing coloured contact lenses. His body looked perfectly sculpted in his clothes that he chose so carelessly and yet always got right. Only Teresa saw the paunch that he allowed to sag in the privacy of their bedroom.

She didn't care. Of course she didn't care. Women have never cared about the imperfections of men's bodies. It is horribly unfair. It is the way of the world.

Rod snaked his way round the table, his paper hat hanging over one ear and one eyebrow, making him look boyish.

'*Your* chocolate biscuits? And who went out at two o'clock

every morning and raided every locker in halls to steal you those chocolate biscuits?'

Teresa held up her hands in a feeble defence against the onslaught of his massive hands.

'Well, maybe, but I didn't have any grant left either. I'd spent it all on that silver eye shadow that I thought made me look like Suzi Quatro!'

'You were far more lovely than Suzi Quatro,' he whispered.

Rod lifted her out of her seat as if she weighed nothing and, in one fluid movement, carried her over to the fire and eased her down on to the rug before it. Once their laughter had subsided, Rod stroked Teresa's face with a tenderness that made her cry.

'Why the tears?' Rod asked.

Teresa breathed deeply to stop any more damage being done to her foundation and blusher. 'I don't know why you love me so much.'

Rod held her tight. 'That's easy. I love you for the same reason I loved you when you were nineteen. You're clever and funny and rude and wild and loving and kind and . . .'

'But not pretty.'

Rod let go of her and stood up. 'Not this again.'

Teresa tried to undo the damage. She jumped up and put her arms around his middle from behind. 'Sorry, darling. I didn't mean to start. It's just . . .'

Rod turned and faced her angrily. 'It's just that, if I don't tell you twenty times a day that you are beautiful and sexy, then I obviously don't love you and must be having an affair with some imaginary, skinny, young bimbo.'

He removed Teresa's arms from his waist and poured himself a Scotch.

Teresa rushed to him and buried her face in his chest. He made no move to touch her and his coldness killed her. 'I'm sorry, I really am. I promise I will never do it again. I'll stop mentioning it. Honestly, I'll really try.'

Rod exhaled with a frustration that frightened his wife. He looked at her in disbelief. 'No, you won't try. It's a self-fulfilling prophecy, you know. Eventually you'll wear me down and I'll say what you expect me to say. I'll say it in anger. I won't mean it but

57

you'll never believe that. I'll say it and then that will be it. Over. Nearly twenty years of marriage.'

He caught his breath and softened when he saw the look of total misery on the face of the wife he loved so much. 'Terry, I love you. To me, you will always be the beautiful young girl I met in Brighton. I see only you and I love only you.'

He put his arms around her and she clung to him like a lifebelt. Such beautiful words but she heard only two: 'To me.' She knew what they meant. They acknowledged that only he could possibly find her attractive. They acknowledged her ugliness to any normal, objective person not struck down with terminal loyalty and niceness.

They held each other for a long time, both lost in their own thoughts.

'Merry Christmas Everybody', sang Slade, without a hint of irony.

It was Christmas night in Gail Bathurst's flat.

Jessye Norman sang majestically from the top-of-the-range stereo as Gail draped herself, sated, over the beanbags that peppered her lushly decorated flat. In her Indian robe adorned with images of fertility goddesses, she blended in perfectly with her surroundings. The walls were liberally covered with prints depicting images of corpulent naked women. Everywhere, tasselled tapestries draped over mismatched antique furniture and elaborate Chinese rugs played hopscotch across the terracotta tiled floor.

A toilet flushed somewhere in the flat and a second woman teetered down the hall in click–clack heels towards the living room. 'Move over, Row.'

Gail peered tipsily over her glass of port at the interloper. 'Find your own seat, you old bag,' she said cheerfully to her friend.

Emma Lhamming lowered herself delicately on to a chaise longue like a Jane Austen heroine, less out of dignity than a desire to keep her dinner down. As she prostrated herself, her body spread across the embroidered seat and spilled over the sides. An onlooker would have been surprised to see so much flesh emerge because Emma hid her weight with great skill under very expensive clothes.

Emma was twenty-nine and her life had never extended tentacles beyond the realm of her weight. There was no tiny part of her life that was unaffected by her obesity. It had started early.

She had entered the world at eleven pounds ten ounces. All her family were big. They blamed it on the genes, an excuse Emma happily accepted until she started having dinner at schoolfriends' houses and learned that not everyone cooked meals the way her mum did. She'd thought it was normal to have pies or fry-ups every night, accompanied by doorsteps of bread with butter slapped on in artery-clogging chunks. She'd thought that potatoes only came in chip form. She learned that some people ate vegetables. Some people had meat without pastry. Some people stopped eating when they were full. Some people only ate three meals a day.

She was eleven when she knew that she was inevitably going to get and stay fat if she continued the way she was going. She ate too much and had done so since she was weaned. She blamed her parents, her mother in particular, for their ignorance. She hated them for giving her an enormous insatiable appetite and an addiction to food that she could not seem to overcome. Most of all, she hated the whole family for refusing to believe her and continue on their stupid, stupid path to heart attacks and premature deaths. As for her, this penchant for self-destruction, which was a family trait rather like a love of the arts or the outdoors in healthier families, manifested itself in extreme eating disorders.

Swinging violently from anorexia to bulimia, from bingeing to starving, Emma had come close to death on a few occasions and longed for death on many others.

She even made a living from her sickness. During a spell in a psychiatric unit when she was nineteen, one of her doctors suggested she write about her relationship with food as an exercise in self-learning. The doctor was so impressed by her honest, lucid and painfully funny account that he persuaded her to allow a magazine to publish it. It was the beginning of a career in journalism that was to see her freelancing across all the major women's magazines and broadsheet press. She wrote about the broad spectrum of women's issues but always returned to the issue of weight and food-related problems.

She weighed a little over fourteen stone and had just made a serious suicide attempt when she interviewed Gail at the inception of 5F. She joined 5F immediately. That was eighteen months ago.

'Aren't you going to phone your mum and dad, Emma?'

Emma shifted uncomfortably to turn her face away from Gail's. 'There's no point. They'll all be round my nan's and she hasn't got a phone. Anyway, Dad'll be drunk and Mum'll be snoring in an armchair with her skirt undone. What about you? Aren't you going to phone anyone?'

'Nobody to phone, Em,' Gail answered shortly.

Emma didn't press her. Their friendship had developed quickly during the early days of 5F. They detected in each other a squashed working class accent that each had only partially obliterated and they respected each other's barriers. It was just that Gail's barriers were much thicker and higher than Emma's. Sometimes, Emma found Gail a little hypocritical in her insistence on the confession and self-revelation of new members when she exposed so little of herself. Still, she was grateful for the friendship as well as the camaraderie of 5F that made her feel less alone, less of a freak.

They spent several minutes in companionable silence before Emma restarted a conversation that they had begun over their enormous lunch.

'So are you really saying that you wouldn't take a fat pill, under any circumstances, when everyone else is?'

Gail pulled herself up to make her point more forcefully. ' You know, much as I like Marina Riesenthal, and I really think she has a lot to offer as well as gain from our organisation, we could do without these seeds of subversion undermining our united resolve and commitment.'

Emma felt the need to defend Marina in her absence. 'She wasn't saying that it was necessarily a good thing, just that it was going to happen and we were all going to have make a decision, one way or another, as to how we felt about it.'

Gail reached with effort for the bottle of port to top up her glass, picking up a couple of chocolate liqueurs on passing. 'The point is, that we *know* how we feel about it.'

'Do we?'

'For God's sake, Emma, you helped me formulate our

philosophy, our mission statement. We agreed that we were no longer going to conform to anyone's stereotype of acceptable female form. That means that we are not going to make ourselves thin just because someone says we should be thin. So *that* means that we are not going to take pills to make ourselves thin just because someone says we should be thin. It's simple. Isn't it simple?'

Emma swallowed her gin quickly to drown the rising doubt that threatened to escape from her throat.

'You're right, Gail. Turkey sandwich?'

It was Boxing Day morning at Rick Gifford's Buckinghamshire house. All was orderly, festive and lush. The children took their noise out in the huge garden where it wouldn't intrude on the grown-up self-satisfaction in the sitting room.

Rick and his wife, Gilly, were curled up in oversized comfortable armchairs. Each was engrossed in a book selected by the other as the ideal Christmas present. They'd studied Philosophy together at Cambridge and knew each other's literary tastes perfectly. They drank a chilled Pouilly Fumé and nibbled at marrons glacés. The music was Mahler and the atmosphere one of utter mutual knowledge. Every so often one of them would look up. At exactly the same moment, the other would do likewise and they'd exchange a look of understanding, contentment, rightness.

There was no tension, no undercurrent, no threat to this idyll. All was as life was supposed to be.

Except that Rick no longer loved his wife. Or his job. Or his kids, particularly. It wasn't a recent feeling, either. It had been building over five years. He'd become accomplished at masking his growing unhappiness. As he smiled at his beautiful, loving, sensitive, intelligent, perfect wife, he was dreaming about opening a beach café in Cornwall.

He had it all worked out. He would wear clothes that didn't match any of his other clothes. He wouldn't shave. He'd eat baked beans out of the tin. He'd read all night and walk aimlessly on Sundays. He'd change his name. Learn the names of all the wild flowers and birds. Talk to strangers. Talk to himself. Listen to himself.

Wonderful, foreign, English, alien, wild, old and ageless,

unpredictable Cornwall. He was dreaming of reinventing himself there. No, not dreaming. Planning. No, not planning, dreaming.

This was his life. A reality and a dream co-existing in conflict. And he had a really, really bad headache.

It was Boxing Day evening in David Sandhurst's laboratory.

He had got rid of the girl who had seen him through the conventions of Christmas which demanded that he not be alone. He fingered Susie's watch. He was already compiling a mental list of little and not-so-little treats to buy himself with the money he got from selling it. Or maybe he'd pay off one of his credit cards. He loved the thought that he had financial choices. It was a rare joy.

He looked over his notes for the umpteenth time. He had cut a lot of corners to reach the stage where testing on humans could proceed. Changing the odd figure and swapping the odd result didn't cause him any moral qualms. His pill worked, he knew it did. He had taken it himself with no serious side-effects (or none that he thought the average overweight woman wouldn't endure for the sake of weight loss). Besides, Perrico had already carried out the preliminary safety testing when Oxymetabulin was still just a potential asthma treatment. That knocked five years off the testing process.

But the testing of Oxymetabulin as a slimming pill was proving to be trickier than he could ever have imagined. Generally when testing a drug, one group will take the actual pill and the second group will be given the placebo. As both groups go about their similar lifestyles, any effects can be attributed directly to the medication.

But these women with their weird eating habits! He couldn't find a single woman who ate in what could be considered a normal way. In fact, all the overweight women he had encountered seemed to have acquired their weight problem as a result of their erratic eating regimes and obsessions.

How the hell was he going to be able to see how the pill worked on a fat woman if she was going to binge or starve midprogramme? To complicate matters, he had read an article by a journalist called Emma Lamington, who said that it was futile asking overweight women to test diet products, because they always controlled their food intake meticulously during the test in their eagerness to make the product seem effective and make themselves look good.

He had been stumped until he met Marina Riesenthal who mentioned 5F. Could they be for real? Overweight women who didn't care about public perceptions of their weight? Women who ate whatever they wanted without any of the bizarre psychological motivations that had previously distorted their appetites? Women whose weight (though substantial) stayed constant as they had given up yo-yo dieting?

As he began writing up the testing protocol, he put aside thoughts of Nobel Prizes and enjoyed a philanthropic glow as he thought of the monumental gift he was about to bestow on these wretched unfortunates. He couldn't wait to start. He pondered on the changes that he would wreak on these women's lives. Judging by what he had read, they had been fat throughout all their adult years.

He was going to make them slim for the first time in their lives. He wondered momentarily what effect this transformation would have on them. Whether their troubled, damaged psyches would be able to bear this abduction of what appeared to be a security blanket. He shrugged to himself. They'll be bloody grateful to me for giving them a shot at happiness, he decided. Then he put all further thoughts of the subjects out of his mind and concentrated on his work.

David Sandhurst was a contented man. He had found his rats.

Chapter Six

'Good Christmas?' Andy poked his head around Marina's door, quickly assessing what was going on in his rival's office and on her computer screen. He was rewarded by the sight of the bureaucratic Vesuvius that Marina was struggling to scale.

Marina looked at him. Then she looked away. 'Go away and die somewhere.'

'It was business, nothing personal.' Andy Cline shrugged his shoulders and walked away, not even bothering to seal the lie with his trademark lopsided smile. Marina wondered how it was that slim people felt tiny when they were belittled whereas a fat person felt bigger than ever.

She grabbed a wedge from her vast wall of paper and stormed into Rick Gifford's office without knocking.

'Does nobody bother knocking any more?' he said laconically, without looking up.

Marina snorted. 'I do apologise. For a moment I thought I was Andy Cline. Would you like me to go out and come in again as myself.'

Rick sighed. 'Do we have to do this so soon after Christmas? I can tell from your tone that you're going to sap the last scraps of my Yuletide goodwill.'

Marina thumped the pile of paperwork on to Rick's desk.

'I presume you knew all about this, Andy being your own personal performing monkey and all that?'

'You may have brought in a big chunk of business, Marina, but you brought it in to *my* agency.' The warning was clear but unspoken. He didn't actually order her to address him as 'sir' in future but he might as well have done so.

Marina willed her face not to redden. It didn't work. She felt the flush ripple through the waves of her chin all the way to her chest. 'OK, maybe I shouldn't have said that but, really Rick, do you have any idea what he's landed me with?'

'Yes I do and I can assure you that the decision to go with his proposal wasn't taken lightly. But Paul Jerome was keen and I had to agree that it added a dimension to the campaign that hadn't been there before.'

'Ouch.' Marina flinched at this attack on her original strategy.

'I'm not saying that there was anything wrong with your ideas, just that Andy has managed to come up with something to complement them. The media are already showing interest in the sexy squeegee girls. And boys, of course. It's all good PR for Sparkleeze. Paul is really pleased.'

He suddenly felt sorry for Marina who was visibly sagging. 'Can you handle this? The fall-out, I mean.'

Marina thought of her desk that was buckling under the weight of the 'fall-out'. 'Well, let me see. I have to call 107 different publications, poster companies, radio and TV stations, tell them that we have to cancel eighteen per cent of our bookings with them, even though we are outside cancellation dates, but can we keep to the original prices and will you still be nice to us and trust us when we come back to book the next campaign? Can I handle it? Yes. But I shouldn't have to. And you know it, you smarmy, ex-public school in-bred.'

Teresa stopped mid-mouthful. 'You didn't call him that?'

'Of course I didn't. I thought it but I didn't say it. God, it makes me feel physically sick to watch all my hard work undone by some oily underling who has achieved the same position as me purely because of some mysterious hold he has over the MD. I said nothing. But I was seething. So I did what any senior executive would do after a personal challenge to her professional credibility.'

Teresa nodded knowingly. 'You bought a large box of Belgian chocolates and ate them all ...'

'Except the hard centres ...' interrupted Marina.

'Except the hard centres, of course,' conceded Teresa, 'and ate them in the toilet so that nobody would see you . . .'

'And put the box and wrappings in the exceptionally noisy sanitary disposal unit so that no evidence remained . . .'

'And then cleaned your teeth with the handbag-sized toothbrush and toothpaste set that is always in your handbag . . .'

Marina swallowed a profiterole before continuing. 'And swilled my mouth out with industrial-strength mouthwash . . .'

'And went back to work and calculated how many calories you'd just ingested ...'

'Three thousand five hundred approximately, which produces about . . .'

A weight gain of almost exactly one pound,' Teresa calculated instantly.

'So I worked out that I would have to do about ten hours of aerobics to lose it ...'

'And of course, that's out of the question because only fit and skinny people can *do* ten hours of aerobics . . .'

'Without having a heart attack ...' agreed Marina.

'And you look like a Lycra porpoise in a leotard . . .'

'Which they don't make in a size 156 anyway . . .'

'So you began to have a panic attack . . .'

'Which I welcomed because the rising heart beat must surely burn off more calories . . .'

'And then you realised that your anger had finally abated only to be replaced by utter, profound depression which could only be cured by . . .'

'More chocolate!' Marina and Teresa chanted in unison.

They laughed even though it was the saddest truth that either of them had ever spoken.

They shared a moment of sweet, comfortable intimacy, each in tune with the other, knowing and understanding all the unspoken bits.

Neither of them finished their puddings.

Marina appraised her new friend's flawlessly made-up face. Even the most expensive Chanel concealer could not hide the stress lines that had not been there before Christmas.

'So how was your Christmas, Teresa?'

Teresa picked up her spoon and began viciously mutilating her remaining profiteroles.

'Great.' She ladled a mass of eclair and chocolate sauce into her mouth without pleasure. Marina looked at her and saw herself. She decided to take a chance that their incipient friendship was already solid enough for a confrontation.

'Doesn't sound it.'

Teresa dropped her spoon on to the plate noisily and sat back in her chair. 'That's because it wasn't. I have the world's most fabulous husband. He bought me a diamond bracelet and a complete set of Teletubbies. We had a fabulous lunch that we cooked together. We got drunk on fabulous champagne and listened to old records.'

Marina raised her eyebrows. 'Sounds awful. I hate you, I'm so jealous.'

'It only got awful when I opened my big mouth, the one part of my body that never gets any smaller no matter how much I diet.'

'What did you say?'

'I asked him if he thought I was pretty.'

Marina exhaled sharply. 'Not that!'

Teresa nodded in shame. 'I do it every time. Just when things couldn't be more perfect, I ask myself how so many good things could possibly be happening to me, to plain, fat me.'

Marina didn't bother contradicting her. She knew from personal experience how pointless that would be. Self-hatred was a quagmire and jolly joshing would be like trying to stick a plaster on a broken heart.

'So what did Rod do?'

'What he does every time I lay this on him. I know how he's going to react, I know what he's going to say and I still do it. He froze, pulled away and we spent the rest of the holiday watching Christmas sitcom specials and eating made-for-one ready meals.'

'Tell me to mind my own business if you don't want to answer, but how much did you weigh when you met Rod?'

Teresa laughed. 'I know what you're thinking and you couldn't be more wrong. You're thinking that this is the classic story of a man marrying a slim girl who lets herself go and becomes tortured by doubts that her husband preferred the old slim wife.'

Marina cursed herself for having watched too much Oprah Winfrey as a substitute for having a life of her own. She had really come to believe that people actually fell into the succinctly-captioned categories so loved by US chat shows: 'My wife used to be a corker, but now she's a porker!' (There was always an exclamation mark. It offered the promise of drama where there was generally none.) She smiled apologetically.

Teresa brushed off Marina's embarrassment. 'Don't worry. *I* fell for that myth as well. No, when Rod met me, I was even bigger than I am now. It's OK, you don't have to try and hide your shock, even I was surprised when I got a little slimmer over the years.'

Marina looked puzzled. 'I don't see what the problem is then. You must be the single most fortunate woman in the Western world. You've found a fantastic man who sees beyond a woman's figure to the person underneath. I've read about such men in articles by worthy-looking journalists of dubious sexuality, but I never really believed they existed.'

Teresa became animated. 'That's my point! I never believed they existed either. And I still don't.'

Marina shook her head. 'Now you've really lost me. The man's been married to you for, what . . . ?'

'Almost twenty years.'

'Twenty years! My God! You're married to Paul Newman! So he's loved you and stayed faithful to you for twenty years and doesn't care about your weight . . .'

'*Says* he doesn't care about my weight,' Teresa corrected Marina.

'Well, in my opinion, I think twenty years of devotion is proof enough. What more does he have to do?'

Teresa considered the question which seemed reasonable. 'I suppose I'd like him to cut himself off from the rest of womankind and spend every second of his waking life telling me that I'm beautiful. Oh, and never touch my thighs, abdomen or hips during lovemaking. Oh, and never say that Meg Ryan is really attractive and then quickly retract it for fear of making me feel inadequate. That sort of thing.'

She snapped out of her reverie to find Marina staring past her at another table. She turned around to try and find out what the object of attention was. Everyone looked the same to her. They were all professionals with shiny faces. The women wore red, the men wore their life stories in their choice of ties.

The table on which Marina's gaze focused was covered in the detritus that only a boy's lunch could have produced. The plates were still piled high with half-eaten food but the glasses were drained of every drop of wine. Rolls had been selected from the bread basket and then ignored. The pudding menu sat unread like a Gideon Bible.

But Marina wasn't looking at the food. She was looking at the diners.

'Cheers, Paul!' Andy Cline clinked his brandy balloon delicately against Paul Jerome's heavy crystal whisky tumbler.

'Cheers, Andy. That was a good lunch. Thanks a lot.'

Andy sat back in satisfaction, pleased with the relationship with Paul that he felt had been consolidated in this blokes' lunch. In three weeks, despite the extended holiday, he had set himself the task of forming a friendship with this client and he believed he had succeeded, as far as a man with little altruism or empathy can define a friendship.

'So, Paul, what did you do for Christmas? The usual deathly duty calls *chez* Mater and Pater or holed up for five days with the lady of your choice if not your dreams?'

Paul Jerome didn't succumb to the inducement to laddish repartee as eagerly as Andy would have wished.

'I did go home but it certainly wasn't a "deathly duty call". Christmas is the only time all my brothers and sisters get together. We spend the whole holiday sitting around, catching up on the year, watching old black and white home movies and singing songs from the musicals. In fact, it's my idea of heaven.'

Andy's consummate acting skills produced a facial expression that betrayed no hint of the horror he felt. If heaven was truly as this strange man was describing, then he was going to step up his avowed commitment to a life of sin so that he might guarantee his place in an eternity where NOBODY sang extracts from *Fiddler On The Roof*.

'Sounds great!' Andy enthused, a maniacal smile slashing across his face.

Paul warmed to the subject. 'What about you? What did you do for Christmas? Go home to your folks?'

Andy thought of his 'folks': his father, whose idea of family loyalty was always to leave his wedding ring at home when he went to visit his mistress; his mother, who went to church every single day of her life to pray for forgiveness in advance for the hatred towards her husband that would fill her otherwise vacant mind for every minute of her day; his sister, Perpetua, who punished her parents for saddling her with an embarrassing name and a loveless childhood by sleeping with all their friends.

He thought about his Christmas; the compulsory attendance at Midnight Mass where they all prayed with their eyes closed in case the neighbours were watching; the present-opening ceremony where Asprey and Tiffany trinkets were exchanged to courteous oohs and aahs; the obscenely lavish lunch endured to a background of recorded carols from King's played at a high enough volume to make conversation thankfully impossible.

'My Christmas?' he reflected. 'Just like yours. All the family together doing what we always do.' He downed his cognac in one gulp before steering into safer waters. 'So, how are the bods in the boardroom taking to my new idea?'

Paul fingered his glass thoughtfully. 'Well, they were all impressed with the document you sent each of them. No doubt the generous bottle of single malt you sent with it helped to win them over. Really, you didn't need to bribe them, the proposal stood on its own merits.'

Andy laughed. 'It wasn't a bribe, it was a Christmas gift. You can't expect directors who are weighed down from weeks of Christmas lunches to plough through some dull old statistics without offering them a chaser . . . ' He stopped talking when he realised that his client was not listening to him. He had turned round to look for a waiter and suddenly spotted Marina across the room.

'I say, have you seen who's over there?'

Andy craned his neck conspicuously until he spotted the object

70

of Paul's attention. It didn't take long because he knew exactly where Marina was sitting. He had known since Marina's secretary made the booking a few days earlier. It had led to the 'spur-of-the-moment' lunch invitation to Paul and the careful choice of table location after a discreet word with the head waiter.

His surprise sounded convincingly sincere. 'Good Lord, it's Marina! I didn't realise this was one of her haunts. What a coincidence!'

'Who are you staring at?' Teresa twisted round to follow Marina's gaze.

'You know the oily usurper who's trying to steal my client? That's him. With my client.'

'Wow! They look a bit buddy-buddy. I can see why you're so paranoid.'

'I shouldn't be. I mean, the account is not my possession. Andy and I are supposed to be sharing the handling.'

Teresa nodded shrewdly. 'But is he the sharing type?'

Marina started back on her pudding with gusto. 'Exactly.'

Teresa clumsily pretended to drop her napkin and stole another glance. 'I'm sorry if this makes me a traitor but I think he's quite attractive.'

Marina smiled. 'You mean Paul Jerome. Yes he is. But then, by what you tell me about your husband, you have a thing for tall men.'

Teresa laughed out loud. 'God no! Not the tall one. I mean, he's OK, but Rod has spoiled tall men for me, they just can't compete with him. No, the other one, the oily usurper. He's got that Jack Nicholson roguishness about him.'

Marina lost her appetite as quickly as she gained it. 'Terrific. He's the MD's best friend, he has no morals and he has a Jack Nicholson roguishness. What sort of fair fight is this going to be?'

Teresa took her hand and patted it conspiratorially. 'Fights are only fair in Errol Flynn films. In reality, they're all bare-knuckle.'

Paul looked puzzled. 'They seem to be holding hands. Marina's not . . . you know, is she?'

Andy improvised, delighted at the twist unfolding before him.

71

'Well, I've always suspected but I've never said anything, being pretty much a "live-and-let-live" sort of chap. You know these big girls. I have this theory that some of them deliberately make themselves unattractive so that men won't get the wrong idea, if you catch my drift.'

Paul was horrified by this cavalier stereotyping but didn't know how to counter it, not wishing to admit that, actually, he had found Marina not so unattractive. Such an admission surprised himself since she was such a long way from his usual 'type'. In fact, he was ashamed to find himself embarrassed about being attracted, however mildly, to a fat woman. He was sure that it made him appear a freak, a figure of fun to be mocked by men with socially acceptable tastes. He said nothing. Muddled thoughts ricocheted around his head.

Andy spotted Paul's discomfort and decided to exploit it. He raised his arm and started to wave to Marina. 'I'll ask them to come and join us for a drink, shall I?'

Paul grabbed his hand and pulled it down, holding it firmly down on the table. He needed some time to assimilate these new possibilities and wanted to defer meeting Marina until he was more composed. 'No! I mean, not right now. I mean, I have to be getting back. A meeting, you know,' he mumbled. He realised that Marina was looking at him so he waved awkwardly.

Teresa looked puzzled. 'They seem to be holding hands. They're not . . . you know, are they?'

Marina looked doubtful. 'Andy Cline has slept with every woman in advertising who weighs less than nine stone.'

Teresa snorted. 'That proves nothing! And you said there was some kind of thing with your MD. It all makes sense to me.'

Marina was indifferent to Andy's preferences. She was inwardly reeling with disappointment at this possible discovery about Paul. While she knew that he could not possibly have any interest in a blob such as herself, she had at least been enjoying the fantasy.

She waved back at Paul. Under her breath she muttered thoughtfully, 'This puts a completely different light on things.'

Chapter Seven

Marina surveyed the mountain of clothes piled on her bed like a Technicolor Everest. She was trying to put together a wardrobe for the conference in New York and the task was depressing. Her suitcase would inevitably be twice the size of those of the other female delegates, since it took a lot of effort to make her look effortlessly professional and stylish.

The doorbell rang. Marina wasn't expecting visitors. She instinctively panicked and rushed around the flat looking for the food wrappers that normally littered the floor. There were none. Calming down as she reached for the intercom, she marvelled at the way control over food had begun to tiptoe into her life while she wasn't looking. Three cheers for 5F, she thought.

'Hello?' She adopted a weak tone to her voice so that she had the option of using illness as an excuse to drive away market researchers, Jehovah's Witnesses or earnest canvassers for the Liberal Democrats. Any of these were real possibilities since none of her acquaintances would ever make an unannounced visit – they all knew how much she hated surprises.

Not that she'd anticipated a surprise quite like this one.

'Hi Marina. It's David Sandhurst.'

It meant nothing to Marina until she remembered Susie's appalling dinner party when she was paired with the handsome scientist. The shock of this man turning up on her doorstep was so great that she completely forgot her well-rehearsed speech for getting rid of unwelcome visitors (a rota of migraine, flooded washing machine and dengue fever depending on the persistence of the caller). Instead she found herself answering in the girly voice that she had first used on her initial introduction to David.

'Oh hi! What a lovely surprise!'

There was an elongated pause while Marina silently role-played several scenarios at fast-forward speed for this encounter. While halfway through the scenario where she'd lost seven stone and David asked her to marry him, her daydream was interrupted by a slightly impatient voice. 'Well, are you going to let me in? It's snowing out here.'

She apologised slightly hysterically and quickly pressed the buzzer to open the downstairs door. Looking in the mirror and facing the fact that there was no time for cosmetic surgery, she smoothed her wild hair down with a bit of spit between the palms and expertly applied one coat of extra-extra-won't-budge-with-out-oxyacetaline-make-up-remover red lipstick.

She opened her front door to find David Sandhurst looking casually divine. She mimicked his casualness, knowing it to be an appealing demeanour, and invited him in. He sauntered through to her sitting room, glorying in his massive physical superiority over this wretched woman who was not hiding her attraction towards him very well.

He looked around her flat which he grudgingly admitted to himself was very stylish. He was going to have a place like this when he had the money. You needed money to have taste, of that much he was sure. The ache of material envy stabbed him in the stomach. Or was it just hunger? It was *that* time of the month again. Pre-payday.

'Nice flat,' he called out, fingering the silver frame of her 'You're The Top' sheet music cover signed by Cole Porter.

'Thanks,' Marina simpered, cursing herself for being so woefully inadequate in any form of contact with men outside of her professional domain. She decided to overcome her awkwardness by pretending that David was a client and assuming the executive persona that won her business and friends. She cleared the adolescent phlegm from her throat and started again.

'Can I get you a tea or coffee or something stronger? I've got some wine in the fridge.'

David smiled and Marina would have swooned if her innate

good sense had not confirmed that such a reaction was only appropriate for a Jane Austen heroine wearing a corset that impeded circulation.

'I'd love a glass of wine. Thanks.'

Marina hurried to the kitchen, desperate to get the wine out of the fridge before her guest had a chance to follow and catch a glimpse of the fridge's contents. That morning, she'd had a difficult choice to make. A 5F meeting was scheduled for the evening and she wasn't sure if she'd be able to go. The day was always going to be stressful with the trawl through her wardrobe and its depressing reminder of the difficulties of being fat.

The choice was twofold: to squirrel away her tension into a hermetically sealed compartment far away from her appetite-governing glands until she could release it safely into the understanding bosom of her sisters; or to stuff food obscenely into her mouth until staggeringly horrible waves of nausea overwhelmed her being, leaving no room for burgeoning emotions to break through. A difficult choice indeed, but for the first time in her bingeing life, she *had* a choice. Unfortunately, while she had hope, she had no resolve. The thought of the trip to New York had filled her with a dread that could only be assuaged by the purchase of twelve chocolate eclairs. She had deliberately avoided the fridge until the moment when the cakes' succour would be desperately called upon to serve like cream-engorged Prozac.

'Great kitchen!' David's voice, inches behind Marina, almost made her scream. Marina slammed the fridge door shut and spun around to face him, a bottle of chilled Chablis held aloft like a truncheon. She saw the alarm on his face and lowered the bottle with what she hoped was a disarming laugh. 'Just testing my reflexes,' she mumbled weakly.

David didn't look convinced and backed out of the kitchen quickly. Marina took the opportunity of his turned back to wipe the bottle over her forehead in a futile attempt to stop sweat from flooding her already glowing face. Taking a deep breath, she composed herself and followed her guest into the living room.

She poured the glass into two glasses, wishing she'd eaten something sensible to line her stomach rather than a glass of Slim-Fast and a handful of bran pills that were supposed to swell up and make her feel full. I know, I know, she replied to her conscience. What happened to my new healthy, unneurotic approach to food? Well, I've only been with 5F for five minutes. Allow me to hang on to my comfort blanket for a bit longer.

'Cheers,' she toasted with a forced smile, as her planned sip of wine turned to a half-glass gulp.

'Cheers,' David replied, appreciating the beautiful wine. It had been a long while since he'd tasted wine that did not come from an Eastern Bloc bargain basement. 'So, Marina. It's good to see you again. I'd wanted to have a proper chat with you after dinner at Susie's but you left in a bit of a hurry.'

He paused and Marina realised that he was waiting for an explanation of her swift departure.

'Yes, sorry I didn't say goodbye.' She would have used the popular excuse about a dodgy tummy, but only thin people are allowed to have dodgy tummies – fat people daren't admit to any disorder remotely related to eating. That would be inviting judgement. 'I had a headache.'

David tried to look as if he cared. 'Sorry to hear that. Mind you, I didn't know whether you'd want to speak to me anyway. You seemed a little uncomfortable at the topic of conversation unless I was mistaken.'

Marina considered this. Uncomfortable? The thought of it! Just because all eyes stripped me naked and pored over every flabby surplus pound on my hideous body, just because I had to watch everyone's repulsion bouncing off my springy flesh as my life was pronounced an abomination. Uncomfortable? I wanted to die. I mean, *really* wanted to die. Is that uncomfortable enough for you? 'Uncomfortable?' She laughed unconvincingly. 'Not at all. I'm aware that my weight is an issue but it isn't a problem.' Good line, she thought, I almost believe it myself. Almost, but not quite.

David was thinking exactly the same thing but he needed this woman's support so he didn't challenge her. 'Well, that's good, then. I'm really relieved to hear that it's not a problem because it's what I wanted to talk to you about.'

Marina tried to look surprised. Gosh, no! You want to talk to me about my weight? Well, blow me down! I thought you'd come to discuss the role played by Quentin Tarantino in the history of post-modern film-making. She edited the thought down to one word. 'Really?'

David continued eagerly. 'It was what you were saying about that group. Five F, I think you said it was called.'

'That's right. Although I'm not an expert. I've only been attending for a few months.'

'Yes, yes.' David hated being interrupted, especially when he'd rehearsed this presentation so thoroughly, allowing no pauses for hecklers. 'What really interested me was what you said about the members eating normally, well at least as normally as someone who's very …, I mean … you know.' He paused, hoping for an encouraging smile or at least some reassurance that he hadn't caused offence. None came. He continued his speech.

'You see, I have a problem.'

Marina stifled a series of replies ranging from facetious to abusive.

'As you know, I have this drug that looks as if it's going to solve the world's weight prob—' he cleared his throat, 'issues without the need for dieting or exercise.'

At this point, his audience usually gasped with admiration. Marina had no air left in her lungs for a gasp since all her energy was being expended on sucking her stomach and cheeks in. She settled for a professional nod which appeased David's constant need for acknowledgement, if not idolisation.

'So, anyway, we're at the testing stage now and that's where the dilemma is. There are protocols, you see.' He hesitated.

Yes, thought Marina, I know what a protocol is. But I bet you're going to explain it just in case I am as stupid as I am fat.

'The protocols are agreed standards and methodologies for testing new drugs,' David explained. 'Like rules and regulations,' he added, just in case the other words were a bit too long.

Marina gave up the cheek-sucking. Not only did it not make her look thin, it clearly didn't make her look intelligent, either.

'Normally it's a straightforward procedure. You take a group of people who share a common problem, or issue in this case,' he added hastily. 'Then you give half of them the real drug and the other half a placebo.'

Now he's going to tell me what a placebo is, Marina thought glumly.

'A placebo is a dummy pill, in other words, not a real one.'

Thank you.

'And the reason we do this is so that, if the problems ... or issues ... seem to improve, we will know for certain whether it is the actual drug bringing about a cure or simply some powerful but psychological effect of popping pills, any pills.'

'I do know all this.' Marina couldn't suppress her irritation. The man might have been gorgeous but if he didn't stem this patronising deluge very quickly, she was going to have to drop her girly mask and hit him.

'Oh, sorry!' David backtracked quickly to the moment when Marina had been drooling over him. I must be losing my touch, he cursed to himself, stunned by the thought that, for an astonishing second, this repulsive woman actually seemed repulsed by him. 'I just wanted to be sure that you understood exactly why your 5F connection is so important to me.'

'Which is?' Marina asked coldly.

David shivered at this icy response before continuing. 'When I started to set out the protocol, I hadn't realised that the vagaries of appetite and, more specifically, eating disorders meant that it was not going to be easy to select people to take part in the test.'

'But surely you just choose people of similar weights and backgrounds?' Marina found that she was getting interested in the subject.

'It's not that easy. Think about it. What is your eating pattern on an average day?'

Marina exhaled loudly. She hated the question, knowing that she couldn't evade its directness. She decided to answer honestly, no longer caring what David thought of her personally. 'You're talking about my pre-5F days. Now I'm close to ironing out the extremes of my food preoccupations.' She crossed her fingers behind her back as she recalled the mountain of chocolate eclairs in the fridge. 'But in the past, I suppose the answer is that I never had an average day. I either dieted, restricting my calories to the point of starvation or I overate substantially.' She didn't expand on the overeating, sensing that he would find a description of a typical binge utterly grotesque. What little remained of her pride restrained her from elaborating.

'Exactly!' David pronounced excitedly. 'So that must mean that your weight went up and down all the time.'

God, she hated it when anyone referred to her weight. 'Well, I stopped weighing myself years ago but, yes, I would estimate that it probably fluctuated by as much as a couple of stone in either direction over the course of a month.'

This took David by surprise. He couldn't imagine the bizarre lifestyle that would cause such enormous rises and dips. It implied variations of thousands of calories from day to day. He composed himself. 'Right. A couple of stone. So you can see the difficulty. If we have two groups of women, one taking the real pill, the other taking the placebo, how are we to discover whether the Oxymetabulin is effective when *all* the women's weight will be zooming up and down simply because of their irregular eating habits?'

Marina was beginning to see the picture. 'So what you need is a group of women, two groups of women in fact, who have relatively stable eating patterns so that any change in weight can be attributed directly to the medication?'

'Precisely! But then, you hit the wall: if they are eating in a stable fashion then they probably won't be clinically overweight in the first place.'

Marina continued the thought. 'Unless they are already overweight and their stable eating merely allows them to maintain their size, neither reducing nor increasing it. The 5F philosophy.'

David sat back, his message delivered and understood. He allowed the theory to sink in for a few moments before moving on to the sales pitch. 'And that's why I'm here. You see, 5F is the answer. If I understand it correctly, it is made up of women who have resigned themselves to their condition.'

'You make it sound as if they've come to terms with a terminal illness. They – we – accept our bodies and have simply agreed to stop allowing an obsession with physical change to dominate our lives.' (I really need a chocolate eclair.) 'We eat what we want, whenever we want and, consequently, food has lost its importance in our lives. So, yes, we do eat in a stable, or normal if you prefer the term, way.' (I'll sneak one into my bra when I go to the kitchen and eat it in the loo.)

David watched the dreamy look washing over Marina's face and mistook it for feminist fervour. 'That's fantastic! That's exactly what I wanted to hear. So what do you think?'

(I think I might be able to get four eclairs into my bra if I squash them between the cups.) 'Sorry? Erm, what do I think about what?'

'Do you think the 5F members will agree to take part in the drugs trial?'

'Absolutely not.' Gail Bathurst could barely suppress her fury. 'I can't believe you would even come to me with such an idea. Have you not listened to a word any of us have said to you, Marina?'

'Of course I have. Haven't you listened to a word that *I've* said? David Sandhurst simply asked me to put this proposition to you and that's what I've done. You have to admit it makes sense. Where else is he going to find overweight women with relatively stable eating patterns?'

Gail threw up her hands in exasperation. 'And why have we got stable eating patterns? Because we've turned our back on society's preoccupation with arbitrary definitions of an ideal weight for women. So what are you planning to do? Give them all pills that might or might not make them thin. Have weigh-ins. Compete with each other over weight loss.'

'It won't be like that.'

'It will be exactly like that! We've fought for years to separate our self-esteem from our weight and now you're suggesting that we all become dieting guinea pigs so that, once more, everything becomes focused on gaining and losing pounds. Well, take it from me, no one is going to want to get involved in this.'

'I will.'

The two words, spoken quietly but firmly, came from an unexpected source. Emma was Gail's staunchest ally as well as her closest friend. Her commitment to 5F was all the stronger since the fellowship and support offered by the group had probably saved her life. Gail was stung by the betrayal.

'What are you saying, Em? That you want to take this pill? Start up the old diet and binge routine again, the humiliation of being weighed every week, of having your body scrutinised in the name of science?'

'I'm just saying that if there's a chance that a pill could make us thin, *without* having to diet, then where's the harm? I mean, it's the diets, the obsessions with food that cause the problems. Well, with this pill, we'll just carry on as usual and see what happens. What's wrong with that?'

'Emma, *everything's* wrong with that. Agreeing to take part in this trial is admitting that our entire philosophy is based on a lie. It would be saying to the world that despite years of campaigning to persuade a sceptical world that women can be happy and fat, we would be even happier if we could be thin.'

'But isn't that true?'

Gail looked at Emma and all mutual understanding crumbled as they took up their positions on opposite ends of a psychological see-saw. Marina intervened before the debate became personal and nasty. 'Gail, I came to you as a courtesy because 5F is *your* organisation, your baby. I'm still new to the group and I'm not yet fully immersed in all the aims and beliefs. I assumed that you could speak on behalf of the rest of the members. But even you and Emma have opposing views on the subject.'

'And your point is?'

'I think we have to put the idea to all the members so that they can make up their mind for themselves.'

When she reported this back to David Sandhurst, he had wanted to address the women personally. Marina had quickly vetoed this, recognising that his clear distaste at the voluptuous female form would antagonise the gathering. She volunteered to make the presentation herself.

Facing the room which recorded a record turnout for a 5F meeting, she was grateful for her ten years' experience of presentations in advertising. Nonetheless, she was nervous and still ambivalent about the moral values of the proposition she was about to put to them.

The reception was surprisingly muted. A few half-hearted judgemental tuts were offered by Gail's more loyal cohorts but the general response was of troubled introspection. The questions put up in the ensuing debate were of the practical sort - how long would the trials last, what were the anticipated side-effects, could you really eat whatever you liked etc. Then the vote, although it was hardly necessary. Even Gail had interpreted the lack of heat in the discussion as an immediate acceptance of the concept. The vote was carried. Sixty-three women declared that they wanted to take part in the trials. That included Marina, Emma and Teresa. Five women declined including Gail. Everything was different after that.

Chapter Eight

It was the 24th March. The day before all the subjects presented themselves at Perrico's laboratories to be weighed, assessed and given their first supply of pills, whether real or dummy. It had taken over two months to set up the protocols according to strict guidelines. In fact, the process should have taken longer but David had speeded things up with some carefully judged misrepresentations to the relevant authorities (forged documents, fraudulently-obtained authorisations, faked safety reports etc.).

It wasn't that he wanted to cheat. He was proud of his work and wanted it be acknowledged, respected and comprehensively accredited. But he was running out of time. The borrowing doors were rapidly closing to him and each month it was getting tougher just to meet demands.

He needed the promised bonus. His bank had told him that they would extend his overdraft if Perrico could confirm that the bonus was definitely forthcoming. Perrico would only do that once the trial was producing results. Hence the rush, the need to cut corners, the need to cheat. It wasn't his fault, it was the bank's.

The build-up to the trial had led to fractures within 5F. Attendance at meetings had dwindled as members questioned their own commitment to the cause while they became more and more seduced by the potential promises of a miracle pill.

Marina had answered Susie's urgent call for a girls' night out. Suspecting that Susie was going to pour out the truth about her marriage problems, she had cancelled a longstanding planned dinner with Paul Jerome to offer solidarity to her friend.

Wearing her most sympathetic face, she was totally unprepared for the direction of the conversation that Susie instigated.

'Have you really thought this through, Moo? How much do you know about this drug? I mean, you could die or get a thrombosis or anything. You don't know what kind of side-effects these pills could cause. And at your size, you can't take chances with your health. It wouldn't take much to give you a heart attack or a stroke. And besides, I thought you were happy with your weight. And if it doesn't work or you get the placebo, then you'll have your hopes raised for nothing. What is the point of putting yourself through all this misery?'

'There speaks the woman who didn't even go over nine stone when pregnant.'

Susie looked at Marina in amazement. 'Bitter! Do I detect a *soupçon* of jealousy?'

'Would that be so surprising?'

Susie was thrown by this admission. 'But what on earth for? You've got everything: a career, a gorgeous flat, loads of money and no one to think of but yourself.'

Marina finished the description. 'And I'm as big as a house. And maybe, just maybe, I've had enough of being fat.'

Susie knew Marina well enough not to react to that.

Marina went on. 'There's more to this. Look, it's not that I'm jealous of you. Not as such.' Lie number one. 'If it turns out to be possible to lose some weight safely and easily then I owe it to myself to give it a try for the sake of my future health.' Lie number two. 'And anyway, why is this such a problem to you? If we weren't such old friends, I might think that you wanted me to stay fat so that the balance of power in our relationship isn't toppled over in my favour.'

'I suppose all this psycho-babble comes from your new 5F friends. What have they told you? That thin women like to have fat friends because it makes them look all the more beautiful? That we don't want our friends to lose weight in case they become more attractive than us?'

Marina had the grace to look sheepish. That was precisely what most of the women at 5F believed to be the truth. But Marina *had* come to recognise a degree of that in her long history with Susie. Maybe it wasn't deliberate on Susie's part. Maybe that was just the way their history had evolved.

Marina looked back on all the nights out at the beautiful places, the 'in' bars and restaurants, the nightclubs and discos frequented by A-list celebrities. She remembered the sidelong glances of men at the two of them. She recalled lipreading as pairs of men squabbled over who was going to ask Susie to dance while the other unfortunate would have to occupy the fat friend. On more than one occasion she saw coins being tossed and silent prayers being spoken through barely moving lips as anxious men begged God to save them from having to spend three minutes with the elephant in the ridiculous dress.

She took a deep breath before answering. Careless words could destroy a friendship that, despite its faults, was still the most enduring relationship in Marina's life. (She didn't define the blood bond with her parents as a relationship. People don't.)

'Susie, don't get paranoid about all this. The honest answer is that I don't know why I'm doing it. I know I said that I wouldn't take this pill when David first mentioned it at your dinner party but I changed my mind. Maybe I'm just weak and shallow and as vain as . . . ' She donned her most professional smile and changed the subject. 'Anyway, what's going on between you and Ken? There's definitely some tension in your house. Come on, spit it out.'

They were fourteen years old again, comparing breasts and David Bowie posters, swooning over Radio Luxembourg DJs and giggling when a teacher referred to a lesson as a period. Susie leaned forward and spat it out. 'I'm having an affair. There! Now I've shocked you.'

'You haven't shocked me at all. I guessed ages ago. Before Christmas at that dinner, actually.'

Susie looked up sharply. 'What exactly did you guess?'

'Just that you were looking particularly radiant and that Ken was not the recipient of any particular loving attention. So who's the lucky man? Anyone I might know?'

Susie exhaled in relief. 'No, no. Just someone I met at . . . at the gym.'

'So, is it serious?'

'It might be. What am I saying? Of course it's not serious, I'm married with two kids. No, it's just a bit of fun.'

Marina was an accomplished enough liar to recognise a fellow champion. She ached to see Susie so clearly in pain. She experienced one of those acute moments of insight when she understood that even thin people have problems. But there was another, more piercing insight. It was triggered by Susie's uncharitable attitude to Marina's weight loss plans. It seemed so out of character. Until she noticed ... Could it be? No, surely not. Yes, it was. Underneath that Lycra dress that had almost draped over Susie's tiny frame a few weeks earlier, flesh was beginning to press for attention. Susie was putting on weight.

'How many times do I have to tell you? It's been tested thoroughly. There are no side-effects. It's perfectly safe.' Teresa stirred the pesto sauce with unnecessary aggression as she found herself stuck in the same argument that had dominated their evenings for two months.

'Terry, I'm begging you! Don't do it. I've been asking around about this David Sandhurst and I don't like what I hear.'

'And *I* don't like what *I'm* hearing, largely because I've heard it a hundred times already.'

Rod ran his fingers through his hair, hoping that inspiration might flake out. He settled for cliché. 'Terry, I'm only being like this because I care about you. I don't like what this is doing to you.'

'And what is it doing to me? Apart from giving me hope for a normal life, that is?'

'Listen to yourself! You're not abnormal. You're not deformed. You're not sick. You're just you, the same you I fell in love with and married and I don't want you to change.'

'Ah ha, now we have it!' Teresa pointed the spoon at her husband and watched a stream of green sauce splatter across his white shirt in a perfect arc. Her anger was diluted by the unwanted intrusion of her subconscious urging her to get some water on that stain before it became impossible to shift. This, in turn, made her even angrier. 'Now look what you've made me do!'

'What is "now we have it" supposed to mean?' Rod asked as Teresa jabbed at his shirt with a damp cloth.

'It all makes sense now, that's what. You're just like all the other men.'

'What other men?'

'The ones you always read about in the slimming magazines who stop their partners from losing weight because they like the security of knowing that their women couldn't find anybody else while they're fat and ugly.'

Rod pulled away from Teresa. For perhaps the thousandth time in her marriage, Teresa knew that she had said too much and wished she could rewind time to a few minutes earlier.

When Rod spoke this time, it was with more sadness than indignation.

'Do you know what really hurts me? It's that I think that you really believe this. Nobody could have given you, *shown* you more love than I have over the years and yet you still doubt me. It's hopeless.'

As he walked away, Teresa plunged into a familiar despair of self-hatred. One thought alone cushioned her from falling to the bottom and shattering her hopes completely. In a few months time, I could be slim. Then everything will be all right again.

'Oh, it's you.' Gail was tempted to slam the door in Emma's face but she had too few friends to be able to indulge herself in pointless gestures. She hesitated just long enough to make Emma think that maybe she *was* going to be rejected (OK, so some gestures can't be resisted) then opened the door just wide enough to let her guest in at a squeeze.

Emma followed Gail into the front room where they had shared such a companionable Christmas a short while ago. Now they were worse than strangers, they were ex-friends where the awkward silences were pregnant with unspoken accusations and shared intimacies made the space between them all the more poignant.

'So, tomorrow's the big day, I hear?'

'Gail, I wish it didn't have to be like this.'

'How can it be any different? Our friendship was based on a

common understanding, a commitment to changing attitudes that would ultimately benefit all women, including ourselves. It used to be us against them. And now you're one of them again.'

She walked into the kitchen while Emma tagged along like a neglected cat. She opened the fridge and stood there for what seemed like an age, unable to choose a snack that would fill the emptiness that was opening up inside her.

'But, Gail, it isn't how it seems. I told you, I'm only taking part in the trial so that I can write about it. It'll be the biggest story of my life. I've got every women's magazine on the market fighting for the rights to it. I've got to do it. You *must* understand, you always said that my writing was important for our cause.'

Gail didn't even notice that she had eaten half a pork pie while Emma was pleading for empathy. She was surprised that, when she spoke, crumbs of pastry fell from her mouth. Emma hid her disgust with all the skills of a woman who was revolted by every aspect of her own existence.

'Em, at least have the decency to be honest with yourself if not with me. I saw your face when Marina first mentioned the pill. I saw that desperation in your eyes, that possibility for change that you had been denying yourself all this time. You want to be thin. That's it, isn't it? Tell me if it's not true, I'd love to hear it, but you can't, can you?'

'Of course I want to be thin! Everyone wants to be thin, for Christ's sake. Even you do, whatever you might say or think. Perhaps you've deluded yourself into thinking that you're happy to be fat, but you're not, you can't be! All 5F is about is making the best of a bad situation. Why can't you just face it and join the trial, give it a go. Just think, Gail, we could both be thin, we could go shopping for clothes, we could go dancing and swimming, we could swap jeans with each other and wear bikinis on Mediterranean beaches. Think about it Gail, please come with me! I want us to do this together.'

Gail looked at the woman in front of her. 'I have absolutely no idea who you are any more and you certainly have no idea who I am. I think you should go.'

Emma left and stumbled along the street, unembarrassed by the tears forming rainbow ripples through her make-up. Her anguish and isolation were compounded by the absence of her usual outlet for dealing with misery. She would normally go home and eat until her stomach was too distended to hold any more. She couldn't do this because her mind was already full of worries about the following day's weigh-in. After all, tomorrow was going to be the start of her new life and she wanted to celebrate by hitting the scales at below fourteen stone for the first time in some years.

If that meant taking a few dozen laxatives and throwing up a couple of times just before she was weighed, then that was what she would do. It was not as if she hadn't done that many, many times before.

'So how was your day, Rick?'

Gilly served up one of their favourite pasta recipes on their casual china which had been, ironically, more expensive than their best china.

'Fine. The usual. Andy's still on at me to swing the board appointment for him.'

Gilly frowned. 'That's hardly fair of him. It's not your decision alone and Marina has done far more than him to deserve it, surely even he can see that.'

Rick rubbed his temples roughly. He couldn't take any more painkillers for an hour. 'Of course he can. Maybe I'm just being over-sensitive. He hasn't actually come out and *asked* me to push things his way as such. It's just that, us being friends for so many years … I don't know. I just get the feeling that he thinks I'm holding things back for him so that I can remain his superior. In the professional sense, that is.'

Gilly tutted indulgently. 'Silly! Surely he knows you better than that. You're not that sort of man.'

Yes, I am, he thought. I love holding the upper hand over Andy. It's my cosmic restitution for all those years when I was his social inferior. And it's the only thing that permits me to bear my jealousy of his freedom. I hate myself for gloating, hate what it says about me, my friendship. I want to say all these things to you, Gilly, share yet another part of my hidden self that I've revealed to you bit by tiny bit over the years. But I can't. I have to start holding back. Halt the evolution of our spiritual union to make it easier for me to break away.

For I have to break away, darling Gilly. And there's no point in me saying anything to you because you won't understand. How can you? I don't understand myself.

And as Gilly told him about her day at college, where she had gone back as a mature postgraduate, Rick ate quickly. He wanted to get to his study as quickly as possible, lock the door and go through the details of properties that he'd received at TNSW today. Details of beach properties in Cornwall.

Chapter Nine

It was like being in a gynaecologist's waiting room. Nobody had any reason to be embarrassed or ashamed to be there and yet, at the same time, each woman's identity was shoved without dignity into second place by her Womanness. This involuntary division of attributes split her into person and gender in a way that had enraged and inspired feminist thinkers for centuries.

In this case, the womb was innocent of all crimes. It was that other female 'W' curse.

Marina was feeling sick. Like most of the other women, and totally in contradiction to the explicit instructions given by David to eat normally, she had not eaten any breakfast. Indeed, she had been quietly dieting over the previous two months so that the ignominies of the scales might be diminished. Her brain told her that this defeated the whole purpose of enlisting 5F members with their professed anti-dieting attitudes in this trial. But she couldn't help herself. None of them could. They were terrified of what the scales were going to tell them. Anything they could do to lessen the torment had to be indulged.

She saw Emma bunched up in an armchair close to the door. She was preoccupied with the buttons on her huge overcoat and her lips seemed to be moving. Marina wanted to talk to her but it was not that kind of occasion. She had never really got to know Emma during her time at 5F. Before the breakaway, Emma and Gail had been a double act, joined at the kaftan. Therefore one could only have drawn the conclusion that they shared an equal degree of militancy and the same uncompromising stance on the merits of fat.

And yet ... And yet ... Marina had read some of Emma's magazine articles and watched her eyes as her mouth articulated some of the glib aphorisms created and evangelised by her mentor. She saw something there, something she only saw when she looked at her own face in a mirror. She saw unresolved tragedy, a simmering stew of trauma that threatened to boil over if not addressed soon.

Marina laughed at herself. Who was she to judge? If there *were* any tragedy in her own life, it was certainly nothing worthy of a sensational tabloid exposé. No abuse, no hideous family skeletons (she even conceded that her mother was probably no worse than anyone else's mother), no sexual scars. There was nothing in her past to cause such self-destructive desperation apart from a seemingly neverending series of petty insults from parents and peers, each one chipping away one more shard of her limited self-esteem until none was left.

Or perhaps this was the greatest tragedy of all.

Marina realised that she was staring at Emma and quickly looked away. Fortunately Emma hadn't noticed. At that point, the door opened and Teresa came out of the consulting room looking shaky. She walked over to Marina and collapsed into a chair. 'God, that was awful!'

Marina looked alarmed. 'Why, what did he do?' She imagined needles and probes.

'Oh, it was nothing like that! Actually, it was probably worse than having physical pain inflicted. First of all, he weighed me. Twelve and a half stone. I could have died. The last time I was weighed, I was only eight stone nine.'

'When was that?'

'When I was eleven.'

Marina laughed, wishing that Teresa hadn't been so open. Did this mean that she would have to tell Teresa what she weighed too? It was going to be more than twelve and a half stone, that was certain. No one likes to swap weights with someone lighter than herself.

'But then he produced a hideous instrument of torture, some sort of calliper device.'

'What on earth for?'

'To measure the percentage of body fat. I told him he didn't have to bother. Just put me down for 100 per cent and you won't be far off the mark, I told him. But he insisted. He sticks your rolls of fat between the callipers and writes down the reading. I got the feeling that he didn't like touching my skin but maybe I'm just being paranoid.'

Or maybe not, thought Marina, remembering David's condemning eyes as he appraised her own body.

Marina was relieved when Teresa declined to reveal her percentage of body fat. At least she was to be allowed some secrets.

'So what happened next?'

'Oh, the usual. There was a doctor in there. He listened to my heart, took my blood pressure, asked me about my history. I think he was disappointed at just how healthy I was. Then I got the pills.'

She opened her handbag and took out a plain white box with unmarked white tablets inside. They looked like unbranded painkillers. How could so many hopes be resting on something so small and insignificant?

Marina asked the obvious question, already knowing the answer. 'Did you get any clue as to whether you have the real thing or the placebo?'

Teresa shook her head. 'Apparently, even David Sandhurst doesn't know. It's called a double blind experiment. The idea is that, if he knew who was getting the Oxymetabulin, he might unconsciously encourage those subjects to behave differently to those receiving the placebo. Or something like that. Anyway, I don't care. You read all the time about people taking sugar pills or whatever and being cured of cancer just because they *believe* that they will be cured by the pills. That's going to be me. I *believe* that I've got the real thing and I'm going to be as skinny as a supermodel in a few months just to prove it.'

Marina felt unaccountably sad at Teresa's prediction. It struck a flat note of similarity to her own unspoken wishes. Was that why she was doing it, to be as skinny as a supermodel? Surely she wanted more from life?

There was no time to analyse her motives further because she heard her own name being called.

* * *

Please let me weigh less than fourteen stone. Please let me weigh less than fourteen stone. Please let me weigh less than fourteen stone. Emma chanted the mantra quietly as she twirled the button one way and then the other, encouraging the strong thread to fray, unravel and finally split.

Underneath the massive coat, she wore a flimsy dress, ludicrous for the sub-zero temperature on this bitter March day. She had weighed all her clothes until she found her lightest garment (three ounces). She wore no underwear or tights (two ounces) and, underneath her Annie Hall hat, she sported a severe bob, the result of having had a drastic haircut the day before (at least another four ounces, she estimated). All in all, she was reasonably optimistic. Even happy.

Chapter Ten

New York was beautiful in April. The tormenting summer humidity had not yet descended and all was blue and sharp and panoramic.

Marina looked out of her hotel window in silence, unable to find any words that were not hackneyed to describe the view. She hadn't been to New York before but she had travelled widely. She had witnessed scenes of more brilliant natural beauty and, having lived in London all her life, was familiar with the vibrant music of a happening, modern city. But this was different.

It was different because *she* was different. In the four weeks since she weighed in at Perrico at a humiliating fourteen stone thirteen pounds, she had lost twenty pounds and dropped three generous dress sizes. She understood the mathematics of dieting and knew that early dramatic weight loss consisted mainly of excess water but it didn't matter. To lose such a large amount in such a short time was exhilarating.

The month had soared by, mainly because of the pressures of work. It had taken her two weeks to cancel all the advertising necessary to release funds for Andy Cline's Junction Jostle. She had been on the phone for ten hours a day, occasionally having to dash off for a personal intervention with a particularly intransigent client. Opportunity for exercise had been minimal but she calculated that her greatest calorie expenditure had been in kicking the wall opposite her desk and imagining that it was a fleshy, sensitive part of Andy's anatomy.

She found that she hadn't needed to pay too much heed to

David's instruction to eat as normal. Her life had been so hectic that food had taken a back seat to her more pressing professional needs. And, for the first time in her life, her personal life was spilling over into the office.

Paul Jerome. Since that awkward encounter in the restaurant when Teresa had first pointed out the possibility that he was gay, she had not been able to recapture the spontaneous casualness of their relationship. When she kissed him on greeting, she deflected her lips ever so slightly so that it became an air kiss of the type that she despised in socialites. When they chatted, the silences were more noticeable and less comfortable.

She missed the blossoming friendship that had fed her dulled imagination with such delicious possibilities over her usual arid Christmas. She knew that she had no right to feel cheated if he was gay. After all, she had already concluded that he was out of her league. Or rather, out of her league when she weighed fifteen stone. But at thirteen stone and going down all the time, well, who knew?

She managed to quell the customary self-pity from taking over by indulging in a pleasurably unfamiliar pastime. She looked in the mirror. And she liked what she saw. She saw a woman, very definitely overweight but no longer grotesque. She saw a suit – yes – two pieces of clothing; a skirt without *any* elastic on the waist that actually fastened with a button without cutting off circulation to her upper body. And a jacket which she could either do up comfortably or leave open, unashamed for her skirt's waistband to be seen. She luxuriated in the new sensation of options that this initial weight loss had opened up for her. Then, confident and calm, she went downstairs to join the rest of the delegation for the opening night dinner.

'Marina, you look fabulous!'

Paul Jerome rushed over to greet her. She knew that he was being sincere with his compliment. She didn't even turn her cheek away from his enthusiastic kiss. She couldn't. She couldn't move. Because she'd seen it as soon as she walked in.

Paul had been standing in a corner, deep in intimate conversation with Marina's secretary, Eleanor. Thin Eleanor. Female

Eleanor. And the body language between the two of them was unmistakably heterosexual and consummated.

This wasn't supposed to happen. She'd lost weight. It was her turn. Bad enough that Paul wasn't gay. (Or was it a good thing?) But maybe it was even worse that he should turn out not to be gay but, just like all the others, bewitched by a size ten body and a vacuous face.

She composed herself quickly and produced an epic smile. 'Thanks Paul. So, when did you arrive?'

'I got here yesterday. Thought I'd take a day to enjoy the city.'

Of course you did, Marina thought. And when Eleanor had asked if she could go a day early to meet up with a friend, Marina had gladly agreed, eager to share her new-found goodwill with her loyal secretary.

'That's great!' she said, a little too enthusiastically. 'Anyway, I'd better mingle. I'll catch up with you over dinner. Do excuse me.'

As she left, clenching her buttock muscles with such force that she minced, Eleanor walked over to join Paul. She touched his fingers with the discreet gesture that their not-yet-public liaison dictated. 'She's looking fantastic, isn't she?'

Paul appreciated the generosity of Eleanor's comment and squeezed her hand fondly. She really was a nice girl. Not the brightest but certainly the most uncomplicated and unbitchy he had met in a long time. It was a rare combination in his experience.

'Yes, she is. Has she lost weight, or is it my imagination?'

'No, it's not your imagination. She has lost weight although I don't think she's been dieting. I think it's just the strain of the last few weeks. That decision of yours and Andy's to do that windscreen washing thing really landed her in it. She's lost a lot of friends in the media because of it. It's been tough for her.'

Paul felt guilty. Andy had underplayed the level of difficulty that it was going to cause Marina. Over recent months, he had attained a deep awareness of the politics at TNSW and the ongoing battle for a seat on the board. He'd had some admittedly enjoyable lunches and dinners with Andy but had begun to see the machinations behind the buddy-bonding. Andy was so arrogant that he had falsely convinced himself that he had succeeded in transferring Paul's allegiance away from Marina.

Paul had allowed him to believe this, partly because he had become ambivalent about his feelings for Marina: stunned by the faint tickle of attraction that he had felt for this large woman and then confused by Andy's hints that she was a lesbian. Little wonder that he had fallen into the arms of the straightforward and lovely Eleanor.

'Eleanor, can I ask you a really appalling question, one that I shouldn't ask and you will be well within your rights not to answer?'

'Now I'm really intrigued! What is it?'

'Is Marina a lesbian?'

Eleanor laughed as if he had told her an old joke with a new punchline. 'What on earth makes you think that? Is it because she's overweight? Don't tell me you think all large women are closet lesbians! I thought you were more worldly than that?'

Paul blushed as proof of his decency. 'No, no, it's nothing like that. It's just something that ... well, it's something that Andy Cline sort of hinted.'

'I might have guessed! The bastard! That's just the sort of stunt he'd play. He'd do anything to discredit Marina although that's even lower than I'd have thought of him. And what would be the point of it? It's not as if her sexuality would make you feel any different about ... Oh, I see. He was right, wasn't he? It made you feel awkward. Just the thought of her being gay changed the way you saw her. What a disappointment you are.'

Her sadness was more wounding than any harsh condemnation could have been. He couldn't defend himself, nor could he put into words his feelings when Eleanor had confirmed that Marina was about as gay as he was.

Rick and Andy stood by the bar. Observing and companionable. Such moments gave substance to their friendship.

'How's Gilly?' Andy asked the question with the neutrality founded on twenty years' practice. Because he always felt that Gilly should have been his. They had both met Gilly at the same time at Cambridge. To this day, he didn't understand how Rick had won her over. Another iniquity.

I don't love her any more, Rick wanted to say. I don't need her any more. I don't want her to need me any more. The kids are their own people. I've done my job there, been the proper father. I have absolutely no right to these feelings. I am the luckiest man alive. I have everything any man could want. Nothing to complain about. My life's easy. Maybe too easy. I don't like the house any more. It's too comfortable. It's a designer mausoleum. I'm dying here, Andy. I'm dying.

But men don't say such things to each other. They share a drink, smile and take codeine for the headaches that are becoming a daily presence.

'She's fine.'

'And the kids?'

'Fine. Sam's planning a year's backpacking after his A levels. Lorna's got her GCSEs coming up. Should get all As like her brother. Everyone's fine.' He changed the subject quickly before he said something honest. 'You know we had a board meeting just before the trip?'

Andy knew. And he knew that he had to wait for Rick to tell him what transpired. Those were the rules to having a friend in high places.

Rick went on, 'As I'm sure you've guessed, the main topic of discussion was the next board member. As I'm sure you've also guessed, Marina is way ahead of you as things stand right now.'

Andy bristled. 'That's not really fair. I know she brought in the Sparkleeze business but this completely ignores all the years' contributions I've made to existing business. The decision shouldn't be made on such an arbitrary criterion.'

'Andy, there's nothing arbitrary about three million pounds.'

'So is that it? The decision's made. She's in and I'm out?'

Rick shook his head. 'No. There's another six months before the final appointment is made. That's enough time to get some business of your own in.'

Andy considered this. 'And that's what it's going to take? I'm going to have to bring in an equally big account?'

Rick nodded. 'That's about it. Unless Marina does something completely appalling to damage the company in the next six months.'

A smile crept into Andy's being at this casual comment. At last.

Language he related to. Doing appalling things was right up his street.

'So, how's it going, Marina?'

Marina found herself sitting next to Andy at dinner and it was an effective appetite suppressant. She kept clutching at the memory of her reflection upstairs. I am no longer unworthy. I was always this man's professional equal and now I am close to being his social equal. She pulled herself up and began eating the stringy chicken before her without shame.

'It's going fine, Andy. I've salvaged a difficult position for you at no small cost to myself. Your budget is secure and mine is cut. But enjoy the victory while you can. Sparkleeze is *my* client, Paul Jerome is *my* client. Any little games you play, any devious tricks you intend to surprise me with in the future, those facts will never change. When the annual report is produced, *my* name will be the one next to the three million pound income figure. *Bon appetit.*'

Andy stared at her for a second more than was polite. Marina shuddered at the silent threat. She was right to do so.

At midnight, the view from her room was as beautiful as before, but different. Like me, she thought wryly. The dark night and dazzling lights of the street theatre forced her to squint in order to find recognisable shapes and activities. Here we go again, she thought, as she found herself crying. How strange that my tears should be the same size as before.

She grabbed her coat and recklessly set off into the mahogany New York sub-culture. Her irritation mounted at each corner. Where the hell are all those 24-hour supermarkets where people get shot in *NYPD Blue* ? Finally she saw one, seedy and uninviting. Uninviting, that is, unless you were hungry. Desperately hungry.

Back in the hotel, she tore the wrappers off the candy bars and cookies and cakes with names straight out of *Happy Days*, the Twinkies and Oreos and Tootsie Rolls and Hershey bars. She shoved things into her mouth without bothering to see what they were. But then it happened. She felt full. Not just full because there was no more room in her stomach, but full, sated, bereft of the need to carry on eating. Physically and emotionally unable to continue. She had $47' worth of US junk food in front of her and she had only managed to eat a few hundred calories.

Bloody pills! She couldn't even binge properly any more! Now what was she supposed to do? She watched non-stop episodes of *The Waltons* on her TV and cried as the perfect family enjoyed homecooked, homely food and homespun platitudes around a homemade table. They were all so bloody happy and so bloody thin. Why couldn't she have been born into poverty in the Midwest during the Depression? Life was so unfair!

The vast meeting room could have been in any hotel anywhere on the M25. One wall of the room consisted of an enormous, neutral blind. As Marina looked at it, wondering what was behind it, a miracle happened. Someone pressed a button and, as if it were opening night, the blind rose, ever so slowly.

New York light is different. It shimmers with possibility and nudges the soul of every visitor as if to say: 'Hey, don't I know you? Haven't I been in your dreams a million times in your life? Weren't you the one who saw *42nd Street* ten times and pretended you were tap dancing on a Broadway stage every time you stood at the photocopier? So, what do you think? Isn't it just like you always thought it would be? All silver and tall and loud and expansive? All funny and musical and Technicolor? Don't you just love it?'

Marina loved it. She wondered how anyone could be depressed in this city. She had quickly forgotten her misery from the previous night. She'd slept well (eventually) and woken up to find herself filled with the thought that anything could happen here. She found herself breathing irregularly and chose to put it down to the spectacle unfolding before her rather than a nagging suspicion that the pills were messing about with her heart.

She looked at the other delegates who thronged around the room, noisy and intense. They came from Sparkleeze subsidiaries all over the world but they all wore the same resigned expression common to marketing executives globally of squashed creativity and enforced bureaucracy. The reality of their number-crunching existences was never going to live up to the glamour of their job titles.

Still, they were in New York. Marina scrutinised the sea of faces to look for the barely-concealed excitement that might reflect her own.

There was none. No one looked at the magnificent vista that was clamouring for attention outside the window. She shook her head in disbelief and started scouring the room for Paul Jerome. All right, so it turned out he was a bastard man, just like all the rest, but he had a soul, Marina was sure of that. He would understand and share her emotional response to their surroundings and she really wanted, needed to share this with someone.

He was thinking and doing the same thing. But the moment when the eyes meet across the room in a freeze-frame of life-transforming empathy belonged to a different film. In this movie, someone clinked a spoon across a coffee cup and brought the meeting to order. Both Paul and Marina sat down, their sense of isolation heightened and sense of wonder a little deflated.

After the Chairman of Sparkleeze had delivered the opening comments, Rick Gifford stood up to say a few words on behalf of TNSW.

'As you all know, this is the first year that TNSW has had the privilege of attending the Sparkleeze annual global brand strategy conference. I would like to thank you on behalf of my team for inviting us and allowing to participate actively in this crucial event.'

There was enthusiastic applause from the brand managers who truly believed that this was a *crucial* event. Sad, thought Marina. Rick continued after acknowledging the clapping with his winning smile.

'As Sparkleeze Window Cleaner launches throughout the UK in a few months, we look forward to helping it achieve the same success that has been seen in every other country of launch over the last seven years . . .'

Marina stopped listening and stared out of the window. It was so, so beautiful and she couldn't concentrate on anything else. How could the others be so oblivious to it? Before she knew it,

Rick had finished his speech to an embarrassingly rapturous reception of whoops and whistles. A suit was now standing up and summing up the aims of the five-day conference.

There was one key aim. Fifteen million dollars' worth of research and development had led to the development of a new floral fragrance that was to be added to all Sparkleeze products in every country. Everyone was happy about it but it threw up a problem that only a global conference could resolve: when they printed new labels for the Sparkleeze range, should the label depict a flower to reflect the new floral aroma or a twinkling star to reinforce the message that Sparkleeze leaves surfaces shiny?

Marina thought she must be going mad. I am in New York, I am drowning in this spectacular skyline before me. I can hardly breathe from the explosion that is rocking my emotions.

Look at these people! They can't even see it! They care, they actually *care* whether the label on their floor cleaner has a star or a flower on it. It's not just because this is their job, no. I can see in their eyes that they are concerned. Look at the French delegates, scribbling angry little notes and sliding them across the table to the Swiss. One wants the flower, one wants the star. They've all brought multi-media presentations along to communicate their point of view. They will spend every minute of the week immersed in a campaign to try and talk their international opponents round to another opinion.

They won't go to the theatre in the evening. Or the museums. They won't go for walks at twilight or open their windows at night and listen to the music of the traffic. They won't breathe in the life beyond the hotel walls. They won't give New York the opportunity to change them. Sad, mad them.

And mad, mad me for sitting here with a chumpy grin, pretending to listen to these automata droning on about stars and flowers.

For one deliciously crazy second of insanity, she considered walking out of the meeting and rushing to Central Park. She would act out her own screenplay, rowing on the lake, rollerblading down the winding paths, roly-polying down the gentle slopes . . .

'Marina! Marina!' Eleanor was hissing into her ear *sotto voce*.

Marina jumped out of her reverie back into the meeting. 'What?' she hissed back, irritated both at the interruption to her fantasy and Eleanor's prettiness that had so captivated Paul Jerome.

Eleanor was stung by the tone and drew back a little before whispering again. 'Something terrible has happened.'

Of course, it could never be proved that Andy Cline had 'mislaid' the slides for Marina's keynote presentation that morning. Or all the hard copies of the handouts. No court would ever convict on the evidence of a look that Marina witnessed in Andy's eyes as he watched Eleanor deliver the bad news. But Marina knew.

She did her best. She stayed up all night typing up a new presentation on her laptop and had some acetate slides printed in the hotel's conference office. But the roughness showed, as did the absence of numbers to back all of her points. Everyone expressed sympathy at the 'loss' of the original presentation, but deep down, she knew that they weren't impressed. If she cared as much as we care, they would be thinking, she'd have slept with those slides under her pillow. She's just not one of us. She would have wept at the cool response to her work but she was too tired from a night with absolutely no sleep.

There were only twenty or so people at 5F that night at the end of April. But it was not just the attendance that was down. It was like a holiday camp at the end of the summer season. People talked in loud voices in an attempt to fill the room. Little enclaves gathered in corners to discuss the taboo subject.

There was a jagged line of judgement dividing the room into two. On one side stood the new members and the militants who had declined Perrico's invitation. On the other stood the guinea pigs. They were divided by more than philosophy. The women on the drug programme had changed. They all seemed to have lost weight although, in some cases, it might just have been the careful way they had dressed or a new hair and make-up style. The union of sisterhood had become 'them and us'.

When Marina walked in, the silence crept around the room like a virus. Her obvious weight loss screamed accusingly at the condemning audience. She felt herself drawn inexorably towards her fellow Perrico experimentees. Looking at her shiny comrades who had visibly begun to obey the grooming pages of women's magazines, she immediately spotted a difference between herself and the others.

For the first time in her life, she had consciously dressed down. Marina had spent longer choosing her clothes for this occasion than ever before. If she hadn't been so nervous, she would have laughed at her frantic efforts to find an outfit that camouflaged her emerging figure. Why I am doing this? she asked herself as she drowned herself in a parachute of synthetic silk. She even damped down her trademark curls and scrunched them into a maiden aunt's bun. Her make-up was functional and succeeded in downplaying the cheekbones that were starting to poke up like meerkats. Not dwelling too long on her reflection, she had left her flat, too preoccupied with other thoughts to analyse her strange behaviour.

Actually, she was embarrassed by the person, the body, that she was becoming. She despised the feeling of elation that soared through her, uninvited, every time she stepped on her newly-purchased top-of-the-range digital bathroom scales and registered further weight loss. She felt vain and shallow, flaunting her femaleness like a girl entering puberty. She wanted to wear a placard around her neck explaining to everyone she met that she wasn't on a diet, that she was shrinking for the sake of science, not beauty. After a lifetime of thinking about being thin, she realised that, in fact, she hadn't given it any serious thought at all. Until it became a reality.

Well, it was happening now but she wasn't ready for it. So she tried to hide it. Unfortunately, she didn't succeed. She was entering a female domain where an inch off a thigh can be spotted with radar-like precision at a hundred yards. As soon as she moved across the room, her shape left subtle imprints in the flimsy fabric that sheathed her, leaving no doubt to onlookers that there was less Marina than before.

She was welcomed into her enclave of shrinkees with varying degrees of warmth. While the women were relieved to have their numbers swelled to repel the wave of resentment that was emanating from the other side of the room, each one of them also found herself nervously estimating Marina's weight loss and comparing it with her own. Stomachs were pulled in and flattering facial profiles were posed so that each might look thinner than the rest.

'Teresa, thank God you're here!'

Marina grabbed Teresa's hand and pulled her away from the group. Teresa welcomed the diversion, particularly since she calculated that she had lost at least half a stone more than her friend.

'Marina, you look terrible! Has somebody died?'

Marina had to think about that for a few seconds before dismissing the criticism. 'No, I was just in a hurry to get here. I got held up at work and didn't get home until the last minute.' Wow, I've become an accomplished liar. I actually believe it myself.

'So, tell me, how was New York? I meant to call last night but I was at the gym.'

'Since when have you been going to the gym? I mean, didn't David Sandhurst say that we're supposed to be living our normal lives and not undertaking new activities?'

'I know all that but the thing is he has to accept that, once you lose weight, your normal range of activities expands. I wasn't physically able to use the gym before but now I've got all this extra energy and I don't know what to do with it.'

Marina looked at Teresa carefully. She took in the extra-bright sparkle in her eyes, the heightened colour of her cheeks which owed nothing to blusher. She was gesticulating awkwardly, presumably to conceal the perceptible shaking of her hands. All in all, she looked like one of those painted actresses in *Valley of the Dolls*, showing the stereotypical effects of drugs. What am I thinking? Of course, she's showing the effects of drugs. She's *taking* drugs. We all are. She shook her head, angry that her brain was not working as efficiently as usual. The processing mechanisms were all being short-circuited and her judgement was showing deep flaws.

'Well, you're looking fantastic,' Marina admitted.

'Thanks! I feel fantastic. It's incredible. All of my old clothes are too big and I'm into size sixteen jeans and even they're a bit baggy around the waist. These pills are amazing!'

'And how's Rod taking all these changes?'

Teresa's high spirits flip-flopped for a moment before soaring back to chemical ecstasy. 'Oh Mr Stick-in-the-mud. Keeps giving me the old 'I-loved-you-the-way-you-were speech.'

'Maybe because he *did* love you the way you were?' Marina dared to suggest.

'Don't *you* start! You of all people know what it's like to be fat. How many men have you ever met who found you attractive?'

Marina wondered if cruelty was a quality that she, too, would acquire as she became slimmer.

'But from what you've told me, Rod really loves you. I just wonder if you might be turning your back on the one-in-a-million man who isn't caught up in the "thin-is-best" meritocracy.'

Teresa snorted unattractively. 'Time will tell. I guarantee that, when Rod sees me swanning around the bedroom in size ten silk pyjamas, his *true* feelings will be revealed. Besides, you're starting to sound like Gail again. You take everything far too seriously. Why don't you join me at the gym tomorrow? It'll make a new woman of you!'

Before Marina could find a suitable reply that wouldn't cast an indelible shadow over their friendship, Gail stormed into their gathering like Boadicea. Her greeting was less than sisterly. 'So, Marina, glad to see you could squeeze us in between aerobics classes and facials. How is life as a weightwatcher? Exactly the same as it always was, I'd wager. Counting the calories in your lipstick? Pretending that cottage cheese is really very tasty? Spending every last possible moment before a weigh-in on the loo, so that you can wee just one more cc of ugliness out of you? Have you yet bought that obligatory size twelve skirt that "one day" you will slide into?'

Marina hated her. She hated her because she didn't like having saliva sprayed across her face and she hated her because everything she was saying was true. Admittedly, the weight was falling off her without any effort. She rarely felt hungry and seldom experienced the obsessive cravings that had put her in this position in the first place. But it was as if the pills allowed her to invent another, sensible person to take over the food intake into her particular body while the other self-destructive Marina still weighed fifteen stone and fantasised about chocolate buttons. The schism that separated her body from her neurosis was beginning to scare her. She pulled herself together.

'It's not like that, Gail. I wish you wouldn't be so aggressive about all this. Don't you see that Perrico coming to 5F is a tribute to your accomplishment in guiding us to the stability that set us apart from other overweight women.'

'We don't say overweight here!' Gail yelled. 'And stop patronising me. Just because you've lost weight doesn't make you better than me. And what have you come back here for, anyway? Have you just come here to gloat? To flaunt your skinny calves and show off your bone structure? You must have spent ages choosing clothes that would draw attention to yourself so dramatically!'

Marina was stunned by the outburst. Although the words revealed more about Gail than they did about herself, she still felt exposed and vulnerable. How can this be? she thought. Why is it that I'm attracting more insults, more sheer nastiness and resentment than I did when I was bigger? I think I was happier when people talked about me behind my back, when I could pretend that I hadn't quite heard the sniggers. Suddenly I'm fair game. Except it's not fair.

'Gail, I'm not pretending to be better than you and I'm sorry if I gave you that impression . . .'

'There you go again, patronising me!'

'For God's sake, will you listen to me for just one minute? If you could only stop fighting battles that don't exist, you might find that there is as much common ground between us as there ever was. In fact, my experiences over the last couple of months have actually reinforced some of the principles that I learned from you and,' she held up her hand to stop Gail from repeating the 'patronising' accusation again, 'I came to 5F tonight because I still need your support. In fact, I need it more than ever. So much is happening that I don't understand and I have nowhere to go to get help to deal with it all. Except here.'

Gail considered the speech then morphed into Earth Mother, smothering Marina in an overwhelming but welcome embrace.

'I don't get it. What exactly do you mean by "couldn't binge"? '

The perfectly valid question came from one of the newer

members (who had tried not to reveal her disappointment at discovering that applications to join the trials with Perrico were now closed).

Marina struggled to put the strange feeling into words. 'It's as if the connection that sends the "eat" message from the desperate part of my mind to my mouth was broken. I looked at the food. All that gorgeous, terrible, claggy food sat before me. I established the ambience; I found a channel on the radio that played non-stop hits of the Seventies; I found *Fawlty Towers* on the TV and turned the volume down; I turned the lights down in my room and opened the curtains; I put the comfiest chair right by the window so that I could look out on to the Manhattan skyline and placed all the food on a bedside table within my reach.'

She could almost hear the wet plops of salivation dripping from the jowls of the needy women around her. 'And?' Gail prompted impatiently.

'And ... nothing. I picked up a Twinkie, a bit like a swiss roll really, and looked at it and then ... I put it down. It's not that I didn't want it, it's more that I couldn't force myself to eat it. I wasn't hungry, I wasn't not hungry, I was just not able to focus on food. It was irrelevant. That's it, it just wasn't necessary.'

Lucky you, her resentful listeners thought, while not having the slightest clue as to what her problem was.

'My problem,' Marina said, 'is that all my problems remain the same but I no longer have the mechanism of dealing with them. That's my problem.'

Chapter Eleven

The waiting room at Perrico was a colourful place that June. Weighing-in had become a time of optimism rather than terror and these women were enjoying the emergence of summer for the first time in their lives. The tyranny of heat no longer enslaved them. They were able to wear short sleeves without feeling mortified by the wobbly tops of their arms. They could wear skirts without tights and actually walk without their thighs chafing together and causing open, weeping sore patches.

The fabrics chosen mirrored their new freedom. They wore vertical stripes and huge dominant prints, they wore (good grief!) Lycra and denim, they wore whites and pastels.

They chitter-chattered about their new lives, their new experiences and, inevitably, the new friends who'd supplanted the old. Many longstanding friendships had crumbled as balances toppled in unexpected directions. Old friends didn't know how to talk to these new people. It was a shame. And a revelation.

But in the waiting room, there was one topic of conversation that was taboo. Nobody mentioned the side-effects that were cursing their lives since starting the trial. Most of them had suffered recurrent headaches, acute stomach pain, dizziness, nausea, the whole range of physical screams that served as warning signs that something was wrong. They each invented the reassurance that it was probably the weight loss causing the problems rather than the medication. After all, they might be on the placebo and then they'd feel stupid if they complained of side-effects.

Nobody was going to complain about the tablets. They might not be given any more.

This was a room of women who had almost all lost weight and the sight depressed David Sandhurst beyond the point of consolation. Because only half of these women had been given the Oxymetabulin. The other half had been given placebos and there was absolutely no chemical reason why they should have lost an ounce.

'Well, you've lost half a stone.'

'What else? Tell me the good news.'

The doctor looked at the results carefully. 'That depends on what you mean by good news. For some people, any diagnosis, however ominous, is preferable to none. If you know what is wrong with you, you can at least try and fight it.'

'In other words, there's nothing wrong with me.' Rick sat back, both relieved and disappointed. The doctor was right. Rick had almost wanted to be able to blame his reckless, irresponsible flights of fancy on a brain tumour or some frightful disease that messed around with your hormones. It wasn't to be.

The headaches were almost certainly caused by stress as was the weight loss and all the other symptoms. Rick had briefly, self-consciously mentioned his dissatisfactions with his life. The doctor had laughed without sympathy. 'Mr Gifford, if there were a pill I could prescribe for a mid-life crisis, I'd be prescribing it for myself. What you're feeling is nothing new. Take up a new hobby. Go away for a romantic weekend with your wife. Play golf. That's what I do. It'll pass.'

What Rick didn't tell the doctor was that he had been having these feelings for a long time now. He'd controlled them and kept them to himself because that was the sort of man he was. Decent, sensible. He had a wife and children. He had responsibilities. But they were feeling more dilute in power with every passing year. Every day, on his way to the office, he had to drive past the junction for the M4. Every day, he had to yank the wheel round to stop his arm from gently swerving the car towards the West Country and a new life.

He'd tried new hobbies. Had romantic weekends with his wife. He was running out of answers. And resolve.

'So tell me the good news.'

Emma stepped off the scales almost bouncing with euphoria. She didn't need David to tell her how much she had lost. She had weighed herself at least three times a day since beginning the trial and knew the exact amount in both pounds and kilograms.

She had lost four stone in three months and now weighed just under ten stone, a good weight for her five-feet ten-inch height, but she looked dreadful. The massive strain that this transformation had placed on her ravaged body was evident. David felt himself repulsed by the hawk-like creature before him. Certainly, she had lost a lot of her excess weight, but at what cost? The speed of shrinkage had left her burdened with flaps of empty flesh sagging over her emerging framework like turkey wattles. Pockets of resisting fat clung like fists to her hips and thighs. Her face had thinned to the point where her unattractive bone structure was making its presence known. The shadows below her eyes were dark blue and her eyes were bloodshot but glittering.

David hated this woman. He could see this whole trial going down the tubes if she continued to destroy herself this way. She would soon be entering the realms of the painfully thin, when the dreaded 'anorexia' rumours would begin to be connected with his project.

'Emma, are you eating normally?' He asked the question wearily, knowing that she would lie since she was so obviously starving herself.

'Oh, absolutely! I mean, I understood what you said about how important it was for us to carry on as before. Absolutely!' Her hysterical enthusiasm was in response to a potential threat to her supply of pills. She was intelligent enough to realise that she might be pulled out of the trial if she was seen to be abusing the protocols. 'I know I've lost a lot of weight but I think that's just because of my natural metabolism. I mean, I think I'm naturally supposed to be thin and your Oxymetabulin has just managed to kick-start my metabolism out of its unnatural rate and now I'm the person nature meant me to be. That would explain why it's all coming off so quickly, wouldn't it?'

David struggled to find the right words. ' I am a little concerned at your rate of weight loss and your blood pressure is far too high as well. Emma, you're not looking too good, I have to say and, if this is because of the tablets, then ethically I really have no choice but to—'

'You can't take me off the tablets! You can't! Just wait and see. I bet, next month, I'll have stabilised, you'll see. I'll eat normally and you'll see that it's all natural, that I'm supposed to be like this. I'll be your greatest success story.'

Her innate cunning and instinctive understanding of the devious Dr Sandhurst led her to mention another thought. 'Just think what it will be like when I syndicate the story across the US as well as all through Britain. I have the contacts, as you yourself pointed out. There's no way that this story will get out without at least one editor asking me to do a feature on it. I am *the* authority on slimming stories. And when the press find out that I was an original guinea pig ... What a story it's going to be! Every daytime chat show in the Western world is going to want my "before-and-after" pictures.' She looked at him levelly and spoke without a hint of threat. 'You really want me on your side, you know.'

David recognised the resoluteness of this kindred spirit. He knew that she would stop at nothing to stay on this programme. She was determined to continue with the tablets, regardless of the effects on her general health.

There was one possibility, however, that would absolve him of any guilt for allowing this self-destruction to continue. If he could know, for certain, that Emma was taking the placebo, that her excessive weight reduction could be attributed to her neurotic faith in the power of dummy pills, then he could not be blamed for the consequences. Oxymetabulin's reputation and efficacy would be untainted.

But how could he find out what she was taking when the secrecy of the triallists' identities was protected so assiduously by a computer programme to which he had no access? All the data had been input in such a way that no single person could connect the names of each triallist with the drug type prescribed. Only when

113

the trial was complete could the password be implemented to activate the list of names and treatment. Or at least that was the theory. David knew enough about computers to understand that no system was impenetrable and if anyone had a mind cunning enough to outwit a machine, it was him. He laughed quietly.

'What's so funny?' Emma asked, wrapping her arms about herself in anticipation of bad news.

David looked at her with distaste. 'Private joke, nothing personal.' He cleared his throat and pretended to read through his notes before making a decision. 'Well, I suppose we can give it another month, see if things settle down.'

Emma almost fainted with relief as he handed over the white box of pills marked only with a computer-generated number. 'I won't let you down. Just watch. I'll be fine next time,' she added.

She stood up and left quickly before he could change his mind and possibly snatch the pills back. She treated the other women in the waiting room to a slightly hysterical smile. She rushed over to Marina and Teresa who were sitting together gossiping nervously as they awaited their appointment.

'Hi, you two!' The effusiveness of the greeting was alarming and Marina took a few seconds before speaking.

'Hi, Emma. Everything OK?'

This vague question didn't really demand an answer but Emma was too hyped up to restrain herself. 'Four stone. Isn't it fantastic! I've never felt so great. Of course I need to tone myself a bit, get myself in shape, but I've started exercising and if you really commit yourself to an exercise programme, you can firm up everything in six weeks and I reckon it'll only be a few more weeks before I'm down to nine stone.'

Her eyes darted maniacally from Marina to Teresa and she closed her mouth abruptly when she saw the expression on their faces. She'd been seeing that same expression on a lot of faces recently. It was something about her that was making people look at her like this. She understood. It was the pure joy of being almost slim that was overstimulating her. She wanted to walk down the street shouting 'Look at me! Look at me!' but her madness hadn't taken her that far yet. Instead she stored up her joy inside her, weaving it into a continuum of delirious communication that she would spray at whoever expressed the slightest interest.

She was talking too much and too fast, she realised. She resolved to try and curb her excesses and present a more reasonable portrait of her new self. At this stage, she still retained a modicum of objectivity and was slightly bothered herself by some aspects of her behaviour.

'So, how about the three of us going out for lunch after this? Girls' outing, that sort of thing?' Suddenly terrified that they were going to reject her overture of friendship, she switched tack. 'It's for my article. I'm doing a huge feature for the *Sunday Times* on the drugs trial and I could do with some other people's experiences to add some balance to my own. My treat.'

Her desperation was so obvious that Marina and Teresa found it impossible to refuse. Teresa spoke first. 'That sounds fine, Emma. We could be another half an hour, though. It seems to be going really slowly today.'

Marina jumped in to support her friend. 'Would it be best if we met you somewhere? Save you hanging around here?'

'No, I'm quite happy to wait here. I like it here. It's got good associations for me! You take your time.'

She put some headphones in her ears, switched on her personal stereo and drifted off into her own special world where she was thin and beautiful and happy.

'Why is she smiling like that?' Marina whispered.

Teresa shuddered. 'I don't know but she's giving me the creeps. Why on earth did we agree to go out with her?'

'If I remember rightly, *you* agreed.'

'Well, I *had* to. It would have been like kicking Bambi to say no. Anyway, why does she want to hang around with us, all of a sudden? She's never been that interested up to now.'

Marina shrugged. 'Hard to say. But, by all accounts, she and Gail aren't speaking at all any more. She's stopped going to 5F completely. Perhaps she hasn't got any other friends.'

'Well, we'll do this once, but if she thinks we're going to become a regular, cosy little girly threesome, she can think again. I'd hoped to have a good old chat with you.'

'More rows with Rod?'

'Not exactly. It's impossible to have a row when I never see him. He's out all hours at the moment. Following up new business leads, so he says.'

'You don't believe him?'

'I don't know what to believe. I can't blame him for wanting to stay out of my way. I'm a complete bitch. I know that everything will be fine once I'm slim, but it's the getting there that's making me ratty.'

'But you already look terrific, you know you do. You don't want to go down that much further, surely?'

'Oh, Marina, don't tell me that you're going to resort to that old cop out, the old "you-don't-want-to-get-*too*-thin" routine! I normally put that one down to jealousy but I know that you're not like that.'

Marina looked pained. 'I suppose some people say it because they mean it, because it's true. You do look great. Even you, with your subterranean self-esteem, have to admit that. And you also have to admit that once someone goes below a certain weight, the balance of their features can be compromised.'

'I don't know what you're talking about but, if you're saying that it's better to be a bit fat, then you'll never get me to agree with you.'

Marina was tempted to abandon her argument. She couldn't. She had to have one more attempt at persuading Teresa away from this course.

'I'm not saying anything about fat. I'm saying that every woman has her own individual ideal body make-up. You know what I mean: the woman whose face becomes haggard and drawn when she loses that last tiny padding from her hips. Or the woman whose calves look bandy when she shaves the last inch from her thighs.'

'So, in other words, I have to keep my disgusting belly if I'm not going to have the face of a decrepit old shrew?'

Marina held up her hands in defeat. 'OK. You win. Let's change the subject before we fall out.'

'Good idea.'

They both stared into space blankly looking for a safe, neutral subject. This was difficult since their friendship had been built on their common concerns with their weight. Everything else had branched out from this shared stem, in tacit acknowledgement of the fact that not a single area of their lives was untouched by their sense of physiological inadequacy.

Fortunately, they were spared from having to face this truth by Marina's name being called from the consulting room. Teresa squeezed her hand and wished her luck. Marina stood up and walked off, uncertain of what sort of luck Teresa had in mind.

They were close to finishing their second bottle of Sancerre.

Teresa looked worried. 'I know I've said it before, but we *were* told not to mix alcohol with these drugs.'

Emma giggled as she tipped the last drops of the bottle into her glass. 'It's a bit late now. Anyway, I explained to you, they always say that on these trials. It's to protect themselves in case you have a bad reaction. That way, they can say that it wasn't their fault. But, deep down, they're really pleased because it means that they've established that there *is* a reaction between alcohol and the pills so they can then print a warning on their packet.'

Teresa and Marina looked confused. It made even less sense this time than it had the previous two times. And yet, in their increasing drunkenness, the logic was becoming unimpeachable. Still, they were reassured by Emma's confidence in her own explanation and ordered another bottle.

They all wore that wonky smile prevalent among the mildly drunk. Somehow, they had become generally unkempt and their posture had folded into zig-zag slumps in their woefully uncomfortable chrome chairs.

The alcohol had deleted all of Teresa's inhibitions and the intrusive questions were about to begin. 'So Emma, what's happening with you and Gaïl? You used to be a double helix, weaving your way around the foundations of 5F, a single entity, and now she seems to have excommunicated you.'

Emma was too drunk to be either offended or discreet. 'She's so uptight, that's her problem. Do you know her problem?' Nobody did. 'She's scared of being thin, that's her problem! And she knows it. And she knows *I* know it. Have you ever been to her flat?' They hadn't. 'Well, I have and I've seen all her photos. She was thin until she was sixteen and she showed me some holiday snaps from that time. Then it all made sense.'

She paused for dramatic effect, although she was so drunk that her audience actually interpreted the pause as a conscious effort to keep from throwing up or passing out.

'What on earth did she look like?' Marina asked, hoping for some lurid description of an adolescent beset by all the juvenile torments of skin and hair horrors. Rather like her own teenage self, except she was fat as well.

'Well that's just it. She just looked ordinary. Not pretty. Not ugly. Everything in the right place, so to speak. A bit big on the bosom front, but not as big as some girls I knew at school. No, she looked, well, fine. The only odd thing was her hair. It was tied back in plaits, a bit ridiculous on a girl that age. And it was an ordinary sort of brown. Amazing when you see what her hair's like now.'

She sat back in satisfaction of an anecdote well told.

'Did I miss something?' Teresa asked, still waiting for the story's climax. 'Where was the bit that made sense of Gail's fear of being thin? Am I so inebriated that I can't even follow a conversation now?'

Marina shrugged her shoulders. 'You and me both. Emma, what was the point of all that? You say that Gail was a totally normal, average teenager. So what?'

Emma waved her arms about in exasperation. 'Don't you see?' They didn't.

'The point is that, when Gail *was* slim, she was ordinary. She was never going to be a raving beauty or a head turner. In fact, by the time the bloom of youth left her when she hit her twenties, she was probably going to be plain. Imagine! A lifetime of being plain!'

She beckoned Marina and Teresa to lean closer so that she could present her masterclass in female psychology in the hushed tones that such serious academic endeavour warranted. They complied reluctantly, already horrified by her searing condemnation of the vast majority of womankind who failed to meet her rigid standards of conventional beauty.

'So what did she do? She got fat. And what is the great thing about being fat? The only great thing about being fat?'

No idea.

'The great thing about being fat is that you can create a thin image of yourself in your imagination. The ideal you. You can be beautiful and popular and funny and loved. You can have perfectly formed breasts. You can have hips and thighs that follow whatever line is currently popular. When you're fat, you can saunter through life, smug in the knowledge that, underneath the big exterior, there is someone who could have anything she wanted, *be* anyone she wanted. And one day ... one day ... you'll be that person.'

She stopped to swallow an undignified amount of wine before continuing. 'Unless, of course, you *know* what you'd be like as a thin person. Imagine knowing that even at eight stone you still won't be special. What do you do? You stay fat. You paint yourself into a caricature. You become special as a fat woman. Not pretty. Not beautiful. But special, noticeable. And when you meet people who sigh sadly and say: 'You could be so attractive if you lost weight,' you smile inside because you know it's not true. *That's* why Gail doesn't want to be thin.'

There was no applause although she seemed to be expecting some kind of accolade. Marina cleared her throat. 'Maybe you're right, Emma. I mean, you know her better than we do, so we can't really say one way or another. But if what you're saying is true, then hardly anybody would diet. Or if they did, when they discovered that they were no raving beauties, they'd put the weight straight back on.'

Emma banged the table triumphantly. 'Exactly! Over ninety per cent of people who lose weight put it all back on again. Why do you think that is?'

She didn't wait for an answer this time. She'd written this article a thousand times and would not be distracted from completing her thesis.

'It's because the reality of being thin didn't come close to matching the fantasy that had kept them sane through their fat years. They didn't meet the man of their dreams, or if they did, they never felt truly worthy of him. They didn't get a big pay rise. Their family and friends didn't love them any more than before. Their bodies were never perfect in their own eyes. Or if they

119

were, they noticed imperfections elsewhere. True and everlasting happiness did not come to call. There never came the time when all was as it was meant to be.

'This is something that slim people have known all along. They assimilate the disappointment and get on with their lives, making the best of it. When a fat person is faced with this reality, they deal with the disappointment in the only way they know how. They eat.'

She sat back, depressed by her own philosophy. While she was talking, she had been unable to prevent herself calculating that she had ingested over 1000 calories in wine. Panic was beginning to set in.

Teresa was also depressed. She wondered where Rod was this lunchtime. He hadn't answered his mobile when she'd tried to phone him to convey the news that she was down to ten and a half stone.

Marina was also depressed. All the joy she had experienced at being officially weighed at just under eleven stone had dissipated. Her own thought processes were dulled by the wine and she was having difficulty in coming up with an argument to counter Emma's theories. If she was right ...

'Moo Cow!'

As if she wasn't depressed enough already.

Susie had just walked into the restaurant with David Sandhurst. There was no time to wonder whether this was a strange occurrence or not. Marina stood up to greet Susie. She spotted that harassed, barely-reined panic that marked Susie out as a working mother with too many commitments. She was loaded with carrier bags from Peter Jones and had her left sleeve rolled up so that her watch was always visible.

'Not working today?' Marina asked in amusement.

'No. I had to take the day off. Alice had a dentist's appointment. Frederick had to see the child psychologist (don't ask, Moo, that's a long story), we've got ten people coming to dinner tonight from the school governors (fingers crossed, I could be a governor this time next year) and I need to do all the cooking and ...'

While Susie discharged her life on to Marina, they hugged awkwardly. Suddenly Susie pulled away in shock.

'My God, Moo Cow! Look at all the weight you've lost. I mean, it's great and congratulations and all that. But you're not anorexic, are you? I hardly recognise you! Your face! You're not going to take this too far are you? I'm not being negative or anything but ...'

'Thank you, Susie,' Marina replied dryly. 'You look great too.' Susie drew back as if she had been shot. It was only at this point that Marina really looked at her friend. After a shared lifetime where only her own body was on permanent inspection, she had always taken Susie's perfection for granted. But then she recalled her own suspicion at their last meeting. She looked more closely and exhaled sharply as she saw the unmistakable truth: Susie was getting fat.

Susie had seen the look of surprise and, could it be, pleasure creeping over Marina's face. No, surely not. Friends weren't like that. Before Marina had the chance to put her observations into words that could not be unsaid, Susie started explaining her situation breathlessly.

'I know what you're thinking. You're wondering if I'm pregnant!'

Marina said nothing. She had seen Susie through pregnancy and knew that this was different.

'Well, I'm not. Although I must say I thought I was myself. You know me, I never put on an ounce. No, I think I've got some sort of glandular problem. Or hormonal. I'm going to have some tests done, of course. It could be my thyroid. Or diabetes. Anything. It could be something serious, you just can't tell, can you? Because this is just not acceptable. Not for me anyway. I'm not supposed to be overweight. Not me.'

The three other women were embarrassed by this speech. Susie was making a massive mistake in trying to make excuses for her weight gain to three women who knew every excuse there was. They felt terribly sorry for her as she struggled to cope with a problem that she had never faced before.

Was there also a little bit of gloating as they acknowledged themselves shrinking in size while this poor creature watched herself swell? Of course there was. Female solidarity is a very admirable concept but when you've suffered a lifetime of torment at the hands of thin women like Susie, well, can you blame them?

Then something awful happened. Susie burst into tears. She turned her face quickly to see where David was. He was unaware of Susie's distress. He was sitting at the bar, flirting lasciviously with the waitress. This made Susie even more miserable. 'Moo Cow, what am I going to do? I'll never be able to make my special sauce again!'

Chapter Twelve

'Am I imagining it or did she just say that she'd never be able to make her special sauce again?' Teresa asked Emma.

'That's what it sounded like.'

Susie stood up abruptly. 'Come with me. I'll show you in the Ladies. It's a nightmare!'

She'd actually been addressing Marina but the other two decided to trot along as well. In their state it was probably a good idea to stay close to the toilets anyway.

The four women lurched towards the toilets, all displaying gaits at various stages of drunkenness and hysteria.

They walked into the empty cloakroom. Susie went straight into one of the cubicles and shut the door behind her. 'Just wait and I'll show you the problem,' she muttered.

There is a common myth that women like nothing better than to have a bonding session in the toilets. This is perhaps true for women under thirty who have nothing to hide, either physically or emotionally. Once over thirty, however, bathrooms become places of refuge where cunning make-up tricks can be employed to conceal the flaws that betray the onslaught of age. They become cocoons where a woman can undo her waistband and loosen her stomach muscles for a few gloriously relaxed minutes. They are havens where teeth can be picked, spots painted over and tights hitched up. And most women prefer to be alone on such occasions.

As Marina, Emma and Teresa stood in the cramped washbasin area, they found their easy conversation had dried up. They read the beautifully calligraphed instructions regarding disposal of sanitary products. They looked in the mirror with a cautious degree of casualness so as not to appear vain. Then they became distracted by the noises emanating from Susie's cubicle. First of all, there was the rummaging sound of a handbag being opened and upturned. Then a box was opened. Then they heard it.

It was the unmistakable sound of a battery-operated appliance being switched on. The humming buzz zhoozhed up and down the register. The three woman were dumbstruck. They looked at each other in shock and disbelief. No one wanted to be the first to offer an opinion as to what Susie was doing in there. The possibilities were just too horrible to bear thinking about.

Suddenly Susie slammed open the door. Recoiling in alarm, Marina saw that Susie was topless and was holding out some kind of plastic bottle for her scrutiny. An empty bottle.

Marina took it reluctantly. She looked at it, deeply concerned for Susie's sanity. 'It's a bottle?' she opined carefully, anxious not to say the wrong thing to the madwoman.

Wrong answer. Susie snatched it back roughly. 'It's not a bottle. It's an *empty* bottle. Don't you see? It's an empty bottle.'

Emma was less concerned about saying the wrong thing. 'We can all see it's empty. But, and I hate to ask this because I'm not sure I really want to know the answer, what is supposed to be in it?'

Susie breathed out sharply, stunned by the stupidity of these people. 'Milk, of course. My breast milk.'

It took a while for this information to be digested. As Marina made the connection between this pronouncement and the countless dinners she had consumed, all lavishly embellished with Susie's special sauce, she felt very, very sick.

'Are you saying that you have been using breast milk in your special sauce for the last ...?'

'Seven years, yes. Since the twins were born.'

Emma shook her head. She thought she'd heard every bizarre food ritual there was, but breast milk in the white sauce? 'But why? What on earth made you do it?'

Susie couldn't belief how uninformed this person was. 'I thought you were supposed to be some sort of expert on slimming. Well has nobody ever told you that you can burn up to about two thousand extra calories a day when you're breastfeeding?'

Of course, they all thought simultaneously. It was so insanely logical that they wondered why more women didn't do it. Or perhaps they did. None of them would ever touch a white sauce prepared by a mother again.

Susie went on. 'It was a miracle. I hated having all that extra weight after the twins but once I got going with the breastfeeding, it all just fell off me. I was eating masses and masses but I was still losing a couple of pounds a week. I couldn't believe that there were actually women who didn't breastfeed. I mean, didn't they realise the advantages?

'So, anyway, eventually the twins went on to solids and they didn't even want my milk in bottles. I was desperate. A few odd pounds started to creep on, even when I dieted. Then the answer was obvious.'

She went back into the cubicle and returned with the device that had made all the noise earlier. Nobody recognised it.

'It's a breast pump!' Susie exclaimed.

'Oh!' the other three chorused, seeing everything clearly for the first time that day. And it was clear. It made perfect sense. Yet it was totally potty.

For seven years, Susie had been using a breast pump to maintain production of her breast milk. Quite when and where she was accomplishing this epic feat was a bit of a mystery. Perhaps Ken thought she had a weak bladder and needed to spend inordinate amounts of time on the loo. Who knew?

Teresa was obviously bothered by something. 'You mentioned that you had twins. They must have taken a lot of feeding. Just how much milk have you been making every day since you stopped feeding the babies?'

Susie thought for a moment. 'About one and a half litres.'

The others almost choked with astonishment.

'Good God! What did you do with the stuff that you didn't put in the sauce?' Marina asked.

'I made rice pudding, ice cream, milk shakes for the kids, that sort of thing. Oh and I discovered it frothed really well in Ken's new cappuccino machine. You'd be amazed how easy it was to find ways to use it up.'

'You're pumping one and a half litres from your breasts *every day*?' Emma asked, still reeling from the image that this presented.

'That's the point. Not any more. I used to but now it's stopped.'

She was talking to people who knew nothing about milk starting or finishing. They didn't have a clue what she was talking about. So she rammed the point home. 'I've dried up! There's no more milk. It was taking me longer and longer to produce less and less milk. That's when I started to put on weight. Then a couple of weeks ago it just stopped. What am I going to do?'

'Why not ask David for some of his pills?' Marina said it before she could stop herself. It was a stupid thing to say. Stupid because it was so appealingly simple. Stupid because it was wrong. Stupid because Susie would now be obsessed with the only 'quick-fix' solution available. Marina was about to try and take the words back when something struck her.

'Was I imagining it, or was that David coming into the restaurant with you?'

Susie's inner alarm bells rang and she acted quickly to deflect suspicion. 'My secret's out! You were absolutely right, Moo. I was thinking along the same lines as you and came to the same conclusion. I invited David to see if he could put me on the Oxymetabulin trial.'

'But Susie, that's impossible, you must see that. I know I suggested it but that was just a silly knee-jerk reaction. For one thing, the trial is now underway, they can't just add people at this stage. And secondly, you're completely the wrong sort of person for this trial. David chose 5F members precisely because we would be more likely to eat in a stable fashion and not skew the results.'

Along with Emma and Teresa, she had the good grace to blush at the blatant lie she was evangelising. Still, that was the story and she had to stick to it.

Susie had calmed down (and put her top back on) and was now anxious to return to David. She hadn't even thought about asking him for the pills before. It wasn't that kind of a relationship, they tended not to talk about serious things. They tended not to talk much, full stop. But now that Marina had put the idea in her head, she was gripped by the possibility.

'You're right, it's just me getting desperate. I won't embarrass David by asking him. Although now I'm going to have to come up with a reason for inviting him. I'll just have to use my charm on him!' She laughed unconvincingly. 'Oh, and Moo Cow, I feel a bit foolish about all this. You won't mention to Ken that ... well, you know?'

Marina agreed hastily, eager to end this whole encounter that was giving her a headache. She'd been having a lot of headaches recently. Not that she'd told David about them. She didn't want to be taken off the programme any more than Emma.

'Incidentally,' Susie asked, 'what are you doing in this particular restaurant? It's a long way from your patch, isn't it?'

Emma answered eagerly on everyone's behalf. 'We all got weighed at Perrico today. I've lost four stone and Marina and Teresa have lost nearly as much. Mind you, they had more to lose than me in the first place.' She stopped talking, knowing she'd gone too far again.

'Oh right. Well done, then. Is that the right thing to say? I don't know. Well, must dash. Thanks Moo Cow. For everything.' Susie kissed Marina gratefully, searching without success for the usual expansive patch of cheek into which to sink her thin (definitely not overweight) lips. She settled for an air kiss rather than confront physical evidence that her friend was changing.

After Susie had left, Emma, Teresa and Marina just stood there, incapable of deciding what to do next. There was only one thing to do in this situation. They each went into one of the cubicles and tried to flush the madness into the toilet pan.

'Where the hell have you been?' David hissed at Susie, furious with her for not being as beautiful as she was when they first started their affair.

'Didn't you see Marina and the others? I had to come up with some kind of explanation for why I was with you.'

This made David even angrier. He knew Marina was a frequent visitor at Susie and Ken's house and he didn't like the thought of Marina mentioning something to Ken. Not that he had any feelings of loyalty towards him. He worked with Ken, they weren't soul mates. No, it was just that he needed him.

Ken, bless him, had never been much of a lad. He was never invited to stag nights or secretaries' birthday drinks. Nobody asked him if he'd had a good weekend or if he thought that Cameron Diaz was a babe. So he'd been flattered when David Sandhurst offered him friendship. David was everything he wasn't: confident, handsome and popular with women. By teaming up with him, some of David's popularity reflected on to Ken. And he liked it.

So that when David asked him, mate to mate, man to man, if he'd do a couple of favours, well, of course he agreed. So far, Ken had been amenable to the grey invoices that David had asked him to pass. And the questionable expenses claims. But he made it clear that he didn't feel right about doing it. David had to keep on 'wooing' Ken as meticulously as he could until he could find another stooge in the accounts department.

'You stupid cow!' he muttered through clenched teeth. 'Why did you insist on coming to this place if you knew your chums might be here? Do you want Ken to find about about us? Is that why you're being such a moron?'

Susie felt tears jabbing her eyelids. 'How was I to know she'd be here? I chose it because it was close to Perrico. You didn't tell me they were all weighing in today or I might have anticipated that they'd have lunch nearby afterwards. You never tell me anything.' She sounded like a brat, she knew, but she couldn't help it. 'Oh David, I'm sorry I'm such a bitch. It's just that I've got lots on my mind. In fact there was something, in particular, that I wanted to talk to you about. Why are you looking at me like that?'

'You've put on weight, haven't you. On your face, that is. The rest of you's been getting bigger for a while but it wasn't too objectionable. You always were a little on the scrawny side. But now it's hitting your face. I hate it when women let themselves go. It always shows in the face. Look, you're starting to get a double chin.'

He squeezed a tiny fold of flesh between his finger and thumb. It hurt and Susie cried out. 'Funnily enough, that's what I wanted to talk to you about. It's the oddest thing, not even my idea, no, it was Marina's . . . '

'Stop wittering, Susie! I hate it when you witter.'

She stopped wittering abruptly. Before she could restart her campaign for joining the Oxymetabulin trial, David's mobile phone rang. He stood up and walked to the other side of the restaurant before answering it. Susie hated it when he did that. It forced her to imagine who might be on the other end of the phone, someone he didn't want her to know about. Of course it could be something to do with work, something underhand. She knew enough about David to suspect that his working methods were probably as shady as the rest of his moral existence.

But it was more likely to be a woman.

When he returned to the table, she scoured his face for a clue. There was none. This was not a soap opera where the villains have shifty eyes and the good guys wear open smiles. In the real world, everyone acted from the day they learned to communicate and, consequently, most people were very good at it. David was better than most.

'Sorry, Susie, crisis back at the lab. Must dash. Take care. I'll call.'

He ruffled her hair as if she were a Labrador puppy and then left. He didn't kiss me, Susie thought. And he said 'call me' but he didn't say when. She knew what this meant. Women of thirty-one know these things.

He's never going to call me again.

It wasn't a woman on the phone. David had other things on his mind. He cursed himself for lashing out at Susie. Although he meant what he said about her weight, it was foolish to alienate her when she was still his most reliable meal ticket. Still, he'd find someone else. He always did. That was how his life worked out.

But his life was slipping more than a little out of control. And he wasn't used to it. With each passing month, his debts mounted while his salary stayed constant. Interest on outstanding loans and credit cards was getting higher and for the last two months his entire take-home pay had not been sufficient to meet all of his creditors' demands.

He was beginning to panic. He'd taken a whole load of his clothes to a specialist shop for resale. That had raised enough to pay outstanding gas and electricity bills and not a lot more. He wasn't sleeping properly. It didn't matter that there was no money for food because he was losing his appetite.

He had been waiting for his bank to come to a decision about extending his overdraft on the guarantee of the end-of-trial bonus from Perrico. There had been umpteen calls between his bank manager (a man, damn) and Geoff Perriam, Perrico's MD. David didn't know what was being said but, whatever it was, it was sowing doubts in the bank's mind.

The call in the restaurant was from the bank manager. Could David pop round for a quick chat? Was it convenient? You bet it was.

David felt sick. Partly because he hadn't eaten for twenty-four hours and had just swallowed a glass of wine in one gulp. But mainly because this ghastly man in a suit was cutting up David's cheque card into humiliating little pieces.

'I'm really sorry to have to do this but we feel that we have to impose some control over your spending in the only way we can.'

David was having difficulty in controlling his breathing just now, never mind his spending. 'I don't understand. I mean, I know the overdraft is a bit on the large side but didn't my company explain about the bonus coming within the year?'

The manager looked at David thoughtfully. Judgingly. 'I've spoken to Mr Perriam at length and his story was somewhat different to yours.'

David was confused by this. This was one of the rare occasions where he had (as far as he knew) been honest and upfront about a situation. 'In what way?' he asked.

'Well, you assured me that your bonus was guaranteed on the drugs trial simply taking part and being completed.'

'That's correct.'

'Not according to Mr Perriam. According to him, the bonus is dependent on the trial being *successfully* concluded. Now, we're not happy with this "successfully" proviso.'

'Yes, but that's just a formality. I mean, they always say that.

But it goes without saying that, once a trial is up and running, it will be successfully completed. I mean, even if someone drops dead, the trial will usually still go ahead.'

The manager smiled. 'You see, there's that word "usually" that we also don't like. We like words like "guaranteed", "definite". You're asking us to lend you a lot of money, *more* money I should say, with no cast-iron guarantee that you will be able to repay it in the foreseeable future. And frankly, Mr Sandhurst, your track record does not bode well for your long-term financial dependability. Of course, we'll look at your request again if your situation should change or Mr Perriam can assure us that the bonus is actually guaranteed.'

David sat for a few seconds, waiting for the thunderbolt of good fortune that normally intervened in his life at such desperate moments to show itself.

It didn't. That was that. His last legitimate source of money had just been shut off permanently. And there was a long, long time until December when the trial was officially over.

He would have to look elsewhere for money.

Chapter Thirteen

'Junction Jostle' was scheduled for 29th August which also happened to be Marina's thirty-second birthday. Now that the event was about to happen, Marina was quite excited about it. She was aware that this was Andy's brainchild and that its success could be a useful weapon in his armoury when he contended for the seat on the board. But she was also aware that its success would consolidate the Sparkleeze account within TNSW. And *she* had brought the account into the agency in the first place.

The media had become interested in the idea, not least because of the guaranteed appearance of the ten most gorgeous nonentities in Great Britain. Goodness, one of the leggy lovelies was rumoured to be 'seeing' a cousin of the Prime Minister. Golly, gosh, thought Marina, amused when she read the press release.

There was no doubt that her mood had improved considerably since hitting nine and a half stone. And the magical size twelve. And she was still losing weight.

She looked fantastic and she knew it. On the day her weight was due to be confirmed at Perrico, she booked an appointment for a complete makeover at Harrods. She already knew what David was going to say (she was weighing herself twice a day at this stage) but it meant a lot to see it entered into her computer record. And she saw the look on David's face when he measured her fat ratio. It was a clear expression of attraction. It was an expression that she getting used to.

That was a week earlier and she had invested in a complete new wardrobe for her new figure. She redefined herself through a new choice of style. No longer fettered by the need to cover up her overabundant curves, she chose clothes just because she liked them. She chose clothes that she'd seen in magazines, confident that they'd look equally good on her.

When she walked into TNSW the day after her makeover, the agency came to a standstill. Although her swift weight loss had not gone unnoticed, in the eyes of her colleagues who saw her on a daily basis she remained fat Marina (who was not as fat as she used to be). While her size was reducing, she hadn't bothered buying many new clothes. Since most of her wardrobe was of the floaty-marquee variety, they had seen her through the period of evolution.

Indeed during those months she had deliberately not changed any other aspect of her appearance, looking forward to the moment of absolute reinvention.

It was worth the wait. She walked through the agency corridors like Gloria Swanson floating down the staircase in *Sunset Boulevard*. It was another person that onlookers observed. It wasn't that big Marina Riesenthal who used to pass unnoticed through their lives. No, it was someone else. Someone half the size but with twice the presence.

From top to toe she was changed. Her trademark pre-Raphaelite curls had all been cut to a bob. This drastic chop had uncovered a beautifully-shaped head, curved and sculpted and not seen since she was a baby. The short layers of her cut revealed natural highlights in graduated shades of red that not even the most skilled hairdresser could replicate.

Her face was stripped of all its surplus padding and in its raw, unadorned state was conventionally pretty. But when it was made up according to the perceptive training of the make-up artist who handled her makeover, the pretty became stunning. She'd always had big eyes but they had always been lost in the gargantuan proportions of the rest of the face and body. Likewise her full lips. When she'd been big, they'd just seemed inflated. Now they were striking and impactful.

Her figure fulfilled all of the fantasies that Emma seemed to believe were unfulfillable in most overweight women who achieve their target weight. Her shoulders and hips were balanced by a waist, a waist! And she had a bust that no longer needed reinforced steel to keep it from sweeping across the floor. And her legs? As you would expect from someone of her height, they were long, long, long. Any slight bulge around the top of the thighs was imperceptible when seen in the context of an otherwise flawless line from waist to ankle. She was utterly, perfectly slim.

In her clothes.

Anyone who did their calculations and worked out just how quickly Marina had lost the weight would have realised that she had lost too much too quickly. And anyone who knows anything about the cruel behaviour of fat would know what was really going on under those designer clothes.

Deflated tyres sat around her middle, worn out from the constant flux. Her breasts were beach balls with slow punctures. And her legs looked like stockings held up by poorly-fitting suspenders, with ripples of skin pleating down towards her knees. Only her face had kept up with the flow. As if in relief, her natural beauty had burst out of its prison and relaxed into its new, comfortable state. Yes, I like it like this, this is just fine, thank you, her face seemed to say to the world.

Marina was given the best advice by her fashion consultants. Get the foundation right, they said, and the building can go up anyhow it pleases. In other words, sort your undies out first and the rest of your clothes will sit perfectly on top.

She was restrained from her chest to her knees, every flaccid fold strapped firmly against her torso like stonecladding. An all-in-one girdle moulded her bust and stomach into an hour-glass mannequin. Occasionally Marina wondered where all those spare inches went to. She felt desperately sorry for her inner organs which must surely be competing for space with her surplus skin right now. Support tights performed their magic on her helter-skelter legs, squeezing them into slender cylinders that tapered down to an apparent full stop. So perfect on the outside, so flawed on the inside. Even at nine and a half stone, she was two people.

The outer Marina felt wonderful. Sure, she wished she could firm up the flab more quickly but she was too enraptured by the reflection that she faced every time she looked in the mirror to be much worried by the state of her naked body.

Anyway, she went to the gym every day now so she felt certain that it was only a matter of time before she had the muscular tone and definition that represented total perfection.

On the day of Junction Jostle, she took advantage of the scorching temperatures to wear a skimpy empire-line sundress, modified only by a chiffon bolero that concealed her still-slightly-floppy upper arms. She accentuated her slim calves with strappy gold sandals that perched on teetering heels. Only willpower kept her vertical.

Her make-up consultant had taught her a number of different faces and today she was wearing number three: the Casual But Formal Look. Low on drama but high on natural appeal, she looked like a twenty-four-year-old girl who had just spent a week in the country.

The launch was held on a patch of land near the beginning of the Hammersmith Flyover in West London. A permanently busy stretch of road which carries traffic into and out of the capital, it was a popular location for particularly eye-catching advertising hoardings. Its main appeal to advertisers was that traffic was almost always slow, which allowed drivers the time to absorb the sales pitch being screamed down at them from the massive posters.

Traffic was especially slow in the approach to the constant stream of traffic lights that you were forced to confront if you wanted to escape from this nightmare road. It was the perfect location for Junction Jostle. What could make better television than the picture of a frustrated, motorway-weary motorist being revitalised by the sight of a Gorgeous Blonde-who-might-be-seeing-a-cousin-of-the Prime-Minister slapping Sparkleeze over their windscreen?

And for the first twenty minutes or so, everything went according to prediction. The trouble with these particular Gorgeous Blondes whose skills didn't extend far beyond the stylish presentation of prizes on game shows, was that they had not been trained in the efficient washing of windscreens. And the windscreens in question had just been assaulted by over a hundred miles of

135

penetrating M4 grime and grit. They needed more than a scant squirt of Sparkleeze and a couple of sweeps with a wet rag that were designed simply to give the lucky driver the fullest possible view of the Gorgeous Blonde's chest.

The windscreens were, without exception, left with worse visibility than they had displayed before the Sparkleeze. It was all right with the English drivers. They were so used to enduring appalling service with a stoic silence that they smiled politely for the press and waited until they had driven out of camera range before pulling over and finishing the cleaning process themselves.

The trouble with this location was that it also carried a heavy load of traffic going to and from Heathrow, both tourists and business travellers. Foreigners. Those really annoying un-British people with no manners who have standards that they expect to be met. It was with an American businessman in a brand-new Saab that it all began to go wrong.

Gorgeous Blonde-who-was-recently-the-face-of-National-Frankfurter-Day stepped out in front of the driver who had just switched to third gear in a failed attempt to get past the media roadblock. He was forced to perform an emergency stop which caused an ominous clunking sound in the gearbox. He wasn't happy.

'Good morning sir. Welcome to Junction Jostle! We are offering motorists a complimentary windscreen clean using new Sparkleeze, the only window cleaner with lavender extract. Just three squirts of concentrated Sparkleeze and daily dirt is wiped away like window wizardry. There, isn't that super? Have a Sparkleeze day!'

Gorgeous Blonde didn't bother waiting for a reply. She had already spotted her next hapless victim in an equally expensive car and was planning her route through three lanes of moving vehicles.

The American stared through a muddy blur where once had been a relatively clean piece of glass. The cameras were about to move on when the driver got out of the car and examined the state of his windscreen with a delicate sweep of his little finger. For a second, he looked as if he was about to cry. He was actually inflating himself into a rage of cosmic proportions.

'Who is in charge here? I want to speak to someone in charge!'

Paul Jerome had been basking in the glow of all the publicity and had allowed himself a little too much champagne. He had been watching this little scene act itself out before him with the objective pleasure of a cinemagoer. Suddenly Marina and Andy were looking towards him, inclining their heads in the direction of the increasingly irate motorist. 'He wants to speak to someone in charge,' Marina whispered. 'That's you,' Andy added.

They sat back down and watched, not too concerned with the outcome, as Paul tried to pacify the furious American. If he had only had more experience in customer relations, he would have known that the best approach was to let the man bluster until he was blustered out. Then Paul could have apologised profusely, offered a suitable gesture of compensation (like a bottle of champagne) and justice would have been seen to be done in the eyes of the customer.

But Paul was a marketing man who had never met a customer. He decided to reason with this man, asking him to see things from the Sparkleeze perspective. He interrupted his complainant's arguments and even touched the man's car! The final straw was when he offered the man (who turned out to be chairman of a multinational oil corporation) a full-size bottle of Sparkleeze as a token gesture. It was only Paul's height advantage that dissuaded the American from hitting him.

But the police didn't have to be called for another twenty minutes. Paul was still arguing with the oilman when the pile-up happened across all three lanes. It transpired that a car was attempting to manoeuvre from the outside to the inside lane without being able to see through his Sparkleeze-cleaned windscreen. The smears across his line of vision meant that the driver didn't see the taxi in the middle lane trying to cross into the outside lane.

No-one was hurt but seven cars were slightly damaged and it took two hours to get traffic moving again. On the news that night, a reporter announced that the motorists involved in the pile-up were planning to sue Sparkleeze for damage to their cars while dozens of others were going to sue for causing unnecessary delays to their essential journeys.

'Look on the bright side, you got Sparkleeze on national TV for an entire day and evening.' Marina tried to coax a smile from

Andy, who would not be encouraged out of his crater of misery. It was eleven o'clock at night and the two of them were sitting in a pub near Sparkleeze's head office where the debrief had finally ended.

All in all, Paul Jerome had shown remarkable fairness in not attributing all the blame to Andy. Yes, it was Andy's idea and yes, it was Andy who had hired the Gorgeous Blondes (or at least the agency who supplied the Blondes). But Paul acknowledged that he had approved the event at every stage and must therefore take a certain amount of responsibility for the dreadful outcome. On the plus side, the male beefcake window cleaners had proved a huge success before the pile-up. In fact, one of the men had cleaned the screen of a theatrical producer who had offered him an audition for a mime version of *Les Misérables* that he was putting together.

The conclusion was simple: Junction Jostle had been a disaster. In PR terms alone, it would cost hundreds of thousands of pounds to protect the company's reputation. At the same time, Sparkleeze was now a nationally-recognised brand name. The Blondes were already entering the annals of popular satire as topical comedians everywhere prepared original jokes around the old dumb-blonde theme.

The Sparkleeze strategy was finalised that night. It was effective but morally bankrupt. The blame was to be placed squarely at the feet of the incompetent bimbos wielding the rags. The (reduced-scale) TV advertising was due to launch in a few days and Sparkleeze's efficacy would be demonstrated in a convincing but creatively bankrupt side-by-side demonstration of Sparkleeze versus its leading rival. This, coupled with a nationwide distribution of free samples, should serve to convince consumers that this was a demonstrably good product.

Andy was nevertheless depressed beyond the point of consolation. He would have to go into Rick Gifford's office first thing in the office and explain what had happened. Their years of friendship would count for nothing if Rick felt that the standing of TNSW had been compromised by the poorly thought-out campaign.

'Rick's going to kill me. Or, even worse, fire me.'

Marina took his hand sympathetically. 'Hardly, you two go back too far. He'll throw a few crushing blows of irony at you, remind you that he's the MD whereas you're ... not, and then you'll remind him of some spiffing caper or whatever that you shared at Eton and you'll be all buddy-buddy again.'

Andy couldn't help himself. He had to smile at Marina's clumsy attempts to cheer him up. 'Spiffing caper? Is that what the girls got up to in all those boarding school books that I bet you used to read?'

'How dare you!' Marina exclaimed in mock-annoyance. 'I was strictly a Brontë-type girl. Anything involving doomed, complicated relationships that still ended in relative happiness, that was my sort of thing.'

'I can imagine that,' Andy said, amused by the image of a fat girl picturing herself as a tormented heroine. 'Now me, I was strictly a Thomas Hardy-type boy. Anything involving doomed, complicated relationships that always ended in complete misery, that was *my* sort of thing.'

Marina laughed. 'Now you're talking. But surely Thomas Hardy comes after the Brontës in the adolescent reader's sequence?'

'I know what you're saying. Firstly the dream then the reality.'

'It says a lot about a person when the person defines a dream as a happy ending.'

'Whereas the reality ...'

They both had their own experiences of reality to draw upon. Each was as disappointed as the other. Both felt that they had left it all too late and that they would have to settle for a level of achievement that didn't reflect their potential.

'I haven't mentioned it before, Marina, because I thought you'd bite my head off, but you look really, really good.' He saw the look of doubt on her face. 'I mean it. You know how great you look now. I can tell by the way you walk and the way you smile when you think no one is looking at you.'

Marina found it strange to think of her previous adversary looking at her with anything other than a professional interest. She was trying to decide whether it was pleasant-strange or stalker-strange when she saw that Andy had closed his hand around hers. She quickly totted up the number of drinks they'd both had. No more than four, she was certain. Just enough to loosen inhibitions, not so much that very wrong decisions might be taken.

She was on the awful verge of liking this monster and, before she leapt into the abyss of conciliation, she had to know something.

'It was you who "lost" my presentation in New York, wasn't it?'

He didn't answer. He didn't have to.

Marina shrugged. 'It's OK. I know it was you. I'm actually flattered that you were so threatened by me that you had to resort to clumsy sabotage to scupper me.'

'I resent that! There was nothing clumsy about that sabotage!'

Marina giggled like the drunk that she was becoming. She was beginning to see what Teresa had found attractive in Andy. All the bullying tyranny he'd subjected her to over the years melted away in her memory with her fat. And she was in control here.

'How did that New Business presentation go yesterday, by the way?'

Andy cheered up slightly. 'It went well. They've more or less promised us the account. But it's only small. Quarter of a million. Not in the Sparkleeze league.'

Marina knew what he was talking about. After his sabotage attempt in New York, Andy had surprised himself by feeling ashamed. Unable to apologise, he instead concentrated on the more positive approach to improving his standing in the race-for-promotion contest. He worked like a beaver at attracting new accounts into the agency. But while he was certainly making inroads, he was still in a poor second place to Marina, that much he knew.

He needed this promotion in a way that he sensed Marina didn't. She was younger than him. And she'd already enjoyed a magnificent achievement this year. Her new appearance would surely open many more doors for her. And there would inevitably be another place on the board in a few more years' time.

She had the time but Andy didn't.

Marina had watched him slog away and admired his determination. She was confident that the promotion would still be hers and could afford such generosity. Also her hatred for him had diminished along with her weight.

Tonight he was suffering. Marina didn't want him to sink even further into his pit. 'It's my birthday today,' she said inconsequentially.

'Happy birthday.' Andy raised his glass to toast her and saw that both their glasses were empty. 'Listen, it's your birthday and I've had the worst day of my whole career. Why don't we get a bottle of fizz, drown today and baptise ourselves into tomorrow? My flat's only five minutes away from here. What do you think?'

It was 5.59 in the morning when a mobile phone began to ring. They both reached out with flailing arms to locate the offending device. It was Marina's. She sat up, very awake. 'Hello?' she said, worried about the reason for a call this early.

'Oh Moo Cow, where have you been all night? I've been ringing and ringing your home number. No don't bother explaining, there's no time. Thank God you're awake! I've been up half the night and you weren't there and I forgot about your mobile until just now. Oh Moo, it's awful, I don't know what to do . . .'

'Susie, calm down and tell me what's wrong.' She felt the man next to her turning to face her. 'It's not the kids is it? Or Ken? Is everyone OK?'

'Yes, they're all fine. They're always bloody fine. It's me, I'm not fine.'

'What is it? If you don't tell me I can't help you.'

'Moo, I weigh eleven stone!'

To someone else, perhaps this would not be classified as an emergency warranting an early-morning call, but Marina understood perfectly. At five feet four, eleven stone was not going to be an easy weight to conceal, however cleverly she dressed. And there was was something about those milestone weights. It was like milestone birthdays. Turning thirty or forty or fifty may each be just another day in your life but they are heavy with significance. A significant birthday forces you to confront the future, tot up your past, evaluate and restructure or simply accept. Likewise, when Susie was ten stone thirteen, she could fool herself that maybe she wasn't overweight. But eleven stone . . .

Marina hadn't seen Susie since that encounter in the restaurant. While she had been amused by the thought of Susie breastfeeding for seven years to stay slim, she was also struck by the psychosis of this behaviour. She was no expert but she also wondered what this false lactation over such a vast period of time had done to Susie's hormones. And now that she'd stopped? Her body must be delirious with freedom; those hormones must be turning cartwheels making their presence felt, registering their disapproval at being mistreated for all those years. No wonder she couldn't control her body any more; it was grabbing the opportunity to control *her* at last.

'Oh Susie, I'm so sorry. I know how rotten you must be feeling. I've spent most of my life feeling like that so I really understand. But you've got to stop panicking. Why don't we meet up for lunch?'

'Lunch?' Susie screamed. 'And watch me get even fatter? Are you mad? It's all David's fault.'

Marina shifted uncomfortably. 'Why? What's he done?'

Susie checked herself from revealing the details of the affair even though it was over. Anyway, that wasn't the main source of her anguish. 'He won't give me the pills. I mean, I've seen what they've done for the rest of you and I'm only a little bit overweight so he wouldn't have to give me many but the bastard won't! I've begged him, I've threatened him ...'

'What have you threatened him with?'

'Oh ... nothing. I just said I'd tell Ken that he was fiddling his expenses or something. He just gave me the spiel about ethics, very rich coming from him, don't you think?'

'Susie, go and make yourself a cup of tea and I'll call you when I'm up and about. It'll all be all right, I know it will.'

'No it won't, it'll never be all right again. Unless – of course, that's it!'

'What's it?' Marina asked, suspicious and alarmed at the same time. 'What are you going to do?'

'It's so obvious I don't know why I didn't think of it before! I'll have another baby! When you're pregnant, nobody notices your weight and once the thing is born ...', a dreamy note entered her voice as she uttered her favourite word, 'Breastfeeding. Must go, Moo. Ken is waking up. Have I got a surprise for him!'

The phone went dead. Marina slumped back on the pillow, exhausted.

'I take it that was Susie?' he said ironically.

Marina looked at the handsome face that was only inches away from hers and felt elated once more. She lay down next to him and stroked his hair even though he'd told her that he found that annoying. She was thin now. When you're thin, you're allowed to be annoying. People, men, still like you even when you're annoying. Marina was empowered and she loved it.

'No more talking,' she whispered. And as she kissed David Sandhurst without inhibition, she knew she was completely happy.

Chapter Fourteen

Within ten days, Marina had slept with both Andy Cline and David Sandhurst. That took her total number of lovers up to three.

Her first and only previous boyfriend was the traditional university cohort. His name was Frank and he had no endearing qualities of any sort. She met him on the first day and stayed with him until the last. They slept together, cooked mince in a hundred different ways on a hotplate, helped each other with revision, said 'I love you' politely, twice a day, then Frank went off to process planning permissions for Basildon Council while Marina moved to London.

She had always been grateful for his attention, having resigned herself at the age of thirteen to a life of lonely chastity. He had been grateful for her sexual compliance and had never appeared to be bothered by her weight. It was this indifference that had given her the confidence to apply for the job at TNSW. Over the four years at university, she had come to believe that it *was* possible to rise above one's body image. She had allowed herself to develop a personality that grew into the expansive, self-deprecating 'one-of-the-lads' version that had made her popular in the advertising world. Because Frank never mentioned her weight, she forgot that it was an issue. It wasn't long before she remembered.

Sex with Frank had been adventurous but she had always been passive, always worried about squashing him or confronting him with the harsh photographic truth of her naked body. She didn't enjoy it and she didn't *not* enjoy it. But it made her feel normal and that was a rare feeling for Marina.

She was amazed at how easy it was to fall into bed with Andy Cline. She hadn't been in this situation for ten years and watching the evolution of sex in the movies had convinced her that it had all become a lot more aerobic and acrobatic than she remembered from the cramped single beds in digs.

Funnily enough there was a filmic quality to the whole night. The background music was Supertramp (conventional for thirty-nine-year-old Andy), the lighting was subdued. Andy even lit candles. This flattered Marina enormously. To her, it meant that Andy was regarding her as a firefly that might or might not be caught. She was no sure thing. She was no longer the affection-starved creature who'd sleep with anyone who showed her an ounce of kindness. Andy recognised that Marina was a woman who loved herself at last. She no longer required affirmation from anyone else. She required courtship.

He courted her into a bedroom which was surprisingly free of macho statements and showed a cultured approach to decor. The whole room was toned in contrasting shades of green and the total effect was light, unthreatening and smile-making.

Marina allowed him to undress her but she clenched every muscle of her body tightly, still worried that the rolls of fat might spill out from their hidey-hole. She couldn't relax totally. She found herself feeling as if she was nineteen again. She tried not to lie on her side, knowing that her stomach would cascade on to the mattress in a gelatinous river. She arched her head back to eliminate the (now non-existent) double chins and she crossed one thigh over the other to create the semblance of a long, lean body line.

Gradually, she came to accept that she didn't need to contort herself to please Andy. He was so delighted with Marina that he didn't mind that she guided his hands away from the fleshy areas towards safer regions. He even interpreted it as a gesture of control that he found massively appealing.

Afterwards, Marina waited for the awkwardness to set in. This was, after all, a colleague and someone who had treated her

145

viciously in recent times. They were both chasing the same promotion and vying for leadership of the same account. But there was no awkwardness. They had enjoyed each other's company in every respect. They had laughed together, talked about books and films and family trivia. Perhaps it was the newness of Marina that made it possible for them to connect in such an unexpected way.

The only hint of darkness appeared at breakfast. Marina remembered that she'd left her pills at home. Something inside her wibble-wobbled as she wondered if her appetite would kaleidoscope out of control without her unmarked little white pill. When Andy pulled croissants out of the freezer along with butter (real, not low-fat substitute) and strawberry conserve (more sugar not less) and even poured full-fat milk into her tea, she wanted to upturn the table and run.

Andy saw her reluctance to touch anything and became mildly irritated. 'Don't tell me you're still dieting. I mean, it's admirable what you've done, Marina, and you look amazing but don't take it too far.' He softened when he saw how upset she was becoming. 'We've had a great night. Let's not spoil it. Let's share breakfast and gaze stupidly across the table just like in the muesli ads! Besides, don't you think we burned off enough calories last night to justify a little indulgence?'

She forced herself to eat a croissant but she refused absolutely to touch the butter.

Marina had to go home to change and, when she got to the office, they both acted as if the night had not happened. They'd agreed that this was sensible while there was so much division at the agency. Andy drank two cups of very strong coffee before facing Rick Gifford.

'You really blew it, didn't you?'

Andy assumed his most winning smile, hoping to limit the extent of the dressing down he was about to receive. 'Oh, I don't know, we're on the front page of all the tabloids and even the *Telegraph* puts Sparkleeze on page three.'

'It's not going to work this time, Andy. You can't sweet-talk your way out of it. This was shoddy work, *your* shoddy work. You come up with a dramatic idea like this, sell it to the client then you just sit back and expect it all to work out. You're lazy, Andy, always have been. Being clever just isn't enough at this level. Nor is charming. It's attention to detail that separates winners from losers ... am I boring you?'

Andy couldn't suppress a yawn. 'No, sorry Rick. Late night. Trying to square things with Paul Jerome.'

Rick shook his head. 'You really are the luckiest man in the business. I've just spoken to him and he's being incredibly decent about the whole thing. But I've still had to agree to underwrite Sparkleeze's legal costs when all these idiot drivers sue.'

Andy winced at this. 'Bang goes my bonus, I suppose.'

'Don't you get it? Bang goes everyone's bonus. This will probably eat up the whole year's profits, if not the next five years' worth as well. You've cost us all a lot of money. So, are you going to explain to the rest of the staff that there'll be no bonuses and no pay rises this year?'

It got round the agency by lunchtime. One secretary was in tears. 'I'd budgeted for my bonus to pay for my wedding. Now we'll have to postpone.' Many of the others regularly overspent during the year, piling up debts on credit cards, on the understanding that their bonus would pay it off. Andy was on the receiving end of some murderous side-glances that day. He was still just senior enough that the junior members of staff didn't dare knock him senseless, which would have made them feel much better. Not that physical assault was necessary. For a man who thrived on popularity, the banishment was devastating.

He took consolation in Marina, who was proving to be a source of endless wonder to him. It had been a long time since he really talked with a lover. They even drove down to the coast that first weekend and spent the day engaging in all those idyllic First Weekend pursuits that he had always condemned as soppy: they walked along the beach and made sandcastles with overturned teacups; they screamed on Big Dippers and emptied their pockets into the slot machines; they ate candy floss and chips; they kissed on a clifftop and held hands along the pier.

He hadn't lost four stone but he was easily as transformed as Marina in her eyes. Since she had come to terms with her own newness, she decided that she had to accept that he could also be legitimately different to the Andy who had tormented her for such a long time. It was a cautious acceptance but one that she deemed worth the risk.

It was the best weekend of Andy's life. And Marina's too.

So why did she sleep with David two days later?

He'd invited her to lunch to share his concerns about Emma. She wasn't due to be weighed for another two weeks and he honestly thought that Emma might be dead by then. Since Marina had been his first contact with 5F, he tended to refer to her when he encountered communication problems with any of the subjects.

It was only when Marina sat down at his table that he realised who she was. He hadn't seen her since her makeover after the last weigh-in. Whenever she came in to be weighed, he still saw her as the same massive sexless person introduced to him at Susie's dinner party that last December. He watched her weight go down with satisfaction but never translated the figures into an actual change in the woman before him. Even when he was measuring the fat levels on her arms, legs and abdomen, he didn't associate the diminishing size with an emerging beauty.

So he was effectively seeing, truly seeing Marina for the first time. She had settled easily into her new image and had become used to choosing appropriate outfits with effortless style. She had adapted her ten different make-up faces into an individual routine that achieved the Holy Grail of cosmetics: the comprehensive make-up application that makes a woman look as if she's not wearing any make-up at all.

David stared at her, his eyes drifting down from that unfamiliar face towards the rest of this rebuilt siren. His eyes quickly undressed her. My God, where did that body come from, he asked himself, almost laughing out loud when he worked out the answer. I made her! She is my creation! I am a genius. With my pills, I can turn a dumpling into a fantasy!

Marina was still shining from the glow of being loved and desired. It added another dimension to her loveliness and confirmed David's initial impulse: I must have her.

'Marina! I don't know what to say. You look absolutely divine. I can't believe it. You're a walking advertisement for Oxymetabulin. Wow.'

Marina still enjoyed the jawdropping that she was causing wherever she went. She too was recalling that dinner party where she first met this man who was going to change her life so completely. The balance was so different then. On the social see-saw, Marina was sitting immovably on the bottom while he flew around the stratosphere like an ABC1 Peter Pan. She was unworthy even to be in the same room with him. He followed the rules while she flouted them with her very being.

But now the see-saw had see-sawed and Marina liked peering down at David who could only gaze upwards in her direction, panting with desire. It hadn't taken her long to appreciate the status of a beautiful woman in the sexual marketplace. She had always looked at pretty girls and good-looking boys and assumed that they shared equal platforms, equal attractiveness quotients but she now knew that this was not the case.

No, a beautiful woman is always of higher rank than a handsome man. There doesn't seem to be a good evolutionary reason for this. It seems to be more a consequence of men's transient attacks of lust that need gratification before the man can get on with loftier goals. Those beautiful women are born to be transient, it is their function in the eyes of the desperate men pursuing them. Men don't marry them, good grief no, but they use them until a good marriageable woman comes along.

More enlightened feminist thinkers might be horrified by this superficial indictment of male/female relationships but Marina wasn't horrified at all. It suited her perfectly to be regarded as a figure of transient lust. She still hadn't come to terms fully with her new self and 'en route' relationships were all she wanted to deal with.

But that still didn't explain why she allowed herself to be seduced by David, or for that matter by Andy. Two men who had treated her with contempt when she was fat now fell over themselves to worship her new body. She could have slapped them round the face, shouted 'I am the same person!' and crushed their hypocrisy with a slamming rejection. But instead she plunged into a physical exploration of them both, taking intense pleasure from the pleasure she was able to give just by being her.

In fact she forgave them because she understood them. She

had despised her own body when she was fat. She had punished herself with food and every insult they had tossed her way, she had self-delivered a million times worse. And she didn't even love her own personality, for it was weak, unable to control even her appetite. All her intelligence, wit and sensitivity meant little to her when she saw herself with her face in a bowl of cold ravioli.

So the new figure *wasn't* just a new outer casing. It signified a whole lot more and the men recognised this. It implied that she was strong and self-disciplined. It meant that she had judged herself worthy of joining the rest of society. It said: 'Hey, don't worry about me! I'm normal, I'm just like you, don't worry.'

The reality that all this had only been achieved with medical intervention seemed irrelevant to Marina as indeed it was to David and Andy.

She pretended not to have noticed David's expression and ignored his flirting eyes. 'So you said you were worried about Emma. What exactly is the problem?'

David had to think back to his original concerns. 'Oh right, yes, Emma. When did you last see her?'

Marina felt guilty when she realised that she hadn't seen her since their lunch together a couple of months earlier. Not that they'd been real friends as such but that was no excuse. Both she and Teresa had sensed that Emma was in trouble, that she was getting much too thin too fast and that all the signs were there for a complete self-destruction. But they had both had problems of their own. Teresa was sure that Rod was seeing someone else and Marina was still embroiled in an increasingly aggressive power struggle with Andy.

They hadn't even been to 5F meetings since then. Too busy, they said. Too thin, they thought.

David was waiting for an answer, although he seemed happy to wait when it gave him extra seconds to analyse this miracle of chemical engineering before him.

'It must be a couple of months, I suppose. It's not as if we're all best friends at 5F,' she added defensively.

'And how did you think she was?'

'A bit hyper. She'd obviously gone overtop with the dieting.'

David winced at the casual introduction of the taboo word. Marina realised her error and tried to backtrack.

'When I say "dieting", I don't mean dieting as such. I know none of us were supposed to be dieting. And I'm sure none of us were. As such. No, I just mean that whatever effect the tablets were having were causing her to ... adjust her food intake a little too ... aggressively.'

David shook his head. 'You women. You must think I'm stupid. I know you've all been modifying your eating at the very least. Don't forget I already had a reasonable idea of the average rate of weight loss that Oxymetabulin could produce and you've all gone way beyond that.'

Marina looked sheepish.

'It's OK, don't panic,' David continued. 'I've managed to explain that away by a natural psychological progression when a woman first experiences substantial mass reduction. I've found a shrink who'll say that all women become motivated to begin or continue with a sensible reducing plan when they've already seen some positive benefit to their appearance. It's like when you get a stomach bug and can't eat for a week. You lose a stone without trying and you think, wow, that was easy, maybe I'll keep going and lose a bit more.'

Marina had to admit that there was an element of truth in what he was saying but even her limited understanding of scientific research could foresee flaws in this justification. It seemed like a blatant manipulation of the results to suit the original premise.

'Anyway, back to Emma. I was already concerned about her appearance. My main worry was that the pills might be having some significant negative effect on her. But I decided to wait another month since she wasn't exactly at death's door.'

'So when did you see her?'

'That's the problem. She didn't turn up for the weigh-in last month. Said she had flu. She was very careful to say that it was nothing that could be attributed to the pills. Lots of flu going round her area, that sort of thing. And since then, nothing.'

'What do you mean, nothing?'

'She stopped answering her phone or returning my messages. I was getting desperate because I simply can't have a gap in my result record. So I went round to her flat yesterday, which was totally unprofessional, but I didn't know what else to do.'

'And?'

'No answer. But when I got back into my car I saw her walking up to the door. I didn't realise it was her until she was practically in front of me. It was a hideous stick-creature. Even though it was a hot day, she wore a coat but it couldn't hide her emaciation.'

'How bad was she?'

'I'd estimate that she weighed around six stone.'

'Oh God. The poor thing.'

'And her hair was dried and matted around her face. I couldn't tell whether it was just in terrible condition or if Emma hadn't washed or combed it for weeks.'

'I should go and see her. See if I can help her.'

'You'll be wasting your time. She looked right through me, refused to speak to me at all.'

'But if she didn't turn up for the last weigh-in, surely she hasn't got any more tablets.'

'That's true but it doesn't help the test. I still have to account for her progress and explain why she is no longer in the trial. I can only come up with one idea that won't jeopardise the programme.'

'Which is?'

'I can say that she's pregnant.'

'But that's an out-and-out lie! Surely the ethics committee, or whatever they call themselves, won't stand for that.'

'They don't have to find out. Marina, think it through. Emma obviously had a disorder of some sort before she started on the programme. Maybe I should have spotted it but I'm a chemist, not a shrink. I had to accept at face value her declaration that she was comfortable with her eating patterns and would maintain this approach throughout the trial.'

Marina remembered making the same declaration as they all did. What a joke, she thought at the time. None of them had got to the size they currently occupied by being comfortable with their eating patterns. All they aimed for was an end to the complete torment of binges and starvation. They still all overate (and secretly fasted occasionally to try and counteract the effects). How could they be comfortable with an eating pattern which gave them sweat rash where their upper arms chafed against their bust, which made them red-faced in the heat and which left them out of breath when they tried to sprint up a few stairs?

She didn't explain this to David, who had enough worries.

'So you can see why pregnancy is the only get-out clause I can get away with. Obviously if any of the triallists did become pregnant, they'd have to drop out immediately. So it's a perfectly valid excuse.'

'And what will you say when Emma doesn't actually produce a baby?'

'That happens, doesn't it?'

Marina shuddered at his effortless dismissal of Emma's imaginary baby. It seemed callous although she felt daft for thinking so. David took her silence as an acceptance of his strategy.

'I knew you'd understand. Look at you. You, of all people, know what a great contribution Oxymetabulin can make to women's lives. It would be a tragedy if the whole thing was scrapped just because one woman's pre-existing eating disorder got the better of her.'

Marina hated this kind of dilemma. The pills had changed her life entirely for the better. And as far she knew, none of the women had experienced any real side-effects. She unconsciously rubbed the front of her head where the recurring headaches had been striking. How could she possibly justify ruining Oxymetabulin's potential for the greater public? At the same time, he was advocating the construction of a complete lie to facilitate a favourable outcome to his research. Surely that was wrong.

She wished she could go away and deal with this situation in the way she knew best. She wished she could go away and eat.

Instead she ended up in bed with David. She drank too much, deliberately ate lightly to compensate for the extra calories from the wine (David didn't make the connection) and got drunk quite quickly. They spent the afternoon in bed. And the evening. And the whole night. Marina called her secretary and cited an urgent Sparkleeze PR issue that she needed to handle. She didn't leave details. She left a vague and cowardly message on Andy's voice-mail so that she wouldn't have to lie to him in person.

Not that she regretted her action. Why should I? she thought. I'm a beautiful, single woman and this is a handsome, single man. Yes, I'm sort of involved with another man and yes, David is bit of a bastard but I'm entitled to indulge in shallow, meaningless sex. I couldn't ten years ago but now I can. So I will.

So she did.

So it was David in bed beside her when she took the hysterical call from Susie. She interpreted his persistent probing about the situation as a (surprising) concern for someone that he too knew.

'Yes, but what did she say?'

'David, I've told you. She's worried about her weight and she is frustrated that you won't let her on the Oxymetabulin pro-gramme. And before you interrupt, it was *me* who told her that it was impossible for you to do that. You don't have to feel guilty about it. I'm seeing her later, I'll explain it all to her again.'

'What are you going to tell her about us?'

'Nothing. Why should I? It was just a one-off, as far as I'm con-cerned.'

David performed a double-take as if he'd been shot. How dare this woman, this woman that *he'd* rescued and recreated, tell *him* that it was just a one-off? That was *his* line. And maybe he wanted this to be more than a one-off.

Marina loved the look of disbelief that undulated across his face. She knew what he was thinking. It gave her an involuntary glimpse into the mindset of the callous man. Or indeed, woman. It was all about power. It was all about watching someone crum-ble with desire. It was the gratification of knowing that you could *make* someone want you. It was knowing that this person would be struggling to hide their neediness, struggling unsuccessfully since the neediness had already announced its existence to the cruel lover.

She pulled herself back from this line of thought, understanding that only willpower could prevent her from adopting this persona permanently. It was too easy and too safe to be hard, she thought. Nevertheless, she remained pleased that David Sandhurst was probably long overdue a brief but sustained attack on his ego.

'Sorry, David. Must dash. Take care. I'll call.'

She ruffled his hair as if he were a Labrador puppy and then left. She didn't kiss me, David thought. And she said 'I'll call' but she didn't say when. He knew what this meant. Men of thirty-four know these things.

She's never going to call me again.

Things had improved for David in the last two months. He'd discovered companies working out of dank, unmarked offices in East London that gave out loans without needing a hundred conversations with Geoff Perriam of Perrico about the definition of 'usually' and 'almost definitely'.

Sure, the interest rates were outrageous and the unspoken threats a little worrying, but David fell back on his old certainties. Soon he would be rich. He would get his bonus, pay off all his debts, have money left over. All he had to do was tread water. And keep this trial going.

And pray to God that these BLOODY, BLOODY women didn't ruin everything.

Because if the trial was scuppered at any point and he didn't get the bonus ...

He rushed to the bathroom and was violently, thoroughly sick.

Chapter Fifteen

'What do you think?'

Teresa spun around in the bedroom, the gossamer sheath cling-ing to the new angular lines of her body like a silky kiss. The daily three-hour sessions in the gym had paid off in producing the gen-tlest curves of muscular definition. She'd bought the nightdress a few weeks earlier when her goal of physical perfection was in sight. Today, she had reached her goal.

Although she was allegedly twirling for the benefit of Rod, it was when the mirror came into view that her smile was most radi-ant. She couldn't get enough of her own reflection. She had become the person she had always wanted to be. Always. Even when she was a doyenne of 5F and claiming with sincerity that she would not deprive herself of food to conform to unrealistic body stereotypes, she'd prayed silently that she could be naturally, effortlessly slim.

She saw no contradiction in the two standpoints. She wished that she had been born into a world that revered and respected the ample female form. But her world didn't. She wished that she had been born with a modest appetite that enabled her to feel satisfied with small meals. Her appetite was like a two-year-old child hav-ing a tantrum if it didn't get the food it wanted, *when* it wanted. I want it, I want it, I want it! it would scream to her if she tried pleading with it for a little restraint.

So 5F was there for her. It allowed her to face up to her metab-olism, her needs and her personal eating history and accept her current lot. What it didn't do was eradicate her dream.

Oxymetabulin offered the answer to her dream. But 5F would still be there in case the dream didn't work out.

There. That's that little conflict of loyalty all accounted for.

Teresa was becoming impatient. While she had been prepared for Rod being overwhelmed by her display of loveliness, she'd expected some kind of reaction. But nothing. Rod looked at her as if she were his mother asking for an opinion on some matronly frock. There was no desire. No breathless lust.

She felt ill. It had all been for this minute, all the months of pill-popping and exercise. She had deliberately not mentioned to anybody (including David Sandhurst) that she had started getting terrible headaches in case she was taken off the programme. She had ignored the dizzy spells and the nausea. All so that she could stand before Rod, resplendent in bony beauty.

He stared into her face, his interest in her body fleeting at best. 'What do you want me to say?'

Teresa gasped. 'I don't believe it. I've done this all for you! Look at me. Isn't this what you wanted?'

Rod looked at her as if she'd gone mad. 'When did I ever give you that impression? Never. When did I ever say that I preferred skinny women? Never. When did I ever say that I wished you could lose weight? Never. When did I ever say that you, your body, everything about you, was the perfect expression of my ideal? Every single day for nineteen or more years.'

'Yes, but you only said that because you loved me.'

'So you think I lied to you every day? Is that because you lied to me every day and therefore thought that was how people behave in a marriage?'

'I never lied to you!'

'So why would I lie to you?'

'Because you're kind.'

Rod turned around, offended by her words, by her very presence in this new guise. 'I give up. I can only assume that you've done this to drive me away.'

'What are you talking about?' Teresa was beginning to hyperventilate. It was going so, so wrong.

Rod tried to think of a way to get through to her. 'You know how much you love my beard? And how much you hated it that time I shaved it off all those years ago?'

'I remember.' Teresa relaxed slightly now that they were on safer territory. 'It was only when you took the beard off that I discovered that you didn't have a chin!' She giggled at the reminiscence.

'I've often felt like shaving my beard off again since then. Just for a change. Or because it's hot and I fancy getting some air to my face.'

'You never said.'

Rod shrugged. 'There was no point. I knew how much you hated it so I didn't even mention it.'

Teresa saw where this was going. It was a corner from which she was going to have difficulty escaping.

'But I wouldn't have minded if it was just for a short while. A temporary measure,' she said weakly.

Rod shook his head. 'Yes, you would. You'd have refused to kiss me. You'd have sulked viciously and nagged incessantly until I agreed to grow the beard back. Just like the first time. You know that's true, don't you?'

She knew.

'But it didn't matter. I loved you and, if you felt so strongly about my beard, then I would keep it for your sake. Because I loved you.'

That use of the word 'loved'. In the past tense.

'So if I woke up this morning and shaved my beard off and announced that it was staying off for good, what would you think?'

'That you didn't care about what I thought, about my feelings,' Teresa conceded.

'And what if I said that, deep down, I knew that you really hated my beard and that I was shaving it off for your benefit?'

Teresa tried to turn the argument around. 'But you know I really love your beard. How was I supposed to know that you really loved my body?'

'Because I told you so. In every different way. A thousand ways.'

Teresa crumpled on to the bed. 'But you couldn't have loved it.

How could you? I was repulsive. Nobody could have loved me, my body.'

'I did.'

He left without kissing her goodbye. She didn't know where he was going and she was too scared to ask.

'I don't know why you've asked to meet me like this. We really have nothing in common any more. If we ever did before, that is.'

Gail was feeling very uncomfortable in the presence of this slim, beautiful woman. Marina's tininess made her feel like a hippopotamus and she resented her for it. And the restaurant was absolutely not her sort of place. When she'd walked in, she'd experienced a sudden terror that the manager would refuse her admission for not being attractive enough. She just knew that she would be the only fat woman there. She was right.

Marina tried to warm to this abrasive woman. 'Gail, please don't give up on this before you've given it a chance. I told you, I'm really worried about Emma. When did you last see her?'

Gail stiffened even further. 'Can't remember. Must be months. From what I hear, she's never out of the gym. No doubt she's having the time of her life, swanning around town, flaunting her new wardrobe to some new glamorous friends.'

Her childish peevishness would have made Marina laugh if she wasn't so moved by Gail's obvious unhappiness.

'You couldn't be more wrong. She's desperately ill. She hasn't set foot outside her flat for a couple of weeks. I only know she's alive because I go by her flat every day and scream through the letter box until she answers me.'

Gail tried not to appear too interested but her concern was evident in her worried eyes. 'What's the matter with her? Is it those bloody pills? I knew something like this would happen. There's no such thing as a safe slimming pill and there never will be.'

'Actually we don't think it's anything to do with the pills.' She didn't mention that Emma didn't have any more pills. She was implicated too far in David's lies to betray him. 'She's the only one on the trial who's this bad. She's anorexic.'

'How bad?'

'I would guess she's about five stone although it's hard to tell when I just get a glimpse of her through the letter box.'

Gail closed her eyes and assimilated this information for a short while. Her meditation was interrupted by the arrival of a handsome young waiter who salivated over Marina as he waved his order pad before her like a come-on. 'Can I get you two ladies an aperitif?' He said this without even glancing at Gail. She wasn't surprised by his attitude but she *was* surprised at how hurt she felt. Not for the first time, she cursed the day that Marina brought the Perrico promise into 5F.

Marina was going to order a mineral water but she didn't want to alienate Gail who, she was sure, would condemn her for this limp choice. So she ordered a glass of red wine which would give her an even worse headache later. Gail ordered the same. Marina uttered a silent thank you to her instincts that she'd made a choice regarded as acceptable by her difficult companion.

Then food. Why didn't I just suggest a pub? Marina asked herself. She knew what she wanted and she knew what was necessary. She wanted something light, a salad or some fish and steamed vegetables. But it was necessary to be seen to be eating like the person she used to be. For Gail's benefit. She was becoming acutely aware of the complications of maintaining existing friendships when only one party has changed radically.

'I'll have the liver and bacon. And fried potatoes please,' she added, surreptitiously glancing at Gail, hoping for a nod of approval. There was none. Gail was too engrossed in the menu. The waiter reluctantly turned to face her to take her order. 'I'll have grilled Dover sole with an assortment of vegetables. No butter.'

Marina tried to hide her surprise. It didn't work. Gail smiled without pleasure. 'So you expected me to choose the most fattening things on the menu?'

'No, no. Not at all.'

'Yes you did. Have you forgotten everything we taught at 5F? It's not about eating the most calorific things available on any occasion, it's about eating what you like, *when* you like.'

Marina hadn't forgotten, she'd just stopped believing it. She felt a fool. Her reliance on Oxymetabulin (if that was what she was

160

taking) had led her to the belief that her appetite was a false god who had to be appeased with either food or pills. She had lost confidence in the 5F premise that the appetite was merely another body function, not a cruel and fickle master.

'And today, I fancied something light. So that's what I'm going to have. Tell me, when was the last time you ate what you wanted?'

Marina tried to sound convincing. 'I always eat what I fancy now. I just don't fancy as much as I used to. I suppose that's the impact of the tablets.'

'And what happens when you stop the tablets and the wanting comes back?'

This was not the purpose of the meeting and Marina did not feel like confronting these issues right now. As far as she was concerned, she'd taken the pills, she'd lost weight without struggle or trauma and her life was a million times better. She hadn't thought about what she'd do when the trial was over. She'd always assumed that, once she'd lost weight, it would be easy to keep off – it was the initial losing that had always proved impossible.

She knew that she would have to deal with this soon because she was starting to dip ominously below the minimum weight that David's medical advisers had deemed acceptable.

The strategy was simple – each woman would continue taking the pills until the desired healthy weight had been attained. Then it was important to gauge what happened to the body if the pills were continued. It was hoped that, at that point, weight loss would stop (or at least slow to a manageable minimum). David's original assertion was that Oxymetabulin switched the metabolism up to an ideal rate and then adjusted it to cope with the body's varying needs. If it simply kept on cranking it up indefinitely then it would almost certainly send the body into overdrive. A fatality would appear inevitable.

The next stage of the trial, once the target weight was achieved and maintained for a short while, was to monitor what happened once the pills were stopped. In the rats (and in David's own self-administration), the weight loss was maintained after a few minor fluctuations.

Marina's commitment to the ethical integrity of the trial had now, like most of the other women's, been chucked out of her conscience. Once she had reached her goal, she could feel that the rate of loss was not abating. She was getting thinner and thinner and she knew that this would mean the end of her dosage. So she blatantly contravened Perrico's guidelines, continued to take the pills and increased her eating so that the measurable rate of reduction would appear to be slowing. That had satisfied David enough to keep her on the tablets for a few weeks longer.

She knew however that, at her next weigh-in in a few days' time, David would be announcing that it was time for her to come off the pills so that he could see what happened. The thought scared her witless.

'Look Gail, I really want to talk about Emma. You've made it perfectly clear how you feel about Oxymetabulin and we'll just have to agree to disagree on that one. But I dread to think what will happen to Emma if something isn't done. Can't we put aside our differences and work out how we can help her?'

'You're right. Sorry. I don't know what you think I can do, though. If she won't let you in, why would I be any different?'

'Because you were such good friends before . . .'

Oxymetabulin.

Gail sighed. 'From the day she first started taking the pills, she turned her back on me. It was as if I reminded her of a past that she was rejecting for good. I understood in a way. I always knew that 5F was just a prop to help her to get through a particular phase in her life.'

'What do you mean?'

'When I first met her she was in between crises. She was on an artificial high, convinced that her years of self-torture were finally at an end. She really believed that she believed the 5F principles. Only I knew that she was deluding herself. You say she's desperately ill. She's been close to death before.'

'I heard about the suicide attempts but they were years ago, weren't they?'

'Five years, actually. But barely a year has passed in her adult life when she hasn't tried to kill herself in one way or another. Anorexia, bulimia, self-mutilation. She's got scars up and down her arms from where she used to cut herself when she was a teenager.'

Marina was shocked. 'But why? Was her childhood that awful? She wasn't abused by her parents or anything like that, was she?'

'No, she wasn't abused by her parents.' Gail paused. ' Emma was always convinced that there'd been a mix-up at the hospital and she'd been given to the wrong parents. She never laughed when she said that either.'

'We all feel like that to a certain extent though, don't we?'

Gail snorted. 'I'm not talking about a flirtation with adolescent angst or alienation here. Emma never experienced a single day when she felt that she belonged to her family. She had two older sisters and two younger brothers and the whole family bonded in a lifelong closed circle which always excluded her.'

'In what way?' Marina was unimpressed by all this. She didn't have a shred of commonality with her own mother or father. Only loyalty kept her in contact with them at all. So this story was not affecting her. She'd expected more to explain Emma's behaviour.

The waiter came back. Gail waited for him to place the wine down before continuing.

'Thank you,' she said ironically to his back as he managed to avoid acknowledging her existence once more. She took a delicate sip from her glass, registering her approval of the wine with a gentle nod to herself.

'Where was I? Oh, yes, Emma. Well, you have to know what her parents are like. Two people who got married at sixteen because they wanted to have sex and didn't have the imagination to find secret places to get this primal urge out of their system. With no understanding of, or concern for, birth control, they had five children in five years.

'The only way they could assess the success of their parenting was to watch their kids expand physically. They all collapsed into bed each night, weighed down with heavy, greasy food. When Emma first mentioned naively that she wanted to go on a diet, her mum was livid. She saw it as an attack on her own unarticulated standards. So when she dished up the meals each day which were always soused liberally in congealing gravy, she used to dissolve a couple of tablespoons of lard in Emma's.

'When Emma flinched at the taste, her mum said that it was a

163

special slimming recipe that she'd taken from the *Sun*. When the weight really began to pile on, Emma guessed her attempts were being sabotaged and caught her mum in the act. It was the thought of all that lard that she'd eaten that made her force herself to be sick for the first time. She was eleven and she never trusted food again.'

Marina could almost taste the lard and she fought off the rising nausea. She thought about her own mother's attempts to help her slim. Unlike Emma's parents, Marina's mother wanted nothing more than for her daughter to be slim like all of her friends' daughters. She would serve up smaller and smaller meals, unaware that Marina would sneak off to her bedroom and binge until the emptiness in her stomach was filled.

When Marina finally agreed to go on a diet, her mother's laughable ignorance of the principles of calorie counting actually led to Marina putting on even more weight. She would go to school with a hefty lunch bag containing four Energen rolls each filled with about an inch of butter, a slab of cheese and a wedge of fatty ham. Her mother also included a Tupperware container filled with (full-fat) milk so that Marina didn't fade away from lack of nourishment.

Not that Marina hadn't been equally guilty of misunderstanding the effects of so-called slimming foods. She'd once saved up her pocket money and bought a packet of Limmits biscuits. She scanned the writing on the side with great interest but not much analysis of the small print. It seemed straightforward to her. These biscuits helped you to lose weight. That's what it said. So it stood to reason that, the more you ate, the more weight you lost.

Pretty soon, she was eating a packet of the biscuits a day. That is, on top of the rest of her substantial food intake. She must have skipped the bit where it mentioned that the biscuits were supposed to replace meals, not supplement them.

Unlike Emma, she didn't resort to more dramatic purgative methods largely, she suddenly realised in surprise, because she couldn't face hurting her parents.

Well, well, well, she thought, sitting in a posh restaurant, all gorgeous and thin. Maybe I don't hate the old witch after all. What a disappointment! Oh my God! I've just had a thought. I haven't been home since Christmas. Fancy depriving Mum of her moment of triumph, seeing the daughter she always wanted at last!

She shivered with glorious anticipation and arranged a visit in her mental diary for the coming weekend.

Gail was waiting for her companion's attention to return.

'Sorry, Gail, it was something you said, just brought back some memories. I *was* listening, honestly. Please go on.'

'Do say if I'm boring you. I thought you wanted to understand Emma. I have got other places I could be.'

Marina apologised again. It appeased Gail, who finally resumed her story.

'Between them, her mum and dad had a go at every menial job available to two prematurely old young adults who were barely literate or numerate. They favoured jobs with useful perks – transport cleaning which provided free travel for the whole family; factory work where the broken biscuits or offcuts of meat were available to the staff at the end of each day. Emma joked that she never went hungry.'

Marina smiled. 'Some might say that they were showing admirable concern for their family.'

'Or looking for a soft life. Whatever. But they didn't know what to do with Emma. She was always a bright thing, reading early, stuff like that. But there wasn't a book in the house and they wouldn't let Emma go to the library outside of school hours. They suffered from that terrible fear of intellectual pursuits with which some of the intellectually-challenged are afflicted.'

What a dreadful snob you are, Marina thought. Just because I may have thought precisely the same thing about my own parents doesn't make it OK to say these things out loud.

'She was like a changeling to them. She wasn't doing any of the things their other kids were doing. She wasn't messing about with boys or having any discernible fun whatsoever. She didn't even look like the rest of them. She was delicately pretty. And she refused to allow herself to follow the family tendency to a puffy pudginess. They all ate off trays in front of the TV so it was easy to sneak food into her pocket and dispose of it later.

'And, more importantly, she was showing no sign of making any contribution to the family coffers. All the others were working from about the age of eleven. Down the markets, local shops, anywhere the rules weren't too stringently applied.

'But Emma was having none of this. She wanted to get out and she knew the only way out was through education. She studied every spare minute. She didn't have friends because the sort of girl she liked was not the sort of girl she could bring back to her loud, slightly grubby home. Anyway, she had no time for friends. So there she was at thirteen, clever, ambitious, pretty, *slim*.'

Marina looked blank. 'Gail, I've read this story a million times before. Poor, clever, misunderstood girl rises up out of unsupportive, squalid environment and goes on to become brain surgeon or prime minister or something. They call it character-building.'

Gail ignored the interruption.

'So they put her into care.'

Marina was horrified. Gail was satisfied that she'd finally got the reaction she wanted. 'That's right. They put her into care. And not because they thought it would be for her own good but to punish her. You asked me a few moments ago if she was abused by her parents.'

'And you said that she wasn't.'

'That's true. She was abused by her foster parents.'

Marina didn't want to hear this. She wanted to understand Emma without having to hear things she didn't like thinking about. She still hadn't developed a reliable mechanism for dealing with uncomfortable truths. To replace the highly effective previous technique of eating. I'm going to have get drunk, she thought glumly, emptying her glass and catching the eye of the waiter to order a replacement in one fluid movement.

'She was treated like a slave by her first family. It was like something out of *Upstairs Downstairs*. Actually scrubbing floors, handwashing all the family's laundry, darning trousers, yes, *darning*. She ended up in hospital. The foster parents hadn't noticed that she stopped eating. She said that she would kill herself if she was sent back to that house.

'The next family completed the cycle. The mother ignored her and the father systematically guided her through the full range of documented abuse. He beat her by day and raped her at night. She

166

stayed there until she was sixteen having decided that she deserved this treatment for alienating her own family. If she had made more of an effort to fit in with them, then she could have stayed at home and enjoyed a life of blissful, untormented mediocrity.'

Marina was appalled by the story. She marvelled at how Emma had triumphed over her tragic past to become an acclaimed, accomplished journalist. Then it struck her – Emma hadn't triumphed over her past at all. Her past was a victory banner, flaunted in front of her haunted eyes every time she dared to think she had escaped. 'You can't run away from me, grubby fat girl, I saw you, I'll tell,' it read in big bold red letters.

'Did she ever see her family again? Her real family that is?'

'Oh yes, that's the really funny bit. She was seeing her family every week while she was being fostered. She ate everything that was put in front of her, to please her parents, then returned to her foster home and vomited it all up, to please herself.

'When she turned sixteen and finally freed herself from council care, she went to college and got her own flat but she still went home every week.

'Imagine the scene. Emma, all pretty and clever and messed up, sitting there in her crushed velvet jeans and kohl make-up. Among her siblings. All four of them left school at sixteen with not an O level between them. They all bear the coarse features bequeathed to them courtesy of the unfortunate genetic soup blended by their parents. They sit there chain-smoking, belching, hating her for being better than them.'

'What on earth do they talk about?' Marina asked.

'Emma tells them about her life. She shows them copies of her articles in the glossy magazines. She knows they resent her even more for her success but she can't help herself. She takes them unsuitable presents from Harvey Nicks that they go on to sell at boot sales. She wants either acceptance or closure from her family and they're simply not articulate enough to give her either.'

They both sat in silence for a while, wondering if there was anything at all they could do to prevent Emma from destroying herself when outside circumstances had done so much to bring about this end.

The food arrived. Marina looked at the plate which shimmered with oil and felt the old nausea rising up again. She threw a jealous glance towards Gail's fish and vegetables which were smiling with freshness.

She took some deep breaths before picking up her knife and fork. To put off the inevitable for just a few more seconds, she twisted her head to examine the other diners. It was a habit she'd acquired from her now-regular lunches and dinners with Teresa when they would conjure up outlandish background stories for the strangers around them.

Except they weren't all strangers. Sitting in a little cubicle at the back of a restaurant sat two people who, by their body language, were most definitely not just good friends. She knew the man even though she'd only been introduced to him a couple of times. It was Rod, Teresa's husband, all big and ginger-bearded and unmistakable.

At first she thought that it was Teresa with him. She even lifted her hand to wave only to yank it back on to the table with a thud.

It was not Teresa but it looked exactly like Teresa. Or rather, it looked exactly like the Teresa of six months earlier. For Teresa was now a long, lean sylph who dressed to play upon her increasing resemblance to a young Audrey Hepburn. She had unveiled a delicate frame that she showed off with waisted dresses and tight skirts and trousers.

No, Rod's current dining companion was nothing like that. She was tall, yes, but she was ample where Teresa had become spare. She had curves where Teresa had bones and she had smiles and bosoms where Teresa had worries and a ribcage.

But in every other respect, Rod was cheating on Teresa with her photofit twin. Marina quickly turned away. How could Teresa ever cope with the fact that she had lost all that weight for Rod, only to find that he had told the truth – he preferred big women all along?

'So what are we going to do about Emma?' Gail asked.

Marina thought of Emma, sitting at home starving herself to death. She thought of Teresa, who'd lost all that weight for all the wrong reasons. She thought about Gail, so perceptive and sensitive to her friend's situation and so blind to her own. She thought of Susie, growing uncontrollably like Alice in

Wonderland after drinking from the wrong bottle. She thought about herself, about to have the security blanket of Oxymetabulin snatched away from her. What are we going to do about any of us? she thought.

Chapter Sixteen

'I love a woman who's as clever as she is gorgeous,' David purred to the plain woman sitting half-dressed in front of his computer.

Her name was Jane and she oozed ordinariness. Not a single feature was big enough to qualify either as ugly or beautiful. She'd probably been a pretty child with that regular prettiness that many girls exhibit up to the age of five. But then everything grew and established, stubbornly refusing to settle in those proportions so often quoted by pseudoscientists as representing the mathematical formula of beauty.

David had invited her to dinner at his flat. She was hugely flattered that this man was going to cook for her and thrilled at the promise of what might happen later. In fact, David had chosen a home-cooked meal because he was broke. Also because the whole point of the exercise was to get her on the computer.

David was the most attractive man Jane had ever slept with. He was an achievement and the glow of pride overruled her instincts that maybe he didn't just want her for her body. The dinner had been from M & S (he'd taken back a jumper given to him by another woman and used the refund to pay for the food) but very efficiently reheated with the same garnish as recommended in the picture on the box. Yes, he was thorough.

The sex had been equally satisfactory. He had rushed through the encounter, giving her the impression that it was her seduction technique that made his passion so uncontrollable. He had already prepared the script for the precise ten minutes that he'd allocated for post-coital endearments. 'Do you know, Jane, right now all I want to do is spend the whole night with you and maybe most of tomorrow as well, but I'm afraid I'm going to have to love and leave you.'

Her despondent face confirmed that he'd hit the right tone. 'But it's 10.30! Where have you got to go at this time?'

'To the office. I know it's a pain, but I have no choice. Someone is going to be phoning me first thing tomorrow, expecting some figures, and I've left the information on my computer at the lab.'

'But I saw you've got a modem in the living room. Why don't you just access your work computer from here?'

David delivered his hopeless–little–boy smile with roguish style. 'Easier said than done. Give me a chemistry lab and I'll knock up a life-changing drug in minutes. But put me in front of a computer and I'm a bumbling buffoon. At the office, all the instructions are written out for me in idiot-proof language. Frankly, I don't know why I bothered having the modem put in at home. I haven't got the faintest idea how to use it.'

Jane shook her head indulgently. 'Have you got the details of your computer at Perrico?'

David leapt out of bed and pretended to fumble around his paperwork until he came across the specifications exactly where he'd placed them a few hours earlier. 'Is this any use?' he asked hopefully.

Jane took the wedge of paper and quickly scanned the text. 'Perfect! I'll tell you what, make me a cup of coffee, and I'll get your computer here to make contact with your computer at the office.'

'Is it that easy?' David asked, hoping he was conveying a suitable display of awe.

'I do this for a living, didn't you know?'

'You're kidding! I mean, I knew you did something with Perrico's computers but I didn't realise you were that technically accomplished. I'm impressed! But I think that the lab computers are on a separate loop, or whatever, to the rest of the Perrico computers. For security, I imagine.'

Jane laughed. 'I know. I installed that security myself! But don't worry, it's designed to keep outsiders out, not you absent-minded professors.'

David lowered his eyes sheepishly. Jane kissed him with the confidence that her newly-revealed power gave her and allowed him to guide her to his desk with tenderness. 'How do you take your coffee?' he asked.

'Right, we're in. What do you need to know?'

David sat down on the chair with Jane, nudging her hips over with an intimacy that would have made her rob a bank for him.

'It's that folder there. Oxymetab.data. I need the whole folder printed out.'

Jane's fingers played fluently across the keyboard. 'Right. Oh. Slight problem. This file needs a password. What is it?'

David groaned and hit his head in a graphic depiction of stupidity. 'I don't believe it. After all your hard work and I'm going to have to go in to work anyway. The password is written down in my desk diary.'

'Don't you know it offhand?' Jane looked baffled by David's ignorance.

'Now you must really think I'm an idiot! I can remember a formula twenty lines long, but passwords – never. I think it's because I don't need to remember them. I always have them written down, so my brain doesn't bother processing them.'

'That must be the scientist in you. Where are you going?' Jane looked alarmed.

'I told you. I have to go to the office. To get that password.'

Jane grabbed his hand and pulled him back to the chair. A little too aggressively for David, who had become very nervous of sudden movements recently. The people who had lent him money were being less than professional in their response to his flexible approach to repayment. In fact he was even detecting a note of ... threat in their recent warnings. It bothered him.

'Sit down!' Jane cried enthusiastically. 'I'll find the password.'

'How can you do that? They're supposed to be highly confidential.'

'And they are. Except to people like me. Watch this.'

He watched fascinated as she trawled through databases and screens filled with meaningless symbols and random letters. He felt a grudging respect for her ability and, if she'd only been more attractive, he might have agreed to see her a few more times.

It took her a while and he was getting impatient. 'Bingo,' she at last announced triumphantly.

There it was before his eyes. The name of every woman taking part in the Oxymetabulin trial along with the product she was taking. O for Oxymetabulin. P for placebo. He didn't spend too long looking at the screen. It was time to pay for this service. He put his arms around Jane and gazed into her eyes. 'You are a genius. Let me show you how grateful I am.'

As he led her back to the bedroom, he pressed the key that sent the document to his printer in the back room. It would print out silently while he distracted Jane.

Deciding to get the most out of his one-night investment he asked one more question. 'By the way, Jane, what was the password? Not that I'll remember it, of course, but just out of interest.'

She laughed. 'Actually, I was going to ask you about that. Did you really create that password yourself?'

'Of course I did,' he answered, his defences up.

'I like that in a man.'

'What?' David hated enigmas. He had so much to hide that he always worried that one of his many dark secrets was being alluded to.

'A sense of humour.'

David didn't like this. It was Perrico's lab director who created the password and David had long suspected that the man didn't like him very much.

'So what was the password?'

Jane was still laughing when she told him. 'How could you possibly forget it? It's DODGYDAVE!'

Nancy Riesenthal almost slammed the door in Marina's face. 'No canvassers, thank you,' she began before catching her breath in shock. 'Marina! Is that you? It can't be.'

'Well it is, Mum.' Marina stood on the doorstep, feeling ten years old.

Nancy held on to the door for support. It was a long time since she had allowed a stranger into her house and that was what stood before her now. A total stranger.

'I thought you were from the Conservative Party.'

Marina laughed and then stopped, suddenly aware that this was the biggest insult her mother could deliver (after 'fat').

'Who is it, love?' Donald called from somewhere in the house. The knowledge that he was not in the garden took Marina by surprise. For a horrible instant, she wondered if he only spent all his time in the garden when she was home. She'd constructed a thumbnail sketch of her father avoiding Nancy's company as carefully as Marina did herself. Could it be that he and her mother were in reality very happy together and it was Marina herself who divided them?

She didn't like this train of thought one bit and gently pushed the door back so that she could go in and see how her parents lived when they weren't expecting her.

'We weren't expecting you,' Donald said accusingly when he heard her voice. As soon as he saw her, he turned white. Marina thought he was going to collapse.

'Are you OK, Dad?' She rushed over to hold his arm in case he fainted. Before she reached him, her mother had got there first. She stood slightly in front of him, a skeletal wall of emotional protection against surprise.

'Your father's fine. He's just a bit shocked, that's all. We both are. You didn't tell us you were coming. Or that you . . .'

She couldn't finish the sentence. She was only just beginning to take in the scale of her daughter's transformation. Marina was a vision of filial perfection. She was slim, beautiful, unsullied. She was a studio photograph that you scrutinised for signs of chemical correction. She was the sort of woman that any man would choose to possess.

But she wasn't Nancy's daughter any more. Their entire relationship had been built on an oppressor/oppressed balance. Nancy's concept of motherhood had evolved into a Svengali-like determination to change Marina utterly. And now Marina had attained the ideal that Nancy had always wished for her.

But she'd done it herself and that simply wasn't fair. What did it say about Nancy's mothering that her daughter only fulfilled her potential when she was entirely free of maternal input? How could Nancy claim any credit for the person Marina had become? She was an honest woman and could not look her friends in the eye and claim that she had played any part in the creation of this beautiful woman. She had been cheated.

Marina had no idea what her mother was thinking but it was certainly not the reaction that she'd expected. They couldn't continue standing there indefinitely. So she bravely asked the one question that she'd not expected to have to ask.

'So, what do you think?' She extended her arms and twirled like a little girl in a tutu. The swiftness of the motion made her parents jump. They took a step backwards in case she lost balance and fell on top of them. For a second, they'd thought she was that fat, clumsy girl who'd lolloped through this house throughout her childhood.

Donald spoke first. 'You look lovely, love. Just not yourself, if you see what I mean.'

She did. She experienced the same displacement every time she looked in the mirror. She waited for her dad to come and hug her. Or pat her. Or touch her. Surely if ever there was justification for a group hug, this was one. But he just stood there, still slightly blocked by Nancy.

'Mum. You haven't said anything.'

'Have you been ill? We haven't heard from you for so long. We haven't seen you since Christmas, then you turn up out of the blue, all thin. What are we supposed to think?'

Marina tried to suppress her disappointment. Her effort was translated into anger. 'No, I haven't been ill. I haven't been home because I didn't think you were interested in seeing me. I've been busy with my career. You know, that career that you've not once asked me about? I've been travelling around the world, sorting out multi-million pound campaigns, that sort of thing. Not quite as impressive as cooking egg and chips for a husband and five kids but it's my life.'

Nancy bristled from the attack on her values. 'There's no need to get nasty. We're just taken aback, that's all. And worried. You've never been so small. Any mother would be concerned as to how you lost all that weight.'

Marina had thought hard about what she was going to say. She knew that she was going to lie. The whole point of presenting herself to her parents like this was to finally gain a degree of approval. She wanted them to admire her achievement. She knew that they wouldn't be swayed by the profile of a new drugs trial. Discipline, that was the only motivation that they would respect.

'Diet and exercise, that's all.' She felt no guilt at lying. Children lie to their parents continually from the false cries in the cradle to the adolescent whoppers and adult omissions that maintain the facade of family unity.

At that point, Donald stepped forward and stroked her arm proudly. 'Well done, love.'

Now Marina felt guilty for lying.

Nancy also stepped forward, never wanting to stand more than a few feet away from Donald. 'Well done, then, Marina. If it *was* just dieting and exercise, of course.'

The insightful suspicion crushed Marina's spirit instantly. Nancy was simultaneously smug that she'd read her daughter's situation correctly and disturbed at exactly what lengths Marina had gone to in order to attain her new body.

It was Christmas all over again. Donald had escaped to the potting shed. Marina and Nancy sat on opposite sides of the sitting room with food debris scattered between them like an accusation. The television was on and Nancy was punctuating the broadcast with her trademark tuts as global injustices were announced in solemn tones.

Marina's physical conversion had also effected some profound changes on her personality. It gave her the courage to ask questions that she'd never dare pose before. She thought that this was probably because she had removed herself as a target from the world's cutting arrows. She could say anything and she couldn't be hurt. And she had questions. Gaps that she now felt strong enough to fill. The liberation was breathtaking.

'Why did you never go abroad again after Spain, Mum?'

Nancy narrowed her eyes and concentrated more intently on the TV screen, hoping that Marina would interpret this as selective deafness and back off. The old Marina would have cringed at the rejection and retreated to the safety of another cake. But this was the new Marina. She hadn't touched the obscene array of cakes and biscuits that Nancy had placed before her like a shiny poisoned apple. She'd ostentatiously pushed away the sugar bowl as she stirred her tea and lifted the cup to her glossed red lips with ladylike delicacy.

Such restraint was not as easy as it had been recently. Today was her second day without tablets and the struggle had been getting more and more difficult. On the drive up to her parents, the urge had whooshed over her as she approached every petrol station. Sweets and chocolate on sale here! they beckoned in neon. Better come and fill up just in case you crash in the middle of nowhere with nothing to eat for days on end. What if you get stuck in a traffic jam and you get hungry? Your fat stores have been depleted to practically nothing. You could die of starvation. Or you could go into diabetic shock from lack of sugar. Quick, stock up before a national shortage sets in!

Only deep breathing and the rhythmic, obsessive chewing of three packets of sugar-free chewing gum prevented her pulling over and diving into a Creme Egg display with her mouth open.

This is crazy, she told herself. It is barely forty-eight hours since my last pill. There must be some residue of the chemical compound in my body. And my stomach must be a fraction of the size it was. This is all psychological. I have become psychologically addicted to the pills and my motivation has crumbled now that the crutch has been taken away from me.

And suppose I wasn't even taking the Oxymetabulin? Suppose I was taking the placebo? I mean, half of us were on the dummy pills and look at us all as a group. We all lost some weight. It's all in the mind, not in the pill. So all I have to do is convince myself that I lost all that weight by my own willpower and that those pills had nothing but powder in them. And what I never had, I can't miss.

That was the theory. Like most theories, it sounded great and meant nothing. Sitting opposite her mother, all her insecurities disappeared somewhere else. She was empowered by her own physical superiority, knowing that she conformed to her mother's ideal of womanly beauty to a degree that Nancy herself could never attain. Nancy could not guess that Marina's grasp on perfection was increasingly tenuous; she could merely bow to the invasive presence of her new daughter.

'Did you hear what I said, Mum? Why did you never go abroad again after Spain?'

In less than an hour, Nancy had come to an understanding of this exotic being who claimed to be her daughter. She was confident, pushy and stubborn. A bit like Nancy when she was younger. A lot younger. She wasn't going to give up until the question was answered. To Marina's satisfaction.

She sighed, exhaling fifty years of dusty excuses that were a bit feeble even when she made them up. She picked up her knitting and started clicking the needles ferociously. 'I didn't go abroad again because there wasn't any point. Spain had been a silly teenage adventure. I accomplished nothing. Got my fingers well and truly burned. So I learned from my mistakes and stayed here.'

'But what did you accomplish by *not* going away again?'

'I made a life here. Are you saying that teaching accomplishes nothing?'

'Don't go all defensive on me, Mum. I'm trying to understand you. You were a brilliant teacher. Everybody said so.'

'Well, there you go then.' A needle of light flickered from behind Nancy's eye, giving a hint of the spirit and drive that once sent the girl to a war that had nothing to do with her.

Marina decided to persevere despite her mother's determination not to get drawn into the sort of conversation Marina wanted. 'You were a great teacher. You've read everything. You must have felt smothered by suburban existence, watching your pupils grow up and move on, doing all the things that you could have done but didn't even try.'

'Everything is so easy for you. So simple.' Her bitterness was transparent. She caught the astonishment in Marina's eye and quickly backtracked. 'All right, I admit you must have had a few problems adjusting to the world with your ... ' She didn't finish the sentence. Couldn't. 'But that was a self-inflicted problem. You could have eliminated that disadvantage at any time you chose, as you've now proved so ably. That's why I always pushed you so hard on the matter. It was such an easy one to resolve but you wouldn't even try.'

'It was never that easy, Mum. That's something you never understood.'

Nancy inclined her head. As she continued with her knitting, her tone changed. 'Maybe you're right. But I've read quite a lot about that 5F you mentioned at Christmas. I went to the library and got some articles out of back issues from magazines.'

Marina laughed out loud. 'Just when I think I've got you all worked out, you go and do something like that. I didn't think you were listening.'

Nancy tightened her lips at this regular accusation. 'Marina, I always listen to you. I often don't respond because I don't know what to say. You always bit my head off when I tried to talk to you. You used to ask me things then throw a tantrum when you didn't like my advice.'

'That's because the advice was always the same: lose weight, find a man. In that order.'

'That's because I thought you would be happier if you found someone. And I didn't think you'd find a man if—'

'I was a big, fat blimp?'

'I didn't say that.'

'But you thought it. Anyway what difference does it make?'

'I didn't want you to make the same mistakes I made. Mothers are like that, as I hope you'll find out for yourself one day.'

This was getting dangerously close to an open and frank discussion and Nancy was feeling uncomfortable. She turned up the TV volume on the remote control.

Marina wanted more, needed more, hungered for more. 'What mistakes, Mum?'

Nancy looked at her daughter coldly, crossly. 'Marina, I know what you want from me. You want me to be the fourteen-year-old girl that your nan told you about. The one that ran away. The exciting, dangerous one. Well I'm not. I'm the other one. The boring retired teacher. The mum who doesn't understand what it's like to be young. Or feel different. That's who I am. That's who you're stuck with.'

'What mistakes, Mum?' Marina refused to be distracted.

Nancy dropped a stitch and cursed her clumsiness. Irritably, she answered Marina. 'Living alone. Building walls around yourself. Saying to the world: "Stay away from me! I don't want your happiness, no sir. Leave me alone. I'd rather be miserable. And alone."'

Marina had never thought of her mother's twenty years of life after Spain and before marriage. Twenty years. A long time. She guessed that she would never find out what her mother's life was like during those years. But she suspected they were painful. Empty. Wasted.

She shook her head. 'But Mum, it's not like that. Things are different nowadays. People are happy to live alone. My weight's not got anything to do with it.'

Nancy was tired from having to speak about things she preferred to leave sleeping. 'Maybe. That's why I was so interested in that 5F group. Perhaps you were right all those times when you accused me of not accepting you the way you were. I didn't. But then I wasn't convinced you were so happy about it yourself.'

I wasn't, Mum, oh I wasn't. And if only you'd once told me that you understood how I was feeling, I could have talked to you. Maybe we could have made things better.

That's what Marina wanted to say. She didn't say anything.

Nancy shrugged. She tried to bring the conversation to a neat conclusion. She didn't have many more words left inside her. 'Anyway it all became a bit clearer to me. You and your friends were happy the way you were. It was the rest of us who had the problem, wanting to change you so that we could all look the same. I just had to accept it. So I did.'

Please God, don't let me cry, Marina thought. It wouldn't have mattered if she had. Nancy's voice was starting to sound sharp once more.

'That's why I was so shocked when I saw you today. The way you were. There was I, ready to welcome you as you. And there *you* were, somebody else. I didn't understand. I *don't* understand. Which one is the one you want to be, the one you want me to understand? Just tell me and I'll do it.'

Nancy became the accuser once more, the where-have-I-gone-wrong mother. The long-suffering martyr. Someone who'd interpreted a daughter's outstanding life achievement as a personal challenge against her mother.

Marina wanted to explain it all. She wanted to tell her how men, attractive men, wanted to have sex with her now she was slim. And how women who used to recoil from her now flocked round to share intimate secrets. And how her fat friends didn't want to know her at all any more. And how everything was different now except what was inside. But she didn't think Nancy would be able to relate to these disconnected feelings. Now it was Marina's turn to be proven wrong in her judgement.

'You asked me why I never went abroad again,' Nancy said. 'The real reason is that I learned something on my one great adventure. I went to Spain to change myself, not the world. To turn myself into a glamorous, feisty heroine a million miles removed from a West Midlands schoolgirl.'

'And you *were* a heroine, Mum.'

'No, Marina. I was a West Midlands schoolgirl in a rebel's uniform. It was just clothing. I was the same underneath. Just as you're the same underneath whether you're fat or thin. I was a dull, suburban, ordinary person who would never be anything else no matter how many wars I tried to fight. I learned something that perhaps you've yet to find out – that you can't change yourself, you can only put on different clothes.'

Marina didn't reply. It was too big an observation to diminish with a glib adage of her own. And she didn't want to acknowledge that it was possibly true. It would make a nonsense of all that she'd achieved.

She could only think of one thing. The plate of cakes that were tormenting her, only inches from her manicured fingers. They were fondant fancies. They *had* to be fondant fancies, life was like that.

I want them, I want them, I want them.

Nancy was grateful for Marina's retreat from this awkward conversation. She couldn't stop herself from perforating the silence with the standard mother's line. 'What have you got to say for yourself now, Marina?'

Marina was drained by this unfamiliar exchange that bordered on intimacy. She just wanted to go back to London. To her flat. To her job. To food.

'Just that I'm glad I came home, Mum. And I'm glad we had this talk.'

Liar, liar.

Chapter Seventeen

It was October and nobody was taking the pills any more.

Tuesday was weigh-in day and the waiting room was a sombre place. The summer stripes and shimmers had been replaced by muted autumnal colours that concealed more than they revealed. Talking was quiet and nervous. Knees were crossed and arms folded. There was no Emma.

'What do you mean, she's disappeared?' Teresa asked Marina.

'Just that. She's moved out of her flat and hasn't left a forwarding address. I've called a couple of the magazines that I know she's been freelancing for but they haven't heard from her either. Apparently that's not unusual for her. She's writing up the Oxymetabulin story but they're not expecting the final piece for a few more months when the trial's over and the preliminary results are available.'

'If no one else is worried, does that mean that we shouldn't be worried either?'

'I don't know, Terry. You didn't see her. I thought she was close to death.'

'Well, if she had the energy to move house, she can't have been that weak. Moving takes a hell of a lot out of you, believe me, I should know.'

Marina took her friend's hand. 'Oh Terry, I'm sorry I haven't asked. How did the move go?'

'Well that depends which part you mean. If you mean the part where I packed up the detritus from nineteen years of a broken marriage and piled them into cardboard boxes like old clothes at a jumble sale, then it was like dying without the relief of death at the end. On the other hand, a perfectly efficient removals firm sent a man with a van to transport the said boxes to my new shoe box with minimal breakages at an acceptable cost. So, all in all, can't complain.'

She bowed her head but not before Marina caught sight of the tears. 'I feel terrible. Maybe if I'd said something earlier ...'

Now it was Teresa's turn to console Marina. 'I don't know whether you were right or wrong to say nothing but I do know that I would have done exactly the same thing if the roles had been reversed.'

'Maybe,' Marina said doubtfully. She'd deliberated for a long time before finally deciding not to tell Teresa about seeing Rod with the other woman. She had been forced to make the decision entirely by herself and it had brought home to her how much she needed a good friend. There was Susie but her own life was getting so complex that Marina dreaded speaking to her. Besides, Susie had been involved with another man herself, although Marina hadn't got to the bottom of that one before it was apparently over. Her moral input would inevitably be skewed.

Marina's only other proper friend was Teresa. It was a rotten position to be in. She had read all the magazines, all those agony aunts talking about truth and honesty and the 'right to know'. But there were other things to consider. Perhaps Teresa suspected and didn't want to have her suspicions confirmed. Perhaps it was just a trivial fling that would be over in a few days. Perhaps it was a minor compulsion that Rod needed to get out of his system. Was it worth landing Teresa with a pain that could haunt her and the marriage for ever if it wasn't absolutely necessary? Marina concluded that it was best that she say nothing.

All lies. She said nothing because she was a coward. She was afraid that Teresa would adopt the 'shoot the messenger' attitude. She was afraid that she'd lose her friend.

In the end, Rod told Teresa himself. It wasn't a trivial fling or a minor compulsion. He loved this girl who made him feel comfortable in the way that he had felt with Teresa in their early years. Her name was Mary, which was all wrong to Teresa. It was such a homely name, not the name of a blowsy broad, not the name of a skinny interloper.

It was Marina who told her just what Mary looked like. She thought it might reassure Teresa that her rival could not compete with her in looks. Understanding the insecurity that comes from a lifetime of hating one's body, she thought this consolation prize might at least furnish Teresa with enough self-confidence to begin her life positively.

It didn't work like that. Teresa was devastated. The implications struck her immediately despite Marina's awkward attempts to cloud the fundamental issue.

'So he meant it all along!' she gasped.

'Meant what?' Marina asked, knowing exactly Teresa meant.

'He really did, he really *does* prefer big women. He told me a thousand times and I never believed him.'

Marina had prepared for this confrontation and managed to avoid the temptation to say: 'I told you so.'

'Well, it was an easy mistake.'

'Easy?' Teresa had retorted. 'Easy when you accuse the man you've loved for twenty years, who's always been honest to you about everything else, you accuse him of an enormous lie that he's perpetuated throughout the entire length of the relationship?'

Marina had rehearsed some platitudes that she'd hoped would help. 'That's because you had a problem. We both did, Terry. In fact all of us did. We were so caught up in our own weight problem that it never occurred to us that maybe it wasn't a problem to everyone. It's like an illness.'

'That makes me feel a lot better. It wasn't the fat that made me such an irrational cow, it was the mental illness. That's bound to bring Rod running back.'

'I didn't mean it like that and you know it.'

They hadn't said any more. It was an argument that couldn't be won because neither was particularly certain of their own viewpoint.

Teresa arranged to move out of the house straight away. It was her way of coping with the situation. She found a tiny flat nearby. She couldn't move too far away because she still had to return to the house to work in their shared office. It was an unbearable situation for her, not helped by the removal of her tablets.

Like all the women, both Marina and Teresa were worried about what the scales would reveal. They had both resumed the battle of the weight-watcher, facing a challenge every second of their waking day. Every morsel of unacceptable calorie content that entered their mouth had been fought and resisted until defeat had to be faced. Eating had become the same miserable ordeal that had dominated their fat lives. It was no easier now that they were thin.

The problem had turned out to be the very aid that had enabled them to overcome their food compulsions in the first place. The drugs. It made no difference whether it had been the real pills or the dummies. To the women, they had lost weight because of the pills. Without them, they were fatties again, out of control, arms flailing wildly as they tried not to grasp all the food they'd denied themselves with so much ease in recent months.

The best thing about the drugs programme was that food lost its role as the central character in each woman's life. The worst thing was that food lost its role as the central character in each woman's life. It was a big thing to lose. It was a bereavement. Food didn't taste the same. It wasn't exciting. It wasn't soothing. It wasn't distracting. Fortunately, the euphoria of a new body was sufficient to fill the many gaps that appeared threateningly.

But once the weight loss had petered out and stabilised and the heightened emotions had levelled out to a matter-of-fact acceptance of the new status quo, that hungry soul started reaching out for another security blanket. Without pills, there was only one security blanket tried and tested by these women.

Of course, they tried some of the more popular crutches used by women who managed to maintain their weight. They tried alcohol (too fattening, lowered the resistance to food even further), smoking (only sixty a day would be enough to fill all the needy moments – they were not yet driven to such a death wish) sex (uninvolved sex left them feeling bereft with yet another hollow crying out for attention).

None of it worked. Only food worked because they knew how to handle that. The old, familiar routines coaxed them back once more into the controlled abandon of a binge. Food tasted wonderful again. It tasted sinful and evocative and magical. It kept them company and spoke to the women in a common language. They'd come home.

This is not to say that all the women put on weight. Indeed, as David had predicted, the women on Oxymetabulin were finding it slightly easier to keep the weight off with their reset metabolic rate. But it just wasn't easy enough.

To look at the women sitting in the waiting room, it was difficult to say just how much they weighed. Most people have a twenty-pound window on both sides of their ideal weight, within which they can usually hide any excess gain (or loss!) with judicious choice of clothing. There were some unfortunates who immediately saw the first surplus pounds transported directly to their faces where they sat like doughnuts on the cheeks and under the chin.

Marina was one of them. It was only when she became clinically underweight that her face had finally shed the last of its padding. Although she had to agree with everyone who knew her that her face was more attractive when it bore some under-padding, nonetheless the bare skeleton of her face had become a touchstone for assessing her proximity to perfection.

She'd looked in the mirror that morning and no amount of steamy blur could disguise the fact that her bones were less visible than a few weeks before. She rushed to her wardrobe and snatched out the clothes that fitted the most closely. Her proudest possession was a size ten skirt that she had bought in September. It had fastened on the waist neatly and the linen sat snugly on her hips, creating not a single ripple or snag of fabric. Intense exercise had left her stomach flat enough to continue the smooth line around her middle. She always wore it with a tightfitting silk body so that no seams would dare imprint through the fabric.

That Tuesday, she'd tried to put it on. She couldn't do it up. Not even if she lay on the ground, sucked her stomach in and held her breath. She'd panicked. Stop this, she told herself sharply, trying to sound like her mother. This is a size ten skirt. A small size ten at that. Yes, I must have put on weight but let's not be silly about this. Maybe I was never meant to be a size ten. What's wrong with being a size twelve? It was nice being skinny but I'm obviously not supposed to be *that* skinny.

But that didn't work. She pulled on some jogging bottoms with a drawstring waist and rushed to the shops. Only by pulling her comfort foods from the shelves into her shopping basket could she keep herself from hyperventilating. I won't eat it, she told herself. At least not all of it. No, I'll just look at it then look at the pictures of how I used to be then look at all my new clothes and at my picture of Andy and then make an informed choice.

So she did all that and made the informed choice. The binge was ten times more satisfying since it followed rational debate with herself. It was less impulsive, more relaxed. She was surprised by how much she was able to consume before the bloated feeling of sickness set in. She'd expected her shrunken stomach to say 'no' long before it did.

Unlike her old binges, she didn't end this one in a pool of tears shed in self-recrimination. She was going to be weighed in a few hours and she had no intention of allowing her folly to be a matter of public record.

So she stuck her fingers down her throat and brought it all back up. It was the first time she'd done it and she didn't find it a pleasant experience but it was effective.

'Marina Riesenthal!' the clinical assistant called.

Teresa wished her luck as she walked into David's consulting room.

'So how have you been finding things without the tablets, Marina?'

David's cool tones amused Marina. She knew how peeved he'd been by her refusal to repeat their one night together. He had been assiduous in his pursuit of her, hoping that he wasn't appearing desperate. In fact, he had appeared so desperate that Marina had almost succumbed out of pity for him. But she was developing a real feeling of loyalty to Andy and the only way she could overcome her guilt for having betrayed him was to ensure that the night was forever etched in her moral sketchbook as a moment of madness.

Marina stood on the scales, all of her muscles clenched irrationally to make herself seem smaller.

'Oh fine. No problems really.'

'You've put on fifteen pounds in two weeks.'

Marina let out a little cry. Fifteen pounds! And that was after emptying her stomach just a couple of hours earlier. She hadn't weighed herself since the day she felt that the weight was creeping back on. She didn't want to know. She wanted to live a lie.

'That can't be true! I know I've put on a bit. But it can't be that much. I haven't eaten enough to put on that much. It must be water bloating or something like that! Or maybe it's a side-effect of coming off the pills. Like steroids. Maybe I just need a bit more time to stabilise. Or maybe I should go back on a low dose of the pills. Maybe you shouldn't just stop them like that.'

David enjoyed her distress. His own life was so fraught with troubles that his only consolation came from knowing that others were in pain too. He hadn't paid his mortgage for a couple of months now. He couldn't. In fact he couldn't pay any of his debts except the extortionate payments demanded by the loan sharks.

Of course they were loan sharks. He'd pretended to himself that they were 'independent financial consultants' but the men who called at his flat the first time he was late with his repayment couldn't have spelt 'independent financial consultant'. His priorities were explained to him in words of one syllable. Now that he was late with an instalment, penalty clauses were invoked. This meant that he had to pay *double* the agreed sum.

They didn't specify the consequences if he failed to honour his debts. They didn't have to. He now had to hand over all of his salary to the loan sharks. His other creditors were circling and their letters becoming increasingly threatening. He was supported by a triumvirate of women who fed him and even gave him money, such was his desperation, but they weren't enough. He was in deep, deep trouble. He didn't even know if he'd make it through to his bonus in December.

The trial's successful completion was becoming ever more uncertain. They were killing him, these women.

So while Marina was probably right that she was going through a period of stabilisation, David was happy to let her squirm with worry. As if his debts were not bad enough, this woman had left him with a very slight ego deficit. She was the first woman ever to

189

turn him down. He had only wanted to go out with her again so that *he* could be the one who dumped *her*, the way it was supposed to be.

Still, the trial was more important than causing this woman pain. Just about. He tried to sound reassuring. 'Maybe it's just a temporary gain. But it's still a lot in such a short time. Basically you're putting it on more quickly than you took it off. That's not good.'

Marina laughed nervously. 'It would help if we knew whether I'd been given the real drug or the placebo.'

David glared at her sharply. 'It wouldn't help in the slightest. That is the whole point of the blind aspect of the trial. If you knew what you were taking, it would influence your behaviour and you'd try to produce the results that you believed were expected of you.'

'All I'm saying is that, well, all of us are finding it difficult to manage without the pills. Surely that happens in all drugs trials. You're given pills to take every day for months, they change your life in one way or another and then they take the pills away. There's bound to be a psychological reaction. And surely, that psychological reaction is one that you would wish to prevent. Otherwise even the triallists who are on the Oxymetabulin might resort to comfort eating in response to their withdrawal feelings. That will blow your results completely.'

David was taken aback by this. Just when he thought he had covered every angle of the mindset of the overweight woman, another handicap was swiftly erected for him to leap over. It had all seemed so simple at the outset. Those 5F women were meant to have overcome all those food-related neuroses that beset less enlightened females. They were supposed to be like normal people. That's why he chose them. It was on that basis that he was given authority to carry out the trial.

And now, one of these normal well-adjusted women was tossing out phrases like 'comfort eating' at him. He'd already weighed seven other women and they were all showing similar fluctuations that were way above projections. He couldn't ignore the situation. If Marina was right, then even if these women began the study with a healthy relationship to food, the pills had sparked off a new

190

dependency that could not be separated from their subsequent behaviour.

The one thing that he could not know was that the very premise with which he started was a lie. The second he mooted the possibility of an effortless weight-loss regime, these women regressed to the stance that they had all occupied at one point in their lives – the woman who wanted to be slim whatever the cost.

He slowly began to appreciate this as he watched them all lose weight to a greater or lesser degree, but was hoping that the longer-term results would enable him to salvage some sensible data from the study.

What Marina said made sense but he couldn't see how he could incorporate her thoughts into the study. The protocol was fixed from the outset. Unless some risk to human life had emerged, the protocol could not be changed and certainly not for some tenuous theory put forth by one of the triallists.

Still, he had to ask. 'How would you suggest I deal with that problem – if there is a problem, of course?'

Marina shrugged. 'You're the scientist, not me. All I'm saying is that maybe the tablets could have been phased out gradually. It's probably too late to do anything about that now. Unless there was some way of putting us *back* on the tablets then slowly taking us off.' The hope in her voice was unmistakable.

David shook his head. 'That's completely impossible. Unless . . .'

'Unless what?' Marina asked eagerly.

'There's just one outside possibility but I'm not sure it's appropriate.'

'Why don't you tell me what it is!'

'If there was a medical problem, something that hadn't been predicted, I could then reevaluate the status of the trial and take action.'

Marina caught on quickly. 'Emma.'

'Have you seen her lately?'

'Not for months. I'm assuming nothing terrible's happened to her or we'd have heard. She's pretty high-profile in the media world.'

David took this in carefully. 'Well, that's good news. But she was in a really bad way when I last saw her and you said the same. Now

I'm not saying that this is a direct result of the drugs she was taking. But what if it was a result of coming off the drugs too quickly?'

Marina looked doubtful. 'That can't be the case. She never reached the point where you withdrew the treatment. She was ill way before that stage.'

David held up a cautionary finger. 'As far as we know.'

'I don't understand.'

'Suppose she just stopped taking the tablets for some crazy reason that none of us know about. *Then* she got ill. It would be the withdrawal not the tablets themselves that could be said to have caused the problem.'

'But you have no way of knowing that.'

'And we have no way of *not* knowing that.'

'Hold on a second. I thought you'd decided to say that Emma had become pregnant and that was why she dropped out from the trial?'

'I was but I changed my mind. As you said, she's a high-profile journalist. I couldn't have her writing a completely different story in the press.'

'So what have you done with her case study? How have you accounted for her non-appearance at weigh-ins?'

David's silence communicated the magnitude of his guilt.

'You haven't made up figures for her? Pretended that she was still taking part? Are you mad?'

'Look, no one will notice. Individual results are never released, it would be a breach of confidentiality. She won't even know herself. But she'd certainly find out if she was down as a void due to pregnancy.'

Marina's heart was beating too fast and her empty stomach was screaming for attention. 'I think this has all gone too far, David. You're going to get caught. And then it will all have been for nothing.'

'How can it have been for nothing? The drug works, you know it.'

She did know it but she was so tired. She didn't want to be in this position. She just wanted to be thin and get on with her life. How many battles was she going to have to fight just to live like other women?

'So what you're proposing is to put it to your bosses that Emma stopped the tablets suddenly, without your permission, and started to develop ... problems? Glossing over the fact that she hasn't been on the programme for three months, that you've just pretended she has.'

'Exactly!' He ignored her accusations. 'And therefore, I feel it's best to go back a step and phase out the medication in more cautious stages.' His eyes narrowed with cunning innocence. 'My case would be even stronger if I could produce someone who actually said that they were currently experiencing some symptoms of withdrawal themselves. In Emma's absence, that is.'

He lobbed the ball to Marina. It braked, suspended in the ethical ether between them as she fought with her conscience.

It was all wrong, Marina could see that. And surely he wouldn't be able to get away with it? Surely they would halt the trial at the first sign of serious health concerns? But this wasn't the floor-cleaning market that was suddenly looking a lot more academic and regulated than this make-it-up-as-you-go-along research field. Anyway, she didn't care. Fifteen pounds in two weeks. That was thirty pounds in four weeks. And sixty pounds in eight weeks. She'd be back where she started.

She wanted those pills back. She needed them back. It was like she said, she just needed a bit more time to come off the pills, to readjust to her own appetite, to slowly allow the chemical effects to drift out of her body. She'd be fine if she could have them back for a couple more weeks. That's all. She'd get herself back into her size ten skirt and she'd be fine.

The two desperate people looked at each other. Each wanted peace. Neither wanted constant crisis and stress. Neither had the energy for lengthy moral and philosophical debate. They had their own problems. They could only countenance simple solutions.

Marina sagged with the additional weight that David had loaded on to her conscience. 'I suppose it wouldn't be that much of a lie, really. I mean, putting all that weight on so fast, it's not healthy, is it. It's bad for my heart. And it's not as if I'm eating a lot more than before. So, in a way, I am ill. Something is not working properly in my body, so that means I'm ill, right?'

'Absolutely!' David agreed, who hadn't bothered trying to

follow her warped logic. She was coming round to his way of thinking and he didn't care why. 'So I'll write down here that you've had, shall we say, headaches, not too severe, mind you, sleeplessness, gastric complaints. And that you were perfectly healthy while you were on the pills. That OK?'

That was OK, apart from the fact that the headaches and sleeplessness and gastric complaints were all side-effects that she'd suffered while *on* the pills, side-effects that she'd deliberately withheld from David to stop herself from being taken off the trial.

In fact, since stopping the tablets, she'd felt better than she had done for months but she was not planning to tell David that.

'Fine,' she agreed weakly.

David watched her leave with satisfaction. A difficult situation had been averted and Marina was beginning to get podgy again. The sooner he stopped finding that woman attractive, the happier he would be.

It was a long day with all the women berating him with tales of woe, lying about what they'd eaten, claiming premenstrual bloating was responsible for at least seven pounds of their gain. Looking back over his records he observed that some of these women seemed to be spending three-quarters of their lives menstruating.

By six o'clock, he had a headache. He'd managed to plant the suggestion of withdrawal headaches into some of the other women and now he had to draw up a proposal to get them all back on to the tablets while he worked out what to do next.

It was all going horribly wrong. The printout of names and drugs had not proved very useful in itself. He had found it frustrating to see that some of the most dramatic reductions had come from women on placebos and some of the more up-and-down results from the women on Oxymetabulin. He had considered the idea of subtly implanting suggestions in the relevant women that might encourage them to conform a little closer to expectations, but dismissed it, recognising that he had no clue what motivated or demotivated them.

It was only when he reflected on his good fortune in obtaining the results that the solution became glaringly obvious. The only defence to the results programme on the computer was the password. Once that was cracked, it was just another document. And like any other document, it could be edited. Changed.

Why didn't I think of it before? I'll just change the results that deviate from expectations. I won't be doing anything immoral. The drug works, everyone knows that. Why should the whole thing be ruined by a bunch of crazy women who can't control what they put in their mouths?

That's what I'll do. I'll change the results.

Chapter Eighteen

'I can't believe I'm here!' Susie said for the fifth time in an hour. It was late October and winter hadn't reached Greece yet.

'So you said,' Andy commented miserably. Marina shot him a withering glance. She conjured up a smile that she'd last seen on *Annie* when she was singing 'The sun'll come out tomorrow ...' on the end of the pier in Eastbourne. What it lacked in sincerity, it made up for in teeth.

'I'm glad you came. We both are, aren't we Andy?'

'I've said I'm glad already. How much more glad do you want me to be?'

It was only Friday and they had an entire weekend to get through together. It had seemed such a good idea. To Susie at least. Andy had wanted to spend some time alone with Marina. There were things they needed to talk about, subjects that Marina had been avoiding for a few weeks.

'I've never been to Greece before,' Susie said perkily.

'So you said,' Andy pointed out again. They'd been sitting in the taverna for an hour and Susie was already very drunk. Rather than being a charming, amusing inebriate, she was the boring repetitive sort. She was also getting loud. Fortunately she was deaf to the frequent jibes that Andy had been inflicting on her since they left Heathrow. A dreamy, tearful expression began to creep out from behind her sunglasses.

Oh no, thought Andy. She's going to tell us about Ken and the children again.

'I wonder what Ken and the children are doing now.' Neither

Marina nor Andy bothered wondering. They'd wondered politely the first time Susie delivered this monologue. This time, they just stared out over the Aegean and pursued their private contemplations.

Susie began to wind up into her customary maternal frenzy. 'He's bound to have forgotten Alice's Vitamin C and Frederick's ear drops. Oh God, and the houseplants! This is the weekend I feed them! They'll be yellow by the time I get home! Oh no! Feeding! You can bet he won't make the twins eat properly. I expect they'll all be at McDonald's now. I know what Ken's like when I'm not around. Doesn't give a thought to the twins' cholesterol levels. '

'For heaven's sake, Susie, they're only seven.'

'Yes, but they're *my* children! They'll have inherited my lazy metabolism. And it's never too early to start establishing good habits. I went to a course on child nutrition. It says children can be showing unhealthy cholesterol levels as young as five. But then I went to this talk the other day, I can't remember what it was supposed to be about, and this doctor said you have to careful not to make your children neurotic. Oh, it's a minefield. I just want to do the right thing. I don't want them to end up like me.'

Andy shuddered at the thought of twin Susies being sprung upon the adult world in the new millennium. He was exhausted by her presence. She never slowed down. She was constantly rewinding her past week and fast-forwarding the coming week. He imagined her family slumped in blissful relief without her. Not doing, exploring, fulfilling, evolving, just . . . being.

Marina exploded. 'Susie, if you don't pull yourself together, I'm going to put you on a plane back home tonight. I'm trying to be sympathetic but, really, this is hardly a tragedy we're talking about.'

'It may not be a tragedy to you!' Susie spluttered. 'How could you understand? You don't have children.'

Marina couldn't prevent herself from feeling hurt even though she knew why Susie was lashing out. She'd done it herself for years. Susie's weight gain had made her irascible. She turned her distress in any direction but inwards. And she was entitled to feel aggrieved. She *had* been hurt, very hurt.

Ken and the twins had gone away on a PTA camping weekend in the New Forest. Susie was due to go with them and she had spent a fortune on state-of-the-art camping equipment that would minimise the inconvenience of sleeping in a field. She wanted to do everything right and had approached the challenge the only way she knew how – masses of money and time squeezed out of her already-overpacked schedule.

She'd bought all the magazines in the 'Outdoor' section in W.H. Smiths. She then sat up late at night scanning the articles and ads until she could confidently produce a checklist of essentials and luxuries to cover every eventuality.

The sad truth was that she was doing all this so as not to let the twins down. She wanted to do things properly, to scramble for and maintain her position at the pinnacle of high-achieving motherhood. She couldn't help herself, it was her way. It was with this well-meaning intention bubbling around her carbonated brain that she attacked the gargantuan task of packing. And it was during a serene moment of self-satisfaction as another bag actually closed that she felt Alice and Frederick watching her.

'What is it?' she asked nervously. They'd been staring at her a lot lately and she was getting increasingly unnerved by it.

Alice had drawn the short straw and stood forward as spokeschild. 'Mummy, Freddie and I were wondering, you won't wear those trousers at camp, will you?'

Susie stopped ticking her list and looked from one twin to the other in confusion.

'What do you mean? What trousers?'

Alice wasn't sure why she was about to land in terrible trouble but she took a step backwards in anticipation of a violent reaction to her next words. 'Those pink trousers that Sylvia Roughton-Jones says make you look like Mr Blobby.'

She took one more step backwards as her mother rose up like a volcano, about to spew her anger over the hapless twin like red-hot lava. Alice decided to have a go at pacifying Susie, thereby demonstrating that she'd inherited her mother's skill for never quite getting it right, no matter how hard she tried.

'I don't think you look like Mr Blobby. And neither does Freddie. Mr Blobby's got spots all over and you've only got them on your face and your spots are red and Mr Blobby's are yellow and he hasn't got hair. And your hands aren't fat, only the rest of you is fat but all of Mr Blobby is fat . . . '

She didn't get any further. The reaction she'd feared didn't come. It was far, far worse. Her mummy started to cry. Alice and Frederick didn't know what to do. Mummies weren't meant to cry. 'Go and watch television or something!' Susie bellowed at them.

They ran out gratefully. That was the only good thing about fat Mummy. She let them watch television.

She couldn't go away with them. Not now that she had become a figure of fun among middle-class seven-year-olds throughout southwest London. In fact she vowed not to set foot in public again until she was back down to eight stone. But since she now weighed twelve stone, she was effectively committing herself to house arrest for six months. She hadn't given up on getting hold of some pills from David. The dreadful irony was that David wouldn't look at her while she was fat. So she would have to lose all her weight before she could seduce him into giving her his slimming pills. Ha ha, she thought mirthlessly.

So she was in Athens that weekend instead of Hampshire.

Sparkleeze were having a conference in Athens to analyse the results of the launch in the British market. Marina was thrilled to be flying out a couple of days early with Andy to enjoy the weekend before the meeting began on Monday. It reminded her of the pang of envy she'd felt on seeing Paul Jerome with her secretary in New York.

One of the many insights she'd gained during the turbulent months of change that followed was that she had not just been jealous of Eleanor for being with the man she wanted for herself. OK. That was a bit of a lie. She *was* jealous of Eleanor and Paul. But, more than that, she'd been jealous that Eleanor had found someone with whom she could share New York. That she could pick up the phone and any adventure would then be heightened with the companionship of someone special.

Oh no, I'm starting to think like my mother. But she was beginning to understand what her mother was implying in her fear of aloneness, even though she never put it into words you could embroider on a tapestry. Sitting on the aeroplane next to Andy, not holding hands, each reading their own book, a ring of togetherness allowing each to be separate within the circle, she felt utterly content.

So why did she invite Susie along? Well, she didn't. Not exactly. One minute, Susie was bursting into her flat, dressed in black, a flawless veneer of make-up only just camouflaging the distraught face below. Marina knew that something was wrong because Susie didn't have any carrier bags. She seemed to have effected the journey to Marina's flat without stopping off to buy anything for her eternally needy family. Something *must* be wrong.

Susie collapsed on the sofa and regurgitated a stream of consciousness that Marina couldn't follow. Something about Mr Blobby in the New Forest weighing twelve stone and having red spots.

The next minute, Marina was talking about her forthcoming weekend in Athens, mainly to try and take Susie's crazed mind off her distress. Then Susie started rummaging through her bag. She pulled out a supermarket loyalty card and started gabbling on about air miles.

'You could always have said no,' Andy suggested tightly when she explained that her friend would be joining them on their romantic weekend.

'I couldn't, sweetie. She was in such a state.' She recounted the sad story of skinny Susie who became fat Susie, an embarrassment to her children. She tried to make the story entertaining, saving the secret of her sauce recipe for the comedy climax. Andy didn't laugh. Anything to do with weight was a taboo subject between them, an issue too laden with recent, unresolved history. It reminded Andy of what a mean-minded cruel person he could be. But it also reminded him of how big and unattractive Marina once was.

He thought he loved her but he was aware that she was putting on weight. She was still slim and beautiful and she seemed to have stabilised recently, but he had to ask himself how he would feel if she returned to her original size. Marina never asked him. She knew that he would probably lie anyway. But she also believed that it was unfair to put Andy on the spot like that.

When she fell in love with Andy, it was with the funny, clever man who liked the things she liked. But he was still the man who had once treated her like a leper, undermined her existence at work and barely smothered his disgust at her appearance. If that aspect of his personality should surface again, would she still feel the same about him? So why should he be expected to feel the same way about her if the old insecure, neurotic, tormented being that lived deep down inside her decided to take over once more?

It wasn't just about fat. She knew that now. It never had been. It just made it easier to push people away, to make it difficult for them to get to know her, to like her. True, Andy had never taken the time to find out that fat Marina shared his taste in books but Marina had never considered trying to find out if boorish Andy shared her taste in music.

'So, whoop-di-doop! You'd still love Andy if he was shallow. Now ask the real question. And then answer it.'

Who said that? Marina couldn't remember the first time the voice spoke to her but the shock of hearing it still caused her to shiver. It couldn't have been God, because she felt sure she had buried this particular truth so deep that even He couldn't find it. Therefore it could only be her Self. And it wasn't going to give up until she confronted the question.

So she asked it. The Question. The one you're not allowed to ask. Marina, how would you feel about Andy if he started eating 8,000 calories a day, puffing up visibly day by day until he weighed twenty stone? I'd still love him, you say, he'd still be the same person deep down. No he wouldn't, the voice says. He'd have become a different person, one who overeats grotesquely, distorting his body into one that he knows society condemns as repulsive. He'd have changed himself, consciously or subconsciously, into one who looks and behaves differently. A *different* person.

And it led to more questions. How would you feel about having sex with him, that heaving mass that deposited waves of fat over your trim, lithe body, undulating and rubbing in sweaty irritation? It would be noisier, squelchier, different, surely, to the athletic tumblings that have given you so much pleasure. Put your hand on your heart and swear that it wouldn't matter. See, you can't! She couldn't.

Go on, spew out that old lie about being worried for his long-term health! She was just about to do that when the voice pre-empted her. What about that old chestnut about only wanting him to be happy?

Stop it, stop it, stop it!

There. She'd asked the question. The questions. She hadn't answered them because she didn't need to. I'm just like the rest of them, she thought sadly. Not only do I now look like the rest of them, I think like the rest of them. At least this self-knowledge enabled her to understand Andy's previous cruelty more acutely. However the blame was not evenly apportioned in this case. Andy's crime was a personal aggressive offence whereas Marina's was silent and judgemental. He was the greater transgressor which was why he felt even worse about evading the topic that was always hovering between them like an empty speech bubble.

He and Marina had been together for two months now and they were pretty inseparable. It was now common knowledge within the agency much to the delight of the gossip grapevine, who watched the relationship play itself out before them like a bizarre soap opera.

Nobody mentioned the Berlin Wall that stood before them, guarded assiduously on both sides. Marina and Andy themselves didn't mention it. They weren't expecting a decision on the pro-motion to the board for a few more weeks. But it was no longer as clear-cut as a few months earlier. Andy had brought in a num-ber of small accounts which, although they currently didn't match Marina's three million pound Sparkleeze coup, nonetheless had the long-term potential to exceed it.

His achievement was astonishing and the consequence of noth-ing but hard graft. Ironically, it was his growing love for Marina that had inspired his current commitment to diligence. He laughed to himself when he thought about the effect on his per-sonal development of this woman whom he'd once derided. He tried to forget that she was his rival. His ambition for promotion belonged to a different section of his life. Besides, he didn't want to think what would happen to their relationship when one of them was voted on to the board over the other. That was another day.

They worked easily together, sharing the Sparkleeze business comfortably between them. Marina of course carried the brunt of the responsibility, thus freeing up Andy's time to pursue new business. They alternated lunches and dinners with Paul Jerome, who was finding Marina and Andy's relationship hard to take.

'I just don't get it, Andy.'

'What don't you get?'

'You hated her before. I mean, really hated her. You said some terrible things about her.'

'I never hated her. I just didn't know her. And I may have said some things but that was just office politics. I didn't think you'd noticed. I think you even laughed a few times.'

I laughed so you wouldn't guess just how unfunny I found your callousness. Because I had feelings of my own for Marina.

He'd become adept at keeping his thoughts locked away. He'd watched Marina shrink in size and grow in loveliness before him, and felt unable to step in and claim her for himself as he wished.

He'd played the whole thing like a fool. He was a sensitive man and guessed how she was thinking. All these men who didn't want to know me when I was fat. Now they all swoon before me, the same 'me' I ever was, just with less flesh. Well, stuff them all. I'll find myself a man who loves me for me. That's what I'll do.

But how will you do that, Marina? he wanted to scream. Now that you're beautiful, how will you be able to tell if they love you or just your glittering facade? You can't. But here I am, Marina! I always saw beyond the exterior. I always meant to tell you but I didn't dare. So you'll have to take my word for it. Yes, I know I went out with Eleanor who was your physical opposite, but I did that because I was confused. It was straightforward, uncomplicated in a way that I knew it would never be with you.

It always amazed him that Marina never read his mind and guessed his feelings towards her. He telegraphed them to her every time he was in her presence. But she didn't seem to notice. And women expect men to read *their* minds, he thought huffily.

He was so jealous of Andy that he could scarcely bear to be in his presence for more than a couple of hours. She was too good for him, that was the truth. He consoled himself with the possibility that Andy might be her 'Eleanor', an easygoing buddy to see her through a transitional phase until a more substantial life-partner presented himself. Yes, that must be it, he thought.

'You're wondering what I see in him, aren't you?'

Paul almost choked on his wine. He was enjoying the evening with Marina and he'd been meticulous in his avoidance of any reference to Andy that might betray his jealousy. She was spot-on. That was what he had been thinking. He was sitting opposite this woman who far surpassed his own ideal of the woman he most wished to spend his life with. It galled him that he had been the only one to have spotted her potential and that his own indecision had meant that he missed his chance.

'I wasn't thinking that at all. Well, maybe a bit. You know I've always ... held you in the highest regard and I just want to see you happy. '

Marina was amused at his old-fashioned language. 'And you don't think Andy will make me happy?'

'Oh I've nothing against him as such. I think he's a great guy.'

'Just not good enough for me?'

Yes, yes, yes! 'No, no, no, not at all! Well, maybe a bit. You're laughing at me!'

'Sorry. But it *is* funny, you have to admit. I never thought the day would ever come when I would be regarded as someone who could be too good for anyone. I'd long resigned myself to the reality that I would always be, at best, a "have-to-do" woman.'

'What's a "have-to-do" woman?'

'Oh, you know. You've spent years going out with lots of women, always looking for Miss Perfect, refusing to compromise until you reach your own, personal end of the road, So you look at whoever you're with and you say, "Well, I guess you'll have to do". That was if I was lucky.'

Paul wanted to squeeze her until every inch of her felt safe and secure in his arms. But he didn't because theirs was a professional relationship and he'd lost the opportunity to turn it into something else.

'I just hope that Andy doesn't turn out to be your "have-to-do" man. You really do deserve better.'

Marina was flattered by the implication. She had long been asking herself if Paul found her attractive. He didn't send off any of the signals that she'd come to recognise over recent months. He'd been flirtatious with her since they first met and he couldn't possibly have fancied her then. She'd been looking for subtle alterations in the way he behaved towards her, little endearments, touches, suggestions, anything. But there were none.

Except for this new concern for her happiness and doubts over the role of Andy as saviour/prince. How was she supposed to interpret this other than as an expression of his own interest in her? She had so little faith in her own judgement that she didn't like to take such an assumption for granted. And anyway, even if Paul was attracted to her, she was committed to Andy. Sort of.

She wanted to flirt with this man. She still felt that physical tingle in his presence that she had experienced when they first met. She hadn't been able to shake off the sense that she was not worthy of him. It was odd because, although he wasn't any more handsome than Andy, or David Sandhurst for that matter, he nonetheless occupied a higher perch than his rivals, one that she could never reach no matter how far she spread her wings.

Paul had something that she had not noticed in other men. It was a quality that defied flowery, literary description. It was – she hated using the word as a positive attribute – niceness. He was nice. Decent. Good. Like many women, she had been brainwashed into believing that nice men were weak, boring, inconsequential. As her own self-esteem started to grow out of nothing, she was learning to value niceness, decency and goodness in men. But until that self-esteem reached an optimal level, she would continue to value it from a distance.

Not that Andy wasn't nice. It was just that his capacity for nastiness was always living inches beneath the surface, waiting for a sharp splinter of Marina's inadequacy to return and spear it back into being.

No, Paul was still too good for her and probably always would be.

Marina looked around the conference room and wondered which delegate Susie had slept with the night before. For this had been the object of her trip to Athens. Susie hadn't known that consciously at the time. Marina had known, however, because she'd come to a deeper understanding of her friend as Susie became more vulnerable and open as her weight increased. She could read her mind. Susie had decided that her only chance of escape from the prison of fat was, for her, pregnancy. Marina had watched Susie spending a fortune on pregnancy testing kits. With each failure, Susie had ached more acutely as that little dot refused to appear in the white window. Marina didn't know what was going on in Susie and Ken's bedroom – their friendship had always excluded such intimacies – but she knew that Susie was not prepared to wait for many more months. She was putting on more weight with every passing month.

So was this what Susie was thinking as she cashed in her air miles, Marina wondered? She would have denied it indignantly. She wasn't that sort of woman. But while Greece in October is a temperate, beautiful place, that had not really, *really* been the appeal of the trip.

No, it must surely have been the promise of a hotel full of predominately male delegates from all over the world. And in that mix of nations, Susie would surely find a number of men who a) find the larger woman infinitely more attractive than the smaller and b) will happily exchange bodily fluids without needing to exchange names, life histories or promises.

Marina was spot on in the analysis.

Susie would never have told Marina what she was thinking or planning. She was too ashamed. But her desperation was greater than her shame. Poor Ken was having trouble keeping up with his wife's demands. She hadn't become pregnant in the first two months of trying and Susie had become convinced that she wasn't trying hard enough. Ken was not even sold on the idea of having more children since Alice and Frederick were turning out to be more Addams Family than Brady Bunch.

He had no idea that Susie was motivated purely by the need to restart lactating and would happily give birth to a troll if it started that milk flow off again. And if Ken could not give her a child with the urgency required, she would go elsewhere to speed up the process.

Not that she was planning to be indiscriminate. She was going to have to avoid men who had skin more than a few shades darker than Ken's (although she was sorely tempted to abandon this rule when she saw the Portuguese contingent, she thought in a giggly moment, briefly recognising her freedom from family ties for the first time in years). No, she took this seriously. She wasn't mad, no sir. There was a plan to this that reassured her that she was not being reckless or irresponsible. Or mad.

If only she'd confided in Marina more openly, she might have learned that there was nothing unusual or wrong in feeling that an increased bodyweight had sent her crazy. In some cases, the psychosis can become complete. If only she'd known she wasn't alone in her fear, she might not have been driven to such extreme action.

Instead Susie remained focused on her guaranteed way out of this mess. She didn't have any qualms about her calculated plan to bring a child into the world solely to facilitate weight loss. Or using another man apart from Ken to speed up the process. Why should she? Ken wouldn't be any the wiser. He'd assume the child was his and love it accordingly. The lucky child would be born into an affluent family and, whether it was a boy or girl, would be loved and cared for by the most efficient, devoted, self-sacrificing mother in London. After all, this baby would be a saviour.

Susie did not think that this was trivialising the enormity of pro-creation. Lots of people had children nowadays to provide bone marrow for a sick sibling. Well, this baby would be saving the life of its sick mother.

Marina was pondering Susie's future when she heard her name being mentioned in Rick's introductory speech the following morning.

'... I'm sure Marina won't mind me mentioning, a mixture of ups and downs these past six months, in more ways than one.'

Everyone laughed enthusiastically at this reference to her new look, so different to the one these people first saw in New York six months earlier. As always, Marina hated the attention. She didn't like her appearance being described as a transformation. It was too loaded with memories of the person she once was. She wanted to put that one behind her and be known solely as the slim, dynamic, vibrant woman she now presented.

Rick continued, 'I know that Paul Jerome has appreciated her marvellous professionalism during a difficult time for Sparkleeze. As I'm sure everyone here has heard, we encountered a hiccup, or perhaps I should say a loud belch, during the Sparkleeze launch in the UK.' He raised his eyebrows in Andy's direction and smiled ironically. Only Andy, with his lifetime's knowledge of Rick, knew that the smile was not ironic. It was cold. As death.

Andy blushed furiously. He hadn't expected the Junction Jostle fiasco to pass unnoticed through the launch review but he had hoped that it would not be singled out quite so intrusively. Everyone was looking at him and not with the blatant admiration that had been directed at Marina. Envy shot through him like toothache and he quelled it before it could leave a visible trace on his face.

'Thanks to some great teamwork between our team at TNSW headed up by Marina and Paul's team at Sparkleeze, we managed to turn the negative into a positive. With skilled use of marketing and public relations, Sparkleeze achieved ninety-two per cent recognition among British adults within its first two weeks on the market. This far exceeded projections and demonstrated our combined ability to react to an unforeseen situation as a united force to be reckoned with.'

By that logic, Andy thought resentfully, all the success is due to *my* Junction Jostle. So how come I'm still the class dunce? He devoted a few pleasurable minutes to replaying countless injustices that Rick had imposed on him over the years. He played his favourite mental game of imagining that he'd been the one with the drive to get to the top while Rick had been the also-ran who might-have-been but never-quite-did. He was shocked out of his reverie by Rick's announcement.

'It gives me great pleasure to announce that, effective immediately, Marina Riesenthal has been appointed to the board of TNSW.'

Marina's first thought was for Andy. She glanced across at him and noticed that he appeared as shocked as she felt. I didn't know, she wanted to shout. It's as much a surprise to me as it is to you!

He was mouthing 'Congratulations' to her but she read the betrayal that underscored his insincerity. And now Rick was holding out his arm to Marina as if she were his queen.

She dragged herself out of her chair and walked to the front of the room. On the way, she passed Paul's chair. He jumped up and planted an over-affectionate kiss on her cheek. She was so taken aback that she turned her face and allowed the kiss to land on her lips. Like courting teenagers caught by their parents, they both pulled away and pretended it hadn't happened. But it had happened. And it had meant something. They both knew it. She tried to concentrate her thoughts on Andy, fighting back her disloyalty. But it was Paul's face that was smiling into her soul.

Andy saw the whole thing.

He seethed bitterly as personal anger and jealousy curdled his professional resentment into a soup of fury. And it got worse. Rick gathered Marina into the crook of his right arm like a bride. Then he kissed her too. On the lips like Paul. Yes, it was the sort of kiss that colleagues have been known to exchange at times like these, but that was not how Andy interpreted it. Marina was yet another prize that Rick was going to snatch from Andy's grasp.

Sure, Rick had always been faithful to Gillian. But he'd been acting very strangely of late. He'd been distracted, irritable and secretive. Whenever Andy walked into his office, Rick always seemed to be shoving something into a drawer with the guilty sideways glance of the wrongdoer. If it wasn't another woman, then he was certainly up to something. And he resented like hell the fact that he didn't confide in his best friend – his only friend.

This was what made him suspect that Marina was involved. Surely the only secret that he would need to keep from Andy would be anything that involved Andy's girlfriend?

Poor, poor Andy. It wasn't his fault that he misjudged this situation. His conclusions were quite logical. He was taking the facts as he knew them and drawing them into a dialectic certainty. How was he to know that his friendship with Rick was based entirely on emotional fraud?

That first time Andy burst into his office, Rick had made a split-second decision to conceal his intentions, his plans. He could have involved him, included him, but his discontent with his life was all-encompassing. When he ran away – for that was what his plans amounted to – he was going to run away from everything. That included Andy.

He'd been to Cornwall three times to look at various properties. He'd cashed in his share options and put the capital in a new bank account that he'd opened apart from his joint account with Gilly. He'd contacted the trustees who managed the trust fund left to him by his parents who died when he was fourteen. They'd arranged that the trust fund would be transferrred to Lorna and Sam. Gilly would be all right. She had money of her own.

He had one more surprise left. While it had already been decided that Marina would be appointed to the board, his own departure would mean that they needed a new MD. He'd sworn the board to secrecy, claiming that he was planning to move with his family out of London but wanted to keep the plans quiet until everything was definite. After a lot of heated discussion, he had persuaded the others that Andy would be the best man for the job, especially in the light of his extraordinary efforts in recent months.

But he couldn't tell Andy without revealing the whole story. Things could have been so different if only he'd opened up to his friend.

'How dare you!' Marina shouted at Andy as they dressed for dinner that night. 'Do you really think that I'm like some kind of temp who'll sleep with the MD to get a permanent job? Or that I'd sleep with Rick under any circumstances? He's married, for God's sake, happily married. You're always going on about his perfect marriage and how he's never even looked at another woman. And even if he wasn't, I don't even fancy him. Did you think of that? Or that, even if I did, I wouldn't do anything so stupid as to get involved with my boss?'

Andy snorted. 'Oh, I see. You'll sleep with me, a humble minion, because it won't damage your career but you hold back from throwing yourself at someone of Rick's exalted status. Well, hey, guess what? You're on the board now. So he's not really your boss any more. In fact, now *I* could be damaging *my* career sleeping with you. So maybe you ought to be fluttering your eyelashes a bit more towards the big man, after all.'

Marina pulled on her tights with such force that she stuck her hand through them. She ripped them off and threw them into the bin. 'Now look what you've made me do!' She snatched another pair from her drawer and tried again.

'Of course I made you do it. It couldn't have been your own fault because you, of course, are perfect.'

'Oh grow up, Andy! I'm not going to apologise again. I shouldn't have had to in the first place. I didn't know the board had made the decision and I certainly didn't have a clue that Rick was going to make that announcement. You know I'd have told you first.'

'Maybe. Maybe not. Perhaps you knew but you were too embarrassed to say.'

'Embarrassed about what?'

'About why you got the promotion and not me.'

Marina began to tense up. This was spiralling into dangerous territory. She should have ignored the allusion. But she couldn't.

'So tell me. Why did I get the promotion and not you? I presume it was nothing to do with my bringing in three million pounds' worth of Sparkleeze business. And your failure to match my achievement? Oh and your little marketing brainwave that nearly lost us the Sparkleeze business? And cost us a whole year's profits? It wouldn't be anything to do with that, would it?'

'Well, if that's what you want to think it is down to, you carry on dreaming. Just ask yourself this, Marina. You've been at TNSW for ten years. You've brought in new business before. Is it just coincidence that you get the promotion just when you happen to look like something out of *Baywatch*?'

Marina laughed. 'You think the board gave me the promotion because I'm not fat any more? Not such an embarrassment? I won't even give credence to that by being indignant. I was already up for the promotion before I lost my weight. If you *choose* to believe that my diet swung things my way, ignoring all the facts, then you carry on in your delusion.'

Andy couldn't think of a retort. He changed his shirt, not because he needed to but because it gave him extra time to think. He was being made to look like a fool and he was not going to give up this quarrel until he recovered some face. He decided to try another tack, an argument that he was surer of.

'And did you have to throw yourself at Paul as well? In front of me and everybody else?'

Marina shook her head, pitying him in his desperation. 'I don't believe this! You must think I'm slapper of the year. You forgot to mention that I smiled at the waiter when he put the coffee in front of me.'

'Don't be sarcastic. It doesn't suit you. You know exactly what I'm talking about. When Paul kissed you, you kissed him back. It meant something. Even I could see that. Everyone could see that.'

'Don't be ridiculous,' Marina replied weakly. Romantic deceit was not a skill she'd had much use for in the past and her inexperience showed. She didn't mean to lie. She simply didn't understand herself what the kiss meant.

Andy seized upon her soft reply as a sign of weakness, an acknowledgement that he'd been right. 'It's bad enough that my oldest friend should be after you. But my client as well! And I was beginning to think of him as a friend.'

'I see! So it's all about you! It would be all right if it was the coffee waiter then.'

Andy wasn't listening. He was further on down the track he'd started. 'It all becomes clear now. All those things he said about you and me.'

'What are you talking about?' Marina asked, trying not to sound too interested.

'All that stuff about my not having liked you before you ... you know.'

'You *can* say it. Before I lost weight. It wasn't syphilis. It can be spoken about without upsetting public sensibilities.'

'I know that. I just know that you don't like talking about it.'

'That's a joke and you know it! I've tried hundreds of times to talk to you about my problems. And my doubts about the drugs trial.'

That wasn't strictly true. She had given him a very edited version of her Oxymetabulin history, leaving out the bits about her collusion with David over Emma, the lies she went along with to get herself put back on the pills, her still-erratic eating tendencies. Oh, and the one-night stand with David. She'd left that bit out too. But she'd told him everything else.

212

'I always listened to you sympathetically,' Andy responded.

'Yes, you listened sympathetically and then changed the subject. You've always wanted to ignore the fact that I was once fat.'

'Is this what it's all about? Are you going to try and sleep with as many men as you can to prove that you're no longer dumpy, frumpy Marina the Michelin Man?'

The words slipped out before he could stop them. But they had always been there, skinny-dipping under the surface of his New Man fascia. No matter how many layers of niceness he added to his reality, those words were patiently biding their time, like the naughtiest children in the class putting up their hands to say a rude word in a quiet moment.

Marina was paralysed with pain. She was eleven all over again. And twelve and thirteen and every age up until thirty-one. As she grew older, the insults became more subtle. But her skin never became any thicker. As insults went, 'dumpy, frumpy Marina the Michelin Man' was in the eleven-year-old category of the barely literate playground bully. Maybe that's why it hurt so much. She hadn't even been deemed worthy of a witty epithet, something sophisticated thought up by the TNSW creative department.

'Marina, I'm so, so sorry. I didn't mean to say that.' He grabbed her arms gently, trying to hug here, sensing that if he didn't hold her very tight, he might never get the chance to hold her again.

She wriggled out of his embrace. 'Yes, you did. People don't say things they don't mean. The only thing you regret is the timing. You know that you've killed us. That I will never forgive you for what you've said. You're sorry for that. Nothing else.'

'Don't talk like this! It was a stupid, stupid thing to say and I'd give anything to take it back.'

'You can't take words back. Whenever I look at you, I'll always see those words hiding behind your eyes, a truth that you haven't been able to purge, probably can't purge.'

Andy was frantically trying to retrieve control. 'You've got it all wrong. I just said those things to hurt you because I was jealous of your promotion. There, I've admitted it. I'm a total bastard. But at least I'm being honest.'

Marina felt sorry for him. He had no idea what he was saying. 'Andy, I'm not stupid. I know you're jealous and I know that's why you lashed out. But it's the words. The words you chose. You didn't call me a bitch. Or a devious, conniving cow. You called me fat.'

'Well, perhaps I'm being pedantic but I actually said that you *weren't* fat.'

'You know exactly what I'm saying, Andy. Don't play word games with me. I'll always win. When you were pushed to the limit, when all your defences were down, it was my weight that you lashed out at. Past or present, it makes no difference. It would always be an issue between us, a weapon in your armoury. And it will always hurt me more than I think I can stand.' She took a deep breath before delivering words she'd never spoken before. 'I think we'd better call it a day, don't you?'

Andy went and looked out of the window. He saw the Parthenon standing in the distance like a view on a postcard. He was unmoved by its majesty. 'That's very clever, Marina. You see what you've done?'

'I'm not playing any more games, Andy. I just don't want to let you hurt me again. Or anyone for that matter. I'm not going to be a victim from now on. I don't deserve it.'

'No, that's not it at all. You don't even see it, do you? You're so blind to yourself.'

'Andy. You're mad at me. So say your piece and then maybe you'll feel better.'

Andy snorted unattractively. 'And then you'll move your things into Sordid Susie's room and you'll have one of your girly chats. How will it go, I wonder? Something like: "Oh, Susie! he's just like all the rest! So nasty about my weight. It's so unfair how it always comes down to my weight." And she'll tut and agree with you. But that's not what happened here at all, is it?'

'Isn't it?'

'No, Marina. Yes, I behaved like a boor and said some unforgivable things. But basically we're breaking up because of deeper things, a measure of incompatibility, different goals, different values. Your promotion over me said something fundamental about each of us.'

'What difference does this make?'

'To the final outcome? Nothing at all. But take a good look at yourself in all this, Marina. Look at how you brought it all back to your weight.'

'I didn't do anything of the sort. You were the one who brought it up!'

'Answer me one question, honestly. If you can. When Paul kissed you, when you kissed him back, were you wondering what might happen if only you weren't attached to me?'

'Of course I wasn't.'

They both knew that it was a lie.

'And can you say with true, *true* honesty that you weren't grateful for the get-out-of-jail-free card that I handed you a few minutes ago?'

Marina didn't answer at first. He was accusing her of using cunning that she didn't know she possessed. But the more she thought about it, the more she saw that he was right.

'So you're saying that it's all my fault? That I was just looking for an excuse to break up with you so that I can go and have an affair with my client?'

'I'm saying that you are only capable of dealing with conflict when it's related to your weight. When another issue arises, you twist it until you can force it back into the area you're familiar with. I think we're breaking up because you want to be with someone else. I started the argument. I said the bad things. But that's not why you're going. I just think you should face that.'

But she couldn't. Because he was right. She could only face matters that related to her weight. She was a baby in other areas. She needed time by herself to think this through. But there was no time because they were already late for dinner.

David looked at the urban destruction that was once his home. Everything in his flat that could not be sold had been smashed. Red paint had been sprayed across the carpets like blood. Perhaps that was the impression he was supposed to get. Next time it'll be your blood. He knew who had done it. And why.

His computer and all the peripherals had gone. He wasn't too worried about that. They belonged to Perrico and would be covered by Perrico insurance. But there were other things. Paperwork that outlined, crime by crime, his manipulation of the

Oxymetabulin trial figures. He'd hoped to find them shredded or mutilated but they were gone. The vandals must have thought they were worth taking a closer look at.

He threw up a quick prayer that they would be interpreted as meaningless figures and chucked away. He had enough problems. If those papers got out, he would be fired. His entire career would be over.

And then how would he pay the loan sharks? He felt sick, sick, sick.

Here I am, Lady Luck! Come and do your stuff, like you always do. Please.

Chapter Nineteen

'I'm so sorry,' she said for the fifth time. Or was it the fifteenth? She couldn't remember. She lurched from the bathroom to the bed, falling across the mattress without dignity.

'Don't worry about it,' Paul said for the fifth time, or the fifteenth. He sat next to her on the bed and stroked her face with a cool, damp flannel. She smelled of Estée Lauder's Private Collection and vomit. To him, the combination summed up the mix of her beauty and her fragility. She felt too ill to care what she smelled like.

The soothing touch on her forehead made her want to cry. Normally she'd restrain herself from such unabashed exhibitionism in company. But on this particular night she was paralytically drunk. So she cried. Paul scooped her up like a baby. The sudden motion made her nauseous again. 'Excuse me,' she said, her hand over her mouth. She rushed back to the bathroom where she sank to the floor, her head leaning on the wonderfully cold porcelain of the toilet basin.

With the very first drink, she should have realised that the night was going to end dramatically. Since coming off the Oxymetabulin, she had been watching her food and drink intake fanatically. She was trying to stick to no more than 1200 calories per day. That seemed to keep her weight stable at ten stone. It was higher than she wanted it to be but at least she could sustain the level.

As it was, she was always hungry, always deprived. That night, she'd barely eaten all day apart from a few sociable nibbles during the buffet lunch. The first glass of wine had slipped down as effortlessly as strawberry jelly at a children's party. It had located the pain and started the numbing process with the efficiency of a local anaesthetic.

As her pain became paralysed, however, so did her inhibitions. Grabbing another glass from a waiter, she cast her eye around the room professionally, wondering where she could have the most fun. She spotted Andy blatantly chatting up Eleanor. It should have made her laugh but she'd lost her sense of humour. 'Good,' she caught herself thinking. 'If he's talking to Eleanor, that means Paul isn't.'

But she wasn't ready for Paul yet. Her head was still reeling from Andy's comments and she needed to sort them out before she dealt with them. Or maybe she'd just have another drink. Yes, that was a better idea. It's always so much easier to think things through when you've had three drinks rather than just the two.

It was after the fourth that she finally spotted Paul and moved into his circle. He was delighted to see her and wasn't bothered by her inebriation. They'd shared some fairly heavy drinking sessions over the last year and it hadn't diminished his feelings for her. On the contrary, he had come to regard her as a good friend, someone he liked to spend his time with, notwithstanding his unspoken attraction to her. And everyone likes to get drunk with a good friend.

But Marina was climbing a spiral staircase to a level of drunkenness that goes beyond fun and into trouble. After the drama of 'Flower vs Star' in New York, the marketing dilemma this time was whether to have a tall, slim bottle or a short, fat bottle.

'Well, you've come to the right person to discuss that one!' Marina exclaimed brightly. 'Speaking as someone with insights into public perceptions of size, I would go for the tall, slim version every time. We can't have Sparkleeze held up to public ridicule, can we? You'd have all the other window cleaners jeering: "Oy, fatso! Been overdoing the old anionic surfactants, have we? You'll never pull an aerosol polish with a backside like that." In my opinion, a surface cleaner can never be too thin, too cheap or too floral.'

It was at this point that the other Sparkleeze delegates left Paul and Marina to conduct more earnest discussions in a more sober environment.

'Was it something I said?' Marina asked Paul.

'Maybe we should find a seat,' Paul replied, gently guiding her towards the dining room where he found a couple of adjoining places. Marina sank into her chair like a rag doll. She was feeling dizzy from the up and down movement and it took her a while to focus on the table. Before each setting sat a fat, glistening artichoke.

'Is there something wrong?' Paul asked, concerned by her intense stare. 'Don't you like artichokes? I can get the kitchen to bring something else, if it's a problem.'

But Marina was somewhere else. Sometime else. It was ten years earlier and her first day at TNSW. Rick and Andy had taken her out to lunch. It was her first proper job and this was her first time in a proper restaurant.

She didn't know what to do, what to order, what was right or wrong or expected. Anyone would feel awkward in such a situation but Marina was burdened by additional self-consciousness about her weight. She read the menu over and over again waiting for Rick and Andy to take the lead. Finally they ordered artichokes. 'I'll have the same,' she said confidently. She didn't know what an artichoke was.

The waiter brought along three of the strangest looking plants she'd ever seen. She thanked him politely when he placed it in front of her. Conversation had stopped. Nobody was making a move to eat. Having eliminated the ludicrous possibility that they were waiting for her to say grace, the horrible realisation crept over her that they were waiting for her to start.

But she didn't know what to do with this thing. She tried not to hyperventilate. I'm an intelligent woman. I will not let myself be brought to my knees by a vegetable. If that is what it is.

So she picked up her fork apprehensively and began playing with it, using it to punctuate points in a fatuous conversation that she began. Still, Andy and Rick did nothing. And she couldn't see where she might stick the fork anywhere. And ... could it be ... was that a glint of amusement in their eyes? Did they sense her discomfort? Surely not. That would be too mean.

Then she noticed the finger bowl and she fought to prevent the thought bubble with 'Eureka!' in bold type emerging from her head. She put the fork down as if to make it clear that she'd only been using it for effect.

She looked at the food as if it were for the first time. Then she looked at Rick and Andy's food, the way you do when you've ordered the same. Her master stroke was a jolly '*Bon appetit!*' and a raising of her wine glass. It was an invitation to the others to begin eating, the sort of genteel gesture Miss Manners herself might have recommended.

Rick and Andy ignored it. By now, Marina's nose was getting shiny and she was becoming more vivacious by the second. Her dining companions had their hands clasped firmly before them, elbows on the table. She knew at that point that they knew. She hated them for it.

But if this was an initiation test, a rite of passage that she would have to endure, then she'd go for it. Eventually, she started. She stroked the leaves, looking for a signal from either of them that she was doing the right thing. Nothing. Finally, she plucked a leaf from the stem, then pretended to have a coughing fit. It was only then that Rick took pity on her and began to eat his artichoke.

When Marina began her relationship with Andy she asked him if he remembered the occasion and the humiliation that they made her go through. He chuckled. 'I'd forgotten that. What a scream it was! You were so green. You have to admit, it was quite a laugh!'

She hadn't laughed when it happened, she didn't laugh when Andy replayed the scene and she wasn't laughing that night in Athens. She cried and cried and cried. She was becoming hysterical when Paul decided that she should be taken away from the scene of her distress.

She'd tried to explain to Paul why she was so upset but the story had collapsed in a mass of sobbing incoherence. He'd taken her to his room, mainly because she couldn't remember her own room number. There, she managed to sink into an armchair, the tiniest residue of decorum stopping her from throwing herself on to the bed. Paul had crouched beside her, stroking her arm, her hair, her forehead. He'd comforted his sisters like this on many occasions and knew exactly how much and how little to say.

'I'm so sorry,' Marina cried once more.

'Shh, now. It's all right. It doesn't matter.' Paul put his arms around her and felt Marina's tension dissolve under his hands.

'Why are you so nice?' she asked.

Paul laughed. 'I'm not really. Only when I've got a crying woman in my arms. The rest of the time, I'm just like all the other men – mean, macho and moody.'

'No you're not. You're always nice. That's the way you are.'

Paul drew in his breath in mock concern. 'Now I'm worried. I've read all those women's magazines in dentists' waiting rooms and I know that "nice" is an insult. Nowadays, women go for the "treat 'em mean, keep 'em keen" approach.'

Marina pulled herself up and then slumped down again in dizziness. 'Not me. I'm perfectly capable of inflicting pain upon myself. I've got a lifetime's experience of doing so. I don't need a man to add to the torment. No, I'm strictly a nice-guy sort of girl.'

'That's not how it looks to me. You forget, I know Andy quite well. I'm not saying that he's without charm but I wouldn't put him in the "nice guy" category.'

'There's more to him than you first see. I suppose that goes for all of us. Anyway, it doesn't matter any more. We've split up.'

Paul hid his reaction well. Not that Marina would have noticed if he'd turned cartwheels of delight. She was preoccupied with the sensation of bile rising up through her body like an erupting volcano. She tried to breathe deeply to stem the flow. It didn't work. It happened. All over Paul. His shirt, trousers, shoes. If she'd sat down and programmed a computer to design a flow of vomit that would cover the maximum area of Paul's clothes, it could not have come up with a more efficient design.

The temporary feeling of relief and wellbeing that followed the purge was immediately overtaken by a painful sense of horror. She'd been sick over the nicest man in the world. It was like being sick over Gary Lineker. And although she'd never dared admit to herself that she harboured fantasies of one day . . . , well, she could toss that dream out the window along with the 'happily-ever-after' one. She knew that decent, tolerant men existed. She'd watched Teresa chuck one away. She knew that Paul was one of the best. But all her common sense suggested to her that throwing up over him in a drunken stupor was not going to endear her to him if he *were* to consider her as a possible ...

'Are you OK?'

He thought she'd stopped breathing. She had. She was mourning the death of a possibility that she'd only just permitted herself to articulate in her heart. And she was so, so, tired. She wobbled to her feet and staggered over to the bed as steadily as she could. When she was in stretching distance of the mattress, she keeled over rigidly like a caber that had been mistossed.

'I'm absolutely fine. Really I am. I'm just a bit tired. I just need a little ...'

After Paul had checked that she was actually alive, he sat in the chair by the bed just watching her. He felt warm and happy and privileged to be able to see her like this. He loved being able to look after her, to cover her when she shivered, bathe her face when she became hot, hush her worries when she cried out. He loved watching her sleep, her mouth twitching as her dreams made her happy and sad in split-screen films with perfect internal logic but insane plotlines.

He changed his clothes while she was in a deep sleep. One of the advantages of coming from a large family is that there is no room for squeamishness. There was little privacy in Paul's home. Five children and two parents in a three-bedroomed flat. Paul was the middle child and decided early on that he was going to enjoy the benefits of being part of the eldest three as well as the youngest three.

All the children were encouraged to be good at something. One was academic, one was sporty, one was arty and one was good at making things. Paul was very good at getting on with people and good enough at everything else that he could pretty much have done anything he wanted in life.

The family thrived and protected itself by sharing a common love. They all loved musicals with an unreserved passion. Any spare money (of which there was little) was spent on balcony seats at West End shows. They begged and borrowed soundtracks which they taped on to scratch cassettes. Each child learned a musical instrument so that they could put on impromptu recitals. No matter how far each member grew away from his family base, whether in terms of social change or geographical distance, their core of commonality kept the family unit intact.

The sheer strangeness of the family alienated the children from their peers. Fortunately, they were churchgoers so they'd eventually managed to find friends who were not threatened by their wholesomeness. Most importantly this unusual upbringing gave them all the courage to be unique. It promised them a solid, permanent foundation of love and support that allowed them to be choosy about friends and partners. There was no need to be desperate in the search for love when love had always been a given in your life.

No, there was no desperation in his love for Marina. And yes, he was quite sure that his feelings for her amounted to a real love. The love had grown from an affection and an attraction, blossoming from the smallest seed into a climbing plant of partnership that could conceivably continue to grow unchecked for ever. And he was capable of objectivity when he analysed his emotions. He remembered his shame at feeling an attraction to Marina when she was overweight. He had forgiven himself, taking comfort in a pride that the shame had remained unspoken, been dealt with and then resolved.

For he had inwardly acknowledged his attraction to her long before she lost weight. He had managed to separate himself from society's insistence that there was something perverse, or even perverted, in expressing sexual interest in a fat woman. Yet he'd achieved this without having to separate Marina from her fat. He didn't buy the lie that the person and the body were different entities that should be judged accordingly. To him, the physical and the personal attractions were inextricably linked.

He loved the way Marina's humour shone through her eyes. He loved the way her mouth thinned when she was being ironic. He loved the way she waved her arms around when she was nervous. He loved the way she sat with her legs apart when she was wearing trousers. He loved the way she rested one hand on her stomach when she was eating. He loved the way she looked, the way she walked and talked, he loved it all.

And while he couldn't say that he loved her fat, especially realising that she didn't love it herself, he loved the vulnerability that it represented. Through his sisters, he had come to a rare comprehension of women's complex relationship with food. He'd watched them struggle with diets, seen their weight go up and down (albeit in less extreme arcs than Marina), and come to understand the damage that drives a woman to self-inflicted morbid obesity.

Marina was damaged, that was for sure. And now that her body was perfect, did that mean that the damage was healed? He doubted it, especially given the drunken coma into which she'd just dived. He wanted to heal her himself, with a promised lifetime of hugs and kisses and reassurances. And now that Andy was out of the way, maybe it was time for him to make his move.

'I think I'm going to be sick again,' Marina groaned as she lurched towards the bathroom, just in time.

Paul smoothed out the bedclothes to make them more comfortable for Marina. Yes, it's definitely time I made my move. Then he saw Marina crawl back into bed and pull the sheet over her in slow motion torment.

But not tonight, he thought. Once a nice guy, always a nice guy . . .

'I'm so sorry,' Susie said for the fifth time. Or was it the fifteenth? She couldn't remember. She lurched from the bathroom to the bed, falling across the mattress without dignity.

'Don't worry about it,' the man from Denmark (or was it Sweden?) muttered without sincerity. He wanted her to leave. He had himself sobered up rapidly when the wretched Englishwoman started throwing up in his hotel room. He hadn't been overly enthusiastic about inviting her back in the first place. But she'd been insistent and he'd been drunk and she'd been quite amusing and his wife was hundreds of miles away.

He hadn't even kissed her when she made her first hasty trip to the bathroom. The sound of a woman groaning into a toilet bowl is not the greatest inducement to sexual awakening. He didn't know Susie well enough to care about her. She was just a nuisance, an embarrassment. He wanted her out.

She wanted the same but she didn't feel capable of finding her way back to her room. She couldn't even remember her room number and she'd given Marina her door key after her row with Andy.

As she slumped across the Dane's bed, she cursed her own lack of self-control. Her last thought before she lapsed into a fitful, dehydrated sleep was of her ovulation testing kit that she'd left in London. By accident? She didn't know. Didn't want to think about it. She just wanted Ken.

Chapter Twenty

'I've been looking over this proposal and I'm not happy about it.'

David had anticipated a few doubts when he presented his interim report but he had hoped that his usual persuasive charm would be able to smooth over the glitches. David's confrontational style was hampered by his inability to accept that Geoff Perriam, Perrico's managing director, just didn't like him. Geoff would have fired David a few years earlier, disapproving of his cavalier approach to research. The trouble was, David was gifted. He thought laterally and frequently solved problems that were holding up long-term projects in other Perrico teams.

The Oxymetabulin discovery came only days before Geoff was going to deliver a final warning about sloppy lab procedures and dubious expenses claims. But Oxymetabulin was David's baby. That much could not be disputed. And there was every chance that it could catapult a small pharmaceutical concern into a global billion-dollar player. So they'd all played along with it, caught up in the excitement of media attention.

Geoff had kept a close watch on the progress of the research. He knew that corners had been cut but, as long as none of the strict guidelines were actually being breached, he had been prepared to sit back and let David run the game. But rumours had been drifting about for a few months. First of all, there was talk of one of the subjects being pregnant. He'd broached this with David, who'd been quick to quash the rumour with some broad observation about women and their cycles. Since then, Geoff had

taken to popping in to the lab unannounced, sitting in at occasional weigh-ins and asking for detailed updates at short notice.

Then there had been the break-in at David's flat. At any other
time, for any other employee, he would just have made sympathetic noises and processed the insurance company's claim forms.
But everything that happened around David seemed suspicious to
him. And the man himself? David Sandhurst was a troubled man.
There had been all that business with his bank. What on earth did
he need such an enormous overdraft for anyway?

Geoff had never got to know David well. He didn't want to.
But he could see that he was a man going down fast. Going
where? He had to find that out if he was going to protect Perrico's
interests.

So far, he'd been unable to find fault with David's methodol-
ogy. He'd been concerned at the general weight loss across both
the women receiving the Oxymetabulin and the placebo group,
but he'd accepted David's explanation about the unique psychological profile of women in a weight-related situation. David
assured him that, once the final statistics were correlated after the
post-medication stabilisation period, there should be a clear
demarcation between those on the pills and those on the
dummies.

But now, David was proposing a complete about-turn in the
protocol. Something about unexpected emotional withdrawal
side-effects that were affecting most of the women and therefore
could not be drug-related.

Geoff shrugged. 'You know the rules. If any triallist is displaying any side-effects, you take her off the medication immediately.'

'But I'd have to take them all off! And they're not real side-
effects. If they were real, then they would only be affecting the
women on the drug itself. No, this is a psychological response by
a group of women who have had a crutch taken away from them.
It's not a physiological issue so I don't see that there's any conflict
in slightly altering the protocol to accommodate this observation.'

He wanted to put all the women back on the medication and
gradually reduce the dosage to address this unforeseen problem.

'The thing is, David, you *should* have foreseen it.'

David spluttered indignantly. 'Well, I hardly think that's fair. In all other drugs trials we've conducted, this hasn't been an issue. In fact, the reaction to withdrawal is one of the distinguishing characteristics that we notice between the placebo group and those taking the actual drug. These women assured me that their eating habits were stable and that they had a healthy emotional relationship with their weight. How was I to know that the trial would trigger off this dependence and that they'd all get neurotic on me?'

Geoff saw the distaste that David felt for his guinea pigs and added one more item to his growing list of reasons for neither liking nor trusting the man. 'You brought the idea to us. You were convinced that this 5F organisation would answer all of the specific concerns we had about testing this drug. You researched the group and gave us your word that you had a group of women who were overweight but who ate normally. That was all we asked.'

'All you asked?' David exploded. 'Have you any idea how these women's minds work? Have you any idea how they eat? They're all bonkers, the lot of them! They sit in my room and sing me the 5F "mission statement". "Glad to be fat", "eat what we want, when we want", "come to terms with our lot", all that sort of nonsense. So I believe them. Well excuse me for not concluding that I was dealing with a group of pathological liars. Because that's what they turned out to be!

'As soon as they got a whiff of the possibility that I might turn them into normal, slim women, they chucked all their principles out the window and turned into a simpering gaggle of teenagers, all talking about how many calories are in a slice of cucumber.

'This was our best chance, our only chance of finding a group of women who would not skew the figures by deviating from pre-defined behaviour. No one could have predicted how they were going to react and that's why I think I'm justified in adapting the protocol to meet new circumstances.'

He sat back, satisfied that his argument had been impressively delivered. Geoff was looking more worried than ever.

'If what you are saying is true, then the whole trial has been a waste of time and all the results must be voided. It means that we're going to end up with a load of random weight loss and weight gain figures that we can't possibly attribute to

Oxymetabulin's efficacy. If we can't state categorically that the tri-allists' behaviour was consistent throughout the trial period, then all the outcomes will be meaningless.'

David could not contain his impatience. 'You haven't been listening! Their behaviour *was* consistent! With each other. It just wasn't consistent with their predicted behaviour.'

'Now I'm confused.'

'Geoff, don't worry. When the results are completed, it will all make sense. I can guarantee that we'll see that only the Oxymetabulin group registered a steady weight loss that stabilised after coming off the tablets to maintain an acceptable base weight.'

Geoff looked doubtful. 'How can you guarantee anything? You've just said that all the women are bonkers and are eating erratically. I don't understand how you can be so sure that we're going to end up with meaningful results that will stand up to scrutiny from the pharmaceutical community.'

David looked smug. 'Trust me on this one, Geoff. Just let me put the girls back on the pills for a couple more weeks and everything will be resolved.'

Geoff considered this for a few seconds. 'Leave it with me. I'll think it over and get back to you.'

David was not happy with this. 'But I need to know sooner rather than later.'

Geoff stood up and opened the door for David. 'As I said, I'll get back to you.'

David left reluctantly, unsure whether he had won over his boss. He was seriously worried. Everything depended on the trial completing and delivering his bonus. He'd managed to buy six weeks of leeway from his (legitimate) creditors by promising a repayment of all his arrears when his bonus came through. The only way he'd persuaded them to agree was by sending them all a (forged) letter from Geoff Perriam guaranteeing that the bonus would be paid.

He hadn't been too concerned at expanding his fraudulent enterprises like this. He'd had no choice. They were going to repossess his flat, send in the bailiffs, have him declared bankrupt. All he had to do was hang on with this trial, *make* it work. Then everything would work out the way he'd promised. So it wasn't really *wrong* to forge the letter. No, it was an improvisation born out of necessity.

After David had left, Geoff sat down and started reading through the trial paperwork, not omitting a single word. He was very, very unhappy about the conversation he'd just had. He had no intention of allowing David to put the women back on the medication. He wanted to know what made David so certain that the final results would justify the project and prove Oxymetabulin's value beyond any dispute.

To do this, he needed access to the database. He picked up the phone. 'Jane? It's Geoff Perriam here. I wonder if you could pop in to my office. I need your help in accessing some computer information.'

Rick sat in front of his office computer going through the file that he'd assiduously protected with two passwords. It was his Cornwall file. The only way he'd managed to preserve his sanity in recent months was by making practical plans for his new life. It stopped him from driving to the coast and diving into the ocean.

His work was almost complete. He'd found the perfect place right on the beach at Perranporth and he'd bought it with cash. It was a derelict shack but, in time and with a lot of work, he could make it into a shop or café with a flat attached. His body ached with longing for the physical demands that the renovation would demand of him. His mind screamed out to be emptied of all the pre-occupations that robbed him of grace. He dared not think of Gilly and the children. He knew that he was doing the right thing. If he didn't leave, soon, then he would surely die in one way or another.

They would understand that eventually.

Now all he had to do was tell Gilly that he was leaving. He picked up the phone and dialled his home number. It rang. And rang. And rang. Finally Gilly answered, out of breath from running from the back of the garden. Rick immediately hung up, ashamed of his weakness. His moment of courage passed as quickly as it had attacked. Soon, he thought, I'll tell her very soon.

Andy put the phone back down again. Damn! He had spent ages plucking up the courage to ring Rick and now he was engaged.

He hadn't been in to the office for a couple of weeks, claiming a nasty virus that he couldn't shake off. In fact, he had been attending interviews. Feeling betrayed, this had been the only option available to him after Athens.

He couldn't work at TNSW with Marina as a director over him. He didn't think he could work with Marina in any circumstances. Their break-up had hurt him badly. What was worse, he had this terrible suspicion that he might have driven her away; but he didn't dwell on it.

Andy was a survivor. And he was going to be forty in a few weeks. He'd wanted to speak to Rick before he made a big decision. But maybe it was fortuitous that Rick was busy. He might have tried to talk him out of going. And that was pointless.

He'd considered all the facts and made his decision.

Chapter Twenty-one

'I think I'm having a heart attack,' Marina puffed, slumped over the exercise bike like a sack of rice.

'That's a good sign. I think,' Teresa stammered, trembling from the exertion.

They both dragged themselves from the bikes on to the floor, where they lay limply before starting their abdominal exercises.

'Are you sure this is worth it?' Marina asked. Teresa was spurred into beginning her sit-ups at this hint of weakness. 'Of course it is. I've lost two pounds since last week. What about you?'

'I'm not sure. I've been too scared to weigh myself. I can't have put any weight on, I'm not eating more than 900 calories a day. But my clothes aren't getting any looser. And they're size fourteen! I've got this horrible feeling that the tablets might have messed up my metabolism or something. You know you read about women who lose weight too quickly and it makes their bodies go into starvation mode so that every crumb they eat gets stored as fat just in case there's a famine.'

'Rubbish! It's a scientific fact. If you eat fewer calories than you expend, then you lose weight.'

'Yes, but the whole Oxymetabulin project is based on the premise that you can crank up someone's metabolic rate, fool your body into thinking you're a thin person. So maybe, my body was too clever for that. "You can't fool me," my metabolic rate might be saying. "This lady's a fatty and that's how she's going to stay!" It might even slow down just to spite me for trying to mess around with it in the first place. Trust me to have a bloody-minded metabolism.'

Teresa stopped her sit-ups when she'd counted to a hundred. 'Now you're just being paranoid. I thought we'd worked this out. It's all in the mind. We're missing the pills and letting all the old bad habits slip back. All we have to do is pretend we're still taking them, trick our willpower into thinking we're still in control. And then we will be.'

Marina sighed. 'I'm not in control. I think I'm becoming an alcoholic.'

Teresa snorted. 'Don't be ridiculous! You've got drunk a few times. I'm drunk nearly every night and I don't feel like an alcoholic.'

'Yes, but you have good reason. Andy and I were only together for two months. It's hardly Greek tragedy. And it doesn't begin to compare with your situation.'

Teresa stopped breathing as she concentrated on eliminating pictures of her marriage from her memories. That didn't work so she did some more sit-ups. The pain that rippled through her stomach muscles effectively redirected her mind away from miserable thoughts. 'I'm OK. Rod and I actually manage to have civil conversations now. They're not very long. But if we manage three sentences without swearing or crying, we feel quite mature.'

'Do you miss him?'

Teresa speeded up the sit-ups to a damaging pace. 'No time. I'm busy, busy, busy. I go swimming as soon as I wake up, then work all morning, then aerobics at lunchtime, accounts in the afternoon, then gym in the evening. Home for a few glasses of wine then I collapse into bed.'

Marina ached for Teresa, hearing the loneliness that punctuated the gruelling schedule. 'You don't have to spend your evenings alone. In fact I'd quite appreciate the company myself some nights.'

Teresa was having trouble keeping up the manic pace she'd set herself. 'I'm too tired even to pick to pick up the phone after gym. That's why I suggested you meet me here. No, I'm putting my social life on hold while I sort out my weight once and for all. Then I'll start living again.'

'Teresa, will you stop doing that before you kill yourself!'

Teresa let her upper body drop to the floor. Neither of them spoke for a while. Teresa was trying to get her breath back and Marina was searching for the right thing to say. Then Teresa began to cry. Marina quickly put her arms around her and they hugged on the floor, oblivious to the men and women pumping around them. But since the exercisers were totally preoccupied with their reflections as they sweated themselves into different people, they didn't feel too self-conscious.

'What's up, Terry? It's OK, honestly, everything will be all right.'

'No, it won't. It'll never be all right. It's all over. I've spoiled everything. And now I've missed my chance.'

'What's happened? Tell me!'

Teresa twisted the wedding ring around her finger. It had been loose ever since she'd started losing weight but she hadn't had it adjusted. It would have involved taking the ring off. And then she'd have had to make the decision to put it back on again. By herself.

'She's pregnant.'

Marina's first thought was that she must be referring to Susie, who talked about nothing else apart from her ovulation. Then she thought of someone else. 'You don't mean . . . ?'

Teresa nodded miserably. 'Mary.' She could hardly say the name without spitting. 'Rod's bit on the side. The other woman. Mary, Mary, fatso fairy.'

While Marina understood why Teresa was so upset, she was still shocked by the epithet. She didn't challenge her. 'I'm so sorry, Teresa.' There was nothing else she could say. The whole subject area was taboo and always had been. Quite early in their friendship, Marina had asked Teresa why she didn't have any children.

'Oh, you know how it is. You're in IKEA and you're looking for a new sofa and you see one that is perfect. It's modern and comfortable and stylish – and it's white. So you have to make a decision, then and there.'

Marina thought back to Teresa's house with its beige carpets and white furniture and delicate glass and chinaware placed at toddler level throughout the interior. She had always wanted to ask which came first – the childlessness or the furnishing, but a solid piece of instinct stopped her from asking. She never mentioned the subject again.

But now Teresa was on the floor, sobbing before her. She had to say something. 'How did you find out?'

They'd been working together in the cramped office. It did not happen very often nowadays. Rod tried to arrange his sales calls around the times when he knew Teresa would be in the office. Similarly, Teresa did as much of the administration as she could at home. But she still had to man the phones when their secretary was away and today was such a day.

She'd been surprised to find him sitting in the office when she arrived. He was clearly waiting for her. She blessed her innate attention to grooming that forced her to make herself look her best even when she wasn't expecting to see anyone. She pulled in her stomach, conscious that she was heavier than when she'd paraded her negligée on that fateful day, three months earlier. Then she recalled his heated reaction and exhaled quickly. She'd finally accepted that this man was truly unmoved by the sight of a skinny woman. She even considered sticking her tummy out but she couldn't. Her faith in his taste didn't stretch that far.

'Oh, hello, Rod. I wasn't expecting to see you.' I love you. I want you back. Whoops, that nearly slipped out. Mustn't be too grabby.

'No. I thought I'd just pop in. For a chat.' You're looking much better. You've put on a bit of weight. Not much but enough to make you look at least healthy again. I still love you, you know, you stupid, stupid woman. Why can't you tell what I'm thinking? Oh what's the point? It's too late anyway.

'So what can I do for you?' God, I sound like the manageress of a shoe shop.

'There's something I need to tell you. Well, it's not exactly a case of needing to tell you, it's more that I feel I ought ...' I don't want to do this. It will kill her. She's already in so much pain and now I'm going to twist the knife.

'Just spit it out, then! Why do you have to make such a meal of everything?' What is he going to say? It's going to be bad, I know that. But how bad? I don't want to hear it, whatever it is but, if I have to, let's get it over with quickly.

'Mary's pregnant.' There, I've said it. I wish I hadn't. Oh no. She's going to faint.

'Oh.' Nothing. I feel nothing. Except raw, piercing pain tearing the sanity from me. I'm going to faint. I'm going to take that paper knife and plunge it into his heart, into his eyes, into my heart, my eyes.

'Is that all you've got to say?'

Teresa sprang to life. 'Oh, I'm so sorry. Congratulations! I'm so happy for you! When's the happy event? Perhaps you'd like to tell me everything. The moment of conception, for example. When was that? Where was it? In our bed?'

'Terry, don't. Don't do this.'

'Oh, I'm a naughty girl! Fancy me being so selfish, spoiling the happy moment for you. You must be thrilled. After all, you've always longed for children.' She put a finger to her cheek in mock-puzzlement. 'Oh, no, I must be thinking about someone else! Silly me! No, you're the one who *didn't* want to have children. Not ever. Not at any cost. No matter how strongly I wanted them.'

'It wasn't quite like that and you know it.'

Teresa was pacing ever faster around the room. 'What a dunce I am! It wasn't quite like that? Do tell me how it was! I must have misunderstood. I thought that when you said "I don't ever want to have children", it meant that you didn't ever want to have children. But this isn't the first time that I appear to have totally misinterpreted you. Please correct me.'

Rod tried to hold her arm, to bring her to a halt, to comfort her. It was the worst thing he could do.

'Don't touch me! You've touched her! You've given her a baby! All that talk about loving me for nineteen years and I fell for it! You made me blame myself, made me believe I'd destroyed our marriage just by going on a diet. And all the time, it was a lie. You didn't love me at all.'

'I did, Terry! You must believe me! I've always loved you! I still love you!'

'Just not enough to give me a baby!'

At this, Teresa's knees buckled and she slipped to the floor. Her skirt rode up around the tops of her legs and her hair fell from its sprayed elegance into ratty tails over her tear-streaked face. She didn't care what she looked like. There was nothing worth caring about any more. Rod sank down beside her and put his arms around her. She didn't have the strength to fight him off. She needed consolation, she needed a substantial physical presence to hold her together, keep her from falling apart.

Neither spoke. Both cried.

Eventually the tears ran out. The drama had played itself out and they were back in the office. They were two grown-ups, neither of whom had a terminal disease. They wanted life to be different. They wanted to be somewhere else but all the praying in the world was not going to transport them to a better place. They had to get through this if they going to get out of it.

'Are you OK?' It was Rod who broke the silence.

His voice jolted Teresa back to life. She smoothed her clothes and rushed across to her desk where she kept a mirror. She scrutinised her puffy face topped by a nest of straggled hair. 'Oh, what *do* I look like?'

Rod laughed despite his misery. 'If the house was on fire, you'd put some mascara on before you screamed for help! You never change!'

'That's where you're wrong. I have changed. I thought that was the problem. But it looks like *I* was wrong.'

Rod turned her so that she could see his eyes, see that he was speaking the truth. 'You *are* wrong about one thing. I always loved you. No matter what you looked like, fat or thin, I loved you. I still love you. It's your refusal to believe me that has killed our marriage, nothing else. Do you know what it's been like for me, being accused of not loving you day in, day out, for our whole life together?'

'You've made your point. Your choice of girlfriend is a very clear indicator of your preference in women. So I was wrong. But I've paid the price, haven't I? I end up with nothing and you end up with everything.'

'It doesn't have to be that way.'

Teresa felt a glimmer of hope sticking its head up and she

couldn't push it away. She didn't want to push it away. Come on in, make yourself at home. I haven't seen you for a while, she wanted to say to it. She'd had so little hope for so long.

'What do you mean?'

Rod donned his most encouraging expression. 'Well, look at you. You're feeling much more confident now that you've got your figure the way you've always wanted it to be. You're bound to meet someone else. You're such a lovely person. Any man would be proud to be with you.'

'Except you,' she couldn't stop herself from saying. This wasn't the way it was supposed to go. He was supposed to beg for forgiveness, tell her that he didn't love Mary, that he didn't want the baby, that he wanted Teresa to have his baby, that they could put all this behind them . . .

'It didn't work out between us,' he said, as kindly as he could. It wasn't kind enough.

'Perhaps you might have mentioned it a little sooner. In time to allow me to start a new life.' Her bitterness was squirting out like venom.

Rod tried to appease her, not wanting things to get nasty. 'I kept hoping that things would work out. I wanted you, us, to be happy. I tried everything but nothing I did was enough. *I* wasn't enough for *you*.'

'Well your timing is impeccable. Thank you. In case, you hadn't noticed, women of my age don't meet new men and have kids. They join rambling associations and start doing macramé.'

'Now you're being silly,' Rod pointed out gently. 'You're not old.'

'And how old is Mary?'

Rod didn't answer. They both knew that she was thirty.

Teresa spat the words out. 'Thirty and pregnant. Lucky, lucky her.' She was close to tears again.

'If it makes you feel any better, I don't want this baby. I never did. It was an accident.'

Teresa looked at him as if he were a child. 'Oh really? And don't you think that it's strange that you should have an accident with your new girlfriend and yet not one in nineteen years with me?'

238

'If you're accusing Mary of doing this deliberately, then you're wrong. She even said she'd understand if I didn't want anything to do with it.'

'You really are a fool, aren't you? Of course she said that. She knows that you're too nice to turn your back on your responsibilities. She's trapped you well and truly. Game, set and match to her! I should have done it myself.'

'Why didn't you?' Rod snapped back.

Teresa was stunned by the question. 'What the hell is that supposed to mean? Are you saying that I should have let myself get pregnant, even though you'd made it clear that you didn't want children?'

Rod turned away from her. 'I don't know what I'm saying. Maybe I just wanted you to make the decision. Maybe if you'd just presented me with the *fait accompli*, it would have relieved me of the huge commitment involved in making the decision in the first place. Maybe that was the only thing that held me back, the commitment.'

Teresa stared at him, her mouth wide open in shock. 'I don't believe I'm hearing this. I was supposed to ignore your very definite affirmation that we were not to have children, Do tell, how was I supposed to read your mind and guess that this what was what you wanted?'

Rod faced her, no love left in his eyes. 'Well, for nineteen years, you expected me to read my mind on every subject. I was expected to know exactly what to say to pacify your moods which went up and down without warning. Loving you wasn't enough. Being kind to you wasn't enough. Accepting you, supporting you wasn't enough. Well, now you know how it feels to be unjustly accused. Yes, I did expect you to read my mind and yes, that's unfair. Isn't life a bitch!'

Their marriage was over from that moment. They'd loved each other minutes earlier but they saw that their particular love had reached the finite border where it could only stagnate or self-destruct. They'd both believed that love could conquer all, that love was all it took. They now faced the truth that love could sometimes be no more than a pesky distraction, preventing a couple from acknowledging fundamental incompatibilities which couldn't be resolved while all the loving was going on. And when the loving took a breather, all the sludge rose to the surface for attention.

And some sludge can't be filtered away.

'When did this all happen?' By now, Marina and Teresa were in the juice bar having abandoned exercise for the day. (Although both were secretly resolved to continue the routine in the privacy of their homes later that evening.)

'Last week.'

'Oh Teresa, why didn't you tell me before? You've had to cope with this all by yourself. On top of everything else.'

The 'everything else' was, as always, a new stumbling block in the quest for easy weight loss. There were to be no more pills. The committee had decided against amending the testing protocol to allow the women to be eased off the pills more gradually. What made it so hard to accept was that David had assured all of them that the pills would be forthcoming. The women had responded in typical fashion.

In anticipation of a renewed attack on their escalating weight, they'd decided to permit themselves one final pre-diet, whoops, not supposed to use that word, splurge. (It was a splurge, not a binge, because binges are for dieters.) In the seventy-two hours leading up to the announcement that the trial was over and they would be required to present themselves at the clinic for one final weigh-in, the women put on an average of nine pounds each.

Marina was nominated by the others to break this news to David. He wasn't interested. What happened to the women was no longer relevant to the study (although it wouldn't be helpful from a media point of view if they all ended up as fat as before). Besides, he had worries of his own. The decision not to allow him to resume the trial came to him in a terse two-line memo from above. No explanations, just a veto. In addition, dull Jane from Computing was leaving frantic messages on his answering machine. He hadn't been able to get hold of her yet but he had a bad feeling about what she was going to say.

Whatever she had to say, he didn't want to hear it.

All he could do was focus on pulling the results together in a persuasive report that would settle any doubts his superiors had. It was coming along well. He'd had to adjust some of the figures to play down some of the more dramatic successes obtained by the placebo group. But that wasn't a problem. How could Perrico argue with the results? They'd seen the women for themselves. Geoff had met all of the women, marvelled at their remodelling. David had told many lies, but he didn't need to lie about the genuine, measurable efficacy of his invention.

Surely that alone would be enough to justify releasing his bonus. He needed that bonus. At once. For he was now not only paying the loan sharks an ever-increasing amount of interest on his original loan, he was being blackmailed.

He couldn't work out exactly which of the inarticulate hoodlums who owned him had ploughed through his papers and concluded that something screwy was going on. But one of them had. They'd got to know David Sandhurst very well. They only lent money to someone when they were sure of the payback. They knew about the Oxymetabulin trial and they knew about the conditional bonus.

And while they had no intention of revealing his 'discrepancies' at this point and thus wiping out the possibility of this man ever paying them back, they saw further potential for profit.

They didn't care how he got the extra money. They of all people knew that there was always money to be found if you were really desperate. He was to buy their silence until the bonus came through. Then maybe, just maybe, they'd settle for one big payment to have the matter concluded to both parties' satisfaction.

He knew that would never happen. They would bleed him dry, always holding the weapon of his career's destruction over him. But, right now, he couldn't think that far. Every day was a quicksand. Every night a blessed retreat. He had to sort things out one at a time. Then maybe all the other things would sort themselves out. Like they always used to for him. A long, long time ago.

His panic was tempered only by his bitterness towards the women who he felt had destroyed his trial with their deceits and neuroses. He wanted to kill them all. Instead, he intended to get in touch with the individual women who'd been taking the placebos. He looked forward to picturing their faces when they realised how easily they could be duped, their bodies and minds, into total behaviour modification. Won't some people feel stupid? he thought. It would be a small victory but at this point the only one open to him.

By this stage, he'd abandoned all of his ethical considerations. The trial had been made a mockery by those women. But they weren't going to destroy his work. He knew that Oxymetabulin would not get another chance. And he'd heard on the grapevine that two American drugs had just gone into test. No, this had to work out. He was going to make it work out.

He was so busy that he completely forgot about phoning Jane to see what she wanted.

Teresa, like Marina, was saddled with a slab of extra pounds and no chemical help to try and shift it. They also both had vacuums in their personal lives that were screaming out for food. Marina and Andy's split had not been amicable. Andy had learned that Marina spent the night in Paul's room and didn't believe her tale of spending it on the verge of death. Nor did he believe that Paul had spent the night cleaning up her sick and sleeping in an armchair. What was he, some kind of weirdo? Impossible.

He was enraged that she should have fallen straight into the arms of his rival, only hours after denying any attraction for him. He was even more enraged that Eleanor had rejected him that same night. She was the only attractive girl in TNSW who had refused to sleep with him and the fact that she'd also had a relationship with Paul Jerome made him crazy with jealousy.

The tensions at TNSW had settled down now that Marina had taken her place on the board. After some fierce negotiations, she'd arranged for all members of staff below director level to receive a modest Christmas bonus, paid for out of an additional Sparkleeze budget that she'd won during the Athens conference. It made her the hero of the hour. She was a little worried about Andy's continued absence but put it down to an attack of sour grapes. She knew he wasn't seriously ill because Paul had seen him the other day looking perfectly well and dashing out in his suit.

Marina was enjoying the new responsibilities at work. She had been too busy to give too much thought to that night with Paul.

Since joining the board (and in Andy's absence), one of her colleagues had taken over a lot of the day-to-day running of the account. By mutual agreement, they had temporarily stopped social contact.

She was still in touch with Paul. They spoke on the phone almost every day and Marina always popped her head round the door when he was in the building. But neither had quite known how to play the burgeoning relationship that had rooted on that night in Greece, four weeks earlier.

Marina had been mortified by her own behaviour. When she'd woken up the next morning in Paul's bed, fully dressed, her hair matted with vomit, she'd felt sick once more, this time with shame. His reassurance that he didn't think any the worse of her had made her feel even smaller. At least the presence of all her clothes confirmed that nothing untoward had happened. And anyway, she knew Paul well enough to know that he would not have taken advantage of a woman in a state of near-unconsciousness.

They parted awkwardly, Marina to return to Susie's room where she had decamped after the row with Andy. Susie, needless to say, wasn't there.

For the rest of the conference, she made sure that she was never alone in Paul's company. He gave her no reason to feel uncomfortable but she was finding his irreproachable decency just too hard to stomach in the light of her own plummeting self-esteem.

Which was why she and Teresa found themselves in the gym on Saturday night, with nobody waiting for them at home, nobody to stop them from eating all night, nobody to care if they were fat or thin. Even so, Marina knew that her own position was positively peachy by comparison to Teresa's.

'What will you do?'

'I don't really know. I've never made a single decision in my adult life that didn't involve Rod. I've never even thought of my own life as a separate entity. I've always been part of a double act. And it's forced me to think of other things.'

'Children?' Marina mentioned warily.

'Children. I've had some time to think over what Rod said. That's why I didn't tell you about it sooner. I needed to thrash the anger out of me so that I could pare the whole mess down to the realities.'

'And what are the realities?'

Teresa curled her lower lip pensively. 'That it was me who didn't want children. Rod was right. If I'd really wanted a baby, I could have done it. When you've been together with someone as long as I have with Rod, you do know what's what. You know the unspoken rules as well as the spoken ones. I knew that, if I got pregnant, he'd accept it. Deep down, I knew that. So I have to face the fact that I didn't do it because I didn't want to.'

'It's not too late, even if you do want to.'

Teresa shook her head. 'I know that. That's how I know it's not what I want. He has handled it badly. He should have confronted me. Or maybe I should have confronted him. I don't know when, though. I keep trying to think of a moment when I should have realised that our marriage was based on untruths. But I can't.'

'But it *is* over?' Marina asked.

'Oh yes. Very much so.'

And when Teresa said this, she didn't cry.

Soon, Rick thought, I'll tell her very soon. His head began to throb again. He couldn't take it any more.

Now, he thought, I'll tell her now. As if his gauntlet was being picked up by a merciless god, the front door opened and he heard the girlish running steps of Gilly as she rushed to find him.

'Rick, darling! I'm home. Where are you? I've got some fantastic news!'

'I'm in the study, Gilly. Come and see me. We've got to talk.'

Chapter Twenty-two

It was December when the women finally plucked up the courage to return to 5F. The Perrico guinea pigs had kept in touch with each other over the previous weeks. Their despair had been mounting quickly as they watched their weight creeping back on despite all their best efforts to try and control their food.

It was Marina who had pointed out the obvious. 'Don't you see? That is exactly what we're doing wrong. How many times did Gail explain it to us? She was so right. As soon as you start to try and control the food, it begins to control you. It's not something that *should* be controlled, like a bad habit.'

Everyone sighed as the old diatribe was churned out once more. 'We've heard it all before though, Marina. Nice words but what good do they do?' someone said on behalf of them all.

'Don't you remember what it was like? When you were part of 5F, fully buying into the philosophy, your weight remained stable. Isn't that true for all of us?' It was grudgingly agreed that this was true.

Marina went on. 'So, OK, we've put on some weight but we're, all of us, a lot slimmer than when we started the drugs trial. Maybe we can't get back down to that dream size, but perhaps we can halt the inevitable slide back to where we started.'

It made sense, they all saw that. If they could get back into the 5F frame of mind, they might be able to maintain the weight that they were currently carrying. It was better than nothing, surely.

And that was the proposition they planned to put to Gail when they entered the hall *en masse* that night. They'd chosen this particular meeting because it was one of 5F's open evenings. There would be no food served so a potential area of conflict would be avoided. Also there was no need to let Gail know in advance that they'd all be turning up. They didn't want to give her the opportunity to refuse them admission.

They'd been right to be wary of their reception. Gail would cheerfully have slung them out of the building but there was a large media presence there on this occasion. The results of the Oxymetabulin study were due to be released on 6th January and 5F had been very vocal in advance criticisms of the drug and its value.

Consequently, Gail had become something of a celebrity. Marina scrutinised her face and body, looking for any impact that such intense attention might have made upon her. There was none. Gail looked exactly as she always did. She seemed happy, as always, big but not bigger, full of words. Her smile drooped as she saw the posse of shrunken women lurking nervously by the door. The cameras followed her stare, aware that the upbeat mood of the room had just shifted into a lower gear.

Gail glided towards them, her anger tightly reined in. She moved up close to Marina so that her first words could not be heard by the journalists who were having difficulty keeping up with this dynamic woman.

'What are you doing here? You're not welcome, any of you.'

'Gail, we're here because we need to be here. We need your help. We now know that you've been right all along. There, I've said it. You were right and we were wrong. I'll even tell it to your media chums if you like.'

Gail turned her face so that she was looking at Marina from the corners of her eyes. 'I've heard this all before, remember? When you threw yourself on our mercy after your so-called crisis in New York? "Oh, Gail, it was so terrible! I couldn't binge, even though I wanted to! Only you can get my emotions back on track and help me deal with my conflict!" Do you remember?'

Marina did remember and cringed at the wickedly accurate mimicry. Gail hadn't finished. 'So we all helped you. We talked it out, sympathised, empathised, listened. By the end of the evening, you'd regained some semblance of peace of mind. Isn't that true?'

It was.

'So what did you do then? Took your little tablets, stepped up the exercise programme, dedicated yourself to becoming the Queen of the the Slimming Pill and never came back. We'd sorted out your problem, filled in the vast gap of raw emotional needs that drugs could not address and enabled you to carry on with Perrico's mission to change you. So now you've come back? And you expect us to stop what we're doing and help you stay a size fourteen? Well, try Weightwatchers!'

She walked away, not caring that she was being photographed from unflattering angles. Marina followed her. She grabbed Gail and made her listen.

'You didn't let me finish. The trial is over. We gave it a chance because we wanted it to work. Everything you said was true. The drugs didn't solve anything. The truth is, it all happened too fast. Everything. We all lost weight more quickly than our perceptions could absorb the new realities of our shrinking bodies. But our brains were as fat as ever. Hang on, fat girls, they would shout out, what's happening? Who do you think you are, skipping down the street in your tight jeans?'

Gail pounced on Marina, furious with her ignorance. 'How did a bright woman ever get to be so dumb? Something made you the size you were. And it wasn't a love of food, even if you think it was. You chose to be fat. Unconsciously. You needed to be fat. When you took those pills, you were dissolving a protective cloak that was there for a distinct reason. But the reason didn't go away. It still hasn't. Otherwise you wouldn't be here.

'It's like taking an aspirin when you're bleeding to death. You'll still die, it just won't hurt quite so much. But if you locate the source of the bleeding and stem the flow ...' She held up her arms. There was nothing more to be said.

Marina nodded. She knew all this. She didn't know why she'd chosen to be fat but she was finally ready to find out, to face her own reasons.

'Gail, I need your help. Please help me. I know you must hate me for having sold out so quickly, but I think you're the only person who can pull me out of this quicksand.'

Gail considered this plea. She gave in as she had before.

Because, unlike David and the drugs companies set to make a fortune out of unhappy fat women everywhere, she cared. 'I'm due to start speaking in a few minutes. You'd better grab seats, all of you, before they all get taken. As you can see, there's a full house tonight.'

When she stood up to speak to the audience of nearly 200 women, it was without notes, without hesitation. After her eloquent exposition of the 5F foundations and aims, she spoke more personally.

'I know what you're all thinking. Because I've thought all those thoughts myself. You're thinking that it all sounds great but that the day will never come when you're liberated from food's manacles. That you'll never be able to eat without ringing up the calorie count on your internal calculator that tuts when you go into four figures.

'And I know what you want. Because I've wanted all those things myself. You want to be thin.' There were some murmurs of dissent. 'No, don't fight it. It's what you want, or have wanted. But you have to ask yourself *why* you want to be thin. Is it for yourself? Does your own hand recoil in disgust when it touches your own flesh? I don't think so. You want to be thin because you've been told that you *should* want to be thin.

'Fat girls aren't chosen, are they? Not by the media, not by the netball captain, not by the blokes down the rugby club. Thin girls are. That's the message you hear when you look at yourself in the mirror. So why do you stay fat? For most of you, it's because you can't help yourself. Only you know why you continue in a lifestyle choice that makes you miserable but I have one theory that some of you might recognise.

'I think many of you exclude yourself from society because it's just too bloody tough and competitive out there. How many of you dropped out of sports as soon as you left school because you were no good at it?' Nods all round. 'Well, didn't any of you like sports? Of course you did! All kids like playing games, running around in the sun, being part of a team. So why did you stop? Because you always lost. You let yourself and your team down and were made to suffer as a consequence. No one likes a loser. No one likes *being* a loser.

'You all had an early taste of failing and you didn't like how it felt. So you set up insurance policies to make sure that didn't happen again. You wrote for yourselves an all-encompassing letter excusing you from life's games. Sorry, you said to all your team-mates, can't play today, too fat. Can't dance, too fat. Can't chase that job, too fat. Can't live, too fat.

'But you don't think that's fair, do you? Looking out the window, watching all the other kids playing, having fun. So what do you do? You don't dare go out and join in. You can't. They might laugh at you. They might call you names. So you wish. You wish that the world will change. Yes, that will be the best thing. I'll stay the same and everything else can change to suit my own reality.

'And then you hear about 5F. Hey, you say, that's it! That's the answer. They'll change things. They'll change me and, even if they don't, they might change the world. Either way, I can't lose.

'Well, that's not going to happen. I'm not going to change you. Only you can do that. Only you can face your demons, have the courage to face them and drive them out. It's nothing to do with food. It's all to do with why you *choose* food. And we're not going to change the world. Of course we're not. All these journalists you see, scribbling away. They're all going to rush back to their editors, write a politically correct lead feature about how fat is good and thin is bad. They'll do a one-off fashion feature with women in size sixteen leggings which they'll retouch to protect their readers' sensibilities. But when you walk down the street, those same readers will still pity you.

'No, we can't change the world. All we can do is draw the world's attention to its own cruelty. Help ourselves help each other. But the battle will always be a personal one. Each fat person must struggle with her own fears and each thin person must struggle with her own prejudice.'

Marina was breathless with insight. Gail seemed to be speaking directly to her. But when Marina looked around her, she saw from the rapt faces that she was probably not alone in feeling singled out. The realisation that her deepset unhappiness was not unique, not that complex, both disappointed and comforted her. It made her feel foolish for having spent a lifetime trying to unravel a fairly straightforward knot while she took solace that she was not alone in her foolishness.

As applause rang out, Marina recapped her life, fast-forwarding through the sequential humiliations and disappointments, dazzled by the simplicity of her own motivations. Then Gail asked for questions. As always, her powerful presence and formidable intellect intimidated the audience and nobody dared speak. But Marina was empowered by the window into her own weakness. She raised her hand. Gail acknowledged her apprehensively.

'Gail, I have a question. You obviously understand what makes many women choose to make themselves fat. I presume that you are including yourself in this group.' Gail gestured to indicate that this was the case. Marina went on. 'So how is it that this knowledge has not changed you? You're obviously not scared of life any more. Nobody could accuse you of being a mere observer. So why hasn't the weight dropped off you?'

Gail sighed, shaking her head. 'I'm so disappointed in you, Marina. After your journey, your *futile* journey to bypass your emotional core and hack off the very fat that was innocently obeying your own subconscious' instructions. You still think it's all to do with getting thin.'

Marina bristled. 'No I don't. My question's much simpler than that. All I'm asking is, if *you* no longer *need* to be fat, then why are you?'

Its directness made it sound more contentious than it actually was. It was a perfectly valid question and the audience all sat forward to hear the answer. Gail scanned the faces before her, looking for a single person who understood her position without having to hear it spelled out. She saw none and it confirmed her recently growing suspicion that her years of work with 5F had been for nothing.

'It's amazing that I should have to be explaining myself, especially to all of you who've been attending 5F for some time. It's also amazing that you women, who've devoted years of your lives to the vagaries of dieting, still haven't grasped the physiological maths of losing weight.

'I'm still fat because I refuse to go on a diet. No, I'm not afraid of the world any more. I've opened the door and joined all the clubs, all the teams. When they said they didn't want me, I forced my way in, made them accept me even if they didn't want me. I accepted myself. I *accept* myself. What would be the point of having gone through that agonising process if, at the end of it, I then have to reinvent myself? I might just as well have gone on a diet at the beginning, joined the club by obeying the rules of membership.'

Marina looked confused. Gail read her mind. 'Yes, Marina, what I'm saying is that I'm OK about my weight. I'm fat by choice. *By choice*. I don't mind being fat. I really, genuinely, truly look at myself in the mirror every day and reaffirm my decision to continue being that person. I can tell from your expression that you don't believe me.'

'I just find it difficult to believe that you could remain at your weight if you're not overeating.'

'Are you stupid? Of course I overeat! I eat whatever the hell I want. Because it doesn't matter what I eat. It only matters if your weight matters. And my weight doesn't matter. If I wanted to lose weight, I'd have to watch what I ate. That's how weight loss happens. You do know that, don't you?'

Her sarcasm made Marina blush. She remembered Emma's theory of Gail being afraid to be slim but she no longer believed that. She suddenly envied Gail with an intensity that both scared and inspired her. This was how she wanted to be. Unafraid of life. Unafraid of eating. Unafraid of her body. She felt like jumping up with her arms in the air, as if she had been touched by the Holy Spirit at an evangelist rally. She wanted to kiss Gail, stand by her side ...

Just as she debated this possibility with herself, the door opened at the back of the hall. She glanced round to see who had turned up just as the meeting was drawing to a close. From a distance, it was just another big woman, hunched to avoid attracting too much scrutiny. It was only as the woman drew nearer, looking for an empty seat, that Marina recognised her.

It was Emma.

An hour later Gail, Marina and Emma found themselves in the pub. It had taken a lot of persuasion to convince Gail to join them.

Marina suspected that it would have been even more difficult if Emma had lost as much weight as she'd clearly put on.

Emma was cheerful and animated. Overly so. Unconvincingly so. 'You're looking great, Marina. How much weight have you lost?'

Marina became aware of the skirt waistband cutting into her flesh. She pulled her ribcage up to allow the circulation to start up again. 'Oh, I don't know. I haven't weighed myself since the last session at Perrico. I've put on quite a bit since I came off the tablets. I probably weigh about eleven stone. Something like that.'

'Yes, I put on a bit after the programme as well.'

Gail and Marina exchanged glances. They both knew that she hadn't returned to Perrico since absenting herself from the programme months earlier. They were both concerned at the change in her appearance and behaviour. Marina left it to Gail to broach the subject. She knew her better and was less likely to say something that might traumatise Emma.

Gail was cautious and gentle. 'Where have you been all this time, Em? We were worried. *I* was worried. I thought you might be in trouble.'

Emma laughed with such force that they both jumped. 'Silly! There was nothing to worry about. I had a reaction to those pills, that's all. I lost a bit too much weight and it made me feel a bit unwell.'

Gail looked blank. 'So what did you do?'

'I went home.'

'What do you mean, home?'

Emma laughed again, a disturbing sound, resounding with lack of humour. 'Silly! The same as home means for anyone. Home. Mum and Dad and the others. They were really pleased to see me!'

She was drinking very quickly but it was hard to tell how it was affecting her since she she was already in an altered state. Marina didn't like to break Gail's confidence by revealing that she knew of Emma's difficult home life, so she decided to feign ignorance.

'That's nice. Are you close to them?'

Gail glared at her for pursuing this loaded subject but Marina ignored her. Something was very wrong with Emma and she'd sought them out. It was their duty to encourage her to open up, to offer themselves as sounding-boards for whatever was troubling her. Emma didn't seem to mind the question.

'Oh very! They're really proud of me. They don't actually understand what I do but I send them copies of everything I write and I go back and see them whenever I get the chance. I hadn't been home for a while so I decided to pay them a flying visit, let Mum look after me like when I was a little girl.'

Marina wanted to weep, wanted to hug this poor girl and beg her to drop the pretence. But she couldn't. 'That's nice. And did she look after you?' she asked, hopeful that her appalling parents might have been so moved by the sight of their pitifully thin daughter that they would nurse her with the love she so clearly sought. Emma laughed that laugh again. It was getting louder and shriller and scarier.

She held her arms up to show off her ample body. 'Well, what do you think! Of course she did! Some good old home cooking, that's all I needed. I'd forgotten how much I missed Mum's meals. We all sat around the table. It was just like old times! Of course, the others are all married now. Hey, guess what! I'm an auntie now. They'd forgotten to tell me, too busy I expect!'

Gail took Emma's hand gently. Emma pulled her hand away instantly, pretending she needed it to remove some non-existent lint from her jacket.

'I'm really pleased for you, Emma. You're looking well. How's the writing going? I haven't seen much of your stuff lately. Not in the usual places.'

'No, I've been concentrating on the Oxymetabulin story. No time for all the itsy-bitsy pieces. This is going to be my big break. I've even had the BBC on to me. Want to do a documentary. They were really excited when they heard I'd actually been one of the guinea pigs!'

Marina looked worried. 'Did you tell them that you dropped out of the project?'

Emma looked at her watch and started gathering her things together. 'Sorry? What did you say? Oh, yes. I'm sure I mentioned something along those lines. Anyway, that doesn't really matter. They only wanted one thing from me. It's not a big problem.

253

Quite funny really. And totally reasonable. I understood their point entirely.'

Gail had a sinking feeling in the bottom of her stomach. 'What was that?'

Emma smiled brightly. 'They just said they'd like me to lose some weight.'

She let this hang in the air between them, heavy with implications, as she rummaged in her handbag to occupy her shaking hands.

'Oh, Emma,' Gail said sadly.

'No, it's not a problem. I mean, ask Marina. She'll tell you how quickly it fell off me when I was on the trial. And I'm sure I was taking the placebo because it didn't feel as if I was taking real drugs. So it'll just take a few weeks. And you've got to see it from their point of view. It's a much more interesting story if I've lost weight. They've already asked for some photos of me at my biggest. Everyone loves all that before-and-after stuff.'

'But Emma, if you were on the placebo, then it will be more realistic to show that you didn't lose weight. That was the whole point of the research in the first place.' Marina was trying to be reasonable. But Emma was beyond the reach of reason.

'But I did lose weight. You saw me. I was slim, wasn't I? David said I'd lost more weight, more quickly than anyone else,' she added proudly. 'Anyway, I've made up my mind. No more of Mum's delicious gravy.' A picture pushed its way into Marina's imagination of a wicked woman spooning lard into an already unappetising gravy to punish her daughter for her individuality. 'No, I'm back on to a sensible eating and exercise plan. I'll just get down to eight stone or so and then I'll be fine. Nothing extreme. Don't worry, I won't do anything foolish.'

'So whose is it?' Marina asked Susie.

Susie looked shocked. She and Marina had never spoken about the weekend in Greece. 'It's Ken's of course. Nothing happened in Athens. In fact, it turns out I was already pregnant when I got there! Funny, eh? That must have been why I was acting so crazy!'

Marina bit her lip. Now all she needed was an explanation for every other crazy day of Susie's life and then the whole world would fall into place. She smothered her sarcasm and hugged Susie in congratulations. She was happy (and relieved) to see her friend happy again.

Ken was delighted with the pregnancy, mainly because Susie had been delighted. He'd put her horrendous moods down to the sudden broodiness for a baby that she couldn't satisfy fast enough. He'd come to terms with having a new baby. Anything was preferable to living with the screaming harridan that Susie had become.

Susie started rummaging through her usual mass of carrier bags that she dropped on the floor around her like a cloak. 'Look at this, Moo!'

The bags were full of maternity clothes. There was not a thing for Ken or the children. While Marina was pleased that Susie was spending time and money on herself, she wasn't sure that this was the healthiest manifestation of self-awareness.

Susie had quickly swapped the unflattering leggings and baggy tops that she'd been wearing to cover her expanding girth for designer maternity wear. The best thing about pregnancy was the tacit permission to be fat that it implied. She strutted about, her belly proudly pushed out even though she was only a couple of months into her pregnancy. She willed people to stop her on the street. 'My goodness, Susie,' she wanted them to say, 'haven't you put on weight?' She would laugh at their mistaken judgement. 'Oh yes,' she would say, 'I have put on weight, that's because I'm pregnant!' And they would apologise for their dreadful mistake and ooh and aah over her condition. Yes, the coming months were going to be good.

And at the end of it – breastfeeding!

'So, Moo, how are you? Is it my imagination or have you got news for me too?'

Marina was confused, then she realised what Susie was implying. She blushed in misery and anger. 'No, I'm not pregnant, if that's what you're suggesting.' She put her hands over her stomach defensively. It was larger than a couple of months earlier but not huge. 'I've put on a few pounds since the drugs trial was finished but then, so has nearly everyone else.'

Susie was appalled by her gaffe. 'God, I'm sorry! I didn't mean to …You must be devastated! All that you went through and then you end up back where you started. What sort of wonder drug is that? What was the point of it all?'

'Well, they now know the drug's limitations as well as its abilities. It's all part of the evaluation. And I don't regret taking part. I'm still a ton slimmer than I used to be. And I learned quite a lot from it. About myself. I've been fat and I've been thin. For the first time, I can make informed decisions about the person, the physical person, that I want to be, need to be. And I've learned a lot about other people too.'

'Are you talking about that Andy? There's a really bad side-effect they didn't predict! If you hadn't lost weight you'd never have had to go through that ordeal with the creep.'

Marina raised her eyebrows, amused at this perspective. 'It wasn't all bad, Susie. I had some of my happiest days with Andy. He just turned out to be a bit … muddled, that's all. Like the rest of us. Anyway, he wasn't the only creep.'

'What do you mean? Why, Moo Cow, you've been holding out on me! So who's the other creep?'

'David Sandhurst,' Marina confided with wicked pleasure. She couldn't have predicted the reaction that this would provoke. Susie went pale and began to breathe heavily.

'Are you all right, Susie? What is it? Is it the baby?'

'You slept with David?' Susie asked weakly. 'When did this happen?'

Marina shrugged. 'I don't really remember. It was only a one-off anyway.'

'When?' Susie asked quietly. She began tearing little holes in one of her carrier bags and tapping her toes to an unheard beat.

Marina flinched. She assumed that Susie's hormones were causing this strange behaviour. 'Well, let me see. I was in bed with him that time you phoned me at the crack of dawn, do you remember?'

Susie remembered. She'd spent that endless night watching the clock tick slowly by, tortured by her weight that was expanding even as she sat, tormented by the thought that David had dumped her for someone slimmer and more beautiful. Even in that mood of self-abuse, she couldn't have envisaged that the slimmer, more beautiful rival would be her best friend. Her best friend who just happened to be the dumpy, plain best friend that made the skinny, pretty other friend look even skinnier and prettier. That was the way it had always been with Susie and Marina. She'd never admitted it before but the truth had always been out there floating around, adding shape to their relationship.

While she was ashamed to admit that she felt this way, she reassured herself that most female friendships she knew of had similar iniquitous foundations unable to bear too much scrutiny. In every pairing, one would always be better in some ways than the other.

It didn't alter the warmth of her feelings for Marina. She hadn't consciously chosen a friend who was less attractive than herself? Had she? It was just how it had turned out. And even if she had, surely it didn't detract from the decades of partnership that each woman had invested in the other? Surely the balance must have been right for them to have survived all these years?

Anyway, right now, she felt the injured party. Marina was looking worried.

'Susie, say something! What's the matter?'

'I'll tell you what the matter is. David was *my* lover.'

She delivered the information flatly. There was no need to add a drum roll because the facts were dramatic enough. Marina ran this new information through the newly-developed mental computer that she'd set up to deal with the increasing number of unexpected discoveries coming her way almost daily.

She couldn't help herself. A broad, all-encompassing smile crept up her face until her eyes were almost closed with glee. The smile turned to laughter, a dirty laugh that hadn't been part of her communications repertoire a year earlier.

'I don't see what's so funny!' Susie exclaimed bitterly. 'He broke my heart. And I introduced you to him!'

Marina couldn't tell Susie what was so funny. She still hadn't learned to be cruel even though Susie probably could take a little emotional slap. She'd dished out enough to Marina over the years, whether intentionally or not. Marina was thrilled by the implied justice meted out to Susie in her one night of (not unenjoyable) sexual pleasure with Susie's ex-lover.

Since Susie and Marina had been ten, the imbalance in their friendship had been strictly defined and adhered to. Susie might have envied Marina her professional success but, then again, it was not a success she could attain for herself. In fact, Marina was stunned to learn that there was *anything* in her life that Susie could envy, but there it was. In every other area, however, in all personal ventures, Susie had held the balance of power.

For no matter how much angst Susie had been forced to endure with her husband, children and all her other social successes, Marina still saw her as the incarnation of the way a woman ought to be living her life.

In society's eyes, Susie had won the marathon while Marina had won the egg-and-spoon race.

But now, Marina had pushed Susie off the see-saw once and for all. They'd shared a lover. Even better, the lover in question had demonstrated a preference for Marina over Susie when it came to a direct choice. This laid a mantle of bonding over the women that could never be dislodged. Coupled with the weight problem that had been handed from Marina to Susie like the Olympic flame, it was going to redefine their relationship on equal terms. If it hadn't been for Susie's pregnancy, Marina doubted if they would survive the transition.

But Susie *was* pregnant and her perspective was warped. 'I forgive you, Moo. Even though you've behaved despicably!'

Marina was amused by her friend's madness. 'Thanks, Suse,' she said, hoping she sounded grateful.

It was easy to be generous. Love had that effect.

Chapter Twenty-three

'Do you mean, like a date?' She felt very brave asking the question. After all, if she was wrong, she was going to look really silly. And pushy.

Paul raised his eyebrows in despair. 'Of course I mean a date! What else could it mean?'

Marina blushed. He'd just turned up at her office unannounced. She couldn't have known that he'd spent days plucking up the courage to ask her out. He'd picked up the phone a dozen times. Even got as far as the TNSW building before losing his nerve and asking the taxi to turn around.

'Yes, but I thought you said that you only went to see musicals by yourself, or with your family?'

Paul wagged his finger at her, confident and elated now that she'd accepted his offer. 'I didn't say that. I said that I would rather go and see a musical by myself than see it with someone who didn't appreciate it. It would have to be someone special and there haven't been too many "someone specials" in my life.'

Now Marina knew what it was like to be fifteen and swept away in adolescent fantasy. This was what a crush felt like, warm and physical and distracting, but mellowed and given grown-up substance with the deep and real affection that had grown between them over the last eventful year. She was a 'someone special'. It was only a week until Christmas and, for the first Christmas ever, she was going to be celebrating it with a new status.

Perhaps he'd buy her one of those big cards that said 'Happy Christmas To Someone Special' that she saw happy people buying in newsagents. Perhaps he'd get her a proper present, one that had taken careful thought, the sort you buy for 'someone special'. Even more thrilling was the prospect of buying something for him. For surely, he would also be her 'someone special'?

'Are you crying?' He was crouched next to her chair as he had been that evening in Greece when she was so sick in his room. His question surprised her. She raised a finger to her face to see if she was indeed crying. His finger got there at the same moment and together they found the tear droplet that was rolling down her face, chubby with joy.

'I'm sorry,' she whispered, embarrassed by the display of emotion.

'As long as they're good tears and not sad ones,' Paul said, pulling out a hanky and wiping her cheek gently.

'They are good ones. I was thinking of Christmas.'

'What were you thinking?'

Marina looked at him. 'That I might dare to think it was going to be a happy one?'

Paul was thinking further into the future than Christmas. Much, much further. 'I can promise you it will be a happy one.'

And it was. TNSW effectively shut down for two weeks. Paul and Marina both took the whole period off and spent the entire holiday together apart from Christmas Day.

Even Christmas Day with her parents was a happier occasion than ever before. Nancy and Donald relaxed, both with Marina and with each other. There were still the silences but they were the normal family pauses where each member struggles to remember points of contact that bind relative strangers into a family unit.

'Nice Christmas,' Donald said after dinner. 'I really enjoyed it.' Both Marina and Nancy were blown away by his announcement. By Donald's reticent standards, this was a Shakespearean soliloquy.

Marina dared to say something real. 'That's the first Christmas dinner where there wasn't any nastiness. On anyone's side,' she added, anxious to include herself in the doling out of blame.

Nancy didn't take her eyes away from her knitting. 'Things are different now. Before, we didn't dare say or do anything that might draw attention to ... you know ... you were so sensitive. We were scared of upsetting you.'

Marina reflected on a lifetime of Christmasses and saw the truth in what Nancy was saying. She'd always dreaded Christmas dinner and had monitored every mouthful so that her mother would have no ammunition to fire at her in the traditional post-dinner fight. She would deprive herself, which would make her miserable and angry. Then she would interpret any silence as an accusation that she was obliged to counter.

'Don't look at me like that!' was a typical opening line. The ensuing exchanges varied but usually ended with Marina screaming, 'It's not my fault I'm fat!' and Nancy calmly replying, 'Well, whose fault is it then?'

This Christmas was a different place. But only one person in the cast had changed. Marina had to accept that most of the tensions of past years had been down to her. She had come to regard her family home as a sparring ring where she always had to get the first punch in. And the last. She thought carefully before continuing in the serious tone that her mother had introduced.

'You haven't mentioned that I've put on weight.'

At this, her father made moves to collect his gardening gloves and escape to the potting shed. 'Please don't go, Dad. I'm not going to cause a scene. I just want to clear the air.'

Donald sat down reluctantly. He switched the television on and, as a concession to Nancy's critical glare, turned the sound down and called up the subtitles so that he'd, hopefully, be left out of the conversation.

Nancy took a deep breath before answering. 'Obviously I noticed that you were a bit bigger than when we last saw you. But, to be honest, I was relieved. You were too thin before, you know it yourself. And as I told you before, I've come to accept that your weight is a personal issue, something that you've decided for yourself and that I must respect and not condemn.'

It was a long speech from Nancy and Marina was grateful. She rewarded her mother by confiding in her. 'I wasn't being honest when I saw you. About how I lost all the weight.' She told her parents about the Oxymetabulin trial. She left nothing out (apart from her fling with the scientist who discovered the drug – these were her parents, after all!). Donald even forgot that he was supposed to be watching the television and became engrossed in the tale of corruption and skulduggery. He was only disappointed that there was no sex in the story. That would have added the final element required to create a good mini-series.

Nancy became the protective, indignant mother, ready to go into battle to right the wrongs done to her daughter. 'Mum, forget it. It's all over now. I don't miss the pills any more. I don't even know if I was taking the real thing or the placebo so the whole thing could all have been in my mind. Anyway, I'm not bothered by it any more. I know I told you last year that I'd come to terms with my size and that I had bought into the 5F ethos but that was a lie.'

'I guessed that when I saw how much weight you lost in October.'

'But now, it's all changed. I really have sorted it all out in my head. I really *don't* have a problem with it any more.'

Nancy looked hard and then she saw it, the light that was shining from somewhere way below Marina's skin and the moderate layer of flesh that protected her from easy bruising.

'There's a man.' It was a statement, not a question, and Marina's look of surprise confirmed that she was right. She thrilled that she had divined a new dimension to her daughter's life. She felt like a mother, a proper mother, for the first time since Marina had been a small child.

Marina couldn't hold her news in any longer. 'Oh, Mum, he's wonderful! His name's Paul. You'll like him, I know you will. He's so ... nice. And he loves musicals. And you'll like him too, Dad! He's really keen on gardening. He's only got a patio but he really works at it.' She stopped. 'What?' she asked, wondering why her parents were regarding her so strangely.

'We've never seen you like this before,' Nancy said.

'Like what?'

It was Donald who found the word. 'Happy.'

'I bet you told them I was nice,' Paul grumbled.

Marina kissed his eyes. 'Of course I did. You have to say that to parents. It's compulsory. What was I supposed to say?'

Paul enveloped her in his arms and kissed her from her fingertips to her neck. 'That I was the most magnificent lover you had ever experienced. That I made you squirm with pleasure. That I'd

262

made love to you in every room in the house. That sort of thing.'

Marina closed her eyes and gave herself up to the sensations. She barely spent a waking minute without glorying in the joy that Paul had brought her. He'd taught her how to see her body as a medium of pleasure rather than an instrument of torture. She'd become completely uninhibited in lovemaking concluding that, if this remarkable man loved every inch of her body, then so did she.

She loved him, she knew that. She'd always wondered how you knew if you really loved someone. You'll just know, the old line goes. It's true! she wanted to shout out. You do just know. I know!

She lost other inhibitions as well. On Christmas Eve, they'd gone to the supermarket and spent nearly £100 on indulgent food. They'd bought everything that they fancied. While Marina grabbed cakes and ham and wildly expensive cherries, Paul snatched Belgian chocolates and smoked salmon and Coco Pops and champagne.

They didn't eat proper meals. They regarded the food as commas to the serious business of living and loving. It was in January that Marina looked back over the festive season and made a startling discovery: she'd put on weight. She'd eaten too much and she'd put on weight. Like normal people do at Christmas! And it didn't matter.

Paul asked her to marry him on New Year's Eve.

'What took you so long?' she replied.

'Happy New Year, darling!'

'Happy New Year, Gilly.'

Rick and Gilly clinked glasses. Rick's glass contained champagne at Gilly's insistence. Just because she couldn't drink, there was no reason why he shouldn't celebrate. Especially when they really had something to celebrate!

'I still can't get over the look on your face when I told you!' Gilly repeated delightedly for the hundredth time since she'd broken the news.

Rick smiled, hoping his facial muscles were working well for him. 'Well, it was quite a surprise.'

'I know! Imagine, all these years after Lorna! Those doctors didn't know what they were talking about. Never, indeed! It's so wonderful, isn't it? We've got so much more to offer this time around. I'll give up my studying so I can be a full-time mum. And you could even think about going part-time yourself. You've said yourself that occasionally the work gets on top of you. And it's not as if we need the money any more. You *are* happy, aren't you?'

'Course I am.' Rick pulled Gilly into his arms, held her tightly against his body so that she wouldn't see his eyes.

He replayed for the hundredth time the power it took for his finger to move the Cornwall folder from his computer screen into the computer dustbin. There had been no sense of pride for facing up to this new, unwanted responsibility. In his mind, there had been no choice, no decisions to make. Gilly had presented him with the next eighteen years of his new future. All he could do was accept it.

Well, there *were* other things he could do. He could run away anyway. But of course he couldn't. He wished he were the kind of man who didn't feel moral burdens when they placed themselves on his shoulders. But he wasn't.

He could kill himself. But that would be a melodramatic cliché that suggested that there was something unique, something special about his anguish that no living being could deal with. And, after a Christmas of introspection fuelled by alcohol, he now knew that his greatest tragedy was his ordinariness.

His malaise was merely the human condition. His pain, a growing pain from which none are spared. His crime, that of over-expectation. His punishment? Like the rest of us, he'd have to muddle through, settle for what he'd got, bury his dreams and count his blessings.

Did he feel the pain more sharply than others? How could he tell, he laughed to himself without humour. Perhaps the rest of the world were all burying their feelings as deep and effectively as he was. Perhaps that was the rule, the way everyone survived.

And he would survive. He was that sort of man. Although how he would last another eighteen days, let alone another eighteen years in this life, he had no idea.

Then he did have an idea. He still had the shack in Cornwall. It was paid for. It was real. It wasn't going anywhere. For the time being, neither was he. But he could carry on dreaming. And planning. And dreaming.

Andy spent New Year's Day packing. Once his appointment was confirmed, they'd wanted him to move quickly. As soon as he'd made up his mind, he found that he was actually happy with the prospect. Yes, he knew what they'd all say. He would have said the same himself, a few years earlier. Maybe even a few months earlier.

A big fish in a small pond.

But it was so obvious, so right, once the idea came to him. Go into a smaller agency. Put some money in. Go straight on to the board. Get involved. Be someone. Make your name. Make a new start. Reinvent yourself.

He'd resigned himself to the reality that he couldn't compete with Rick for ever. They were not the same people. They never had been. He would build a career elsewhere. Probably less glittering than Rick's. He would find someone to love and settle down with. Probably not as perfect as Gilly.

He wondered if Rick would miss him. If he would miss Rick. They'd promise to keep in touch, of course. But they wouldn't. Andy laughed at the idea of Rick leaving London to come and spend weekends with him. Rick was the urban king! He was allergic to fresh air, to quiet. No, he wouldn't be making the journey to Andy's new home.

That day, Andy consciously let go of his envy and found himself breathless from the subsequent gale of liberation that blew through his soul.

The next day he was moving to take up his directorship of a small but ambitious advertising agency. In Truro.

Truro, Cornwall.

Chapter Twenty-four

Funerals are never happy occasions but Emma's funeral was particularly laden with pathos as the revelations unravelled.

Marina, Teresa and Gail sat together. There were some other 5F members there as well which made the turn-out a little more substantial. A couple of magazine editors had shown up but, all in all, it was a sad reflection on a successful, professional young woman's life that there were fewer than twenty people who mourned her passing.

Perhaps it was the suicide aspect that put people off. Death is supposed to choose you, not the other way around. And while Emma's reliable method of suicide (pills and slashed wrists in a rented bedsit over Christmas) was most definitely not a cry for help, there was perhaps an unspoken feeling that the whole incident was rather attention-seeking and should be ignored, like an infant's bad behaviour.

As at most funerals, no one appeared to know the social protocols. It seemed inappropriate to initiate social chit-chat with complete strangers who could be mad with grief at losing a member of the family. Fortunately, Emma's family were not bothered by protocol of any kind.

Both parents were there along with four others who were obviously the siblings. They all looked uncomfortable in suits and dresses that had clearly been borrowed from people who were all a good six inches shorter than them. The effort they'd made was superficial. It was as if they'd dragged themselves out of bed after a late night partying, pulled on the alien clothes, seen how ridiculous they'd looked and not bothered taking the grooming process any further.

They looked exactly as Emma had described them to Gail. But then again, she'd been a writer, a good writer, Gail recalled sadly. She knew how to communicate. So why couldn't she communicate when she really needed to? She was overwhelmed by the image of her friend dying alone, slowly, slowly, while the rest of the world pulled crackers and laughed at bad jokes and watched *Only Fools And Horses*. For an insane moment, she wondered if Emma had had anything to eat first.

It was after the service that Emma's parents introduced themselves to their daughter's friends. They extended their hands cheerfully as if they were were sealing the sale of a used car. 'Jack and Ruby Lamming. So, were you in the magazine business with our Em?'

For a second, the women wondered who these people were. It took a while to work out that Emma must have changed her name to Lamington. More reinvention, they thought wryly. Gail took control, as was her habit.

'I'm Gail Bathurst. And this is Marina and Teresa. We were all ... good friends of Emma. We're so sorry for your loss.'

Jack Lamming shook her hand warmly. 'Thanks, love. But to be honest, we're none of us too surprised how it all turned out. She was always a strange one. We couldn't make head nor tail of her. Coming for a drink?'

And so with minimal social graces, the funeral breakfast organised itself at the nearest pub. Marina told Teresa to go on ahead, that she would join them later.

She wasn't sure why she wanted to stay at the church a little longer. Or why she wanted to be by herself. It wasn't as if she believed in anything in particular. And she felt that it would be hypocritical to pray. What would she pray for? It was too late to pray for Emma, and the rest of them would survive. Was it permitted to pray for a life better than just survival?

After ten minutes, she left. She never told anyone about her experience in church. Nothing to tell really. No vision. No divine intervention. Just the miraculous awareness that she'd allowed herself the possibility of something bigger, more meaningful, more purposeful. She'd allowed herself to consider the possibility that there was hope, even salvation, for them all.

While it would be a long time before she allowed herself to explore an expression of faith with any sense of commitment, that day she felt that a door had been opened ever so slightly. And it was the first feeling of peace that she'd ever known in her life.

The Lammings held back at the pub door to allow the women to go in first. Teresa had thanked Jack warmly, always keen to encourage good manners. It was only when he shouted after her, 'Mine's a pint of bitter and a whisky chaser, love, and the wife and kids will all have a pint of lager!' that she realised he'd held back so that he wouldn't have to buy a round.

'He's not even going to put his hand in his pocket for his own daughter's funeral,' Teresa hissed in a stage whisper as Marina came up beside her.

'Ssh! He'll hear you.'

'I don't care if he does. It's disgraceful!'

'Terry, look at them. They probably haven't got a penny between them. And we can afford it.'

'*You* can maybe. I've got to start watching my money. Rod's dissolving our partnership. He's asking me to buy him out so that he can buy a house for himself, the Virgin Mary and the future heir.'

Marina stared at her friend in shock, something she'd done too frequently in the short time that she'd known her. 'Oh, I'm sorry, Terry. It never ends, does it? What are you going to do?'

Teresa downed her drink in one and ordered an instant replacement from the barman. 'Get a bank loan, take on a new salesman, make the business work, survive, that sort of thing.'

Marina had run out of platitudes. She squeezed Teresa's hand and muttered something indistinct and consoling. Teresa brushed her off affectionately. 'Thanks and all that but today is about Emma. At least I'm alive.'

They raised their glasses to Emma, wishing her peace and dignity in death, before returning to her family who were getting impatient. It was an expensive afternoon. Marina ended up handing her credit card to the pub manager and allowing a hefty tab to tot up.

Conversation was strained until the drink loosened everyone's tension. It was Gail who uncovered the saddest truth of all. In the absence of anything more meaningful to say, she brought up Emma's last trip home.

'At least you got to spend time with her shortly before she died. That must be a great comfort to you.'

Jack and Ruby exchanged baffled looks. 'I don't know what you're talking about. We hadn't seen her for, what, five years. She was always sending us stuff, presents, things she'd written, not that we understood any of that but she never came to see us. We were too beneath her, you see.' The rest of the family mumbled agreement. It had evidently been a regular source of disgruntled discussion in their cosy home circle.

Gail, Marina and Teresa sat in silence as they digested this fact. It left them with a question to which they would never find the answer: where had Emma spent those weeks when she'd claimed to be at home, enjoying *Little House On The Prairie* hospitality? Wherever she'd been, she must have spent all her time eating. For she had put on an enormous amount of weight. They also learned from her magazine contacts that she hadn't been doing any work during this time either. She'd missed some deadlines and had effectively been written off in the competitive world of freelancing where unreliability could not be tolerated.

They sat there thinking of everything she'd said during that last evening when she'd turned up at the 5F meeting. All the clues they'd missed. It must have been her last attempt at getting help. Or support. Or anything. Whatever it was she'd wanted or needed from her friends, they had failed tragically. It was a curse that they would never escape and they all resented Emma slightly for leaving them a bequest of everlasting guilt.

She'd left no letter. This was a sign of utter and total despair. She had no point to make, no message to leave. She was separating herself absolutely from life and everything connected with it. She had just made a decision to cease being. She couldn't be bothered to tie up any loose ends. There was only one end that concerned her. Her own.

David Sandhurst read about Emma's suicide in a newspaper as he flew across the Atlantic on 3rd January. Stupid cow, he thought. He wanted to pity her, to feel human. But he couldn't. He only had enough pity to spare for himself. And he was applying that by the bucket-load.

At least they can't blame me for that, he mused. She wasn't even taking the Oxymetabulin. She didn't need it. She was so crazy that her body was probably capable of producing mind-altering substances all by itself. Not that anybody would know. He'd deleted all the research data before leaving the country.

There was always the possibility that his blackmailing loan sharks would try and do something with his stolen paperwork. But that was pointless now. His career was over. The trial was discredited. There was nothing more to gain from this sorry situation.

He'd had to work fast. Jane had finally tracked him down at home on New Year's Day. It had been the first year that he'd spent New Year's Eve alone. He had no social life by this time. Every minute of his life was spent trying to find money, pay money back, dodge those trying to collect money from him. It was that time, the nick of time. Time for the miracle. Because that was what he needed now.

In forty-eight hours, the loan sharks would be coming round for their money. They hadn't actually said 'or else' but that was what they meant. By then, his bonus had to be in the bank. It had to be, he couldn't contemplate an alternative scenario. A couple of days later, the deluge of letters and calls from all his other creditors would begin, swiftly followed by court orders.

All he could do was wait. There was nothing more he could do with the Oxymetabulin data. The report was complete and submitted. He'd done his best and could only hope that it was enough to pass Perrico's definition of 'successful conclusion'.

Did he really think, at that point, that there was any chance of this happening? Yes, he did. He had to. It was his last, his only hope. And, hey, he was born lucky, wasn't he?

So when the phone rang, he'd answered with a smidgen of

optimism. Maybe this would be his long-overdue lucky break.

'You bastard,' the voice opened with.

This didn't help him to pinpoint the caller's identity. Most of the women he'd known would address him so if they were ever to make contact with him again. He fished for further clues. 'Happy New Year to you too! What can I do for you?'

The woman's voice grunted. 'It's really more a case of what I can do for you. And it's not much but it's still more than you deserve. Geoff Perriam is on to you. I almost lost my job over you!'

Jane. In a few sentences, she'd informed him that his career was over. Bitch. 'What's happened?'

'What do you think? He got me to access that file you were so interested in. He spotted that you'd been regularly logging into the research file from which you were *specifically* excluded! You didn't mention that to me, I recall.'

'What exactly does he know?' David was beginning to lose his cool.

'I told you. Everything!' Jane shrieked. 'He knows you've changed figures. He knows you made the changes from your own flat. You can't deny it. At the moment, he's trying to work out if you've broken the law. But whatever happens, you are in big, big trouble. And I'm bloody glad. Thanks for nothing. Happy New Year!' At that she slammed the phone down.

All over. It was all over. The nick of time had just gone. Lady Luck had found someone else's life to build up and then ruin. There would be no bonus. No nothing. No way out.

He'd quickly assessed his life, his priorities and commitments. It didn't take long. On the minus side were his debts. They were unmanageable, dangerously so in the case of the loan sharks.

On the positive side, the only possession he valued was the formula for Oxymetabulin. He was still convinced that it was going to make him a fortune. Some day. Somewhere. The pills worked. Why couldn't the world see that? He'd invented something that would bring happiness to millions and bureaucracy was conspiring to prevent him from taking it to a global marketplace.

So stuff them all. He'd take his ball and go and play in another playground. He'd leave them nothing. He'd learn from his mistakes and next time, he'd *make* the research work for him. The second time around, he'd be armed with knowledge that he didn't have before. He now had the firm conviction that there was no such thing as a woman who could control her relationship with food. If such a woman did exist, then she'd have no use for Oxymetabulin and would, therefore, be a poor subject for testing.

But he'd find a way of making this project succeed and he wouldn't get caught again. He'd already invented the name under which he was going to reinvent himself in South America – David Thynne. Yes, he thought, the women will like that. They're all superstitious, the lot of them.

He would start up again. Maybe with his own laboratory this time. He could borrow money, just to get himself started.

Before he'd left, he'd carried out one final little job, just to satisfy a whim. Those women had wrecked his career with their crazy eating habits. He wanted them to know how stupid they were. So he sent a short note to all the women who'd been taking placebos throughout the research. He didn't stop to think that he might actually be giving them a terrific present, the gift of confidence in their ability to change their own body when they'd thought they were too weak to do it without medical assistance.

It was 4th January when Marina finally returned to her flat. She'd more or less moved in with Paul and was going home to pick up a load of clothes and personal stuff to take back to his house. She picked up the mail which consisted mainly of New Year's greetings cards from people who had forgotten to send Christmas cards and had then been mortified to receive Marina's cards at the last moment.

She resolved to open them with Paul later and share a good laugh as they imagined the Christmas Eve fights: 'I thought you'd sent her one!' 'She's *your* friend, not mine!' 'Well, you'll have to drive by and put a card through her letter box.' 'You can't do that! She'll know that it was an afterthought.' 'Well stick a stamp on it and smudge some Biro over it so it'll look like a postmark.' Many sherries would be downed in despair before the last resort was faced and someone was dispatched down the road to buy the Happy New Year From Your Friend! card.

Still chuckling with anticipation, she spotted a flimsy envelope in the pile. At first she thought it was empty but when she opened it, she saw a post-it note folded inside. She unfolded it. Across the top was printed : FROM THE DESK OF DAVID SANDHURST and across the bottom seven words were scrawled.

You were taking the dummy, you dummy!

It was twenty minutes later when she realised that she'd just been sitting on the floor, staring at the note. Seven words that changed her life. That changed her. She was a different person *again*. She was someone who could lose weight all by herself, with willpower. She was someone who might have put the weight back on, but who could take it off any time she chose.

The mere promise of Oxymetabulin had turned out to be the most effective drug of all.

Thank you, thank you, thank you, she whispered to David wherever he was. She wondered who the other women in the placebo group were. Then she thought of Teresa. Teresa had been convinced that she was taking the dummy pills. Wouldn't it be fantastic if she'd had this note as well! It would give her such a lift. She jumped up and rushed to the phone.

'Hi, Terry, it's Marina. Just a quick call. Have you received anything in the post?'

'Funny you should mention that. I've had a letter from Rod's solicitors, a tax bill and I still haven't opened the thousand cards addressed to both Rod and me from people who haven't heard we'd split up. Is that the sort of thing you were talking about?'

So Teresa hadn't been taking the placebo. Yet she'd always believed that she was, *wanted* to believe it. It was the spur that would keep her going through the next diet and the next diet. She'd convince herself that she had the power within her to control her eating. She would be able to cope with each successive failure if she knew that she could always succeed the next time.

It was a safe non-chemical crutch and Marina didn't have the right to take it away from her.

She lied. Because it was the right thing to do. 'No. It was just I got ... a chain letter. That's all, a stupid chain letter. I was just wondering if you got one.'

'I wish! Just throw it in the bin. That's what I'd do. And don't give it another thought.'

And that's what Marina did.

Chapter Twenty-five

'What did you say? I can't hear you. Don't babies ever stop crying?' Teresa put her fingers in her ears in mock-pain.

Marina hit Teresa's arm teasingly and led her into the garden. It was a chilly December afternoon so they had to walk briskly to keep warm.

'So how's it going, Terry?'

'The divorce was finalised on Wednesday. I'm a free woman. Hip, hip hooray! So how come I don't feel free?'

'It'll take time, you always knew that.'

Teresa looked shy all of a sudden. 'Actually, I went out with a man last night.'

Marina spun round to face her friend. 'And you didn't tell me before! That's fantastic! Who was he? How did it go? I want to know everything!'

Teresa linked arms with Marina and firmly started walking again. 'Don't get all excited. It was a bit of a disaster really. It was a supplier I met at that dinner-dance I told you about last month. I'm lying. It wasn't really a disaster. But nothing happened.'

'So are you going to see him again?'

'I don't know. Maybe.'

'Maybe!' Marina squealed. 'That's wonderful! Six months ago, you were saying that you'd never go out with another man again. And now you're saying "maybe"!'

'The truly funny thing is that he mentioned that he prefers women with fuller figures.'

Marina glanced at Teresa to see how she'd taken this. It was still a very sensitive area. Teresa had put on all the weight she'd lost on Oxymetabulin and a bit more on top. She still looked great and carried the weight well but she was not totally happy with the situation.

A sly smile crawled up her face. 'I believed him. I actually believed him, in a way that I never quite believed Rod.'

'Oh Terry, I'm so pleased for you. That's such an amazing breakthrough. You must be feeling so confident now that you finally accept that a man *can* find you attractive!'

'Oh, I'm going to be impossible to live with now! I'll end up like Susie, only standing next to women who are less pretty than me so that my undisputed beauty will glow even more brightly!'

'Ssh, she'll hear!' Marina whispered, glancing back at the house nervously.

'Oh nonsense. I just saw her creeping into your guest bathroom with her handbag. We both know what that means. You won't see her for half an hour.'

They both folded up in giggles. Then Marina put her hand over her mouth in panic. 'Oh God, I'd better hide the cheese dip in case she's tempted to add her own personal flavouring to it.'

Teresa stuck her finger in her mouth in disgust. 'Too gross! Careful, or you'll make me lose my appetite and I can't let down my admirers by getting thin!'

'Marina! You're needed!' Paul shouted from the house.

'Sorry,' Marina apologised.

'Nonsense,' Teresa replied. They walked back into the house where Paul was waiting with the screaming baby who refused to be pacified. In a fluid, practised movement, Marina grabbed the baby and put her grasping mouth to her breast. She sank into the sofa where Teresa joined her.

'You have to admit, Susie was right about that breastfeeding lark. You're as thin as a rake!'

Marina didn't take her eyes away from the beautiful face below her. 'I couldn't tell you what I weigh now. I hardly get any sleep and the only time I sit still is when I'm feeding so it's probably inevitable that I've lost some weight. But do you know what, I don't care.'

Teresa watched her friend's beatific face with affection. 'I believe you. I'm as jealous as hell, but I believe you. Oh, I forgot to ask, did you see Gail on the box last night?'

Marina's eyes widened. 'Yes, I couldn't believe it. She looked fantastic, didn't she, all strong and wild.'

Teresa agreed. 'It's pretty impressive, isn't it, a BBC documentary all about her. She's done well.'

'She deserves it. She's done a lot of good for a lot for women. I owe her a lot myself.'

'We all do. Did you ever thank her?'

'Yes, I met her at the Perrico press conference. It was all a bit of a letdown. "No conclusive results, research continues apace" and all that. She was really disappointed. She'd planned a major disruption of the presentation and then there was no presentation. Anyway, I told her what a difference she'd made to my life, to our lives. I think she was pleased, but you can't tell with Gail.'

'That's because she doesn't do it for the rewards. She really believes in it all.'

'It's funny, isn't it?' Marina looked off into an opaque distance.

'What's funny?'

'Gail's probably the luckiest of us all. Happy with herself all along. Living her life being honest with herself and with everyone else. She's the winner in all this, always was.'

Teresa considered this. 'So how come we didn't listen to her? I mean, *really* listen to her.'

'People don't listen. It's a fundamental characteristic of us all. Or rather, they listen and then they go and do exactly what they were planning to do all along no matter how destructive their behaviour might be.'

Teresa stroked the baby's head. 'That doesn't bode well for your stint of motherhood. How will you cope with little Sarah refusing to listen to and learn from you?'

Marina tightened her daughter's little body to her chest. 'Sarah will be the exception. Anyway, every day of her life, this little girl will be told that she's beautiful. We'll never use the word "diet" in this house. I'm going to get this right.'

They sat quietly for a while, the only sound being the greedy gurglings of the hungry baby. Teresa broke the silence.

'It was all a bit weird, the Perrico thing, don't you think? And David disappearing like that.'

Marina had returned her concentration to her baby. 'Maybe. I'm not interested any more. I can't believe there was ever a time that it was the most important part of my life.'

'Me neither.'

Marina raised her face to shoot some scepticism Teresa's way. Teresa read the look and held up her hands in defence. 'OK, OK, so I'm lying a little. I'm not saying I wouldn't take another pill, if one should come along. But it won't get in the way of my life next time.'

'Then you did learn something. There was a point to it.'

'Of course, there's a point to everything. Now I've just got one question for you, Marina.'

'Ask away!'

'It's not that I don't trust you, but can you just tell me which dishes in the buffet do not have *any* dairy products in them?'